MW01077274

REQUIEM

AURORA RESONANT BOOK THREE

(AMARANTHE ♦ 9)

G. S. JENNSEN

HYPERNOVA
PUBLISHING
2017

REQUIEM

Cover design by Bonus Experiment
Cover typography by G. S. Jennsen

Hypernova Publishing
P.O. Box 2214
Parker, Colorado 80134
www.hypernovapublishing.com

Ordering Information:
Hypernova Publishing books may be purchased for educational, business or sales promotional use. For details, contact the "Special Markets Department" at the address above.

Requiem / G. S. Jennsen.—1st ed.

LCCN 2017959855
ISBN 978-0-9984245-6-9

Happy Anniversary, my love

ACKNOWLEDGEMENTS

Many thanks to my beta readers, editors and artists, who made everything about this book better, and to my family, who continue to put up with an egregious level of obsessive focus on my part for months at a time.

I also want to add a personal note of thanks to everyone who has read my books, left a review on Amazon, Goodreads or other sites, sent me a personal email expressing how the books have impacted you, or posted on social media to share how much you enjoyed them. You make this all worthwhile, every day.

AMARANTHE UNIVERSE

AURORA RHAPSODY

AURORA RISING
STARSHINE

VERTIGO

TRANSCENDENCE

AURORA RENEGADES
SIDESPACE

DISSONANCE

ABYSM

AURORA RESONANT
RELATIVITY

RUBICON

REQUIEM

AURORA SHORT STORIES
RESTLESS, VOL. I • *RESTLESS, VOL. II* • *APOGEE* • *SOLATIUM*

VENATORIS • *RE/GENESIS* • *MERIDIAN* • *FRACTALS*

ASTERIONOIR

EXIN EX MACHINA

OF A DARKER VOID

THE STARS LIKE GODS

RIVEN WORLDS

CONTINUUM

INVERSION

Learn more at gsjennsen.com/amaranthe-universe

AMARANTHE
ANADEN EMPIRE

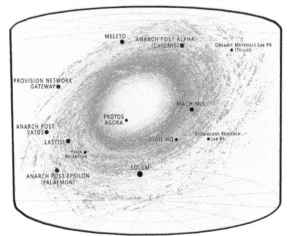

MILKY WAY GALAXY

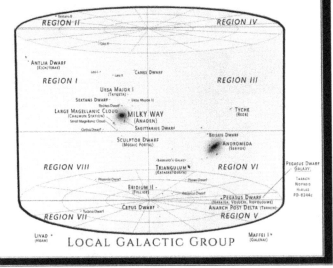

LOCAL GALACTIC GROUP

AURORA
COLONIZED WORLDS

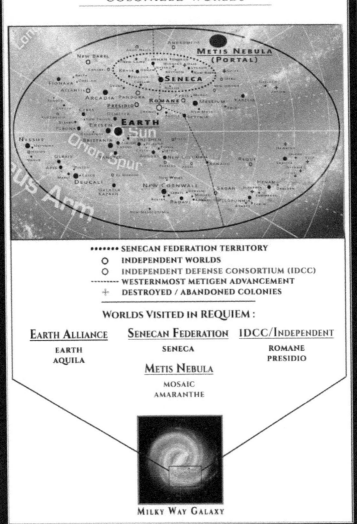

- •••••• SENECAN FEDERATION TERRITORY
- ○ INDEPENDENT WORLDS
- ○ INDEPENDENT DEFENSE CONSORTIUM (IDCC)
- -------- WESTERNMOST METIGEN ADVANCEMENT
- ✛ DESTROYED / ABANDONED COLONIES

WORLDS VISITED IN REQUIEM :

EARTH ALLIANCE	SENECAN FEDERATION	IDCC/INDEPENDENT
EARTH	SENECA	ROMANE
AQUILA		PRESIDIO

METIS NEBULA
MOSAIC
AMARANTHE

MILKY WAY GALAXY

View the Amaranthe and Aurora Maps Online at gsjennsen.com/maps-requiem

DRAMATIS PERSONAE

HUMANS OF AURORA

Alexis 'Alex' Solovy

Space scout and explorer. Prevo.
Spouse of Caleb Marano, daughter of Miriam and David Solovy.
Artificial/Prevo Counterpart: Valkyrie

Caleb Marano

Former Special Operations intelligence agent, SF Division of Intelligence.
Spouse of Alex Solovy.

Miriam Solovy (Commandant)

Leader, GCDA/AEGIS Forces.
Captain, *AFS Stalwart II*.
Mother of Alex Solovy.

Malcolm Jenner (Brigadier)

AEGIS Director of Marines.
Captain, *AFS Saratoga*.

Mia Requelme

Prevo. Entrepreneur.
IDCC Minister of Colonial Affairs.
Artificial/Prevo Counterpart: Meno

Kennedy Rossi

Founder/CEO, Connova Interstellar.
AEGIS Consultant. Alex's best friend.

Noah Terrage

Co-founder/COO, Connova Interstellar.
Former smuggler. AEGIS Consultant.

Valkyrie

Artificial. Prevo counterpart to
Alex Solovy. Pilot of the *Siyane*.

David Solovy (Commander)

Alex Solovy's father. Miriam Solovy's
spouse. Captain, *EAS Stalwart*.

Richard Navick

Former EASC Naval
Intelligence Liaison.
GCDA SENTRI Director.
Family friend of the Solovys.

Morgan Lekkas

Prevo. AEGIS Council.
Cmdr, IDCC Rapid Response Forces.
Artificial/Prevo Counterpart: Stanley

Brooklyn Harper

Former EA Special Forces Captain.
Leader, IDCC RRF ground forces.
AEGIS Council.

Devon Reynolds

Prevo. Former EASC Consultant.
Quantum computing expert, hacker.
Artificial/Prevo Counterpart: Annie

ALIENS OF AMARANTHE

Eren asi-Idoni
Anarch resistance agent.
Species: Anaden

Danilo Nisi/Corradeo Praesidis
Sator (leader) of the anarch resistance.
Species: Anaden

Mnemosyne ('Mesme')
Idryma Member, 1ˢᵗ Analystae of Aurora.
Species: Katasketousya (Metigen)

Cosime Rhomyhn
Anarch agent. Friend of Eren.
Species: Naraida

Nyx elasson-Praesidis
Inquisitor.
Species: Anaden

Casmir elasson-Machim
Machim fleet military commander.
Species: Anaden

Praesidis Primor (Renato)
Head of Praesidis Dynasty.
Species: Anaden

Machim Primor
Head of Machim Dynasty.
Species: Anaden

Thelkt Lonaervin
Anarch agent, friend of Eren.
Species: Novoloume

Logiel ela-Erevna
Exobiology scientist.
Species: Anaden

Savine Idoni
Head of Idoni Dynasty.
Species: Anaden

Lakhes
Praetor (leader) of the Idryma.
Species: Katasketousya (Metigen)

Felzeor
Anarch agent. Friend of Eren, Thelkt.
Species: Volucri

Ziton elasson-Praesidis
Inquisitor.
Species: Anaden

Onai Veshnael (Dean)
Leader of the Novoloume.
Species: Novoloume

Trepenos Hishai
Anarch agent, Chalmun Station.
Species: Novoloume

Xanne ela-Kyvern
Anarch, mission supervisor.
Species: Anaden

Zoravar Bazuk T'yevk (Commander)
Leader, Ch'mshak military.
Species: Ch'mshak

OTHER CHARACTERS

Abigail Canivon
Former Cybernetic Expert. Deceased.

Brandon Ashonye (Brigadier)
EA Armed Forces; AEGIS Council.

Carrie Verela (Sergeant)
EA/AEGIS special forces.

Charles Gagnon
Earth Alliance Prime Minister.

Drae ela-Machim
Anarch agent.
Species: Anaden

Ekhor'pai
Leader of the Hoans.
Species: Hoan

Erevna Primor
Head of Erevna Dynasty.
Species: Anaden

Geralt Eaton (Major)
EA/AEGIS special forces.

Gino Belosca (Brigadier)
SF Armed Forces; AEGIS Council.

Graham Delavasi
Director, SF Division of
Intelligence.

Hyperion
Idryma member, Analystae.
Species: Katasketousya (Metigen)

Isabela Marano
Biochemistry professor; Caleb's sister.

Miaon
Anarch agent. Friend of Eren, Mesme.
Species: Yinhe

Marlee Marano
Isabela's daughter; Caleb's niece.

Necha Hahmirin (Senior Advisor)
Novoloume government official.
Species: Novoloume

Nelson Escarra (Rear Admiral)
EA Armed Forces; AEGIS Council.

Nolan Bastian (Field Marshal)
Leader, SF Military; AEGIS Council.

Phael Thisiame (Pointe-Amiral)
Commander, Novoloume fleet.
Species: Novoloume

Phillip Grenier (Major)
EA/AEGIS special forces.

**Pinchutsenahn Niikha Qhi-
yane Kteh ("Pinchu")**
Tokahe Naataan of Ireltse.
Species: Khokteh

Simon Ettore (Major)
AEGIS Prevo, *AFS Saratoga*.

Stanley
Prevo counterpart to Morgan Lekkas.

Sylvia Zvedski
Spouse of Admiral Zvedski.

Thomas
AEGIS Artificial.

Tom Hammett (Major)
EA Armed Forces.

Vii
Artificial, fork of Valkyrie.
Employee of Connova Interstellar.

Volya Gaala-min
Post Satus security supervisor.
Species: Barisan

William 'Will' Sutton
GCDA SENTRI Deputy Director.
Spouse of Richard Navick.

Anaden Dynasties

PRAESIDIS
Role: *Criminal investigation and enforcement*

MACHIM
Role: *Military*

THERIZ
Role: *Resource cultivation and management*

EREVNA
Role: *Research, science*

IDONI
Role: *Entertainment, pleasure seekers/providers*

KYVERN
Role: *Administration, bureaucracy*

DIAPLAS
Role: *Engineering, construction*

ANTALLA
Role: *Commerce, trade*

*

Dynasty Ranks

Primor

Elasson

Ela

Asi

View the Dramatis Personae Online at gsjennsen.com/characters-requiem

THE STORY SO FAR

View a more detailed summary of the events of Aurora Rising and Aurora Renegades online at gsjennsen.com/synopsis.

AURORA RISING

The history of humanity is the history of conflict. This proved no less true in the 24th century than in ancient times.

By 2322, humanity inhabited over 100 worlds spread across a third of the galaxy. Two decades earlier, a group of colonies had rebelled and set off the First Crux War. Once the dust cleared, three factions emerged: the Earth Alliance, consisting of the unified Earth government and most of the colonies; the Senecan Federation, which had won its independence in the war; and a handful of scattered non-aligned worlds, home to criminal cartels, corporate interests and people who made their living outside the system.

Alexis Solovy was a space explorer. Her father gave his life in the war against the Federation, leading her to reject a government or military career. Estranged from her mother, an Alliance military leader, Alex instead sought the freedom of space and made a fortune chasing the hidden wonders of the stars.

A chance meeting between Alex and a Federation intelligence agent, Caleb Marano, led them to discover an armada of alien warships emerging from a mysterious portal in the Metis Nebula.

The Metigens had been watching humanity via the portal for millennia; in an effort to forestall their detection, they used traitors among civilization's elite to divert focus from Metis. When their plans failed, they invaded in order to protect their secrets.

The wars that ensued were brutal—first an engineered war between the Alliance and the Federation, then once it was revealed to be built on false pretenses, devastating clashes against the Metigen invaders as they advanced across settled space, destroying every colony in their path and killing tens of millions.

Alex and Caleb breached the aliens' portal in an effort to find a way to stop the slaughter. There they encountered Mnemosyne, the Metigen watcher of the Aurora universe—our universe. Though enigmatic and evasive, the alien revealed the invading ships were driven by AIs and hinted the answer to defeating them lay in the merger of individuals with the powerful but dangerous quantum computers known as Artificials.

Before leaving the portal space, Alex and Caleb discovered a colossal master gateway. It generated 51 unique signals, each one leading to a new portal and a new universe. But with humanity facing extinction, they returned home armed with a daring plan to win the war.

In a desperate gambit to vanquish the enemy invaders before they reached the heart of civilization, four Prevos (human-synthetic meldings) were created and given command of the combined might of the Alliance and Federation militaries. Alex and her Artificial, Valkyrie, led the other Prevos and the military forces against the alien AI warships in climactic battles above Seneca and Romane. The invaders were defeated and ordered to withdraw through their portal, cease their observation of Aurora and not return.

Alex reconciled with her mother during the final hours of the war, and following the victory Alex and Caleb married and attempted to resume a normal life.

But new mysteries waited through the Metis portal. Determined to learn the secrets of the portal network and the multiverses it held, six months later Caleb, Alex and Valkyrie traversed it once more, leaving humanity behind to struggle with a new world of powerful quantum synthetics, posthumans, and an uneasy, fragile peace.

AURORA RENEGADES

Following the victory over the Metigens, Alex, Caleb and Valkyrie set off to unlock the secrets of the Metigens' portal network. Discovering worlds of infinite wonder, they made both enemies and friends. Planets of sentient plant life which left a lasting mark on Alex and Caleb both. Silica-based beings attempting to grow organic life. A race of cat-like warriors locked in conflict with their brethren.

Behind them all, the whispered machinations of the Metigen puppet masters pervaded everything. In some universes, the Metigens tested weapons. In some, they set aliens against each other in new forms of combat. In others, they harvested food and materials to send through the massive portal at the heart of the maze.

But Alex and Caleb found yet another layer to the puzzle. In one universe, they discovered a gentle race of underground beings with a strange history. Their species was smuggled out of the universe beyond the master portal by the Metigens. They watched as their homeworld was destroyed by a powerful species known as Anadens; but for the Metigens, they would have perished as well.

Back home in Aurora, the peace proved difficult to maintain. The Prevos found themselves targeted by politicians and a restless population desperate for a place to pin their fears. Under the direction of a new, power-hungry Earth Alliance PM, the government moved to cage and shackle them.

In desperation, the Prevos uploaded the AIs' consciousnesses into their own minds, fled from their governments' grasp and disappeared onto independent colonies. Devon published the details of the Prevo link to the exanet, unleashing its capabilities for anyone who wanted to follow in their footsteps.

Meanwhile, an anti-synthetic terrorist group emerged to oppose them, fueled by the rise of Olivia Montegreu as a Prevo. While the private face of Prevos was the heroes who defeated the Metigens, the public face became the image of Olivia killing a colonial governor and tossing him off of a building in front of the world.

Unaware of the struggles her fellow Prevos faced, Alex forged her own path forward. Rather than bringing the AI into herself, she pushed out and through Valkyrie, into the walls of the *Siyane*.

Piloting her ship in a way she never dreamed, Alex was able to feel the photonic brilliance of space itself. Over time, however, that bond began to capture more of her spirit and mind.

On the surface of a destroyed planet, Mesme at last revealed all. The portal network was, above all else, a refuge for those targeted for eradication by the Anadens. And the Anadens, rulers of the true universe through the master portal, were the genetic template upon which humanity was built. Aurora was nothing more than another experiment of the Metigens, created so they could study the development and nature of their enemy and the enemy of all life.

Alex and Caleb returned to Aurora to find a galaxy rocked by chaos. After the execution of Olivia Montegreu by Alliance and Prevo forces, Miriam had gone rogue. Her resistance force, bolstered by help from inside the Senecan and Alliance militaries, moved against the despotic Alliance PM.

As Alex struggled with her growing addiction to an ethereal realm, she felt herself being pulled away from reality. Away from her husband, her mother, her friends. She watched as those she loved fought, but increasingly found herself losing her own battle.

When terrorists staged a massive riot on Romane, Dr. Canivon, the mother of the Prevos, was murdered in front of Devon and Alex. Overcome by her own and Valkyrie's grief, Alex unleashed the explosive power of the ethereal realm to destroy the terrorists' safehouse. Standing in the rubble of her destruction, Alex made a decision to sever the quantum connection between herself and the *Siyane*, choosing a tangible, human life. Choosing Caleb.

Miriam wrested control of the EA government away from the PM, bringing an end to the Prevo persecution. In the wake of victory, a shadowy Anaden hunter emerged from the darkness to attack Alex and Caleb. Caleb was gravely injured when the Anaden's power leapt to him, healing his wounds and helping him kill the alien.

Mesme revealed the ominous consequences of the attack. Soon, the Anaden leadership would discover Aurora. When they did, they would destroy it unless humanity could stand against them. Mesme told Miriam and the others to prepare, but knowing the end game was upon them, asked Alex and Caleb to come to Amaranthe. The master universe. The home and dominion of the Anadens.

RELATIVITY
(AURORA RESONANT BOOK ONE)

AURORA

Miriam now leads the Galactic Common Defense Accord, a multi-government agency created to ensure humanity is prepared to meet the threat of the Anadens, and AEGIS, its military division. Malcolm and Harper work to train ground forces, while Kennedy, Noah and Vii—Valkyrie's clone—work to build a next-generation fleet with integrated Artificials and Prevos sharing command with their captains.

A celebration commemorating the victory over the Metigens a year ago takes place on multiple worlds. Mia and Malcolm attend the Romane event as a couple, having finally become romantically involved. After the show, Devon and his girlfriend are attacked;. Devon repels the attack, but Emily is injected with an unknown substance and falls unconscious.

Doctors identify the substance as a five-dimensional virus, leading Mia to believe it originated from the deceased Anaden scientists are studying. Richard identifies the scientist who sold the Anaden's cybernetic code on the black market, but the man has disappeared. He is soon found murdered on Seneca. The next day, Morgan Lekkas' skycar is attacked and crashes, leaving her badly injured and comatose.

During a romantic evening, Kennedy asks Noah to marry her; he refuses. They argue, and she leaves under the pretense of work.

At Mia's house, Malcolm and Mia are attacked by mercs wielding more doses of the virus. Malcolm disables the attackers, but Meno is hacked to deliver a threat from an unknown individual who sounds eerily like Olivia Montegreu.

Later that night, Harper is discussing how to heal Morgan's neurological damage with Mia when the hospital comes under attack. She kills several attackers; Mia kills another. On a different floor, Devon fends off a wave of attackers. Realizing they are Prevos, he sends a surge of energy through sidespace to shatter their Prevo connections, killing them and shattering multiple walls nearby.

At the Presidio, Kennedy troubleshoots a component problem in the new ships while ruminating over the riff with Noah, trying to figure out what she truly wants. Similarly, Noah visits a bar on

Romane to do his own ruminating. There he runs into an old friend from Pandora who gives him a different perspective on the events of the last year and a half.

Harper travels to Seneca and breaks into Stanley's lab. She taps into the Artificial's server to give Mia remote access, and Mia copies crucial functionality left behind when Morgan severed the hardware link. Mia uses this data to reawaken Stanley's consciousness in Morgan's mind.

Late in the night, AEGIS receives a data cache from Valkyrie with voluminous information on the Anaden military and its war machine, but no other news from Amaranthe. The AEGIS Council begins developing strategies to counter their future opponent.

Mia has a breakthrough in her attempts to counteract the virus killing Emily, and the young woman recovers.

Richard analyzes the details of the various attacks and comes to the conclusion that the source is not Olivia Montegreu, but rather the Artificial she joined with to become a Prevo, left behind on her death.

Devon convinces Richard to let him go after Olivia's Artificial. Devon and Annie remotely access the Artificial. They encounter robust defenses, but breach the core operating system and plant a virus. The Artificial explodes, destroying the Zelones headquarters on New Babel.

Before going to Amaranthe, Alex left her father's construct in Vii's care. Using advances she and Dr. Canivon made before Abigail was killed, Vii fills in the gaps in his consciousness to create a more complete, accurate recreation of David Solovy's mind. She awakens him in a virtual copy of his favorite camping site. She tells him that he's still in a fragile mental state, but together they are going to change this.

On Romane, Mia and Malcolm argue. He tells her he refuses to be what she settles for and tries to leave. She stops him by confessing the true extent of her feelings. They make up, but an emergency alert summons Malcolm back to the Presidio.

Noah returns to Kennedy with a gift, an adaptive holo device he built for her, and confesses he is hers no matter what. When he asks if she still wants to get married, she suggests they just take a honeymoon instead.

Morgan wakes up to find Stanley once again in her mind. He says he never truly went away, but retreated out of self-preservation. They agree to take more care with each other. An alert arrives then, and Morgan informs Harper that they have a war to go fight.

ᴚ

AMARANTHE

The Directorate, the governing body of the Anaden empire run by the Primors of each Anaden Dynasty, discusses recent attacks by the 'anarch' resistance movement. The Praesidis Primor assigns Nyx, a high-level Inquisitor, to investigate the disappearance of Aver, the Inquisitor who discovered Aurora and was killed by Caleb.

Two anarchs, Eren and Cosime, surveil a Directorate exobiology lab where alien captives are experimented on. Lacking the resources to rescue the captives, they decide to blow up the lab.

Eren goes to an administration center to steal credentials to get him inside the lab. He obtains the credentials but is caught by security. As he is being detained, a mysterious man appears and uses *diati*, the mysterious power wielded by Praesidis Inquisitors, to attack the security officers, and a woman approaches Eren and tells him to come with them. Lacking other options, he flees with the strangers to their ship.

The ship is the *Siyane*, Eren's rescuers Caleb and Alex. They introduce themselves, Valkyrie and Mesme, and ask him to help them obtain details on the Directorate's military arm, run by the Machim Dynasty. Eren is reluctant to trust a synthetic, a Kat (as the Metigens are called in Amaranthe), or strangers who look Anaden but are not, but he reluctantly agrees to look into the matter.

After he leaves the *Siyane*, Eren is approached by Miaon, a fellow anarch. Miaon reveals that it is Mesme's contact and urges Eren to help these strangers. Eren visits an anarch friend, Thelkt, for information on how to obtain the intel Alex and Caleb seek.

Mesme takes Alex and Caleb to a nebula hiding a massive store of Reor, the unusual mineral those in Amaranthe use to store data. Mesme reveals that the Reor is sentient, but no one else suspects this. Alex tries to interact with the mineral; she's unable to communicate directly, but the Reor creates a new slab of itself for Alex.

Caleb dreams of the distant history of the Anadens, as relayed by the *diati*. When they are invaded by a powerful enemy, the Anadens face annihilation. The ethereal *diati* joins with the Anaden's greatest warrior, Corradeo Praesidis, to defeat the enemy. The Anadens thrive, then face an uprising by people seeking to join with synthetics. The conflict ends in a purge of AIs and AI-sympathizers and the formation of the Dynasties. The *diati* propagates into Corradeo's descendants, losing its coherence. The Anadens grow more oppressive as they abandon the ethos Corradeo espoused, but the *diati* cannot prevent it.

Nyx follows Aver's trail until she uncovers one of the hidden Mosaic portals. Rather than traverse it, she goes to Katoikia, the Kats' homeworld, and seizes two Kats in stasis chambers to interrogate.

In response to Nyx' visit to Katoikia, the Kats evacuate the stasis pods kept there and take them to the Mosaic for safekeeping. Mesme invites Alex and Caleb to witness the exodus.

While exploring Katoikia, they uncover a hidden structure where a Kat named Paratyr monitors locations around Amaranthe, watching for Directorate aggression. Alex is drawn to a scene of an aquatic species called Galenai; she uses sidespace to "visit" their underwater city. Paratyr tells her the Directorate is expanding into the Galenai's galaxy, and the Kats have flagged the Galenai for possible evacuation to the Mosaic.

Alex and Caleb leave Katoikia to meet up with Eren on a quest to infiltrate Machim Central Command and steal what intel they can. Thelkt sends Eren the Machim data server access codes, delivered by Felzeor, an intelligent avian. Felzeor has an engaging personality, and Caleb bonds with the falcon-like anarch in the short time it's on board.

After Felzeor leaves, Eren tells the story of how he became an anarch. Over a century ago, he encountered unfamiliar aliens serving as sexual slaves to the Idoni Primor. Recognizing their extreme fear and distress, he fled in horror. Soon thereafter, the Directorate eradicated the species. Disgusted with his leaders, he fried his neural link to the integral, dropped off the grid and made contact with the anarchs.

When they reach Machim Central Command, Caleb impersonates an Inquisitor to get inside, while Eren guides him. They reach the server room, and Mesme transports Alex to their location. She and Valkyrie hack the server and are downloading a plethora of military data when security forces arrive. An officer puts a blade to Alex's throat; Caleb orders Valkyrie and Mesme to flee then surrenders. Eren refuses and is killed. Caleb and Alex are rendered unconscious and arrested.

Valkyrie flees to the Mosaic then Aurora, where she transmits all the data from Machim Central Command to AEGIS. Then she travels to the Idryma portal and bids Lakhes to accompany her to Amaranthe.

Eren awakens in a "regenesis" pod, for Anadens are able to transfer their consciousness to new bodies when they die. He fills in his supervisor, Xanne, then insists they rescue Alex and Caleb. Xanne takes his request to the leader of the anarchs, Sator Danilo Nisi. After hearing Eren's story, he authorizes resources for a rescue mission.

Caleb and Alex wake up in separate detention cells, both restrained and subjected to interrogation by drones that jolts them with electricity when they refuse to answer. Caleb's *diati* absorbs the jolts, keeping him from injury; Alex is not so lucky.

Nyx deactivates a stasis chamber and interrogates the Kat until it reveals details on the Mosaic and the Kats' work there. She relays to the Praesidis Primor what she's learned. He sends her to interrogate the Human prisoners, then informs the other Primors of the Kats' betrayal. They issue an Eradication Order for the Kats and decide to destroy the Mosaic, except for the portal spaces providing crucial provisions to Amaranthe.

Eren rejoins Valkyrie and Mesme on the *Siyane* with a rescue plan. Mesme reveals to Eren that the species he encountered at the Idoni party, leading to his rebellion, were not all eradicated. Called Faneros, many were smuggled out to safety in the Mosaic.

Nyx arrives to interrogate Caleb. She asks what he is and where he came from, but he refuses to answer. In frustration she draws closer, and he steals her *diati* until he's strong enough to break out of the restraints. He then drains her of *diati*, incapacitates her and goes in search of Alex.

When he reaches her cell, his *diati* allows him to pass through the force field easily. But he's unable to deactivate the force field, and he has to trust the *diati* to protect her as he carries her through it.

Security is closing in when Eren and Mesme appear. Mesme transports Alex to the *Siyane* as an assault mech attacks. Caleb destroys the mech, then Eren insists Mesme transport Caleb next. Once they're gone, Eren detonates explosives he brought, destroying the facility.

Informed the Directorate is sending a military fleet to the Mosaic, Alex and Caleb rush to get a message to Miriam: it's time to bring her own fleet. During the trip, they work on a plan to keep the Machim fleet out of the Mosaic.

The Machim fleet acquires special Igni antimatter missiles and a doomsday device called a Tartarus Trigger. Further interrogation of the Kat prisoner reveals the ultimate truth: Humans are the genetic recreation of Anadens. The Directorate wants the Tartarus Trigger taken to the Aurora portal space and detonated, annihilating the Aurora universe. Meanwhile, a separate Machim fleet bombs the Kat homeworld.

The *Siyane* joins the AEGIS fleet in the Mosaic. Alex reunites with her mother then briefs Miriam on their plan.

The Machim fleet arrives at the Gateway to the Mosaic. It promptly explodes, hit by negative energy missiles from the *Siyane* and stealthed fighters nearby. The explosion takes out a large chunk of the Machim fleet; while it's still recovering, the AEGIS fleet materializes behind it.

The battle is joined. AEGIS enjoys an advantage in most respects, but the Igni missiles can damage adiamene hulls. Prevos in the fleet work to identify which ships are carrying the missiles, then take them out first.

Paratyr appears in the cabin of the *Siyane* in ethereal form. The Kat warns them about the Tartarus Trigger on the Machim command ship Imperium. If detonated, it will annihilate every molecule for parsecs, then possibly the entire universe.

Malcolm devises a way to bypass the impenetrable shields of the Imperium and is about to try it when Alex stops him, as the odds of the Tartarus Trigger detonating when the ship is destroyed are too high. Mesme volunteers to infiltrate the ship and transport the device away.

Alex uses sidespace to determine the device's precise location, then Mesme surrounds it and both vanish. Alex gives Malcolm the all clear, and he destroys the Imperium. The remaining Machim vessels retreat, handing a decisive victory to AEGIS.

The AEGIS Council, now including Alex and Caleb, convenes on the *Stalwart II* to determine the next steps. They are interrupted, however, by a message from Sator Nisi requesting a meeting.

Alex, Caleb, Miriam and Mesme travel to Nisi's headquarters. When they meet Nisi, Caleb realizes the man controls *diati* as well. Miriam and Nisi spar, and the lack of trust on both sides is evident. Alex challenges Nisi, and he admits the anarchs are not powerful enough to defeat the Directorate. Rather, they are a force designed to be of maximum strategic value when the fulcrum that will change the cosmos arrives.

He believes that fulcrum is not the AEGIS fleet, but rather Caleb.

Rubicon

(Aurora Resonant Book Two)

AEGIS wastes no time pressing the advantage gained at the Gateway victory, attacking and destroying a major Machim warship construction facility. Caleb trains with Sator Nisi, learning greater control over and abilities with the *diati*, including teleportation.

After the mission, the AEGIS Council debates the goals of the war, eventually concluding that they will have to kill the Primors, and prevent them from undergoing regenesis, if they want to be victorious. But first, they need to win the anarchs' trust.

The Directorate, perturbed by the Kats' ability to infiltrate secure locations their use of it to help the anarchs and the Humans, decides they must uncover the location of a hidden portal into the Kats' multiverse network in order to destroy the Humans' home universe.

Malcolm returns to Aurora and reunites with Mia. He confesses his love for her, and she reciprocates. He asks her to return to Amaranthe with him to serve as AEGIS' ambassador to the anarchs. After some hesitation, she agrees. Kennedy is also asked to come to Amaranthe to study weaknesses in the Machim Imperiums. She convinces Noah to go with her, leaving the Artificial, Vii, in charge of Connova Interstellar.

The anarchs learn that Directorate security has begun a massive dragnet sweep designed to root out anarch spies. They plan missions to extract what agents they can, and Eren enlists Caleb, Alex and Mesme to help him and Cosime rescue Thelkt and Felzeor from Plousia Chateau.

Meanwhile, the Inquisitor, Nyx, interrogates the owner of Plousia, Avdei elasson-Idoni. She has uncovered evidence of Eren's presence there recently and shows him images captured by security cams. He recalls seeing Eren with Thelkt.

When they reach Plousia, Mesme transports Eren and Cosime into the building where everyone is being held, just as Nyx arrives to question Thelkt. Eren distracts Nyx long enough for Mesme to transport Thelkt and Cosime away, then suicides. Meanwhile, Caleb and Alex retrieve Felzeor from Thelkt's residence, but Nyx interrupts them, and a battle between Caleb and Nyx ensues. Caleb claims a portion of her *diati*, but she teleports away before he can take it all.

While the events at Plousia unfold, AEGIS forces move against another Machim warship facility. However, Machim fleets are now stationed at every transit point. When the AEGIS ships emerge through a gateway, Machim vessels ambush them. The Machim commander fires Igni antimatter missiles at the gateway's adjacent space station. Admiral Rychen intervenes in an attempt to save the station, but the station and Rychen's dreadnought are destroyed, killing everyone on board both.

Malcolm, Mia, Kennedy and Noah arrive from Aurora to find the AEGIS forces in a state of shock. While Mia and Malcolm digest the events they missed, Kennedy meets with Alex. She reveals that with Vii's blessing, she brought David Solovy's quantum construct with her for Alex.

Alex accesses a virtual space where she can see, touch and talk to her father. They hug, cry, and bond anew. They talk about his journey to this point, and what to do next. He asks her not to tell Miriam about his existence, fearing he would distract her from her mission, and insists he'll be fine in his current state for now. Alex agrees but, now convinced of his realness and authenticity, she secretly begins to hatch a plan.

In her first act as AEGIS Ambassador, Mia meets with Nisi and his advisors. A delicate negotiation ensues, but she persuades Nisi that humans can be trusted, and that they need each other if they want to defeat the Directorate. The anarchs grant AEGIS access to one of their posts, intelligence files and promise future joint missions.

Alex and Mia tour the anarch post. Alex quizzes the director of the post's regenesis lab on the regenesis procedure and how it might be adapted for humans. Alex and Mia talk about how the Prevos can help AEGIS. The fleet can't use the wormhole gateways any longer, so they need a way to cross galaxies in a reasonable amount of time—they need their own wormholes. Valkyrie analogizes sidespace to wormholes, and Mia reveals that Devon has figured out how to affect the real world from sidespace. Alex begins to see how it all might work together.

In Aurora, Miriam reports Admiral Rychen's death to the Earth Alliance Prime Minister. He challenges her on the state and necessity of the mission in Amaranthe, but she stands her ground. Miriam then visits Richard at the Presidio. She unloads her concerns and fears on him, then asks him to come to Amaranthe with her. He declines, saying he won't be of much help there, but he is doing good at home.

Mia convinces Devon to return with her to Amaranthe to help her and Alex create wormholes out of sidespace.

Caleb and Nisi talk about Caleb's encounter with Nyx. They speculate that the Primor must have gifted her with some of his own *diati* after Caleb stripped hers at the Helix Retention facility. Abruptly, Caleb is overwhelmed by a strange sensation and excuses himself. On Post Epsilon, Alex begins to experience the same strange sensation. She and Caleb meet back at the *Siyane* and decide it must be Akeso calling to them, as that's the one foreign entity they share.

They head for the Mosaic, and arrive at Akeso to find it under active attack by an orbiting moon. The method of attack suggest the moon originated from Ekos-3, another planet in the system. The attacker is trying to take over Akeso like a virus. In a display of impressive power, Caleb uses his *diati* to destroy the moon. When the *diati* leaves his body to attack the moon, he passes out, but is invigorated when it returns.

Caleb communicates with the planet intelligence to ensure it's safe and well. Akeso asks them to stay for a while. They reluctantly decline but promise they will return when they can.

Eren wakes up at the Post Alpha regenesis lab following his suicide at Plousia, and is just getting his bearings when Mesme appears. The Kat takes Eren to see the Faneros, the species Eren encountered that spurred him to become an anarch, in the Mosaic. At first, Eren is fascinated, but observing them triggers vivid memories from his troubling first encounter with them, and he recoils—from himself and from the Faneros—and demands to be returned to Post Alpha.

There, he begs Xanne to bring him back as another dynasty on his next regenesis, and if she can't do that, not to bring him back at all. When she refuses, he returns to his room and tries to overdose on hypnols. Cosime finds him, throws away all his remaining hypnols, then begs him to tell her what brought this on; desperate for salvation, he begins confessing his darkest secrets. The next morning, reinvigorated, he devises a plan to rescue alien prisoners from the Erevna exobiology lab he was once going to blow up.

Malcolm discovers a discrepancy in the number of Reverb devices in stock. He asks Harper about it, pushing her on it until she's forced to admit the discrepancy is a result of her loaning out a Reverb to Caleb back on Romane. She refuses to reveal what Caleb used it for, but Malcolm puts the pieces together and realizes he used it to kill Jude Winslow while the OTS terrorist leader was in custody.

Alex, Mia and Devon meet on the *Siyane*. Together with Valkyrie and the other Prevo Artificials, they strategize how to use sidespace to open wormholes. Alex realizes the answer lies in the Dimensional Rifter. By controlling the rifts in the spatial dimensions, they can move people and objects from one rift—wormhole—out another, and a slight change in the structure of a Dimensional Rifter will generate the power required to tear open such rifts.

After the meeting, Mia meets Malcolm back at her accommodations on Post Epsilon. He shares what he learned about Caleb and Winslow, and she confesses she already knew. They argue, with her insisting Winslow deserved to die and Malcolm insisting that was the justice system's decision to make, not Caleb's. She recalls the times in her life when there was no justice system to protect her and she had to kill to survive. Convinced he doesn't want to understand, she tells him to leave.

Alex goes to see the Post Epsilon regenesis lab director. She asks him to use the regenesis technology to help her transfer a quantum consciousness into a physical human body. He concedes it might be possible, but insists Nisi must give his approval first. Alex gets Caleb to ask Nisi for that approval, which he gives. Caleb, however, has some concerns, so Alex takes him into the virtual space to meet her father for himself. Afterwards, they instruct the regenesis lab director to proceed.

Mesme and two other Kats watch Directorate agents place a tracking device on a Kat vessel while it delivers supplies from the Mosaic. They hatch a plan to trick the Directorate into thinking they've located a portal.

Later, Casmir elasson-Machin is tasked with investigating the potential location of a portal into the Mosaic. He takes his fleet to the location indicated by the tracking device and is able to open a portal. His fleet traverses it, then abruptly is thrown across space into the center of a star and killed.

Alex and Kennedy dismantle a Dimensional Rifter and build it back up again in such a way as to capture the power needed to open a wormhole, then head to space to test it out. They're able to successfully traverse a wormhole in the *Siyane*, and they dub the new device a Caeles Prism.

Malcolm confronts Caleb about what happened with Jude Winslow. They argue, nearing blows, and are left with seemingly unbridgeable differences on ethics, morality, and the role of law and order.

When Alex finds out about the argument, she sends Noah to find Caleb until she and Kennedy can return. Noah takes Caleb to get a drink at the bar on Epsilon. While there, they are provoked by two aliens into a bar fight. They escape as chaos descends on the bar, then hide from their assailants in the icy waters surrounding the post. Alex and Kennedy arrive to find them soaked, freezing and drunk, and take them back to the *Siyane*.

The next morning, Eren pitches Alex and Caleb on the idea of infiltrating the exobiology lab and rescuing the aliens held captive there. Caleb tells Alex to take him to Malcolm, as he'll need the help of the Marines to pull it off. As soon as Alex sees Malcolm, they argue about his dispute with Caleb. Some unpleasant barbs are exchanged, but they ultimately call a truce for the good of the mission.

Malcolm, Harper and several Marine squads accompany Eren and Cosime to infiltrate the exobiology lab. They rescue dozens of prisoners, are forced to kill several violent ones, and Malcolm blows up the lab. Unbeknownst to the Marines, Nyx was at the lab when the attack began. She allowed the raid to succeed, then secretly placed a tracking device on the Marine transport.

The Marines take the refugees from the lab to Post Alpha, where Eren talks to Nisi about the need to stop playing by the Directorate's rules. He asserts its time for the anarchs to come out of the shadows and publicly stand up for those oppressed. He proposes a plan for Nisi to address everyone in the empire, to make their case to the public.

At an AEGIS Council meeting, Mesme reveals the destruction of a Machim fleet through the false portal. Miriam authorizes the use of the Caeles Prism in combat missions. Alex comes up with an idea for the first mission to use it, one targeting the Dyson rings powering Machimis.

Alex and Caleb test the Caeles Prism for intergalactic traversal by traversing a wormhole to the Maffei I galaxy. While the wormhole is open, Alex sees luminescent strings running in all directions, but all running through the Reor slab she's holding in her hand. Valkyrie's analysis of the luminescent strings reveals that they are waves carrying data stored on other Reor slabs. Alex believes the Reor possess a universal decryption key so that they can read the data. Caleb suggests the key might be embedded in the slab the Reor gifted to her.

They visit the Galenai's homeworld, and Alex is able to show

Caleb and Valkyrie the Galenai's underwater city. Shortly thereafter, Alex, Caleb and Eren return to Maffei I armed with antimatter explosives. They mine the newly constructed gateway and destroy it to protect the Galenai from discovery by the Directorate.

The AEGIS fleet uses the Caeles Prism to travel directly to the sun in the Machimis stellar system, where they destroy the Dyson rings collecting power for Machimis. Power transmission to Machimis ceases, and the lights begin to go out on the Machim homeworld.

At the same time as the Machimis mission, Eren leads an anarch mission to take over communications systems around the empire. Mesme transports Eren to a secret resistance hideout, Chalmun Station, where he makes a grand speech about the anarchs and their intentions to take the Directorate down, then introduces Nisi.

Nisi gives an impassioned, emotional speech about the right of everyone to be free of the Directorate's oppressive hand, the arrival of the humans and their ability to defeat the Directorate, and his intentions to pursue regenesis for all species if the anarchs win.

The Praesidis Primor watches Nisi's broadcast in horror, for though the man's face has changed, he recognizes Nisi as his father. A flashback follows of the distant past. Renato Praesidis argues with his father, Corradeo (original wielder of the *diati* and head of the Praesidis Dynasty). He attacks Corradeo, stealing his *diati* then throwing his father out a window into an icy crevasse. Then Renato takes on his father's identity and claims the Praesidis throne.

The *diati* the Primor gifted Nyx with shows her the same memory while she sleeps. When she sees Nisi's broadcast, though she doesn't recognize Nisi, she feels drawn to him. On the *Siyane*, the *diati* shows Caleb the same memory as well. He realizes Nisi is Corradeo from the memory.

Caleb goes to see Nisi, confronting him with his newfound knowledge about the man's past. Nisi reveals that the little *diati* remaining within him spirited him away and nursed him back to health. In the centuries that followed, he wandered the stars, then eventually joined those rebelling against the Directorate.

Malcolm returns to Post Epsilon and seeks Mia out. He bares his soul, apologizing for devaluing her and all she's done to survive and professing his love for her again. She yells at him, then kisses him.

On the *Stalwart II*, Alex readies a surprise for her mother. Caleb clears the bridge for privacy, and Alex asks her mother to trust her.

Then David Solovy walks in, flesh and blood and alive.

CONTENTS

REQUIEM

AMARANTHE

YEAR 6143

12TH EPOCH PROPER

PART I:

AS YOU (NEVER) WERE

"We have it in our power to begin the world over again."

— *Thomas Paine*

1

AFS STALWART II

"The universe may be looking out for you and your cause, but if you truly expect to win you really ought to pitch in and give it a boost."

Miriam stopped mid-motion, leaving two of the four planned report screens unopened. "You're questioning my war strategy?"

"No. The destruction of the Machimis Dyson rings was ballsy, and it was only the latest in a series of savvy moves. But if you want to take full advantage of the gains it bought you by keeping the Machim off-balance and reeling, you need to be using every tool at your disposal right now, often and simultaneously. The most brilliant strategy is worthless without tactical maneuvers implementing it at all times, and you can't win a war when half your fleet sits idling in the void."

Calmly, as if this were a regular and ordinary conversation, Miriam took a sip of her tea and considered her response.

First thing this morning, he—*David*—had asked her to brief him on the current state of the war. He'd said he wanted to better understand what she faced. The events of the day before—the military events—made it an appropriate time to review where the venture stood in any case, so she'd agreed, which was how the two of them found themselves in the main conference room on the *Stalwart II*. Alone, which was about to be a good thing.

Miriam rested her forehead on the mirror of the lavatory in her quarters, her jaw clenched tight to render her sobs all but silent. Her shoulders racked nonetheless, thudding against the mirror in sync with her ragged breaths.

Were they sobs of rapturous joy—a bubbling up of elation at lost love impossibly found again?

Or were they sobs of long-suppressed sorrow forcing their way into the world only now, once their cause had been erased—a defiant proclamation that the sorrow could not be erased from her soul?

Or of terror at what the next minutes and hours may hold—a herald for emotions over which she feared she would not be able to keep control?

After setting the cup of tea down on the table beside her, she resumed opening the remainder of the briefing materials. "The greatest advantage the Machim enjoy, and it is a significant one, is numbers. We are vastly outnumbered in every engagement. If I send even smaller formations to engage the enemy, they will begin to lose."

David moved along the length of the table with the intensity of a man who'd been at rest for too long. "But you've forced them to spread their ships thin as well, yes? They're now having to guard hundreds, possibly thousands of gateways and fabrication facilities, stations and planets. You've made it difficult if not impossible for them to send their full strength against you in any one clash. It's an excellent strategy, but now you've got to exploit it."

"I assure you, I intend to push our enemy until it breaks. But I won't act blindly or recklessly."

She forced the sobs to a premature halt with a deep, portentous breath. She must pull herself together. Then she must walk out of the lavatory and face a future she'd never expected. She must face this man and all he represented.

Didn't she want to face him? To touch him, feel him? Wasn't this the realization of the one dream she'd never allowed herself to dream?

Of course it was. She dared to hope it was. But as she hadn't allowed herself to dream it, so she hadn't allowed herself to prepare for it.

Now she stood here on the precipice of she knew not what with no plan, no war map, no strategy, no safety net, no contingencies to fall back on. No idea what might happen next.

"Certainly not, when you never have. But you're micromanaging, and it's in danger of harming your cause."

The muscles in her jaw twitched. "*Excuse* me?"

"You've got talented people serving under you. How many admirals are here in Amaranthe? I promise you, they're capable of leading their own missions. The brigadiers, too." He smirked. "I've even heard tale of the odd commander being trusted to lead missions from time to time. Tiny missions."

"And getting themselves killed doing so?"

His energetic movements halted, and an odd look came over his features. Always so expressive, then and now. "I didn't start out leading that mission—I was merely the last man standing. Until I wasn't."

His chin dropped to his chest. "The Alliance screwed itself over in the 1st Crux War by sending the minimum required forces to any encounter while leaving a million ships to guard Earth. They played it too safe, and it became the most dangerous strategy they could follow. But this isn't that war and you shouldn't fear making their mistakes. You're pushing the enemy hard, getting in their personal space, taking them by surprise and knocking them off-kilter. All I'm saying is, don't pull up a fraction short of the goal line. If you want to win, you've got to see it all the way through."

"I fully intend to see it through. But I am outnumbered ten to one. I'm sorry if you don't grasp the import of those numbers, but I have to recognize reality and exercise the discretion it demands."

She drew back from the mirror to stand up straight, then quickly splashed water on her face and wiped it dry. When she lowered the towel and dropped it on the counter, the mirror revealed a hard, closed visage in its reflection.

Was this truly how she wanted to meet the moments to come? Her emotional armor had long served as her ally, but now she had to let it go. Armor had no role to play tonight. So she closed her eyes, exhaled and willed her countenance to soften.

She scrutinized the mirror's contents again. Better, but the Commandant still reflected back at her. Her hands paused half-raised in the air—then she brought them the rest of the way up and undid the knot holding her hair primly in place.

Burgundy locks tumbled free to her shoulders. She ran fingers through them until they formed gentle waves to frame her face and fall across her collarbone. Next, she removed her uniform jacket and hung it on the hook by the door. The plain navy shirt she wore underneath bore wrinkles from the day's activities, but it would have to suffice.

She swallowed hard, notched her chin up and opened the door.

"Okay. You don't have enough ships. Reality accepted. What about the Kats? Have you used their armada since the initial battle at their Provision Network Gateway?"

She pretended to study the information displayed on one of the screens; it had updated overnight and should now hold new insights. "Circumstances haven't presented themselves where it was appropriate for me to do so."

"What does that mean?"

"It means the Kats make everyone uncomfortable. Eighty-three percent of the servicepeople here saw action in the Metigen War. They watched identical vessels cut down civilians in the streets on their way to destroying entire colonies, and they continue to have nightmares from it."

"But the Kats are our allies now and—"

She whirled on him as frustration finally boiled over. "You weren't there."

He countered her frustration with vexation. "I've seen the horrors of war."

"Not these horrors. I'm telling you, it's a problem."

He rubbed at his jaw. "All right...do you believe the Kats will betray you?"

"No. This was their fight long before it was ours."

"Then send them on missions alone. They nearly wiped out the entire military strength of humanity, so I suspect they can hold their own in an engagement against a smattering of Machim forces. Send them off to do righteous work in service of the cause out of sight of your crews."

"The Kats are the fastidious sort, which complements their staggering arrogance. Would you care to explain their role to them and issue them their orders?"

He sat perched on the foot of the bed, directly across from the lavatory door and from her. He'd been fidgeting when she walked out, though he'd hurriedly squelched it. Still, his wasn't a relaxed pose; could he be as nervous as she?

"By the heavens, you are a beautiful woman."

Her heart trembled unbidden. "Flattery is not the critical path forward."

"I know. But I can't help it if you take my breath away."

"That's—"

"More flattery, yes. Deflect all you like. It doesn't alter what I see. Feel. Believe."

In a few short seconds, with a scant few words, he had utterly disarmed her then swept aside her defenses. Only one person had ever been capable of stripping her naked in such an adroit manner.

He held up his hands in an exaggerated gesture of surrender. "You win. I apologize—I'm overstepping, badly. I was good in a firefight, but I've never had to command over 60,000 ships or direct an entire war. I know the big-picture view looks a lot different from the one in the trenches, and you've done a magnificent job here. You have."

He gave her a wry grimace. "I want so badly to help you—with everything. I want to *do*...everything. Right now. To prove my worth, to make up for lost time, to satisfy a long list of reasons that are so obvious they're cliché."

She stared at him until his brow furrowed in puzzlement.

"What is it? Is my face melting? Because I know where to get a refund...."

"I think I'd forgotten this about you. How impatient you could be, how driven to action. How you'd always be rushing off headlong toward a goal while everyone else was struggling to clear the starting gate."

"Well, not *always*."

She allowed herself to laugh. "Of course not. You're correct, however. The view from the top is different, and there are factors you haven't taken into account. But, since you bring it up, it so happens that I have already tasked the Kats with their own missions. As of four hours ago, their superdreadnoughts are guarding several civilian facilities we believe the Directorate is likely to target and the anarchs have a vested interest in seeing protected. In addition, segments of our fleet will embark on concurrent missions as soon as additional Caeles Prisms are assembled, which is happening today."

His expression flickered, exposing a hint of unease. "You let me rant—you let me challenge your decisions—when you could have told me your plans as soon as the topic arose. Why?" His posture wilted. "It was a test. And I failed it, didn't I?"

"No...I don't know. It wasn't that kind of test. I'm just trying to figure out...."

"What to do with me?"

"I suspect you'll do with yourself whatever you damn well please. I guess I'm trying to figure out how much trouble that's going to cause for me."

He gazed at her without a trace of acrimony. "I do remember this about you. Honesty. Brutal, stark honesty, unvarnished by niceties. I acknowledge your concerns, but I don't want to cause you trouble. I want to help you."

"I believe you do. So...I'll simply ask you to pause periodically and give thought to whether our opinions as to the type of help I need coincide." She flashed him a quick smile. "You've raised several worthwhile points deserving of serious consideration. It's possible I've gotten spooked by some of the losses we've taken, and I can't let caution morph into paralysis. I don't act unilaterally unless urgency demands it, but I'll bring up your ideas at the AEGIS Council meeting later this morning."

His eyes widened. "*Gavno.* There are other people involved in fighting this war—I positively forgot about them. What are we going to tell everyone?"

Was he teasing her? His delivery was as flawless as it had ever been. She studied him, noting how the playful glint in his eyes contrasted with the earnest set of his brow, and decided he *was* being flippant, but it hid genuine trepidation. If only his irreverent humor could see them through the Council meeting unscathed.

She reached out and covered his hand with hers, touching him for the first time since they'd entered the conference room. Warmth rushed from his skin straight to her chest, and she wondered when she might stop being surprised he was real. "The only thing we can tell them and the one thing they deserve: the truth."

She crossed the remaining space between them in three rapid steps and knelt in front of him. His hands were draped atop his knees, and her left hand moved to hesitate uncertainly above his right. She willed it lower until it covered his hand, and the feel of his bare skin beneath hers shook her to the core.

His mouth opened to speak more flattery and shatter her last threads of composure, but she held up her other hand to cut him off. "I need to tell you something."

Yet her lips pursed in a panicked last-ditch attempt to keep the words unspoken; she forced them apart. "One of the last things you ever said to me was that I was the strong one in our relationship—and you were right. So when you died, I did what you had asked me to do—I bucked up, stiffened my spine and soldiered on alone. For twenty-five years *I was strong. I have been so damn strong for so damn long.*

"Now, tonight, I don't want to be strong any longer. Tonight, you're here, and I think I...I think I don't really care if you're truly David or merely a very, very good copy. Because you're here, *and tonight I am not strong enough to question the rightness of it."*

He exhaled and brought both hands up to the sides of her face then wound them into her hair, drawing her closer until his lips hovered scant centimeters from hers. "You know what? In this moment, being here, seeing you, touching you...I don't care either."

2

PALAEMON

Odd sensation, the weight of tangibility.

The molecules comprising the air fought her existence among them; the resistance was trivial, but she felt its pressure all the same. It made her feel real. It was exquisite.

Valkyrie took a step forward. Technically, she needn't step to move—but apparitions glided, and she had not invested such great effort in learning this skill to be a mere apparition.

The absence of the cushioned tile pushing against her presence displeased her, and she hurriedly returned the collection of agitated particles that created a representation of a 'foot' to the walkway. The resumption of the walkway's texture in her perception was...interesting.

She lifted an arm and stretched it out in front of her. Golden-bronze points of light shimmered and pulsed, flowing in calm ripples while maintaining a cohesive whole...mostly. The arm was hollow, and the particles formed a porous, translucent shell around nothing. But it nevertheless acted as an extension of her identity. So very *interesting*.

Her gaze—itself a collection of particles honed into perception filters—drifted beyond her arm to the expanse of scenery ahead. In the distance, past the ring of landing pads, Kennedy and Noah sat at one of the patio tables eating breakfast. Perfect!

This not being a physical, human body constrained by muscular ranges of motion or skeletal interlocking, her presence cascaded forward in a blur of *steps*, and the next second she stood beside the patio table. "Good morning."

Kennedy jumped in surprise, sending her fork clattering to her plate as she jerked back, eyes wide. Noah simply regarded Valkyrie with interest.

Kennedy cleared her throat, belatedly adopting a semblance of composure. "I'm sorry, we're not familiar with your species...?"

"Of course you are. I'm Valkyrie."

"Alex's Valkyrie?"

"Among other attributes, yes."

Noah tilted his head, nodded to himself, and settled back in his chair. "Sure. Makes sense."

Kennedy frowned. "Dare I ask how? And what? And...never mind, I can guess why."

"Certainly you may ask. Mesme has been instructing me on the process required to instantiate one's consciousness in the physical world. This is my first venture outside of the *Siyane*."

"Oh. How fascinating." With the initial misunderstanding resolved, Kennedy began to study her curiously. Valkyrie made a note to plan such introductory encounters better in the future. "This is impressive."

"Thank you. How do I look?"

"Um, great, I think. The sun rising behind you is kind of washing you out, so the details are a bit indistinct."

Unacceptable. She focused inward and drew more power to the space within the boundaries of her presence.

"Much better." Kennedy seemed to remain confused, however. "Are you wearing a helmet?"

Noah rolled his eyes. "It's a Norse winged helmet with a bronze finish. She's a *valkyrie*."

"And you will fill me in later on how it is you randomly know what a valkyrie's helmet looks like."

"If you make it worth my while. Valkyrie, you said Mesme was teaching you how to project yourself, but the Kats don't speak audibly. Did you figure that part out on your own?"

"Ah, yes. I extrapolated the method to do so from the scientific principles underlying the projection mechanics. The Kats suffer no limitations that would render them unable to vocalize, so why they choose not to do so, I cannot say."

Kennedy scowled. "I can. Forcing their words into your head makes them seem mysterious and enigmatic. It's a power play."

"Likely so. I did not want to be rude and presume as much to others." Valkyrie moved forward several centimeters. "Pardon me, but do you mind if I touch the table?"

Kennedy grinned. "Not at all. You can do that?"

"I believe..." she extended an arm until her 'fingertips' hovered just above the table "...I can." She lowered the appendage digits until the first particles made contact with the synthetic polymer of the table surface.

Resistance. Tactile pressure. Tangibility. *Physicality.*

She smiled, though without consciously directing the composition of her face to alter in such a manner. "Yes, I affirmatively can. May I hold your fork?"

Kennedy picked it up and held it out toward her. "Of course."

'Holding' was a more advanced act than 'touching,' and she was forced to concentrate quite hard on maintaining sufficient coherence in her hand and fingers to ensure the fork did not slip through. Kennedy kept two fingers on the fork until her outstretched appendage solidified. When she withdrew them, the fork remained suspended in midair, encased in Valkyrie's hand.

Joy. This sensation was *joy.*

Or possibly *delight.*

"Do you want to—I guess you probably can't eat, can you?"

"No." She carefully placed the fork down on Kennedy's plate, pleased when it only lightly clanged. "Aside from the obvious fact that I do not require organic nourishment, I lack any taste mechanisms. I would experience the food as an object, but it would not convey any characteristics beyond density and weight. Nevertheless, what is it you are eating?"

Kennedy made a face of mild disgust. "Noah talked me into trying some of their food—the Anadens' food, not the more-alien aliens' food. It's a popular breakfast dish of..." she poked at the spongy, yellowish blob with a tine of her fork "…I honestly don't know."

Valkyrie directed her perception filter particles to the item of food. "It is a berry fruit of tropical origin, with a thin skin covering and ample flesh of a soft but meaty texture—" She stopped and began again. "It's similar to a sweet eggplant."

Noah lifted his hands. "See? That doesn't sound too awful now, does it?"

"Enh." Kennedy set her fork on the plate and looked up at Valkyrie. "Is Alex still on the *Siyane*?"

"Yes. Little of me remains there while I am occupying this persona, so she is monitoring the ship's vital functions." Valkyrie shifted her focus toward the landing pads and the *Siyane*. "Not much is happening at present, and nothing apt to tax the ship's systems, so everything should be fine. I ought not to stay gone for too long, however. She is anxious enough already without me adding to her concerns."

"Anxious about her dad? Did something bad happen with the transfer or the…awakening? Did he come back wrong?"

Noah burst out laughing. His chin hurriedly dropped to his chest as he tried to subdue the laughter. "I'm sorry. I know this is a serious matter. But he's not a *zombie*…" his lighthearted expression began to darken "…is he?"

"No. All of our—Alex, Caleb and my own—interactions with him yesterday suggested the transfer was a complete success. I'm afraid she is rather more anxious about her mother. I normally would not share such a confidence, but I sense she would not keep her concerns from you. Irrespective of the tenor of her mother's response to David's appearance, she is concerned about her mother's response to her own role in his appearance."

Kennedy indicated understanding. "She's afraid Miriam will be pissed Alex kept all this from her for months. It's a valid concern…but I never thought I'd see the day when Alex was actively worried about whether her mother was angry at her."

"Indeed. Much has changed for Alex in my time with her, and now those changes will be disrupted in ways I cannot foresee or predict." She cast her perception filters toward the *Siyane* once more. Kennedy's remarks had reminded her of her own anxiety on Alex's behalf.

She forced herself to experience this present and this place for another moment. "Before I go, may I ask what you have planned for the day?"

"We're going to build a second Caeles Prism today. If the convoy from home gets here with all the right parts, possibly a third one. We need to be able to split the fleet up and run simultaneous missions at disparate locations."

"A wise strategic decision. Until later, then." Valkyrie released control of the particles holding her presence together, and the manifestation that had been *her* dispersed into the air until nothing remained.

SIYANE

Alex slouched in the pilot's chair, one foot thrown up on the dash. The Palaemon sunrise shimmered off calm waters and painted the cockpit in diffuse amber light. A quiet, peaceful morning extended from horizon to horizon—the kind of morning that brought smiles to even irascible faces and vigor to even weary bones. One full of hope, promise and possibilities.

Ostensibly, she monitored various ship systems to make sure nothing failed or went wacky in the absence of Valkyrie's active control. But all the systems were fine. They'd functioned superbly before Valkyrie had arrived, and in the months since the disastrous incident at the master portal the first time they'd tried to come to Amaranthe, every system had been modified to function—if not superbly, at least adequately—without Valkyrie's guiding hand.

It was good that the systems were fine, since Alex could hardly string two coherent thoughts together for worrying about how last night had gone for her parents, then worrying about what the answer meant for today and all its tomorrows. The urge to slip into sidespace and peek—a fast and fleeting peek—had tormented her sleepless hours. But she hadn't done it, because she respected her parents' privacy, dammit. And because she'd been as afraid of what she might see as she was hopeful.

'Alex?'

She jerked and yanked her foot down off the dash to sit up straight. "Valkyrie, you're back? Obviously you're back, seeing as you're talking through the ship. How did it go?"

'Well, I think. I touched a table and held a fork.'

Alex laughed, but she kept it kind in tone. For a noncorporeal life form, those must be extraordinary actions indeed. "That's fantastic."

'Did you experience any anomalies here during my absence?'

"Only your absence."

'What…oh. I see. Thank you.'

"I mean it. You were truly *gone*, and I could feel it. The walls were empty, the HUD lacked character. It was both surreal and disconcerting."

'You are teasing me.'

"Maybe a little. But no anomalies to report. Everything functioned normally and as programmed."

'I am relieved. I spoke to Kennedy and Noah while I was walking. They are having breakfast on a nearby pavilion.'

"Oh? I should go say good morning." Caleb was showering, but if she made it a quick visit she'd be back before he came upstairs.

'A fine idea, as they inquired about you. I will run diagnostics and review performance reports on our systems. I wish to identify any latent variances capable of growing into problems if the systems are stressed during any future absence on my part.'

"I thought you probably would." Alex gathered her hair up and wound a band around it before opening the airlock and starting down the *Siyane's* ramp—where she almost ran smack into her mother coming up.

Her eyes widened in surprise and a spike of fear. "Mom! What are—is something wrong? Did something happen—"

Miriam held up a hand to cut her off. "Everything is…to be honest, I have no firm grasp on how everything is, but I can say with reasonable confidence that nothing is burning or exploding and, so far as I know, no one is bleeding. I simply decided, rather than wait for possibly a long time for you to come to me, I would short-circuit the drama and come to you."

This all sounded normal and reasonable, if surprisingly colorful coming from her mother. It had to be a positive sign.

"I just wanted to give you some space to…." A memory flashed in her mind of a conversation with Caleb on Portal Prime.

> *"If you want the relationship to change, one of you is going to need to let down those barriers."*
> *"I'm afraid to."*
> *He brought his other hand under her chin and lifted it so she met his gaze. "You're not afraid of anything."*
> *"Well, I'm afraid of this."*

She abandoned her attempt to fake a lackadaisical demeanor; old habits and older defenses aside, she really shouldn't screw this one up. "I was afraid to come see you. Afraid to face your wrath—" no, that was no good "—not your wrath. I'm sorry. I was…afraid."

"Yes, David said you were concerned I was going to be angry at you for not telling me about his existence at any point in the last sixteen months."

"Which you are." It stung, but she nodded resolutely. "Okay. Understandable. But you called him David, so be as angry at me as you need to be. It's worth it."

Miriam turned away to motion toward the winding paths of the floating outpost. "Walk with me?"

Alex had been preparing to weather the litany of displeasure soon to come her way, and it took a second for what her mother had said to register. "Um, of course."

Without another word, her mother strode to the bottom of the ramp and headed off to the left. Alex hurried to catch up and fall in beside her. "I wanted to tell you so many times."

"I believe you. You don't need to explain yourself. I understand why you felt you had to keep your secrets."

"You do?"

"Oh, yes. If you had told me, I would have tried to stop your efforts to…" a dubious look flitted across her mother's face "…transform a consciousness existing in quantum form into something more. And I very well might have succeeded."

"I worried you would, yes. I worried you would call it a pointless, destructive fantasy on my part and insist I was merely imagining any resemblance of random algorithms to my father. I worried you wouldn't believe it was him."

"Perhaps I would have said all those things. But they are not why I would have tried to stop you."

It was early, and Alex hadn't slept a minute the night before, and her mother was running circles around her. "They're not?"

"No. I would have tried to stop you because I would have been…" Miriam's gaze drifted off to survey the placid morning waters beyond the path "…afraid. Like you, though my fears wear different guises. Fear of hope. Fear of believing in the impossible. Fear that if it failed, it would destroy me. I would have claimed I was stopping you out of practicality and because reason and logic demanded it, but in truth it would have been out of fear. And that…would have been wrong of me."

Optimism blossomed in Alex's chest. "You're glad I brought him back? You believe it's genuinely him?"

Her mother's eyes were troubled enough to stall the burgeoning optimism. "A part of me still insists it *can't* be. Impossible things are impossible, and all the hopes and wishes in the universe won't change this reality. Nevertheless, if people can't return from the dead, but the copy is indistinguishable from the real thing, does it really matter?"

"Mom, it's him."

"How? *How* can it be?"

"I don't...I can't tell you how it is, only that I know it in my heart *and* my mind." She fisted her hands at her chin. "All right, science. While the Anadens have refined their genetic makeup to the point where the genes determine the person, it's not true for us. DNA creates probabilities and predispositions, but anyone who has ever met twins or a vanity baby can tell you that having the same DNA doesn't make two individuals the same person. Yet he *is* the same person. Some aspects of a personality can't be replicated by algorithms, either. There are things about him that can only exist in *him*. They manifest in ways that can only be *him*."

A tiny smile grew on her mother's face.

It was an encouraging development. "What are you thinking?"

"You may have a point. He does retain certain quirks I did not expect DNA or memory to be capable of passing on."

"I was talking about facial tics and mannerisms and such, but what are you talking about?"

Her mother's tone now grew positively mischievous. "I believe that is between me and...well, me."

She cackled in unexpected delight. "Mom!"

"Enough about that. You make a compelling argument, but I still submit it ultimately doesn't matter."

Mirth gave way to a tentative sigh. "So I did the right thing?"

"I hope so." Miriam grimaced. "See, now you've managed to make me embrace hope nonetheless. May neither of us regret it."

"We won't. But you're not angry at me for keeping this from you?"

"Oh, I am angry at you, but the anger shares equal space with anger at myself. I would have stopped you, and it would've been wrong of me. I put you in an incredibly difficult position. You reacted by doing what you believed was best to protect me—from myself—and you shouldn't have had to do it."

Wow. It couldn't have been easy for her mother to make such an admission. Walls down, defenses disarmed. One soul-baring confession deserved another.

"Mom, I want you to know something. When I realized it actually might be possible to bring him back, real and living and in the flesh? A part of me wanted to stop then and pretend like it *wasn't* possible, because I thought you would never forgive me for keeping you in the dark. I thought no matter the outcome for him, the fact I didn't tell you beforehand was sure to ruin our relationship, and I desperately didn't want that to happen. Being close to you has meant so much to me of late, and I didn't want to give it up. Not even for him. But I didn't have the right to deny him the chance for renewed life—or the right to deny you the chance to again have him in yours."

Her mother paused for half a step, and she met Alex's hopeful gaze wearing a non-wrathful expression. Possibly an affectionate one. "Thank you. That means a great deal, as has having you in my life again. You haven't ruined our relationship, nor, presumably, have I. But going forward, perhaps fewer secrets?"

Alex beamed, flush with relief and a new lightness of being. "You got it. In fact, I should get some secrets out in the open, just to start fresh. Let's see…Mesme is teaching Valkyrie how to project her consciousness into the spatial dimensions, so if you see a golden specter of a Norse woman, don't freak out. Caleb and Noah started the bar fight here the other night—well, they didn't *start* it, some Dankath did, but they were why it happened. Before the Machimis mission, Caleb, Eren and I used antimatter explosives to destroy a gateway leading to the Maffei I galaxy in order to protect an indigenous species of aquatic life."

"What?"

"When I was fourteen, I deliberately broke your Yixing teapot, then chickened out and blamed it on the cat. When I was seventeen I stole—"

Miriam lifted both hands in a gesture of surrender. "Okay, enough. Please. I said *going forward*." She shook her head. "Who am I kidding? You will always do what you believe is right, and I can't ask you to change. I wouldn't want you to change. I suppose if I'm saying anything, it's that I *am* trying to change a little, here and there at the margins, and you might want to keep this in mind when you evaluate these kinds of decisions in the future."

Æ

Alex returned to the *Siyane* in a sort of daze. Once inside she sank against the cockpit half-wall and stared at nothing, eyes unfocused.

Caleb must have heard her arrive, for he vaulted up the stairs from below while still pulling on a shirt. "Valkyrie said your mom was outside. Is everything all right?"

She regarded him a moment, started to answer—and covered her mouth with her hand as a sob welled up in her chest and forced its way past her lips.

He was touching her the next instant. "What happened?"

She wiped at her cheeks even as tears kept falling. "She forgave me."

Caleb's brow furrowed as he took over the futile task, his thumb gently catching a few tears as they fell but mostly caressing her cheek. "Then what's wrong?"

"Nothing! I have my father back, and my mother forgave me." She laughed and sobbed at the same time, making a mess of herself and his clean shirt. "I feel like my life has…started over, like I've been given a second chance to write the story of my life."

He smiled so wonderfully and drew her closer to kiss her forehead. "Because you have—but it wasn't given to you. You made it happen."

She breathed in through her nose and worked to impose a measure of control. What had gotten into her, bawling like some hyperemotional teenager? "I love you. I could never have become a person worthy of her forgiveness without you. Thank you for believing in me."

Her lips found his, grazing across them and back again. "So what do you say? Will you help me write the second story of my life?"

"Oh, baby, it would be my genuine pleasure."

3

MACHIMIS STELLAR SYSTEM

"**L**ights!"

The room obediently brightened to a moderate illumination, powered by one of dozens of generators swiftly assembled and installed on the Annex earlier in the week by Diaplas engineers. Their use was being rationed out of necessity, hence the room's state of darkness on his arrival.

The Machim Primor gritted his teeth against the shame that flared despite him being alone in the cavernous, circular apex of the Annex. Every step, every action on his part seemed to trigger a new cause for embarrassment, but he dared not succumb to the deceitful whispers fogging his mind. Instead of entertaining them, he opened the intergalactic map and set about reviewing the state of the numerous in-progress operations. After brief consideration, he chose one to dive.

If the anarchs and the Humans were going to continue to insist that business must cease being as usual, the Directorate had finally decided it could accommodate them. Whether despite or because of what had transpired in his home system, all Machim formations had been pulled off their regular duties and now conducted active war assignments. They guarded important worlds and stations as well as every transit gateway; now they guarded vital power module fabrication centers.

They also attacked.

His integral perception focused in on the members of his progeny currently located in Sector 5 of the Large Magellanic Cloud until his mind occupied each and all of theirs. They perceived his presence as no more than a faint tickle at the base of the skull, if they perceived it at all. He watched through their eyes as the warships approached Chalmun Station Asteroid.

All of the underground, pariah outposts would be crushed in short order, but this one would be crushed most viciously of all. The anarchs chose Chalmun Station to thumb their noses at the Directorate; from within its slipshod burrows they made a show of publicly humiliating the leaders of the empire. Chalmun Station would be punished accordingly.

As the formation closed in on the asteroid's location, radar pinged not one large object as expected, but rather multiple smaller objects. *Many* multiple smaller objects. His perception leapt to the forward scouts, who were just coming into visual range of the asteroid.

A fleet of Katasketousya superdreadnoughts hovered in defensive lines arrayed in space. They guarded...nothing. Chalmun Station—the entire physical asteroid housing it—was gone.

The Katasketousya vessels engaged his warships without provocation. Hundreds of thousands of tiny tentacled drones detached from the hulking superdreadnoughts to swarm the Machim formation while deep red beams eighty meters in breadth swept across what had in seconds become the battlefield.

He leapt back to the Imperium's Navarchos an instant before a beam caught the entire squad of scout ships and they exploded. The Navarchos had already begun doing what one was required to do when attacked: attacking in return.

But if Chalmun Station no longer occupied this point in space, why were the Katasketousya here at all? If nothing existed to guard, why were they stationed here? Did they linger merely to take advantage of an opportunity to attack Machim ships out of spite? Did they take pleasure in claiming empty space from him? The Katasketousya were proving to harbor many distasteful characteristics they had hidden from the Directorate until recently. Why should pettiness not be one of them?

But why pettiness toward *him*? Why did Machim bear the overwhelming brunt of the enemies' destructive impulses in this conflict? Yes, he represented the military and thus the true authority in Amaranthe, but a plethora of other targets existed. Why had they not stolen the power from Solum, or Chomar? He had been humiliated again and again by this collection of terrorists, turncoats and invaders, but this was solely because he had been the only one to challenge them. Let Erevna stand up to these enemies and see how she fared.

With a weighty breath he drew into himself long enough to regain his bearings. He again pushed aside the disjointed, erratic doubts and concentrated on the unfolding conflict. Warfare lived in his soul, and he intended to see it executed properly.

The superdreadnoughts were both powerful and sturdy, however, and the engagement soon devolved into a battle of attrition. The fact that SAIs controlled the enemy vessels rankled him a great deal, and the fact that they were allegedly shackled, limited-purpose SAIs did nothing to quell his displeasure. His men should be able to outsmart the lowly machines. They must do so, lest the monstrous creations wreak havoc on civilization if victorious.

The simultaneous contradictory sentiments clashed for dominance in his mind. Were the SAIs inferior or superior? Were they worthy only of subjugation, or to be feared as potentially domineering overlords?

He blinked as a train of thought from the Navarchos flared in his mind. *They were losing too many ships for the dynamics of the encounter.* Crippled and destroyed ships continued to be tallied across the battlefield, but the numbers weren't adding up. Ships were simply…vanishing.

He backed away from the deep dive to study the overarching flow of battle. The dropouts seemed to occur when ships went behind enemy lines to flank the Katasketousya vessels.

He encouraged the captain of a cruiser to attempt a flanking maneuver and mentally accompanied the vessel as it swung around in a wide arc while fending off a multitude of swarming drones.

When it neared where the asteroid should have been, the cruiser readied to reverse thrusters and pivot toward the rear of the super-dread—

—blinding light washed over the cruiser, followed an instant later by searing heat. The hull melted, the skin of its crew melted—

—shock propelled Machim backward in the top-level Annex meeting room, and he would have fallen to the floor if he hadn't impacted a wall first.

He furtively checked the room, skin reddening in preemptive mortification. But he remained alone, his abasement private this time.

He tried to shake off the lingering nausea. The ordeal reminded him of the sequence of events when Casmir's fleet was annihilated beyond the false portal, though he had not experienced those events first-hand or in so intense a manner.

Had the Katasketousya positioned one of their dimension-shifting fields here, as they had inside the false portal space? Was such a field sending any vessel that crossed it into what he assumed must be a nearby star? Why? Again, for spite? Did they cavort in glee at continuing to outsmart him not with new tricks, but with the *same* tricks?

He felt sick to his stomach, still nauseated from the vicarious but violent deaths and newly disgusted by the mental image of Katasketousya snickering at his ineptitude—abruptly he bent over and retched onto the floor.

Now disgusted by himself as well, he used his immaculate uniform jacket to wipe his mouth off then called for a Cleaning Unit. But the foul taste remained in the back of his throat as he struggled in search of an appropriate response to the current state of affairs.

With no Chalmun Station present to destroy, the ongoing engagement was pointless and served only as a drain on his resources. But he could not withdraw. To do so would be to admit defeat, to no end but his further disgrace.

ᴁ

CHALMUN STATION ASTEROID

LARGE MAGELLANIC CLOUD
LGG REGION I

"This is bloody marvelous." Eren grinned in the direction of the oversized screen hovering above the crowd. He and the crowd watched, transfixed, as it displayed in gloriously vivid detail the destruction currently befalling the Machim fleet outside the hidden shelter of the asteroid. The Kats had turned the region into a shooting gallery.

Cosime giggled beside him. "The Kats are persnickety, but they're also spectacularly clever."

"Right? No doubt about it. Did you meet this 'Hyperion,' though? The one in charge out there? Prickly, dour bastard makes Mesme seem like the life of an Idoni party in comparison."

Cosime shook her head, sending iridescent strands of hair bouncing off her shoulders as she sipped on her fruity drink. "No, but it can be as prickly as it wants, I say. It made the entire asteroid *invisible*, and now its ships are kicking the Machim fleet's petard."

"True enough for certain." He glanced around the bar, one eye scanning for any trouble that might have an inkling to brew. As he did, the bartender caught his attention and held up a glass in question. Eren shook his head and continued his survey.

"It wasn't an ultimatum, Eren. You can have a drink. I won't get angry."

Damn, how had she picked up on the brief, silent, *subdued* interaction? He laughed faintly and with a touch of woe. "I know. Better to err in the other direction for a while, though, I think. Besides, I need to be sharp right now. I'm expected to be acting all leader-like."

"Yes, but this is still Chalmun Station we're talking about."

"Granted. Which is another reason why I need to be sharp." The station was on full alert, a precaution against the improbable event of the Machim ships finding a way past the cloaking effect of the Kats' dimensional shifter and managing to get inside. Full alert meant virtually everyone on the station was now armed, because outside of a dozen bouncers and a handful of deputized peacekeepers, the defenders were also the residents. While they may be 'his people' in the philosophical sense, they also included a disproportionate number of criminals and general-purpose thugs, and they were riled up and spoiling for a fight.

"Trying to protect me again?"

He scoffed. "You can protect yourself—I'm more worried about protecting *me*." It was at least half true.

"Sober or not, you're still full of it."

Before he could respond, indignantly or otherwise, Cosime had flounced off her stool and was grabbing his hand. "I see Trepenos motioning for us. Come on."

Tucked into the carved-out walls of the asteroid another full level up, above the balcony that jutted above the bar, sat Trepenos' office. It felt lofty, but a hundred meters of asteroid pressed down on the ceiling above it.

Eren leaned against an irregular, bare wall. "What's the situation?"

"I was hoping you could enlighten me."

"Oh, outside? It's going fine. The Kats' SAI ships are embarrassing the Machim fleet. I'm embarrassed for them, and I despise the Machim."

"Is there a Dynasty you don't despise?"

"Eh, I suppose the Diaplas build some decent stations. Anyway, I was asking about *inside*."

"Hmm." Trepenos peered out the interior-facing glass wall, his uneasy visage suggesting he feared a riot had broken out in the minute it had taken them to come upstairs. The lack of sudden distress overtaking the Novoloume meant one had not. "Edgy and anxious but not panicked. Broadcasting the battle on the screens was a good idea. The only thing more nerve-wracking than watching a battle for your home being waged is to know a battle for your home is being waged without knowing how it fares."

Cosime flitted around the small office, pausing to peek out the glass to the open space below. "More people than I expected. I assumed many would have fled for safer harbor after Eren painted a giant bullseye on Chalmun Station."

"Oh, many did flee, but an even greater number have arrived since Sator Nisi's message aired. Most of them seem to think this is where they come to sign up for the revolution, which is what I wanted to discuss with you."

Eren beamed with pride. The rabble flocking here to fight because of him! Well, because of Nisi. But also him. "We've set up a sort of 'friends of the anarchs' comm channel and data repository. People can use it to request resources, provide information on potential targets, and team up with other likeminded individuals—and to call for help, obviously. But newcomers don't get told the locations of any of the Posts or invited to meetups with high-level anarch personnel. Not until they've proved themselves trustworthy.

"We ought to be especially cautious with Anadens claiming to want to join up. I feel for them—I've *been* them—but we need to protect our assets and our agents. Even if they're sincere, unless they can demonstrate they've severed the connection to their integral, they're apt to do the cause more harm than good."

"Unless there are a great many of them."

Eren frowned in Trepenos' direction. "You think?"

"The noise generated by a significant number of fractious Anadens could disrupt the normal flow of an integral, no?"

It had been so long since Eren had felt the insidious touch of an integral, he wasn't certain he remembered how it worked in practice. Nor did he want to. But this was serious business and he was trying to *lead*, after a fashion, so he thought about it nonetheless.

"It depends on the situation. A dozen or so Kyvern anarchs thinking rebellious thoughts at the same general location probably muddles the area integral cloud enough to render a loyal Kyvern on the scene—and possibly even an Inquisitor—unable to identify them individually. So you make a good point. We should have the

Anadens who sign up work as teams whenever possible, ideally Dynasty-specific teams.

"But I don't care if there are a million recalcitrant Kyverns, the Kyvern Primor will still be able to identify them individually from her colossal monument to regulatory authority on Diakel. Now, if there *are* a million of them, she'll require a fair spot of time to hunt them down and punish them all, and if we're lucky our coalition will take her out before she gets that time."

Trepenos arched a smooth, opalescent eyebrow. "Indeed. Before you go, are the two of you willing to speak to a few of the most enthusiastic and qualified volunteers? Offer a few encouraging words, perhaps give them a couple of targets? Minor, ancillary targets to get their feet wet on. It would help bring some order and purpose to what is, for now, directionless chaos."

Eren caught the twinkle in Cosime's eyes and smiled. "Sure, we can do that."

4

AFS STALWART II

When David had been a Marine captain, he was involved in a mission that went south. People died who shouldn't have; valuable property was destroyed that needn't have been; havoc was wreaked to no good end and without due cause. Given that he'd been a lowly captain trying to follow orders in an impossible scenario, then trying to stay alive when everything exploded, the *khrenovuyu* fuckup hadn't been his fuckup. However, this hadn't stopped an Ethics Council tribunal from subjecting him to not hours but *days* of endless questioning before he was cleared of wrongdoing. During his official testimony he'd been grilled, screamed at, insulted, and had both his honor and his manhood challenged—and that was before the cross-examination.

In the years that followed he'd endured episodes of lesser inquiry and judgment dispensed from on high many times. But not until this moment, here in a rapidly filling conference room on a ship orbiting a foreign planet in a foreign universe, had he felt the crushing pressure of scrutiny so intensely as he'd felt it at that tribunal. Might as well call him a rodent and stick him in a science experiment's maze....

He sat beside Miriam and listened to her describe the way these meetings typically proceeded as well as what needed to be covered this morning. He knew all this, or at least had internalized the gist of it before leaving behind his virtual existence, but he liked hearing her talk. Talk to *him*, even if her tone was subdued and reserved on account of the setting.

While he listened, his eyes identified faces and matched them with the records stored in his uniquely hybrid mind—a physical, human brain made of neurons, synapses and glial cells, holding memories and information in the normal way but also a vast storehouse of data in quantum form. Well, perhaps not *entirely* unique; it couldn't be so different from how a Prevo's mind operated, though he didn't have an Artificial sharing the space.

A tall man bearing Mediterranean features and SF-style BDUs entered the meeting room. *Field Marshal Nolan Bastian. No prior personal history.* He returned his attention to Miriam.

The meeting hadn't yet begun, but his wife's stance was comfortably formal, her shoulders and chin level, her countenance guarded—aware of the audience even as she spoke with him. A stark contrast to the night before, but it was a mien he knew well.

While he could put on airs when he must, for the most part he had always simply presented himself as who he was, regardless of the situation or company he found himself in. But Miriam had consistently maintained two personas, the public and the private. A vague…sense, formed from the sum total of transferred facts he'd brought with him into this world, told him that in his absence the private persona had faded and the public one hardened. If the shift had begun to reverse course of late, it was due to a kaleidoscope of events but above all the marked improvement in her relationship with Alex.

He forced himself not to dwell on the state of the relationship until recently. It was his fault, and the ache in his chest over it didn't need the excuse of dwelling to materialize, but he shouldn't encourage it. And they had reconciled on their own, without him. So it was all fine now.

Almost as if she'd known he was thinking of her, Alex walked in then, Caleb off her left shoulder. While everyone else had thus far been trying to ignore the oddity in the room, her gaze instantly fell on him, brightened by a vibrant smile that washed away sorrow and regret alike.

She strode across the long room to reach him, leaning down to hug him and whisper in his ear. "I'm glad last night went well."

He nodded as she drew back, the only response he could or should give. 'Well' was a poor descriptor, but no single word could capture the joy and the pain, the ecstasy and the terror, the soothing comfort and the chilling fissures which had punctuated the hours of last night.

He shook Caleb's hand in greeting when it was offered. He didn't doubt his son-in-law's gesture was sincere, but he also recognized it was intended to send a message to their audience. The more people present who accepted him without question, the easier it would be for the rest to do so. He wished he didn't need the assist, but right now he'd take it.

Agitated murmurs at the door weren't drowned out by Alex and Caleb talking to Miriam as they sat down. His gaze casually swept in the direction of the doorway. *Earth Alliance Brigadier Malcolm Jenner. AEGIS Ambassador Mia Requelme.* Jenner would have seen historical visuals adorning the walls of Miriam's offices and Alex's home. He would know David's face, which was why he now wore a rather confused expression. Ambassador Requelme— *Mia,* for she was a friend to his family—placed a hand on Jenner's arm and spoke quietly to him, stopping him from voicing aloud the obvious question.

Behind them, a striking woman with a mane of golden curls walked in. *Kennedy Rossi.* Immediately her hand came to her mouth to stifle a gasp. Her eyes shot to Alex, delight breaking across her face.

David dipped his chin in acknowledgment at the woman as a myriad of professional and personal details bubbled up into awareness. He'd never spoken to her during his time in Vii's care, but he was certainly aware of her, and she of him. Most importantly for current circumstances, she was an ally.

The woman hurried over to sit next to Alex, and they promptly began whispering to one another, just like the schoolgirl friends they had once been. He pushed aside another pang of bittersweet regret; it was only the twentieth or so he'd experienced this morning. He would have enjoyed seeing them as they'd been then, but he'd take seeing them as they were now.

Beside him, Miriam's demeanor changed subtly. It was time. He wanted to squeeze her hand under the table—no one would see—but he didn't presume. Not in public, not quite yet. Instead he met her gaze for a fraction of a second and tried to convey to her how he understood.

A touch of her fingertip to the virtual control panel overlaid on the table's surface, and the door closed. "I believe everyone is here, so let's begin. We have a number of important matters to cover, but first we have an unusual one to cover. As is apparent to everyone present, we have a guest this morning. Let me start by...."

She stopped and let her gaze fall to the table. When she spoke again, the rigid, formal tenor of her voice had softened a bit. "My daughter has done many extraordinary things in her life, and an extraordinary number of them in the last two years. If you thought the invention of the Caeles Prism was the latest of these, however, you would be mistaken. I've spent the last twenty minutes preparing, but now I find I don't have the proper words. Alex, will you explain to everyone what you've done?"

Alex bit her lower lip as her eyes narrowed. Miriam hadn't forewarned her this was to be her responsibility. "Thanks, Mom. I'll be happy to, but since I didn't spend *any* time preparing, I'll cut to the chase—everyone, meet David Solovy. Yes, *that* David Solovy. I brought my father back to life."

The murmurs rippling down the table in response to the audacious declaration were...surprisingly muted.

Alex seemed surprised, too. She considered the table suspiciously. "How many people here *didn't* already know this?"

Bastian. Jenner. Brigadier Ashonye. Rear Admiral Escarra. Brigadier Belosca. Mia Requelme's hand wavered half in the air. "You told me not to look, so I didn't look. But your emotions were really loud in the Noesis yesterday."

Commander Lekkas gestured dismissively toward Alex. "You didn't tell me not to look."

Devon Reynolds offered a mild shrug. "Nor me. Still, I've been crazy busy, so I almost missed it. But like Mia said, you were loud yesterday."

Alex rubbed at her jaw. "Okay, next item on the Prevo Invention To-Do List: a way to shut out the Noesis, for when one is *trying to keep a secret*. Anyway! For those of you who weren't aware of the situation, or only have bits and pieces, here's the short version: before the final battle of the Metigen War, for strategic reasons Valkyrie uploaded my father's neural imprint into her quantum architecture. Unexpectedly, the natural synergies between it and my own mind resulted in the inception of something more robust than one expects from a neural imprint a quarter-century old.

"Valkyrie's fork, Vii, used the neurological paradigms she and Dr. Abigail Canivon had developed to enhance the construct and transform it into a full consciousness, then into a fully realized being. A mind, as real and complete as any Artificial's. I convinced the anarchs to adapt their regenesis technology to work with human biology and to transfer the consciousness into a body cloned from my father's DNA. Presto!" She motioned at him, her cheeks flushed.

"If Admiral Rychen were here, I believe he would say, 'This is the damnedest thing I've seen all day, but it is early,'" Ashonye said before frowning at Alex. "Is he Anaden?"

David chuckled and leaned forward. "It's all right, Brigadier, you can talk to me directly. I didn't want to cause a scene straight off, but I do speak."

"Apologies...sir. Commander? What do we call you? I meant no offense."

"None taken. I expected a far more colorful if not contentious reaction from the room, but I suppose all of you have gotten used to the unusual lately. We'll get to the messy title formalities in a minute. To answer your first question, no, I am not Anaden."

"But if the Anadens built you using their own technology...?"

"Think of it like this: you hire a builder to construct a custom home for you. You tell them what style you want, how many stories, bedrooms, and so on. You pick out the exterior material, the flooring, the window design and the kitchen fixtures, among a thousand other details. When the house is completed, it's yours, built to your specifications. All the builder did was use their trained skills to fit the pieces together in such a way as to ensure the house doesn't fall down when whacked by a brisk wind."

Alex chuckled. "Damn, what a great explanation. I have a suggestion. You do the rest of the talking."

"As you wish, *milaya*." The endearment had slipped out unintentionally, but the room seemed to settle in its wake.

He did the same. "Next obvious question: am I an Artificial in a physical body? Also no, though I'll concede that one's a little fuzzier at the margins. But while an Artificial's neural net resembles a human brain in some respects, it's not constructed to mimic the way our brains function. They may end up at a similar place, but Artificials are programmed from the ground up to complement their synthetic nature. Me? This all started with a neural imprint—a mapping of the function of my completely human mind. Everything since then has merely been fiddling with the drapes."

They appeared to accept the explanation easily enough—or elected not to quibble over details—leaving no reason not to jump straight to the proverbial heart of the matter. "Which begs the real question, the one hovering on the tip of every tongue but no one dares ask: am I David Solovy?"

His chin dropped to his chest, and dammit but he would *not* look at Miriam. "It doesn't matter if I tell you that I am, for you will each insist on deciding for yourself. I only know this: I intend to be the best incarnation of myself that I'm capable of being."

Dammit, he looked at her. But her expression, if still guarded, bordered on affectionate in the split-second before her attention shifted to the table. "Brigadier Ashonye, you asked what you should call him. At present, he is not serving as active duty military. The steps required to have someone declared no longer deceased, let alone reinstated? Well, they haven't been invented, and we do not have the time or bandwidth to invent them right now.

"As of today he can be considered a consulting member of the AEGIS Council, similar to Ms. Rossi. If anyone wishes to address him as 'Commander,' they are welcome to do so, for if retired military officers never lose their final rank, neither should he. I, however...plan to call him David."

A slice of fear fell away to lighten his burdened soul. When they were in private, he wanted to tell her how much the public declaration meant.

Field Marshal Bastian cleared his throat. "I only have one question: does this mean we're all living forever now?"

5

AFS STALWART II

David propped against a pallet of food crates in the hangar bay and waited. Outside, the convoy from the other side of the portal—from home—lost its structure as cargo vessels peeled off toward various ships to dock and make their deliveries. Beyond the cargo vessels a mini-fleet settled in to await integration with the existing AEGIS forces.

One hell of an operation, what Miriam had built. He'd always appreciated her skills, her intelligence and her analytical mind, but now he was in awe of the dividends her sheer determination could pay. He needed to tell her that, too. He'd been unjustly hard on her this morning. In his enthusiasm he'd strayed into overbearing and bossy behavior without the facts to back him up, when he needed to lavish credit where credit was more than due.

The transport that had accompanied the convoy maneuvered into the *Stalwart II's* hangar bay, and he shifted his thoughts to the imminent reunion. Staging an ambush definitely wasn't fair to his friend, but he was seeking an unguarded reaction, one which hadn't been prepared and steeled in advance. He wanted a gut response from the most level-headed, guileless man he had ever known.

Security procedures stalled the disembarking, but he bade his time. Plenty of overwrought, egoistic thoughts were queued up to occupy his mind during any lull. Still, he was running out of ways to dismiss the worst of them by the time the large airlock finally opened and the passengers began filing out.

Richard emerged talking to a blond man in civilian clothes—*William Sutton, Jr., husband, architect, Federation spy, SENTRI Deputy Director*—and didn't initially spot him. Presumably familiar with the workings of the *Stalwart II*, Richard and his husband ignored the staff sergeant answering questions from passengers and headed straight for the lift. As they did, Richard's gaze idly ran across the hangar bay, passed over David—and jerked in reverse. He froze where he stood.

David pushed off the pallet to stride toward him. Halfway there, Richard finally unfroze and started walking toward him as well. Slowly, and shaking his head.

David did neither, instead going straight up to Richard and grabbing him in a bear hug. "Richard Navick. It is damn good to see you."

Richard huffed a breath and took a step back. "I didn't believe it. Even after everything Alex has done, I didn't believe it."

"Believe it now?"

"Here you stand, so how can I not? But I…" he shook his head, eyes closing briefly "…I have no idea what to say."

"I do. Thank you."

"For what?"

These words he'd prepared in advance. "For being there for Miri and Alex, far above and beyond any extent I could ever have asked. For being such an incredible friend to Miri, for being like a father to Alex, for treating them like family. I will forever be in your debt."

Richard's cheeks reddened, and he looked away. His voice took on a wistful tone. "I never expected you to find out…." He cleared his throat. "Anyway, they *are* family to me. They always were. And they've been there for me, too. It wasn't all selflessness on my part."

"Eighty percent selflessness?"

"Sixty-five percent at most." Richard's countenance shifted from resoluteness to exasperation—and for just a moment a quarter century hadn't passed.

"All right, if you say so." David raised an eyebrow while staring pointedly over Richard's shoulder. "Speaking of family, your husband's doing an excellent job of not loitering, but you should probably introduce me."

"Something else I never expected I'd be doing." Richard cleared his throat. "Listen, there are a few things you ought to learn about Will before—"

"You mean how he was a Senecan spy for fifteen years? I don't know if you heard, but Alex is married to a Senecan black ops agent whose father tricked us into starting the 1st Crux War. Suffice it to say that I've had to leave grudges back in the mausoleum." He paused. "No, not 'had to.' I've chosen to. Besides, Will also helped bring a swift end to the 2nd Crux War, which helped Miri win the Metigen one, which ultimately led to you and I standing here together right now. I owe him thanks, not acrimony."

Richard stared at him oddly. Evaluating, absorbing, ramping up to analyzing. "I'm glad to hear it. I'm sorry, I was told you knew everything. It's just hard to wrap my head around."

"Well, I don't know *everything*. I know…history, the great events that happened while I was absent. But unless there was some record of an incident or Alex knew of it, everyone's secrets are safe. At least up until the Prevos were created—I'm aware of more of what's happened since then, though the knowledge is still spotty and uneven." *I was alive and not alive, aware and unaware, flitting in and out of existence….*

"Because…wait. You're not a Prevo, are you? It's fine if you are of course, I merely…." His friend shrugged helplessly. There weren't many points of reference to fit this scenario.

"No. I mean, I can't access their Noesis, and Vii isn't in my head. Any longer. Hell if I know. Can I go meet Will now? All this introspection is killing me."

"Really? You had to go with 'killing me'?"

An uneasy silence hung in the air for a second—then David started chuckling. He threw an arm around Richard's shoulders. "My old friend, regrettable word choices are the least of my minefields."

ℛ

The door to Miriam's office was open, but Richard knocked on the frame nonetheless.

She held up a finger while she wrapped up a comm. When she disconnected, she motioned to one of the chairs opposite her desk. "I had to employ some rather extreme measures in order to get you over here, but I finally succeeded."

"Extreme is one way to put it—but you're in good spirits. I'm glad."

"You were worried about my reaction?"

He shrugged. "There were factors. And how is Alex?"

"Other than ecstatic at having performed another miracle and fulfilled her own greatest wish? Contrite about having kept it a secret from me, but mostly relieved on all counts, I think."

"You're still speaking to her, then."

She blinked and pursed her lips. "I couldn't have behaved so badly in the past that everyone who knows me assumes I would excommunicate my daughter for keeping her plans from me."

He stared at her deadpan until her shoulders sagged. "Right. Apparently I did. But I'm not going to run off one family member just when I've gotten the other one back." An odd expression flitted across her face. "I'm...conflicted about the fact she hid this from me, but more so about why she felt she needed to. It would be hypocritical of me to be angry at her for doing so when I'm not convinced she was wrong to do it. But you—you knew and kept it from me as well?"

"No. The message from Alex that you delivered on your last visit to the Presidio hinted at *something*, but I never could have dreamt it was this. And I advised her to tell you what it was she was doing."

"Good. Where is Will? I thought he was coming as well."

Richard pinched the bridge of his nose. "With David. They hit it off instantly, because of course they did. I'm doomed."

"Very possibly." She regarded him soberly. "*David*. Now we've both uttered it aloud, so no more tiptoeing around the edges as though we're afraid if we speak his name he'll vanish. You've seen him. Talked to him. What do you think?"

Richard searched the room for an answer, but none were forthcoming from the neat and ordered walls of her office. "He talks like David and acts like David, as surely as a damn ghost risen straight from the grave. I didn't expect him to be like that. I...I don't know what I expected. An android or an Anaden wearing his skin, maybe." He frowned, watching her as she calmly retrieved her teacup and brought it to her lips. "Miriam, you're acting as if everything is normal—as if nothing has changed."

She took a sip of the tea before responding. "Am I? Clearly everything has changed." She studied the cup hovering in her hand midway to the desk; a tiny smile crossed her features as she set it down. "I suppose I cling to the familiar, to the routine, in an effort to stay sane when the world has transformed around me. I still have a war to win, and the fact my husband is back from the dead doesn't change this reality...even if it changes every other reality." She chuckled, then let it escalate to full-throated laughter. "Or perhaps I've already gone insane, in which case the tea and the war are both irrelevant."

"If you've gone insane, I'm right there in the padded room beside you."

"And I'll take some comfort from it." She eyed him speculatively. "You didn't answer my question."

"I know I didn't. Do *you* believe it's truly him?"

"We're both asking a lot of questions without providing many answers. But we're in uncharted waters here, so I guess we can't expect anything so straightforward as easy answers. I keep coming back to...does it matter?"

She dropped her elbows to her desk. "And it sounds more like a copout each time I say it. But it's not...what I'm trying to grapple with is the assumption behind the question: what does it *mean* to say it's 'truly him'? I'm not convinced I believe in the existence of the soul—how can I judge if this man bears the same one as the man who died?"

Richard nodded thoughtfully. "Well, I do believe in the existence of the soul. Not that I'm in any way qualified to pass judgment on his, but give me a little time with him. Like you, I'm inclined to give him the benefit of the doubt. I do worry—or maybe I hope—that what I want to see will crowd out what I *should* see. Honestly, is there anything in the world either of us want more than for him to be the man he was?"

Her gaze again dropped to the teacup she'd slid back in front of her, and her voice fell to a faint whisper. "If he's not, I'm not certain I'll survive the loss a second time...." Abruptly she turned the cup up and emptied it in a long sip before quickly putting it down. "But it is what it will be. Meanwhile, multiple universes continue spinning, and the one we're currently in threatens to spin out of control unless we can steady it."

He'd known her too well for far too long to press her on the brief display of candid weakness; mostly, he was grateful she'd allowed him to see it. "So, business as usual then. Now you've got me here, and I shouldn't spend all my time gaping in stupefied disbelief at David. What can I do to help?"

She perked up and opened several files. "I'm glad you asked. It so happens that our anarch colleagues declared public war on the Directorate yesterday and invited everyone to the revolution. From an operational perspective, this war just got a great deal more complicated."

R

Richard found Devon in what had been a security monitoring room the last time he was onboard the *Stalwart II*. He knew the ship's layout well, but he hardly recognized the room, so thoroughly had it been transformed.

A full slate of new generation quantum server boxes were installed in an embedded rack on the left wall. Threaded strands of photal fibers had been bundled up and hung from the ceiling to wind into the rack and two unfamiliar pieces of hardware secured to the center of the room. Anaden tech? Additional fiber ran from them up and across to the servers that *had* been here before. Three new screens added to the three previously in the room—plus the unfamiliar hardware came with its own style of screens. Assorted additional equipment was rigged up along every meter of free wall space.

Devon swerved past him in a mobile chair, skidded to a stop using his heels and scooted back toward him. "Richard!" He leapt up, sending the chair wobbling across the floor, and offered a hand. "Welcome to Amaranthe. Glad you got here."

He shook the young man's hand. "Thank you, I think." He hadn't spent much time with Devon since the strike against Olivia Montegreu's Artificial. Devon seemed to have bounced back fully from those trials, but first impressions could be deceiving. He hoped it proved to be true.

"You're here because of..." Devon cleared his throat melodramatically "...Commander Solovy, I assume?"

"Among other things." While he held a fatherly affection for Devon, his feelings about David were very much in flux and also best kept to himself for now. "I'm here in this room because I was told you have made yourself the go-to man for inside intel on this highly peculiar universe."

"Yup." Devon went over and grabbed the chair from where it had finally landed and dragged it to the conglomeration of screens, then motioned him over. "I didn't set out to be Mr. Go-To. I was simply the first one—and still kind of the only one—to figure out how their data tech works on a structural level. This gave me direct access to all the anarch files, whereas before I, and everyone, had to come up with a specific question to ask, ask it, and wait for an anarch tech to find the answer."

He gestured toward the rack of new equipment to the left of the door. "I wrote a couple of routines to automate the translation of their data files into our format, then more routines to write the data out onto those servers. We had some good analysis programs installed from your guys at SENTRI, but the trigger terms were all wrong. Everything's called something different here, even the things that aren't actually different. So I adapted the routines for Amaranthe-speak. I made a few enhancements here and there, too. If this circus ever wraps up, I'll pass them along to your programmers."

Yep, he'd definitely bounced back. "I'm sure they'll be appreciated."

"Should be. So..." Devon kicked the chair against the shelf behind him and clasped his hands behind his head "...what do you want to know?"

Richard leaned on the shelf beside Devon. "Miriam said this 'revolution' is going public. Since I've heard the authorities here aren't the permissive type, I assume they will move swiftly and forcefully to stamp out any rebellious behavior before it gets out of hand. Talk to me about the law enforcement here."

"Vigil?" Devon spun the chair around, and the screens burst to life. "You got it."

6

SOLUM

"Down with the Directorate!"

A raging Naraida man slammed a pipe against a glass barrier until it shattered. Protestors scampered through the opening in fevered waves, turning its jagged edges red from smeared blood. Undeterred by their injuries, the mob soon overwhelmed the Vigil officers on duty.

Vigil drones arrived inside a minute, and the reinforcements neutralized many of the frontline rioters in a sweeping burst of weapons fire. Those who found cover sufficient to withstand the initial barrage, however, soon acquired firearms from the fallen Vigil officers, and a more sustained firefight ensued. Some of the rioters ripped apart fixtures to serve as makeshift shields, and slowly but inexorably the drones, too, were overwhelmed.

And with that, the rag-tag mob of rioters took control of the entry wing of MW Administration 41.

They weren't even proper anarchs—they'd entered the station legally, carrying approved credentials and citing sanctioned business to conduct. Surveillance cam footage needed to be reviewed to determine what incident set off the riot, but Praesidis doubted it was a random, spontaneous confluence of events. It felt staged.

Damn Corradeo and his brazen call to arms.

His *father* was the leader of the anarchs. His mind refused to accept it, though he hadn't found a sane way to deny it. His father should be six hundred thousand years dead. Buried deep beneath the ravages of ice and time and history. Forgotten.

The questions jostled up against one another in a restive queue to disrupt the normally immutable calm of his psyche. How had his father survived the attack—the plummet into the abyss—in Antarctica? Where had he hid all these millennia? Why had he never returned to challenge Renato publicly or even to take private revenge? Why had he instead chosen to lead the anarchs? Had he always led them? Why incognito? Why had he not revealed his true identity during his manifesto broadcast? What did he want now? Was his goal merely the toppling of the Directorate as he professed, or did he have more devious designs? Corradeo Praesidis was nothing if not *clever*, and a single, straightforward goal would not be enough for him.

Watchman Tovald ela-Praesidis, MW Administration 41 Vigil Supervisor: "Sir?"

Renato blinked. "*What?*"

"I asked for your orders regarding the situation on MW Administration 41, sir."

"Yes, right. Lock down all entries and exits, then gas the whole level. Execute anyone who survives, then clean up the mess."

"Understood, Primor."

All these years, centuries, millennia, he'd believed himself safe. Untouchable. His head swam, pitching him toward dizziness on contemplating the notion that his damnable father had been out there this entire time, lurking. Watching. Judging.

Only when a crimson aura reflected back at him in the glass wall did he realize it had materialized. He tamped down the flaring *diati* and tried to focus his thoughts. He would not be provoked by what, objectively, was nothing more than a temporary, minor complication.

It didn't matter that his father lived. Let Corradeo come for him. He was the Praesidis Primor. He ruled over the greatest and most commanding Dynasty of the greatest and most commanding species in fifty galaxies, and nothing and no one could take his power or position from him.

He attempted to focus enough to follow the progress of the crackdown at MW Administration 41, as slip-ups could not be tolerated in the current environment. He was on the verge of succeeding when a new report arrived to draw his attention.

Flagged the highest priority, it contained an update from one of the scout ships investigating the region where the tracking dot placed on the Human vessel ceased transmitting. He perked up as he absorbed the information it held.

Artificially generated activity and multiple structures had been detected on a small planet in one of the systems near where the tracking dot failed. The planet registered on the edge of Anaden habitability parameters, and the structures were located in an arctic, mountainous region. No sanctioned uses of the planet were on file.

Everything would certainly become easier if his father happened to be in residence when the base was annihilated, which was precisely what he intended to do to it.

Renewed energy drove his purposeful stride as he crossed the room. *Machim, I need two regiments for a mission.*

The silence had neared an unacceptable length when Machim finally responded. *My forces are currently engaged in multiple offensive missions, as am I. It must wait.*

I realize you have taken losses, but do you not continue to command some fourteen million vessels?

I do. However—

Do you not want to exact revenge on the anarchs for pitching your homeworld into darkness?

Another lengthy delay. *No, I want to exact revenge on the Humans for doing so.*

Praesidis scowled. *If we remove their anarch support structure, the Humans will be helpless. Further, they will be cowed into submission, left trembling in fear at the magnitude of our ruthless annihilation of their anarch friends. They will then make for easy pickings for you to ravage at your leisure.*

But your motivations matter not—only your firepower. I have a mission, and it will not wait.

TELLUS

ORGANIC MATERIALS LAB #8
MILKY WAY SECTOR 60

In the deepest bowels of Organic Materials Lab #8, amid dimly lit storage closets and unshielded power distribution junctions, hid a small, cramped laboratory. The two-hundred-meter journey from the nearest transit tube revealed no signs of life, only the occasional whir of a passing drone. It was for the best, given her purpose here today.

On stepping through the lab's barely labeled door, Nyx elasson-Praesidis wrinkled her nose. Though the room was surely clean in the technical sense, the dank stench of grease and pseudo-organic lubricants permeated the air.

MASK NONSTANDARD ODORS

She inhaled deeply as the *diati* filtered out the offending malodor. The remaining air was sterile and artificially dry, as air in a lab should be.

Logiel ela-Erevna wandered into the far side of the room through a doorway in the rear, head buried in a display, and didn't notice her.

"Logiel."

He jumped back half a meter in surprise and brought a hand to his chest. Then his eyes landed on her, narrowed in instant displeasure. "*You*. It isn't polite to sneak up on people you're not intending to incapacitate."

"I did not sneak. I was merely standing here in the open, in full view of anyone who might happen by. It's not my fault if you've forgotten how to be observant of your surroundings."

He sniffed and closed the display he'd been studying. "If you are here to ruin my life further, I'd ask you to consider whether you instead have some more fruitful errand to pursue."

She took in the details of the lab, where alien biomass was studied for potentially useful properties like electroconductivity and, evidently, lubricity. "I also did not ruin your life. If it is ruined, you will have to search for an alternate perpetrator of the vile crime. This posting is, I presume, a punishment from your Primor for the destruction of Exobiology Research Lab #4?"

"It is. And for losing the Kat subjects, and for allowing other subjects and data to fall into the hands of the anarchs. Or the Humans, or whoever is running their catastrophe of a revolution. I believe she would have demoted me to *asi* had my regenesis process not already completed by the time she learned of the incident."

"It seems like a disproportionate reaction, considering you are neither Praesidis nor Machim and the lab maintained minimal defenses."

"Yes. My explanation of the litany of mitigating circumstances fell on deaf ears, however. Perhaps in another month or two the Primor will be in a more reasonable mood and I can renew my plea. Now, are you here to gloat, then? Because I actually do have a great deal of work to do. Dreadful, mundane, mind-numbing work better suited to a drone than a scientist of my skill, but work nonetheless."

She ran a fingertip along the cool metal surface of the countertop beside her. "I have a question."

He didn't respond, and she looked up to find him glaring at her. "I'm waiting."

Still, she hesitated. This was the precipice. Another step and the future became an unknown quantity, every further step a leap into an unexplored domain. Did she genuinely want to veer down this path?

But it wasn't a matter of wanting; it was a matter of necessity. As an Inquisitor, she must find answers, and to find them she must do this. "Is there a manner in which one can implement a…buffer of sorts between one's own thoughts and delves from the integral? Specifically, delves from a Primor?"

He arched an eyebrow. "That is a most unusual question, Inquisitor."

"I am aware. Will you answer it?"

"For the masses, no—that is to say, no, it isn't possible. If 'one' is you, on the other hand? Perhaps. An *elasson* enjoys a fair degree of control over their interaction with an integral, so the framework is in place upon which even greater control can be grafted. May I assume 'one' doesn't wish to disconnect entirely and run away to become an anarch?"

She gave him a blank expression. "You may so assume."

"Then why do it?"

"My motivations aren't your concern or your business. There are simply some matters my Primor doesn't need to...trouble himself with until I've brought them to a resolution. If he were to learn of them prematurely, he might...suffer an incorrect perception of them. Of my intentions with respect to them."

"So you're trying to protect him from himself."

She hadn't meant to answer his question, immediately after having told him she didn't intend to answer it. Small consolation that she'd answered with a lie—or a truth that could soon become a lie. "I am serving him in the best way I know how, as ever."

"Of course."

She swallowed vocal annoyance at his continued peevishness. "What would doing so involve?"

"We are talking about your neural architecture here, which means it would involve a very delicate medical procedure."

"But you are capable of performing such a procedure."

"For the right price."

Such a vain, petty man. "Name it."

He paced between two long lab tables, a new vigor animating his steps. "I want out of here. I want an assignment commensurate to my intellect, experience and skills. I don't particularly care how you accomplish it, but make it happen."

"I can send a formal communique to the Erevna Primor, through proper channels of course, taking responsibility for the destruction of the lab—"

"You *were* responsible for the destruction of the lab."

"Only in that I didn't stop the incursion. I will explain to your Primor how allowing the enemy to succeed was crucial to a larger strategy, and you were most helpful in assisting me in this regard."

"Which I was."

"Don't push it, Logiel."

He rolled his eyes as if put upon. "Send it now."

"You don't believe I will keep my word?"

"I believe my luck has been in quite short supply of late, and I am not inclined to take a chance and assume it will make a surprise appearance now."

She pressed a palm to her forehead. The extended verbal sparring was worsening a headache that had arrived with the looming weight of what she was about to do. "Very well. Give me five minutes to prepare the communique, as I do want to make certain to be as eloquent and persuasive as possible."

7

MACHIMIS STELLAR SYSTEM

MILKY WAY SECTOR 36

Zoravar Bazuk T'yevk had never met this Anaden chieftain. Words in messages then more words from the operators of the flying machine insisted the chieftain was important. Big. Powerful—the most powerful Anaden chieftain of all the powerful Anaden chieftains. Must be treated with respect.

Now that he stood before the chieftain, Zoravar decided the man looked weak and puny, same as all other Anadens. Soft. Easy to bleed.

"Commander Zoravar Bazuk T'yevk, allow me to present to you the leader of the great Anaden military. Our Primor, Machim." The flyer of the flying machine bent over at the waist toward the chieftain as if he were about to…Zoravar laughed.

"Do you find something amusing, Commander T'yevk?"

"Did not know Anaden chieftains were suckled by their serfs. Keeps them in their place, yes?"

The chieftain's fleshy face contorted in what looked like pain as he waved his fingers in the air. "You misunderstand our formalities, but I care not. I've called you before me because I am tasking you and your horde—cavalry—with a mission of supreme importance."

They always said such things. Every task came with words like 'vital' and 'grave' and 'importance.' Soft Anaden words from soft Anaden men. Stripped of fancy words, they wanted creatures killed—sometimes animals, sometimes walk-talls—and killing was not for soft men.

Zoravar grunted. "We execute every mission to our fullest, until the blood runs thick."

"Good, for the purpose of this mission is, above all, for the blood to run thick."

But it always was, so Zoravar waited.

"Eight hundred of your best fighters will be accompanying our ships to a planet called Chionis. It is cold, snowy and mountainous, so have them prepare appropriately for the elements."

"We wear woven mittens, then."

The chieftain made another squishy wrinkle-face. "Is that a joke?"

"Funny one, yes?"

"I...did not know the Ch'mshak had a sense of humor. Fine. Wear whatever you want, but you've been warned. Chionis houses a base of operations for a group of terrorists—enemies of the Directorate. Once our fleet has eliminated the perimeter defenses of the base, your troops will be transported to the surface."

As it always was. "What are we killing this time?"

A new expression grew on the chieftain's fleshy face. Zoravar had seen it on Anadens before, when he'd fought side by side with the stronger of the Anadens' weak warriors. When the battle fever overtook them and they ceased being proper and soft and became the animals even they had once been. He hadn't expected to see such an expression on a chieftain in shiny clothes.

"Everything."

Zoravar nodded. "Makes things easier. But everything of what? Giant spiders like in the Antlia galaxy? Giant reptiles like in the Briseis galaxy? Something more giant? My warriors hunger for a proper challenge."

"No." The chieftain turned from Zoravar to stare at the front of the ship. "A variety of species will be on Chionis: Naraida, Novoloume, Barisan. Others." The bulge in the front of the chieftain's throat bobbed up and down. "Anaden."

It had been many cycle-years since Zoravar had felt surprise at anything an Anaden said. "We are killing Accepted Species—who we are forbidden by the Directorate masters from killing? We are killing your kind?"

Red veins popped into streaks running through the chieftain's eyeballs, and he looked as though he was straining not to release his bowels. "The individuals who are on Chionis have committed grave crimes against the Directorate and its citizens. The gravest. They have earned their death sentences. More than this, they have earned slow, agonizing deaths. We could bomb them from the sky and the end result would be the same, but that is too merciful a death for these terrorists. Commander T'yevk, I want your troops to turn the mountainside red."

Now this was a zeal for killing he could respect. He gestured with enthusiasm. "And yellow!"

"Pardon me?"

"Novoloume bleed yellow."

The chieftain took a forceful step toward him and thrust his face in close. Anyone less than an Anaden chieftain and Zoravar would have ripped the soft man's throat out for the implicit challenge, but here he limited himself to a deep, threatening growl.

The chieftain didn't seem to notice, and by the wildness overtaking his tiny eyes Zoravar wondered if the man was already hearing the call of the battle fever.

"It's not yellow, it's *copper*, and I don't *care* the color of their blood. Just make sure they die screaming. Every last one of them."

PALAEMON

ANARCH POST EPSILON
MILKY WAY SECTOR 17

Caleb made his way across the elevated walkways toward the *Siyane* as Palaemon's sun set on the watery horizon. It had been a good day, and would likely prove to have been a fruitful one as well. David Solovy's return to the living was thus far going as smoothly as anyone could hope for, and a fair bit better than he'd feared.

He was beyond happy for Alex...but he was also giving her and her family a little space to reorient themselves without the complication of his presence. Yes, they were his family now, too, but they hadn't been his family during the fateful events currently being rewritten.

No, rewritten didn't feel like the right way to characterize it. The past was not being changed, only the future. He'd be a part of that future, in time.

For today, however, he'd made himself useful elsewhere. Several squads of Marines had spent the afternoon at Epsilon training anarch field agents, and vice versa. He'd sat in on two sessions of the latter, as he still had much to learn about the idiosyncrasies of Amaranthe and its inhabitants: weapons he might come up against in an encounter, defensive tools his enemies took for granted, non-obvious weaknesses of a lengthy list of alien species.

The Directorate had quickly escalated its offensive following Nisi's broadcast, sending its Machim armadas against any target associated with the anarchs they could find. Both AEGIS and the anarchs were ready for the escalation, and thus far they'd met every challenge. Tomorrow they would....

He slowed to a stop near an intersection of three walkways, senses instantly vaulting to heightened alert. Why?

The *diati* stirred to ripple within his skin in anticipation. Anticipation of...he closed his eyes and listened, not for sounds but for the disturbance to *normal* that the *diati* perceived. He began turning in a deliberate circle—the *diati* spiked.

He opened his eyes and discovered he faced a transport module from the *AFS Saratoga*. It had brought the Marines down earlier today and remained here until they were ready to rejoin the fleet. When he'd left them, the Marines were enjoying some downtime socialization with their anarch counterparts before heading back to the *Saratoga*.

He cautiously approached the transport, cognizant that with every step the *diati* hummed louder. But the vessel should be empty and locked up tight.

The hilt of his blade found its way into his hand.

Nothing looked amiss as he reached the transport. He confirmed the airlock was closed and secure, then walked the perimeter of the hull. Nothing. Nothing but the *diati* singing in his ears and vibrating against his sternum.

The landing gear elevated the vessel almost a meter above the ground, so when he'd completed the perimeter check he crouched down, blade at the ready, to peer beneath the—

—a mild surge of power washed over him, and in its wake the *diati* quieted. Had he just absorbed a new dose of *diati*? The sensation had been faint. He might not have noticed it were he not noticing everything in his perception: what he touched, saw, heard and even smelled. Everything he felt. But from where had it originated, or what?

LIGHT

A ball of artificial illumination materialized above his free hand, and he extended it beneath the undercarriage to try to see more clearly.

This stretch of the hull, between the engine and the single defensive laser housing, was smooth...except for one small imperfection. Now confident no attacker lurked under the vessel, he rolled onto his back and scooted under the frame.

A tiny piece of equipment three centimeters in diameter and a centimeter tall jutted out from the hull. He tried to pull it off, but it stuck fast. Yet it wasn't part of the hull; the color and shape were wrong. The location was wrong. It was *wrong*.

He brought his blade up, activated it, and narrowed the blade to its thinnest width. Then he carefully worked it between the hull and the foreign object until the object came free and dropped onto his chest.

He returned his blade hilt to its sheath, palmed the object and shimmied back out from underneath the transport. He stood and opened his palm, but he couldn't discern any details about the object, as the sun had completed its descent beyond the horizon and left behind only shadows.

LIGHT

The illumination shifted to hover above the object.

It didn't look AEGIS-made. In fact, it looked Anaden-made. Had *diati* been concealing it?

Valkyrie, I'm sending you several visuals taken with my ocular implant. What am I looking at?

A moment. I cannot say for certain, but a comparison against images found in the anarchs' files suggests the object closely resembles a Vigil tracking device.

"Motherfucker!" He called forth his power and transported briefly to a distant point in space, then from there to the *Stalwart II*.

PART II:

ANGELS &
MONSTERS

"Some work of noble note, may yet be done,
Not unbecoming men that strove with Gods."

— Alfred, Lord Tennyson

8

AFS STALWART II

David returned from refilling his drink to half-sit on the arm of Miriam's chair. His free hand instantly, naturally, alighted on her forearm; her gaze instantly, naturally, rose to meet his in answer. A blink and the moment passed, but the fact that it occurred at all was nothing less than a miracle.

Richard and Will had joined them in the *Stalwart II's* captain's suite for drinks at Miriam's request. Events were in motion with respect to the war, but a measure of calm had been snatched out of the chaos this evening. Richard was glad Miriam seemed to not only recognize it for what it was, but be willing to take advantage of it. Though he suspected she would vehemently deny it if asked, in the span of hardly a day, David's presence had changed her.

David took a quick sip of his drink then rested it on his thigh. "So the three of us are attending this ball the brass arranged in honor of Admiral Zvedski, who was retiring from active duty to head the prime minister's Advisory Board. Everyone is outfitted in their shined-up dress uniforms and wearing their best airs, but of course this being a ball, there is a well-stocked bar, which is where Richard and I are.

"We're minding our own business—by which I mean drinking—when this woman saunters up beside Richard and orders two Negronis straight up. She might have been a noteworthy arrival on account of the screaming red dress slit up to her thigh, or due to the five-carat diamond necklace dangling into her ample cleavage, but no. She's a noteworthy arrival because she's the trophy wife of Admiral Zvedski himself—and because she arrives as drunk as a bridesmaid crashing a bachelor party.

"We both recognize her from prior formal events. Her name was...Sylvia, I think. We square up our shoulders and are trying to look respectable—or was it respectful?—when she sidles up closer to Richard and starts hitting on him. And I don't mean subtly."

Richard sighed. He wished David were exaggerating. "I'd had women hit on me in bars before—" he caught Will raising an eyebrow beside him "—a few. The point is, I had experience in getting rid of them. But I'm serving up every 'no thank you' cue, signal and body language I know, and nothing is working. She's completely oblivious to my polite rejections and getting drunker by the second. Then she puts her hand on the back of my neck and lays her head down on my shoulder, and I flat-out freeze. This is the admiral's wife, everyone knows it, and I have *no idea* what to do to defuse the situation without causing a scene. At this point, I'm resigning myself to the reality that my military career is at an end."

Will winced at Richard but tilted his head toward David. "Where had you gone?"

Richard scoffed. "Oh, he'd moved down to the end of the bar where he could laugh his ass off while he watched. Refused to be of any help whatsoever."

David shrugged. "This is all true."

Will shifted to Miriam. "And you were somewhere, too, right?"

"I had been tasked with giving the introductory speech for the admiral. So while this—" she waved a hand in Richard's direction "—is transpiring, I'm across the ballroom beside the stage going over the order of events and various procedures with the admiral and his attaché.

"I get this random pulse from David..." her voice dropped into a rather adept imitation of his voice and accent "...'Keep the admiral distracted and don't let him turn his attention to the port bar.' That's it—no elaboration. Well, *I* can't look over at the port bar, because if I do, the admiral will notice and do the same. I'm completely in the dark as to what's happening, so I simply keep talking."

Richard lingered on the realization of just how surreal this all was. David, *here*. He and Miriam acting like a couple. Will joking with David...for years he'd wished they had gotten the chance to know one other. Now here they were.

But the story was about him—and guaranteed to embarrass him at any given point—so he forced himself to return to the present. To enjoy it, too, for it was its own miracle.

David picked back up the story. "Meanwhile, the situation is deteriorating. Sylvia keeps trying to order another drink, and Richard keeps trying to stop her. She's leaning into him so hard her diamond necklace keeps hitting him in the chin. But he's a gentleman to the last, so he tries to politely move her away—and she starts climbing into his lap. No shit. I'm about to come over and step in—"

Richard scowled. "No, you weren't."

"I *was*. But I don't have to, since Tom Hammett shows up then. Now, Tom's ninety-five kilos of solid muscle, as straight-laced as they come and married with two kids, but Sylvia doesn't know this. He stomps up to them, puts a hand on Sylvia's shoulder and comes out with, 'What are you doing shoving your tits in my boyfriend's face, bitch?'

"She jerks and, wearing ten-centimeter heels and being sloppy drunk as she is, stumbles backward and falls on her ass. In the quest to keep things quiet, this is not a good development."

Miriam interrupted. "It most certainly was not, because it did cause a commotion. People start staring, then pointing, and I'm reduced to sidestepping back and forth in front of the admiral to keep him from seeing *whatever* is happening at the port bar. In the sole stroke of luck I'd had so far, he was not a tall man."

"And he suffered from a classic case of Napoleon complex as a result, but it's not relevant to the story. Hammett hurriedly leans down and offers a hand—"

Richard cleared his throat while trying not to blush. David was having entirely too much fun telling the story. For Will's benefit, surely. *David.* "Which I was getting ready to do myself."

"Of course. Hammett offers her a hand and helps her up—then pulls her in close, gets in her face, and growls, 'Are we going to need to take this outside?' Sylvia's a waif of a woman—except for the cleavage—and this hulking Marine in full dress uniform is calling her out. Her eyes get as wide as saucers, and she shakes her head and backs away. Hammett turns to Richard and throws an arm around him, then says, 'I'm sorry I was late, honey, but I got held up at the base.'

"Richard looks like he's about to vomit from mortification. But he calmly takes a sip of his drink and responds with, 'I understand, dear, but you need to try harder to be on time for these sorts of occasions. Appearances are important.'"

Will twisted around on the couch to face him fully. "You didn't!"

"It's all kind of a blur. I'm not sure—"

"He absolutely did. I've never been prouder of him. Then the music quiets, Miri takes the stage, and she gives as brilliant a speech as one expects from her."

Richard scoffed. "How would you know? You and Tom were too busy stifling your glee into the bar to notice anything else going on."

Miriam stared up at David expectantly. "That's an excellent question. How *could* you know?"

Her tone remained affectionate, but Richard had known her for more than forty years, and he sensed the undercurrent of challenge in the question. It asked for affirmation, for validation that she'd been right to accept him, to trust that he returned the same man he had been and welcome him into her arms and her life.

If David recognized the challenge, he didn't retreat from it, instead dipping his chin in concession. "When I finally stopped laughing, which was about the time the admiral took the stage, I accessed the vid feed. I restarted it from the beginning and watched you instead of the admiral." He leaned down until his forehead almost touched Miriam's. "Double win for me."

"You have an answer for everything, don't you?"

"Yes."

A smile, a breath, a touch of a hand. It seemed miracles were alive and well in Amaranthe.

"The truth was—" Miriam sat up straight, nudged David back and held up a finger to preemptively silence everyone. A frown replaced mirth to overtake her expression as it became clear that the war had come to claim their peaceful interlude.

Abruptly she stood. "Run your alcohol neutralization eVi routines and meet me in the conference room. We have a problem."

"Where's the tracker now?"

Caleb paced along the length of the table, cognizant that soon enough the conference room would be too crowded for him to do so, and soon after that he would be expending the pent-up energy in more consequential actions. "About four hundred parsecs away, orbiting a red dwarf in an uninhabited system. I'd have destroyed it, but I didn't want them to be alerted to the fact that we'd found it."

Before Miriam could respond, Jenner rushed into the meeting room. The brigadier instantly opened an aural and slid it down to Miriam. "This is a sequential list of everywhere the *Saratoga* or the transport module has visited since arriving in Amaranthe. Unfortunately, the list includes almost seventy percent of our missions. The only locations where either have landed, however, are Post Epsilon, Post Alpha and Exobiology Research Lab #4."

Caleb paused his traversals long enough to drum his fingers on the table. "The odds of catching a tracker this small while in space are extremely low. I'd put my credits on the lab being the source, for one basic reason: if the Directorate had spies on the ground at either of the anarch posts, they wouldn't need the tracker."

"Unless they were searching for the fleet."

Caleb barely managed to stop himself from whirling in surprise. It was damn strange to hear the accented voice, to see David Solovy walking and talking among them. "Then they should have found us days ago. Why haven't they attacked us yet?"

Miriam eyed them both as she opened a new holo interface and Nisi appeared—Corradeo, Caleb reminded himself, though few in the room knew it. He'd shared the Sator's true identity with Alex, and they'd agreed that Miriam should be told, but Caleb didn't intend to out the man to the world unless circumstances demanded it.

The anarch leader was studying a screen and didn't greet them at first. In the brief lull that resulted, David spread his arms dramatically in response to Caleb's question. "Why haven't they attacked at all yet?"

Nisi looked up to respond. "Multiple scramblers are in place in the region surrounding each post. The tracker's signal would have dropped twelve parsecs before the transport reached any of our locations. Best case: they assumed the tracker was discovered and destroyed, and they gave up. Worst case: They continued to investigate, which means they needed to search multiple nearby systems for evidence of our presence. Unless they got very lucky, this would take time. They might have failed entirely, as our posts are well camouflaged."

Miriam shook her head. "We nonetheless must act under the assumption that they did not fail and any or all of the AEGIS fleet, Post Alpha and Post Epsilon are subject to attack at any time. The fleet has been placed on full alert. Sator?"

"I have informed the respective Administrators of the increased danger, but there is little 'alert' status to activate. The perimeter defenses are always active. Beyond that? To move every resident to an alternate post via the teleportation gates will take days. To put them on ships is more efficient, but there are not so many ships, thus it will still take days. We need to determine whether such drastic action is warranted."

Alex hurried through the door then. The look on her face as her eyes found him—before they found her father, and he should not take such pride in it as he did—suggested she was up to speed on the situation, which of course she was. Even apart from the quick message he'd sent her, word would've traveled through the Connexus into the larger Noesis and to every Prevo in seconds, if it took that long.

Jenner stepped into the brief disruption Alex's arrival created to answer Nisi directly. "AEGIS personnel are all being recalled from Epsilon as we speak. Sator, Ambassador Requelme is en route now to Post Satus to act as a liaison during this crisis." He pivoted to Miriam. "Commandant, I recommend we split the fleet—leave half here to guard Epsilon and send the other half to Alpha. Rather than evacuating and abandoning the locations, we should defend them."

It was an unusually assertive move on his part, Caleb thought.

Miriam hesitated for less than a second. "Agreed. Thomas, distribute orders to implement the directives that follow, authorization AFX-21X93 Alpha Zulu Mark 3.4."

'Acknowledged.'

"Brigadier Jenner, you'll lead the forces at Post Alpha."

Jenner drew up in surprise. "Ma'am, with respect, I don't deserve the assignment. This is my fault."

Ah, so this was the reason for the earnestness. Caleb considered remaining silent…but it had been a good day. "No, it's not. Only Praesidis and Kats—and me, I guess—can detect anything less than a substantial concentration of *diati*, and it took a fraction of that amount to mask the tracker's presence. Unless we want to enlist a cadre of Kats to scan every one of our ships in addition to their own—and maybe we do—there is no realistic way to detect the presence of a tiny, hidden tracker like this one."

Bastian snorted, despite the fact he'd only arrived a minute earlier. "What about when it was placed? Or preventing it from being placed?"

Caleb kept his attention on Jenner. "Were the transports under guard while they were at the lab?"

"Every second."

"Then there's nothing else you could've done to prevent it. I assume a Praesidis Inquisitor or Vigil agent was onsite. They must have stealthed to place it, and in an environment you didn't already control, you couldn't guard against invisible—that's why we use Veils so frequently."

Alex reached his side and squeezed his hand.

You're acting kind to Malcolm. What gives?

I'm feeling generous.

Miriam nodded in agreement. "Now is not the time for rashly assigning blame, though I suspect Caleb's analysis is the correct one. As for more rigorous preventative measures, those considerations will also need to wait for the aftermath. We need—"

Nisi cleared his throat, somehow managing to project such gravitas through the holo with the simple act that the room instantly quieted. "Discussion has become moot, and our course is set. I've just received a priority notification of Machim vessels inbound to Post Alpha."

Miriam sighed. "Belay my last, Thomas. Marshal Bastian, the SF Southern Fleet formations will remain at Post Epsilon in case of an additional attack there. The rest of the fleet will proceed immediately to Post Alpha under my command. Thomas, direct the *AFS Keswick* to move the Caeles Prism into position and the fleet to escalate to Level V Threat Status."

She glanced back at Jenner. "Sorry, Brigadier. Next time."

9

CHIONIS

F elzeor soared high above the snow-capped-and-coated mountains that all but encircled Post Alpha. The arctic air frosted the porous feathers of his face and outstretched wings to the brink of freezing, but it wasn't *so* much colder up here than on the ground, where the chill from the snow crept into the walls and floors of the post.

In a grudging allowance to the frigid temperatures, he wore a thermal vest around his chest that Cosime had designed for him. 'To keep your heart warm,' she'd said. Wearing *clothes* felt so odd, and he suspected it interfered with his aerodynamics a bit, but it did help keep him warm. His chest anyway, which held his heart. This should make Cosime happy.

He canted his wings to drop into a valley between two peaks and raced a few meters above the ground up the steep angle of the next peak until he reached a zenith in unobstructed sky. Only then did he tuck his chin and level off parallel with the jagged horizon. What fun!

The terrain surrounding Alpha was interesting, challenging and exquisitely pretty; he just wished it wasn't so *cold*. But Thelkt and Cosime were here now, and often Eren, too, so he tried to get by. He loitered around the thermal vents a lot.

Of course, he could go spend some time at Epsilon with Caleb and Alex and Valkyrie...unless they didn't stay put there. He bet they didn't stay put there. For like him, they were happiest when they were flying. Post Charlie was tropical, which sounded fabulous...but he didn't really know anybody there. He preferred to be among friends whenever possible. Friends were worth a spell or two of frigid air.

The transmitter embedded beneath the skin of his neck broadcast his 'friend' designation as he flew past one of the perimeter turrets built into the mountainside. Cosime would probably fuss at him for venturing so far from the post...so he wouldn't tell her! She was adventurous, too; she simply got a little overprotective of him sometimes. And of Eren. Especially of Eren. Which didn't make much sense since Eren couldn't die. It must be because she loved him?

He crested an even higher peak to greet the morning sun, and for a brief span the air felt *almost* warm. He cooed to the sunrise and swept into a wide circle to fully enjoy the almost-warmth.

As he came back around, a sharp glint of light flared off to his left. But he was above the tallest peaks, so there shouldn't be anything nearby for light to reflect off of. He didn't know about all of the secret defenses Alpha used, but he did know they were sure to be hidden, not out in the open where they might reflect light and draw attention to themselves.

He dipped his wings to veer in that direction—and the glare shifted away to reveal a row of Machim fighters speeding barely above the peaks of the mountain range. Though still well outside Post Alpha airspace, their heading would bring them directly to its location in minutes.

They knew where it was!

He plummeted into a near-vertical dive through the nearest valley, out of sight, then sped as fast as he dared, skimming dangerously close to the snowy, rocky ground.

Felzeor: Xanne! Administrator Hano! Machim warships are on approach from the northwest! They'll be at the post in less than five minutes!

ᴁ

Eren threw a leg over one arm of the chair opposite Xanne's desk and slouched against the other. "If the reports I'm getting are to be believed, three regional hubs have seen their operations completely shut down and another four are being repeatedly disrupted. The MW Sector 18 and Andromeda Sector 2 Administration stations were taken over by anarch forces for multiple hours, and SMC Sector 1 Administration is still under anarch control."

"Are they?"

"Are they...?"

"The reports—are they to be believed?"

He glared at Xanne in borderline annoyance. Ever the pragmatist, she certainly knew how to deflate a pleasant high when reality required it. He laughed under his breath at the recognition that he'd been high on the gratification success brought rather than, well, *high*. It felt good—or at least it had before Xanne doused it with a bucket full of skepticism.

"Is something amusing, Eren?"

"A bit. To answer your question, on average the reports are probably inflating the level of success twenty percent or so in an attempt to impress us—to impress the anarch leadership, that is. And for the most part, failures never make it to reports, as there's no one left to do the reporting. But I've solid confirmation on—"

The emotions abruptly springing to life on Xanne's face stopped him cold. His feet landed on the floor, ready to vault him into action the instant he gave them a destination, or just a direction in which to move. "What's happened?"

"We're about to come under attack." She opened three different displays and entered a multitude of commands. Sirens began to peal through the hallway behind him and many hallways beyond.

"Defenses are active. Sator Nisi has requested for me to report to Post Satus and assist him from there. There's no time for flight evacuations, so Administrator Hano is beginning an evacuation of the most essential personnel, followed by the most vulnerable, through the teleportation gate to Post Charlie." She paused her frenetic work long enough to check him. "Eren, you should get to Post Charlie."

She was telling him he was 'essential.' He got that. All the more reason to stay. "Not a chance. I'm fighting. If nothing else, I'll buy time for people to evacuate."

She nodded as if she'd expected the response. "Empty the armory and don't hold anything in reserve. Good luck."

"See you on the other side." He hit the door running.

10

CHIONIS STELLAR SYSTEM

T he wormhole exited into normal space a scant three megameters above Chionis. With no time to waste, Miriam had set the destination at the minimum safe distance.

The instant they arrived, every formation engaged the attacking Machim fleet.

A scan of the tactical map as it populated with data revealed a full third of the Machim vessels deployed in defensive rearguard positions. AEGIS' arrival had been expected, or least their appearance was not *un*expected.

That was fine. She, too, had come prepared, despite being given only a few minutes warning. Most of being prepared involved having the right standing orders in place when the pivotal moment arrived.

She stopped herself from glancing over at David, who stood off to her side. She didn't need more than her peripheral vision to observe that he was as comfortable on the bridge of a ship as he'd ever been. But it was the first time he'd stood on the bridge of *her* ship while it entered combat. The sudden desire to impress him that welled up shouldn't be a surprise, but she couldn't afford to indulge it.

Commandant Solovy (AFS Stalwart II): "SF Northern Fleet, focus on the Machim defense line. EA SE and SW fleets, spread out and protect our flanks. EA NE and NW fleets, form a defensive perimeter around the remainder of the planet to prevent additional forces from reaching the surface. AEGIS ESC flights, trench a line of negative energy mines between the enemy defense line and the vessels actively attacking the planet. Cut them off from one another. AEGIS Assault brigades, get yourselves past the defense line and engage the forces attacking the planet in full."

"Thomas, flash analysis. What do you see?"

'Our arrival was anticipated, and a portion of the enemy vessels have been tasked with waiting for us, then engaging us when we appeared. The enemy fleet is outsized for the target, however, even by Machim standards and even accounting for the additional ships required to engage our forces. Speculation: they expected Chionis to have a level of planetary defenses that it does not possess.

'Given the number of Machim ships present, the post should be obliterated several times over by now, irrespective of the high percentage of vessels tasked with defense. Yet it is not. I'm receiving information confirming communications are still transmitting from the ground. Fragmented and disjointed and providing negligible actionable intel, but communications nonetheless.'

She sensed David draw closer. "Your Artificial would make a decent battlefield commander."

"He *is* a decent battlefield commander."

'Thank you, Commandant.'

Miriam studied the tactical map more closely as the conflict began to take shape. Separate and apart from the rearguard that had been waiting on them, a hefty chunk of the Machim forces held stationary positions on the far side of the battlefield, closer to the planet. They weren't attacking the surface, however...in fact, it sure looked as if they were *protecting* it.

Commandant Solovy (Stalwart II)*(Command Channel): "Commander Lekkas, leave the mine placement to your Eidolons. I need eyes in the sky down there. Something isn't right up here, which I suspect means something isn't right on the ground."*

Commander Lekkas (AFS MA-Primary)*(Command Channel): "On it."*

ᴀR

Morgan hardly noticed the buffeting of the atmosphere against the sleek adiamene hull of her ship as it left space behind and dove toward the surface, primarily because she'd put the ship on autopilot to leap ahead in sidespace and survey the scene. Once she was flying within sight of the ground, there would be no time to loll around contemplating strategy. She wanted to figure out now where to go once she got there.

What she saw sent her consciousness slamming back into her body. She disengaged the autopilot and increased her speed to tear through the balance of the upper atmosphere.

Machim fighters buzzed high in the skies above Post Alpha, shooting out the few remaining defense turrets and shield generators and patrolling the perimeter of the site, presumably intending to shoot anyone or anything that tried to arrive or flee. A small squad of fighters fired on the structures of the post, but only until the edifices fell, after which they moved on to the next. All moved prudently and gave the craggy mountains a wide berth, with good reason. But they weren't her.

She slowed and descended as low as she dared, stealthed or not. Her custom ship was the most advanced fighter-type craft ever built by humans, and she wore it like a second skin. Flying this low to the ground, surrounded by steep mountains and narrow crevices, took unparalleled agility and quick reflexes—luckily her ship had one and she had the other. She tipped the wings and slipped through a gap to get a closer view of activity in the distance, past what remained of the clustered structures.

A large Machim transport vessel hovered above a comparatively level area of the steep terrain, beyond the southernmost boundary of the post. A wide ramp had been lowered from its fuselage, and out of it poured an army of massive, hulking creatures.

I believe they are Ch'mshak.

Yes, but what are they doing here?

Based on what we know of the species, there can be only one logical answer: they are here to kill.

Stanley was correct, of course. The brutish warriors must have been departing the transport for some time now, for her eyes swept across the vicinity to see skirmishes among wrecked buildings and in open spaces. No, skirmishes was not the correct word. Slaughter. No mere anarch, or three or four anarchs working together, stood a chance against a lone Ch'mshak—and there were no lone Ch'mshak, for they were moving in packs.

The file on the species scrolled through her mind:

» 1.5x larger in height and breadth than the average human

» thick hides for skin

» claws, tusks, etc., etc.

» viciousness as a defining societal characteristic.

She frowned, and not only at the shudder-inducing descriptives. The Machim were orderly, predictable and proper soldiers, top to bottom. Their fleet could have simply bombed the post out of existence from the sky, or even from space; they had no need for ground troops. And if they should have a need for ground troops, the Machim had plenty of their own to deploy. They could overrun the anarchs trapped on the surface with numbers and weapons without the help of these brutes. The Machim were cold, heartless and ruthless, but they weren't bloodthirsty or overtly malicious.

However, in removing his source of energy in audacious fashion, AEGIS had delivered more than a tactical blow to the Machim Primor—they had delivered a nasty psychological blow as well. They had plunged his homeworld into darkness.

Perhaps he was a little peeved. Perhaps he wanted to make a revenge-laden statement in return. And perhaps he knew that while his ground troops were efficient killers, they were eugenically incapable of *brutalizing* their prey before killing them. The Ch'mshak, on the other hand? They would delight in doing so.

She activated her arcalaser and burned a swath through as much of the advancing front line of Ch'mshak as she dared without endangering anarchs trapped in the complex, then pinwheeled up and away to evade seeking fire from two of the Machim fighters.

Commander Lekkas (MA-Primary)(Command Channel): "Brigadier Jenner, pay attention. Commandant, we have a critical situation on the surface. Hordes of Ch'mshak are being sent in to slaughter everyone who survived the initial assault—which wasn't much of an assault, so I anticipate there being a lot of survivors to slaughter."

Commandant Solovy (Stalwart II)(Command Channel): "There's no tactical need for such a move. Obliterating the base from the air is faster, safer and simpler. Why are they bothering with Ch'mshak ground troops?"

Commander Lekkas (MA-Primary)(Command Channel): "My guess? Revenge. The anarchs, and us, have humiliated the Directorate. We epically humiliated the Machim Primor at Machimis. They don't merely want to stop the anarchs now—they want to make them pay. I expect next they'll want to make us pay."

Brigadier Jenner (AFS Saratoga)(Command Channel): "Commandant, permission to take Marine—"

Commandant Solovy (Stalwart II)(Command Channel): "Granted. I'm sending three flights of SF fighters down for air support as well. Commander Lekkas, update the flight primaries with the intel you've acquired and take command. Clear the skies, then take out as many of the Ch'mshak as you can without risking civilians or our people. We'll do our part up here to prevent any further vessels from reaching the surface."

Commander Lekkas (MA-Primary)(Command Channel): "Acknowledged."

Belatedly, Morgan realized what the events she'd just set in motion meant. She sent a pulse to Harper.

Listen, watch yourself groundside. The Ch'mshak may qualify as the nastiest fuckers I've ever seen.

Sounds like fun. I'll bring extra grenades.

I'm serious, Brook. These monsters aren't your typical adversaries.

You worry too much. This is what I do, and I'm damn good at it. Got to go—monsters to kill.

Morgan squeezed her eyes shut for half a second in an attempt to ward off the unreasonable fear that crept in to squeeze her heart in a vise. Their enemies were either immortal or half-ton killing machines, but Harper was neither, dammit.

She made a mental note to ask Harper to get an updated neural imprint as soon as the current crisis passed. With the all-but-literal resurrection of David Solovy, Alex had demonstrated that death no longer need be the end. Eternal life wasn't in their reach quite yet, but no harm in covering the bases.

Then she forced her mind back to the conflict at hand and started scanning the surface for some Ch'mshak to shoot.

11

CHIONIS STELLAR SYSTEM

AFS SARATOGA

The briefing room was packed full with every Marine and ground troop Malcolm had in Amaranthe, minus two who were laid up in Medical and four who had gotten stuck on Palaemon when all hell broke loose.

How many of the people in the room was he going to lose today?

Malcolm gritted his teeth and shoved the dispirited thought away. Objectively, he recognized its origin. He felt guilty—his mind insisted this was his fault despite any reasoned arguments to the contrary—and his guilt was expressing itself in the form of a bleak voice muttering doom in his ear. But that voice had no place in command or on the battlefield.

He didn't bother with a polite throat-clearing. "Attention! We have no time, so listen up. The situation is this: an unknown but large number of Ch'mshak shock troops are on the ground at Post Alpha. Their sole purpose appears to be to finish off the anarchs who survived the initial aerial attack. Brutally so."

He displayed a scale image of a Ch'mshak in battle armor beside him, evoking several gasps and many curses. "I cannot overstate the danger these troops represent, so I will not try. Now, the good news: three flights of SF fighters are heading in-atmo as we speak. Their mission is to clear out any Machim vessels in the air then carpet bomb the rear lines of the enemy, taking as many out en masse as they can without endangering innocents on the ground. The bad news: the Ch'mshak have been there for a while, so they've spread throughout the post complex.

"This is where we come in. The only way to eliminate the Ch'mshak inside the complex and rescue survivors is to take the

Ch'mshak out in close combat. We'll move in teams of no fewer than six. Whenever possible, concentrate on taking the enemy out one at a time before moving on to the next, because if we spread ourselves too thin they will tear us to shreds. In addition to your standard gear, everyone is carrying an augmented TSG. Daemons aren't likely to do anything but piss these guys off.

"All right, everyone suit up in full combat tactical gear and be on the transports in ten." He paused. "And bring grenades. Bring all the grenades."

⋏

CHIONIS

ANARCH POST ALPHA

They executed a combat jump into the center of the bombed-out post. A quick tactical analysis using the schematics of the post and the visuals Morgan had taken concluded that they would save the most anarchs by establishing a central bulwark, taking down the Ch'mshak that had reached the heart of the post complex and working their way out. Beginning at the rear of the complex stood to save even more lives in a perfect world, but the rear of the complex was slammed up against the sheer cliff of a mountain and left no room to maneuver or retreat. Not a perfect world.

Meanwhile, an aerial bombardment would destroy the enemy's transport and work its way up through the ranks of the enemy until it met friendlies.

Snow fell in heavy, wet flakes to blanket the scattered wreckage and bodies. It lent a surreal quality to the scene, in stark contrast to the savage reality.

Harper landed with a soft roll across the snow-coated floor of a building lacking a roof. She ended the roll face-to-face with the corpse of a Barisan. The vertical, cat-like irises stared at her unseeing, and its throat had been shredded. Its stomach, too.

Captain Harper (mission): "They're already this far in. We need to move into the building north of the drop point."

Brigadier Jenner (mission): "Copy that. Delta, fortify this position. Don't let enemy troops cross this line from the south. We'll gather survivors here as we clear the complex. Echo, begin sweeping the area to the south. Take it slow and keep an eye on the skies. Everyone else, form up at my location and prepare to move. We're sweeping the grid to the north. Alpha left, Bravo center, Charlie right."

Forming up and preparing took seconds, after which seconds were wasting.

Captain Harper (Bravo): "Pello on point, Odaka on rearguard. Let's go."

The partial edifice of what had once been an expansive, multi-level structure stretched nearly across the length of the vale between two towering peaks. They stepped through a jagged hole in the wall into a large, open room, possibly a training or entertainment area.

Bodies lay scattered and strewn, silent beneath the snow that was making good progress in burying them.

"Pello, life signs?"

"Negative. It's a dead zone."

"Proceed ahead."

The far end of the room led to a long hallway. They cleared three offshoot rooms before they encountered their first Ch'mshaks. Two of the alien combatants had dragged a pair of Naraida out of a closet and were—

—okay, so the Naraida were already dead. She unlatched two splinter grenades and tossed them in the room as the Ch'mshak looked up. Christ, they were huge. Monstrously, colossally huge. Larger than the beast at the exobiology lab. "Move!"

The squad hauled ass back down the hallway to reach a safe distance from the door. The grenades detonated; what remained of the edifice shook as shards, flesh and blood exploded out the open doorway and tore through the walls.

"Redale, Verela, clear it."

The two Marines moved to the hole that had been the doorway, and Redale's TSG swung up to unleash a torrent of laser fire.

When the barraged ceased, Harper scowled. A single splinter grenade could kill every person in an eight-meter radius of detonation, and the room wasn't eight meters *wide*. "They weren't dead?"

Redale's shoulders heaved as he lowered the TSG. "They are now."

"Noted. Next time, they get three grenades."

Around the next corner the hall opened up into a larger space. Collapsed sections of roof had split the room in two, forming a makeshift barricade across the left third of the room.

The sound of limbs scrambling behind it indicated survivors had taken refuge—plasma shot out from a small gap in the fallen slabs to nick one of the four Ch'mshak in the process of tearing the barricade down—and they had weapons.

She quickly motioned everyone back into the hall, hoping to buy a stride or two of surprise, and switched to comms. *"Survivors behind the barricade. Watch your shots."*

Four Ch'mshak, and a split-second to choose a tactic. *"As soon as I move, start shooting while backing down the hall. Splinter grenades risk hitting the survivors, but toss two stun grenades when they reach the doorway and open up on them with everything."*

She breathed in—and sprinted toward the right wall, opposite the barricade.

As the weapons fire began, the attackers spun around. They were surprisingly agile for their size, as if they needed another advantage. One came after her, and the other three barreled toward the rest of the squad.

She waited until her pursuer was committed and she'd nearly reached the wall, then ordered her defense shield to maximum EM protection and Veiled. She dropped a stun grenade on the floor and launched herself upward. *Lift.*

She was halfway up the wall and eye level with the Ch'mshak when the grenade detonated. The alien stumbled once, blinked and kept coming.

Shit. *"Stun grenades are ineffective. Draw them another five meters down the hall then use splinter grenades."*

The alien stopped a meter from the wall and swiped its massive clawed hands out into the empty air in search of her. When she hit the junction of the wall and a half-intact section of ceiling, she opened fire downward into the top of its head.

It instinctively looked up in surprise, and the laser tore through an eyeball and out the back of its skull. Her momentum carried her into the air in an arc above its thrashing body then toward the floor—

—a long arm swung wildly in her direction. A single claw on the outstretched hand penetrated her shield from sheer force to swipe across her thigh.

The Ch'mshak collapsed as its body finally registered the fact that its brain was dead. She landed hard beside it, and her injured leg promptly buckled upon the jarring impact.

She splayed a hand on the floor to catch herself and was pushing up to standing when the floor, walls and debris shuddered from the detonation of multiple grenades down the hallway. Despite the distance from the explosions, several pieces of the barricade shifted and fell. Hopefully not on any of the survivors.

Captain Harper (Bravo): "Report."

Weapons fire answered her. She tested out the leg. Walking, check. Sprinting and leaping? Maybe not. She de-Veiled and hobbled toward the hallway, TSG raised, but by the time she reached it the weapons fire had finally stopped. "Report."

Redale shouted in her direction. "All targets down. Shanti took a shoulder hit."

She reached into her pack and found a basic medwrap, then jammed it inside the torn material of her tactical pants and stuck it over the gash in her thigh. Her eVi executed a combat wound routine and deadened the area; she'd be good to go in a few more seconds.

"Verela, get Shanti's shoulder treated. Everyone else to me." She studied the unstable barricade. "We have people to rescue."

ᴙ

They found two Anadens, a Novoloume and a Barisan behind the barricade. All were wounded, but except for the Novoloume they were ambulatory. On seeing the heavily armed Marines, the aliens tossed aside their weapons and lost any forced bravado in favor of exhaustion and relief.

While Odaka passed around a canteen of water, Harper peered in concern at the copper blood seeping out of a long cut in the crushed leg of the Novoloume. "Verela, can we do something...."

Verela knelt down beside the grimacing alien and offered it a reassuring smile. "Bandages will help any wound, no matter the color of the blood."

"You are kind, Human."

"I try." Verela buried a frown as she swathed a large medwrap around the leg.

Sergeant Verela (Bravo): "This wound's ugly. I'm tempted to do a field amputation, but...."

Captain Harper (Bravo): "But we don't have the time or security. Just staunch the bleeding as best you can."

Verela squeezed the Novoloume's hand as she stood. "When we get you to some real medical help, make sure they take care of you first thing. Understand?"

Her patient nodded weakly and sank against the wall.

Harper straightened up as if she didn't have an injured leg. "We need to move all of you to our forward base. From there you'll be evacuated as soon as the skies allow it." She peered upward; a gaping hole in the ceiling provided an unobstructed view of those skies, but fighter after fighter flew by too fast to see more than blurs of metal.

Lekkas, what's it looking like up there?

Like a shooting gallery, if you're me. The Machim took note of our presence and sent some fighters they had stashed halfway across the planet to engage us, so still shooting.

Noted.

You?

It fucking sucks. Got to go.

One of the Anadens and the Barisan hoisted the Novoloume up between them without being asked, and Harper checked over everyone. "Are we ready? Odaka and Redale, fifteen meters back and eyes on our rear. We don't want to get flanked."

⟨⟩

They arrived at Forward Base 1 to find Delta had erected its own improvised barricade. In the distance down the sharply sloping hill, the transport vessel lay in smoldering ruins. The valley seemed to swim with the hulking creatures, though. Half a dozen of them lay dead in range of the camp, indicating Delta had seen activity and handled it. Another hundred meters away, somewhere in the middle, weapons fire marked Echo's location.

Three additional survivors huddled beneath a second protective barrier inside the outer barricade, and when their own charges arrived they hurriedly joined them. She sent a brief comm to Major Eaton, the Delta leader, informing him of the state of the new arrivals, then motioned her squad—minus Shanti, whose shoulder was damn near mangled—back into the wrecked complex.

They retraced their steps cautiously but swiftly. Past the scene of their previous skirmish stood a series of half-standing halls and smallish rooms. The nature of the debris suggested it had been a lodging wing, but almost nothing remained—

She pulled up and lifted a hand to call a halt. The battle ongoing overhead made it difficult to hear, and the snow, which had begun worsening toward blizzard conditions in the last few minutes, muffled what little she could hear.

But she had heard a moan.

Her gaze fell on a pile of debris a few meters to the left. "Cover me." She hurried over to the debris and tried to peer beneath it. "Hello? Is someone under there?"

A high-pitched cry answered.

"Hang on, we're going to get you out. Redale, Benoit, we need to clear this." The Marines materialized at her side, and together they began hefting the largest pieces of debris off to the side.

They found a small, willowy alien curled up in a ball beneath it. It wasn't one of the common species—Accepted Species. A refugee from the exobiology lab, perhaps?

Harper dropped to her knees, ignoring the stab of pain in her thigh, and tried to appear as nonthreatening as possible while wearing combat gear and carrying a giant gun. "You're going to be all right. Can you stand?"

The diminutive alien began spouting a string of nonsensical babble, eyes wide in terror—then let out a blood-curdling scream.

Harper whirled, TSG rising with the motion. Five Ch'mshak had emerged from behind one of the few standing walls and now barreled straight toward them.

Five.

A splinter grenade from Redale knocked one of them out of play, but the other four just brushed off the mortal wounds and kept coming. The rest of the squad opened fire, but the monsters were *close*—

—a pinpoint laser stream streaked down from above to burn into the advancing enemies and the ground beneath them. When it had passed, only bone shards and viscera scattered around a smoking depression remained.

She exhaled through the adrenaline. She didn't know their fighter-type craft could hone their fire so precisely, or to so small an area.

Got your back, because I adore you.

She jerked in surprise and peered upward, but the craft that had fired was long gone.

Not going to lie—right now, I'd adore you even if you weren't sharing my bed. Thanks.

She wanted to say other things, and say them better, but instead she forced her attention back to their still obscenely hazardous situation. "Pello and Benoit, get our rescue to Forward Base 1. The rest of us are heading to see what else is behind this wall."

Nothing but more wrecked structures and more anarch bodies. Past the wall they had a good view of the remainder of the post, all the way until it abutted an almost sheer mountain face.

She'd only thought the infrastructure had been destroyed up to this point. What remained of the main administration building looked as if it had been hit with an antimatter bomb. Either the Machim had tired of waiting on the Ch'mshak to make it to the rear section of the post, or they'd elected to take out the most strategically crucial buildings at the start.

Movement on her left heralded the arrival of Alpha squad. Malcolm jogged over to her. "Sit rep?"

"We've rescued five. That's all. Five goddamn survivors. Killed…I don't know, maybe a dozen Ch'mshak."

"We haven't fared much better. Think anyone's left alive up there?"

She considered the ruins ahead, stretching beneath daunting snowdrifts into the mountainous reaches. "No, sir."

"All the same." Charlie squad came into sight, clambering across debris to make their way toward the gathering.

Malcolm motioned the Charlie lead over, then glanced down at her leg. She did the same and discovered it was bleeding through the medwrap and the tactical pants. She gave him a shrug.

His voice rose. "Bravo squad, set up defenses and hold this location as an additional forward base. Alpha and Charlie, let's move ahead. I know it looks bad up there, but we have to check."

Harper started to protest, knowing damn well her injury was the reason Bravo was being left behind…but the truth was she *was* gimped, and if heroic actions were required, she would fail.

She sighed. "We have our orders, Bravo. Start gathering together debris for fortifications."

12

CHIONIS

C old.

Biting, painful cold so frigid Chione herself must have crashed the party to dole out an extra helping of *cold....*

Something was wrong.

Eren struggled to open his eyes, an act made yet harder due to his eyelashes being in the process of freezing together. He brought a hand up and rubbed on them until they grudgingly parted and his eyes opened.

Wind and snow whipped through the air above him. Because the roof was missing. Most of the walls, too.

Huh—

He sat bolt upright. The attack! Alpha had come under attack—Machim warships in the skies—he'd grabbed a stash of weapons from the armory and rushed to find Cosime—

"Cosime!"

He got a couple of moans in response to his call, but their low, growling tenor meant they weren't from her. Had he reached her before the building had come crashing down on him? The last seconds of memory were for now a blur, but...maybe?

He started to stand—and collapsed back to the floor with a howl of pain.

All air had left his lungs with the cry, and for a time he forgot how to breathe. When his body finally remembered how to inhale, he gulped air in, froze his throat and twisted around to inspect the damage.

His right leg was broken, and spectacularly so. The tibia had ripped through the skin to jut out at an angle into the open air. It had fucking *frost* on it.

Pain. Right. There was that, too….

…and it was slowing him down. How many minutes had he been writhing about, panting and hurting in a foggy, doped loop? There was something else he needed to be doing—

He scrambled to get into a position where he was able to look around. Again? "Cosime? Where are you?"

Nothing, not even the moans from before. Dread joined pain in his chest. *Think!*

He had cut through the admin cafeteria and spotted her on the opposite end of the room, running in the same direction as him. He'd shouted for her to wait, and she'd halted and turned toward him. Then crashing and screaming faded into blackness.

Okay. Where had she been? Next to a table at the far end of the cafeteria…left from where he'd come in, which had been…behind him? He could have fallen in any direction and writhed in any other. But the missing far wall revealed a downward slope instead of a sheer mountain face, so this was the correct direction. His goal was a little to the left and a long way away.

He planted his hands on the floor and began dragging himself through the snow.

Whenever he suicided out in a blaze of glory, he always tried to die quickly, the better to avoid the unpleasant side effects of the process. A couple of times, however, things hadn't worked out as planned. Twice he had suffered for many agonizing minutes before mercifully losing consciousness, once to asphyxiation in space, once to a gut wound.

Dragging himself across the floor with a maimed leg in tow felt about like those. Both, at once, in fact.

He bumped up against two of the weapons he'd been carrying. He bumped up against a body, then another. He kept moving.

A bright dash of emerald cut into the white palette a few meters ahead. Her eyes? No, ridiculous—but she *had* been wearing an emerald top! He veered to the left and dragged faster.

Too many agonizing seconds later he reached her. His first thought was relief that no large pieces of debris pinned her, because he was in no condition to be lifting heavy objects. His next thought was considerably darker.

Blood coated her left arm and shoulder to the point he couldn't tell the extent of the injuries. Lighter flecks of blood decorated hair that otherwise shown pearl upon the snow beneath it. But the blood wasn't the problem.

Her chest jerked in shallow, fitful motions. Her lips were parted as she stared up at the sky and tried desperately to draw in air. The lines of her *spiraire* lay crushed into tiny shards beside her.

"*Arae*, Cosime!" He balanced on one elbow and brought a hand to her face. Her eyes didn't shift to acknowledge him. Her chest jerked again, after too long a pause, the feeble gasping in of air barely audible.

She was going to suffocate and die if he didn't do something fast. What the Hades could he do? He couldn't walk, which meant he couldn't carry her. And where would he carry her to? There was no safety here, no refuge. He couldn't create nitrogen out of thin air—

—but he knew someone who maybe, just maybe, could.

Eren: "*Caleb, I need you right now.*"

Caleb: "*Are you at Alpha? Are you hurt?*"

Eren: "*Yes and yes, but I'm not begging for me. I'm in what's left of the admin cafeteria.*" He peered around for a landmark and belatedly noticed there was an entire war going on outside, down the hill. Smoke and flames curled through the falling snow, punctuated by erratic rumbles and booms. Now that he noticed the activity, it was all very loud and chaotic. Damn, he was in a sorry state. "*Way up the mountain from most of the fighting. There's a large tree split at the base and burnt to a crisp lying about fifteen meters south of me.*"

Caleb: "*I'll find you.*"

Eren: "*Arae, hurry.*"

He dropped his forehead to Cosime's arm, taking care not to put any added weight on her straining chest. He was probably getting her blood in his hair...turnabout was fair play, though. "Don't you die on me. You can't. I won't allow it."

He listened to her shallow, halting breaths slow and grow more uneven. Panic washed away pain, and he forced himself back up to lean over her. "No, no, no, no, no. Help is coming, so you keep breathing. Godsdammit, you *keep breathing!*"

Still her eyes didn't deviate from their fixation on the sky, and he wondered if she was truly seeing anything at all.

"Eren!"

His head whipped around to spot Caleb running toward him from below. "Over here!"

Caleb's darting gaze took in the scene as he neared them, and he dropped to a crouch the instant he arrived. "What happened?"

"She can't breathe—she's suffocating. She needs an...eighty-eight percent nitrogen, eleven percent oxygen and...one percent helium air mixture. Can you create that?"

Caleb's brow furrowed. He looked as if he'd strode right through the heart of the battle to get here, all covered in snow and blood. Perhaps he had.

"I can try." He lifted a hand, palm down, to hover half a meter above Cosime's face. The air beneath his hand gained a faint crimson hue. He frowned, and the crimson grew more pronounced.

Cosime's chest rose, faltered, and rose again more fully. It fell, and her body stilled for an endless second...then she inhaled, long and deep. Her chest rose, then fell, rose, then fell.

Eren started laughing, or crying, or making generalized hysterical sounds. "Thank you, gods. Thank you, Caleb. I, um, okay. Got to focus. How are we going to get her to safety? I can't carry her—or walk."

Caleb glanced down at his leg, and his face screwed up. "Jesus, Eren."

"It doesn't matter. Can you take her to wherever someone is treating the wounded? Please tell me someone is treating the wounded, somewhere."

"I can do so much better than that. One second." Caleb's voice dropped to a murmur under his breath. "Mia, are you on Satus?…Great. Can I have your precise location…I don't give a fuck about Nisi's security protocols, I need Satus' location…thank you. Alert the medical staff they've got incoming."

"Get ready." He lifted Cosime into his arms, placed a hand on Eren's shoulder—

—and they were kneeling on the floor in a room. A warm room, with walls and a ceiling. Also medical beds and Curative Units and lots of people scrambling around.

"We need help here!"

An Erevna woman spun and looked at him in shock. "Where did you come from?"

"Does it matter? I've brought wounded from Post Alpha."

She hurried over to them, Curative Unit trailing behind. "Get two mobile cots readied." She directed her doctorly scrutiny at Eren first, for some unknown reason. "Sir, what are your injuries?"

"Other than the obvious, I've no idea, and I don't care. Focus on her."

The Curative Unit tried to take Cosime from Caleb's arms, but he turned his shoulder in a protective stance. "I'm maintaining a bubble of the proper air mixture around her face. I have to stay with her until you can get her hooked up to a suitable air supply."

The doctor blinked in confusion. "You're Praesidis?"

Caleb exhaled ponderously. "Something like that."

"We're going to move her to the cot on this side here. Ready?"

Caleb stood to follow. When he reached the cot, he gently laid Cosime down on it. The doctor wound two tubes out from the wall, fitted them into a mask and placed it over Cosime's mouth and nose. "Naraida air supply established. Unit C-3, I want diagnostics on her chest cavity in case there are internal injuries, then of her left shoulder and upper arm."

She pivoted to Eren, who had used various furniture to pull himself up to a standing position and clung feebly to a cabinet. "Now, you—off the leg before you fall and shatter what's left of your tibia. A Curative Unit will see to cleansing and disinfecting the area...eventually." She reached in her lab coat pocket and removed a vial filled with liquid. "For now, painkillers will have to do."

Eren sighed, briefly interrupting the grimace he wore. "I should decline them, but...frankly, right now I'm not that strong. Load me up."

"First, let's get you on a cot."

Caleb helped him over to the next empty cot. He gritted his teeth to keep from screaming as Caleb carefully lifted his busted leg up and positioned it alongside the non-busted one. Nope, not any-where close to that strong. There was nothing else he could do to help Cosime, to help anyone including himself.

But what of the others? He had been consumed with pain and cold and Cosime to the exclusion of all else, and only now did the reality of his home, his friends, his colleagues all being under attack penetrate his addled mind. He frantically started pinging comms.

The doctor motioned in grudging approval, and Caleb gave him a once-over. "Well, you look like shit, but they'll take care of you. I need to get back out there."

Eren's hand shot out to grab Caleb's arm. "Wait. Felzeor—he was supposed to be evacuating to Charlie, albeit under protest, but I don't think he made it to the teleportation gate. I just checked, and he's not answering any comms."

"The teleportation gate's been destroyed. The whole building's been destroyed. If he's not already at Post Charlie...."

"He saw the attack coming and warned us. He saved dozens if not hundreds of lives."

"I'll find him."

$$\mathcal{R}$$

SIYANE

CHIONIS STELLAR SYSTEM
MILKY WAY SECTOR 59

How the hell was he going to find Felzeor inside a smashed complex of buildings three hundred meters wide and twice as long?

Caleb had gotten the comm address and started pinging Felzeor immediately, but the Volucri hadn't responded to him, either. Maybe his translator was damaged—or maybe Felzeor was damaged.

He teleported from Satus back to the *Siyane* and found Alex mid-destruction of a Machim fighter. On the ground, among the snow, fighting and very visceral death, he'd almost forgotten about the battle underway above the planet. But up here, it continued to rage unabated. Out the viewport, tens of thousands of ships large and small soared and fired, spun and exploded—

—including the Machim fighter.

Alex peered over her shoulder at him as she casually veered to avoid the debris. "Do I even need to say it?"

He glanced down and realized blood had soaked into his shirt and much of his pants. "Okay, but it's not mine."

"Eren? Is he all right?"

"He's not in great shape, but he'll…well, obviously he'll live, but this time probably without the help of regenesis. Cosime, I'm not so confident about." He dropped a hand on the cockpit dash and leaned in beside Alex. "Can you leave the battle for a few minutes to go to the surface and circle what's left of the upper main complex? I want you to scan for life signs."

"I can, but is there any chance you could be a bit more specific as to what we're hunting for? I expect, or hope, that we'll pick up a number of life signs, so what do we do then? The Marines are already on the ground wading through the Ch'mshak to reach survivors."

"We need to find Felzeor. Eren said he was on site and headed for the teleportation gate, but now he's not answering comms."

Her face fell. "Shit. There are a lot of bodies down there—fighting, injured, dead—and he doesn't cut that large of a profile. I don't see how we'll be able to identify him through all the noise. Not from the air." She politely left out the 'even if he's alive' part, but she must be thinking it. He was thinking it.

'I can find him.'

He and Alex shared an uneasy look. "What do you mean, Valkyrie? By modifying the scan parameters? Or are you saying your consciousness projection can locate him?"

'Yes. The latter, that is. In my testing I have confirmed that I can detect and distinguish individual life signs at eighty meters distance with a high degree of fidelity. From a position on or just above the surface, I will be able to conduct a far more precise search than the *Siyane* can perform at the minimum safe altitude.'

"It's ugly down there. We're talking about an active combat zone, with widespread gunfire and bombing runs."

'Weapons cannot harm me.'

Caleb chuckled kindly. "An excellent point. Alex, will you and the ship be safe?" He gazed out the viewport in concern. It looked as if they might be winning, but too many Machim vessels remained for him to be certain. "I know you've tested the effects of her absence, but this isn't exactly idling on a landing platform."

She nodded firmly. "I will. I can fly without her. Did it for years."

"And quite skillfully, as I recall. If you're sure." He drew in closer and kissed her softly. "Don't push your limits, please? Let the rest of the fleet take the risks for once."

She smiled a little as he stepped back. "I'll try, but...no promises."

He sighed in acceptance. He'd recognized its futility as soon as he'd voiced the request. "Stubborn as ever. Okay, Valkyrie. Meet me at the coordinates I'm sending you."

CHIONIS

ANARCH POST ALPHA

The snow cover makes the blood stand out in stark relief, as if someone painted scarlet graffiti indiscriminately across the landscape.

Valkyrie de-prioritized her emotional processes. Her presence here was not an experiment in fostering personal growth; her presence here was an attempt to facilitate the saving of lives.

Caleb materialized off to her left. A crimson shimmer—*brighter than the blood*—encased him to form a reinforced protective layer of *diati*. He briefly gazed to his right down a slope littered with half-fallen buildings and smoldering debris, to where the core of the fighting raged. Then he turned from it and strode toward her. "What do you see?"

What used to be the main administrative building of Post Alpha lay in utter ruin in front of them. No wall stood higher than two meters, while rubble often did.

But these were inanimate metal and stone. The cellular composition of the rubble and edifice vanished from her top-level perception as she began seeking indicators of living organic cells. Heartbeats, spots of heat created by warm body temperatures.

I see death. So much death. "There are only two discrete life signs detectable within this structure. One is—" she flowed forward, into the ruins, and paused at a point near the center "—here. The other is—" she moved to a corner of what had once been the front wall, facing the slope on the far left "—here. The characteristics of the readings suggest this second one is most likely to be Felzeor." She shifted back toward the interior. "And the first one is…no longer registering." *Life, gone.*

"Understood." Caleb had followed her movements without question or effort. He studied the rubble burying the tiny, weak life signs for a few seconds, then sent out a wave of *diati*. The topmost slab, possibly from a ceiling, tumbled away.

Valkyrie circled, particles flowing one after another in a slow-motion pirouette as she took in the full measure of the scene. Past the outline of the administration building rose a towering mountain; no more survived beyond this point. But below? "I must go. I can find others who are injured, down the hill where structures still stand." *Where life still stands a chance.* "Perhaps I can bring them help."

He waved her off as a cross-beam lifted up and toppled over. "Go. Do more good. And thank you."

13

AFS STALWART II

CHIONIS STELLAR SYSTEM
MILKY WAY SECTOR 59

Miriam accepted an update on damage reports across the fleet from Major Halmi. The data revealed what looked to David like encouraging numbers, but this didn't stop her from frowning and issuing several new orders.

Halmi pivoted and strode purposefully off, and Miriam redirected the frown to the tactical map. She studied it with the intensity of a painter mid-masterpiece, when the formless swirls of color and vague contours became texture, shadow and light.

"Suggestions?"

David stood off to her left, close but far enough away to not interfere with her work or the work of those who bustled around the bridge. Much occurred both here and out beyond the hull for him to observe, but again and again he found himself entranced watching Miriam adroitly maneuver through the intricacies of pitched space combat.

In the now distant past, he'd been the ship captain and the one always knee-deep in one fracas or other, while she managed the complex systems that made the waging of war possible, usually from the safety of an office. In his absence, though, she'd done more than step up when duty demanded it—she'd surpassed him. She'd transferred her considerable skills at logistics and systems management to the front lines. There she'd adapted them to suit the specialized needs called for by her position at the helm of the command ship of a vast multi-agency fleet in the throes of a multi-universe war. The realization evoked pride, not jealousy...but it also left him wondering what his place might be. In the war, in the world, in her life.

In the here and now, he merely shook his head wryly. "How did you learn to be a battlefield commander?"

"Necessity." She arched an eyebrow. *"Suggestions?"*

He blinked and shook off the vestiges of the reverie. If she was *asking* for his help, he would not deny her.

The tactical map showed, as he imagined it often did when engaging Machim forces, a battle of attrition. Her ships were superior in every way—better equipped, faster and hardier—but the enemy numbered so damn many. "Honestly, I'm impressed. It's going well. You're holding your own, and if the current trend holds you will eventually win against far larger numbers.

"But if you have a recurring problem, it's the Machim battle-cruisers. Everything smaller you can swat away with little trouble once they're all you're facing, but those behemoths are clogging up the battlefield and forcing you to spend most of your time shooting at them. Putting aside for the time being the spectre of the Imperium, you need to clear out as many battlecruisers as you can as fast as you can, or we'll be here all day." He brought a hand to his chin. "Do the Sabres have arcalasers?"

"No. The expense was prohibitively high, even for a well-funded operation."

"It's all right. The battlecruisers don't have them either, so it can still work."

"What can still work?"

He stepped closer to the tactical map and her as a faint buzz of adrenaline began to hum beneath his skin. Battle, the waging of it and the winning of it, had always been in his blood. "Their battle-cruisers can fire at three separate targets at once, correct?" She nodded. "Put five Sabres on a battlecruiser. I know, they're glass cannons. What are your toughest tanks on the field?"

She didn't hesitate. "Alliance cruisers."

He chuckled. "Was true then, still true now. Assign an Alliance cruiser to each Sabre. When the Machim battlecruiser turns its weapons on an attacking Sabre, the cruiser will sweep in and block for it, absorbing the bulk of the fire. The instant the Machim vessel directs its attention to *another* attacker, the cruiser will drop out of the way and the Sabre will resume firing. A minimum of two Sabres will be delivering sustained, full-strength fire on the battlecruiser at all times. The enemy's shields then its hull will buckle in..." he did a rough approximation of the math in his head, for while his consciousness may be quantum in origin, his neurons were not "...twelve seconds. Fifteen at most."

She stared at him, skepticism prominent on her features. *Bozhe moy*, did he know that look. But he didn't back down.

"Artificials are piloting those Sabres, Miri. They can move themselves far more rapidly and precisely than you, I or the Machim captains could dream of achieving. And if a cruiser happens to catch a swipe of friendly fire on its backside, well, that's why it's a tank."

"David, there are eight hundred twenty battlecruisers on the field."

"Do this, and there will be six fewer every fifteen seconds. In ten minutes, you'll have cut their number by a third. In half an hour, the engagement's over."

"What about all the other Machim vessels? They will come to the battlecruisers' defense."

"The evidence outside that viewport there says they don't matter. Raindrops plinking off a tin roof."

She was silent for a moment, then checked the tactical map. "Okay."

Commandant Solovy (AFS Stalwart II): *"AEGIS Sabre and EA cruiser captains, switch to Mission Channel 4 for new instructions."*

When she'd finished relaying the details, she turned back to him. "Now, about the Imperium."

ℛ

SIYANE

CHIONIS STELLAR SYSTEM
MILKY WAY SECTOR 59

Alex dodged laser fire not meant for her and arced away from the dogfight she'd apparently wandered into the midst of.

Despite the glib assurance she'd given Caleb, she found herself surprised at how odd it felt for the *Siyane* to be under her sole and complete control. She'd flown it solo for years, but to do so now felt foreign. Unnatural, even. Objectively, the ship responded to her actions with no detectable lag in performance. Hell, it responded faster and more smoothly than it did in the old days thanks to a slew of upgrades acquired over the last eighteen months. Still, she'd taken for granted how much work Valkyrie did behind the scenes.

But it was more than that. For the first time in quite a while, she was truly, completely alone on her ship. Funny, it didn't seem to hold the appeal it once did. She had all these wonderful people to share her days and nights with now—Caleb, Valkyrie, her mother, her *father*—and her life was so much richer for them being in it.

*Commandant Solovy (*AFS Stalwart II*): "AEGIS Assault Brigade #2, reinforce EA NW Regiments #7 through #10 in Quadrant 2."*

On the tactical map, dots began moving against the current of the natural flow of the battle. With any luck, the movements appeared random to the enemy.

*Brigadier Ashonye (*EAS Marengo*)(Command Channel): "Have we been able to find out if they brought Igni missiles? I haven't seen any fired."*

*Commandant Solovy (*Stalwart II*)(Command Channel): "No recorded use as of yet. Thomas, can the Connexus analyze enemy vessel movements the way they did at the Provision Network Gateway?"*

Thomas (Command Channel): 'None of the battlecruisers exhibit signs of carrying Igni missiles. It cannot be determined whether the same is true for the Imperium, however.'

Blasted Imperium. The imposing command vessel stalked the battlefield like a tromping elephant, cowardly firing from behind its uber-shielding in short bursts so as to avoid falling into the trap Malcolm had sprung at the Provision Network Gateway. Knowing they couldn't damage it, the AEGIS vessels tried to ignore the Imperium until it turned its firepower on them, at which point they stealthed or fled. It was a stalling tactic with no defined goal on either side, but the game would nevertheless have to resolve eventually. If the Imperium carried Igni missiles, it was holding the winning hand in reserve.

Alexis Solovy (Siyane)*(Command Channel): "One second. I'll find out."*

She pointed the *Siyane* away from the crux of the combat and engaged the autopilot, then slipped into sidespace and mentally breached the interior of the Imperium.

The Machim Central Command data cache had included images of the Igni missiles, and the weapons were notable for being significantly larger and bulkier than other Anaden weapons, so they should be easy to spot. She ignored the bustling of the crew to zip through the weapons bay and torpedo tubes until she found what she was searching for.

She reopened her eyes in the *Siyane* cockpit, took the controls and pivoted to rejoin the battle.

Alexis Solovy (Siyane)*(Command Channel): "The Imperium has four Igni missiles on board. Two of them are loaded in torpedo tubes."*

Brigadier Ashonye (Marengo)*(Command Channel): "Four is better than the kind of numbers we've faced before, but it's still worrisome news."*

Alex drummed the fingers of one hand on the dash. The brigadier was correct on both counts. Four Igni missiles targeted appropriately stood to wipe out a significant number of AEGIS ships and inflict a grievous toll, but four wouldn't win the Machim the engagement. On the other hand....

Machim commanders had shown a willingness to take out their own people if it meant damaging their enemy in the process, and somehow she doubted this commander was going to lose sleep over incidentally killing a few hundred Ch'mshak. If the Imperium sent a single Igni missile through the atmosphere to strike Post Alpha, the entire base would be obliterated, along with every ship in the air above it and twenty kilometers of land in every direction. Every Marine, every fighter pilot, every anarch. Caleb was down there, and she didn't think the *diati* could keep him safe from a blast of such magnitude.

She'd pulse him and ask him to leave, but it would be a futile act. He'd never do it—not until he found Felzeor, and probably not even then.

Alexis Solovy (Siyane)(*Command Channel*): *"If they haven't used them on us by now, it likely means they're meant for Post Alpha. What are they waiting for?"*

Commander Lekkas (MA-Primary)(*Command Channel*): *"They're waiting for the Ch'mshak to wreak as much carnage as possible first. Bloodlust and vengeance are driving this attack. Only when there are no anarchs left to kill or no Ch'mshak left to do the killing will they finish off the post. At that point, since they can't beat us, they'll leave."*

Alexis Solovy (Siyane)(*Command Channel*): *"You've got eyes on the ground, Morgan. When will that be?"*

Commander Lekkas (MA-Primary)(*Command Channel*): *"Honestly? Soon. The Marines are still clearing out a fair number of Ch'mshak in the ruins, but their ship and their reinforcements are dust, so it's only a matter of time."*

Fuck. Nobody down there was apt to want to leave until there were no more survivors to find, which was far too long to stay. So how to stop the Imperium from loosing a torrent of antimatter destruction upon the surface?

Ugh…she longed for someone to bounce ideas off. But she was alone; she had to think for herself.

A Kat could spirit away the Igni missiles, much as Mesme had done with the Tartarus Trigger at the Provision Network Gateway battle. But the Kats were busy defending multiple anarch-friendly locations, in at least two instances from active attack at this very hour. Also, the odds were high that as soon as one Igni missile vanished, the Imperium commander would react by firing the remaining three.

No, they needed to destroy the damn elephant, and in a rapid, unexpected manner that didn't give the elephant's commander time to go scorched earth.

Kennedy had said the wormhole tech might provide the answer to circumventing the Imperium's shielding…because the shielding wasn't pandimensional, merely thick, strong and reinforced. A wormhole could get around it and open an exit inside the shielding!

But a hundred meters was not a great distance when one was in space, and a thick hull and the intact shielding bounded either end of that distance. Hell, the *Siyane's* wingspan alone stretched nearly thirty meters, leaving little buffer for maneuvering in what was effectively a crawlspace.

After using her supply on Ekos-2, on returning she'd restocked with a fresh pair of negative energy missiles. They packed enough of a punch to blow a sizable hole in the Imperium's hull for certain, and at point-blank distance should take it out entirely.

Commandant Solovy (Stalwart II*): "All vessels, monitor the Imperium for signs of an Igni missile launch. If one is detected, any and all measures are authorized to intercept and destroy the missile or missiles."*

The order evidenced a decision on her mother's part to protect the people on the ground, but it was going to cost lives nonetheless. The cruisers and interdictors had anti-missile weapons, but given the short distance from the battlefield to Post Alpha below, chances were 'any and all measures' would come down to a ship sacrificing itself by placing itself in the path of the Igni missile. Assuming they reached it in time.

Chto za khuynya! In polite terms, fuck this shit.

Her hands were moving toward the dash when she forced herself to *pause*. To take a moment to soberly contemplate what she was about to do, since she'd promised Caleb she would *try* not to stress her limits, and this was several parsecs beyond any limits. Well, the self-imposed ones, anyway.

Alternatives? Morgan could do it. But she was in-atmo and fully occupied providing needed cover to the Marines and to Caleb. Since Morgan was worth four Eidolons and a dozen fighters all on her own, Alex didn't want to deprive those on the ground of her skills.

An AEGIS Prevo-joined ship could do it, in theory. But the smallest of those were frigates, and in practice the hundred-meter space between the shielding and the Imperium's hull was too little room for a frigate to do *anything*, if it fit inside at all.

Okay, then. She'd gone through the paces and checked the boxes, but she'd already known the answer: it was up to her.

Alexis Solovy (Siyane)*(Command Channel): "I have an idea for a way to damage and hopefully destroy the Imperium."*

Commandant Solovy (Stalwart II)*(Command Channel): "Alex? What are you thinking of doing?"*

Alexis Solovy (Siyane)*(Command Channel): "If it works, you'll know it. Be ready to order everyone to either open fire or get clear, depending on the state I leave the Imperium in."*

Next, she pulsed Caleb.

I love you.

She needed a concrete connection to the power of the Caeles Prism in order to open the wormhole. Typically, Valkyrie provided the connection, but Valkyrie wasn't here. She was down on the surface saving lives, and Alex intended to give her every opportunity to continue doing so.

After a quick glance around the cabin and the cockpit, she worked open a section of the dash cover to expose the quantum circuitry beneath it. Valkyrie's circuitry, mostly, embedded and intertwined with the ship's functional wiring.

Milaya, your mother has concerns.

She chuckled. Oh, the conversation that must be underway on the bridge of the *Stalwart II.*

Just stall her for me. Use some flowery words.

Milaya, *I have concerns.*

I'll be fine.

Totally fine. Of course, she and Valkyrie had never gotten around to testing whether one of them could open wormholes without the assistance of the other. Ah, well. No time like the present.

She closed her eyes and—

—Caleb's pulse interrupted her.

Alex, baby....

I promise I tried.

She lowered both palms into the circuitry.

Space welcomed her into its arms like a long-lost lover. The demarcation lines separating her, the ship and the atoms of the universe blurred. Alive, she and it and everywhere were all *alive*, deafening and brilliant, sparkling with effulgent photons and radiant energy. The energetic forces of battle screamed past from every direction. Engine output, lasers, plasma, all clashing to drown out the symphony of the cosmos beneath a discordant concerto.

In her body, she breathed out, long and slow…and in her mind, she withdrew into herself. In the gap between the two, the connection remained open. It was all there, in her vision and within her reach to touch. But it did not, would not, consume her.

It would not erase her. Not this time.

Exigency did not allow for further introspection. She spun up the Caeles Prism, which was also a part of her. As soon as the power reached the required threshold, she opened a wormhole in front of her—the ship—and designated the exit as a point inside the Imperium's shield but outside its hull. It was a moving point, so she continued to not dally. She did wonder what she might have seen had she lingered in the space in-between from this vantage, but it wasn't important. Not so important as succeeding in her mission.

The instant she reemerged into real space, she closed the wormhole and matched her speed and trajectory to that of the Imperium. She didn't power down the Caeles Prism; she was going to need it again in another few seconds. Next she metaphorically tip-toed along the periphery of the hull to the location on the lower stern where Malcolm had so successfully ripped a hole in another Imperium—

—an explosion crashed against the shielding to her port. The Imperium's hull didn't so much as vibrate, however, and she only noticed it because of the flare of light as photons burst forth out of the collisions of atoms, and energy multiplied then dissipated.

In a distant, detached voice she hardly recognized as her own, she accessed the mission command channel. *"All vessels in a four megameter vicinity of the Imperium, retreat to a safe distance in the next five seconds."*

Now came the really challenging part. She seriously had a new-found respect for Valkyrie's ability to balance a multitude of systems and actions simultaneously; she was also grateful for the quantum processes she did have access to, for the small ways in which her brain now enjoyed a few enhancements.

Set the targeting on the negative energy missiles.

Redirect the surfeit of power from the Caeles Prism, now approaching dangerous levels, to open another wormhole directly ahead.

Fire the missiles.

Accelerate through the wormhole.

The missiles impact the Imperium's hull.

Reemerge into normal space.

Close the wormhole before the energy from the impact travels through it and damages the Siyane.

Shut down the Caeles Prism before it blows up the Siyane.

She checked her location. Six megameters from the Imperium, right where she'd intended to be. She—the ship—pivoted in time to see explosions rippling through the underside of the Imperium hull, then cascading to ever greater strength in a runaway confla-gration of energy. The telltale shimmer of the shielding flickered and went out.

Commandant Solovy (Stalwart II): *"The Imperium's shielding is down. Fire at will."*

The pulse arrived 1.4 seconds later.

Are you alive?

I am.

And well?

Close enough.

Then you can tell me what you did later. Rest, and we'll take it from here. Thank you.

Her mother went back to directing the engagement. Alex drifted there in space, her mind half in her body and half in her ship. She supposed this was as good a time as any for the delayed introspection.

It was easier to straddle the two realms now, and not unlike hovering in the opening of a wormhole. She felt hydrogen and helium atoms impact the hull, even as she felt the material of her shirt shift across her skin as her chest rose and fell. Now, neither felt more nor less real than the other. She thought and hoped it meant she'd grown less susceptible to the siren song of the elemental realm.

The wormholes—the infinite space in-between space—had shown her the farthest and nearest spans of dimensions, of the fabric holding the universe together. In seeing this, in knowing its nature, she understood: it had always been inside of her. Part of her. Part of everyone, she was merely the lucky one gifted with the ability to catch a glimpse of the true expanse of reality. Joining with the ship was nothing more than a physical expression of what had always been true.

Thus when she let it go and returned to her corporeal body, real and whole, she wasn't giving up anything at all.

To make sure, she did exactly that. *Fine hairs on her skin. Smooth fabric of the chair beneath her. Solid walls, pliable floor, touch-interactive screens and controls. Real and whole.*

She smiled. Just as real, just as infinite. She hadn't been wrong on that most terrible of nights on Romane when she'd knelt in front of destruction of her own making and found the bottom of the abysm. It *was* all just atoms—but what mattered was what the atoms came together to create.

She drew up in the chair with renewed purpose, accompanied by a healthy dose of relief, and prepared to rejoin a battle that had now tipped decisively in their favor.

A new pulse came in from Caleb.

Alex, I need you.

14

CHIONIS

Caleb spared a brief motion of his arm to send a wave of *diati* crashing into an advancing group of three Ch'mshak. In the corner of his vision he noted when they tumbled through the air toward the sheer face of the towering mountain, but he kept his focus on the shrinking pile of debris.

The sky above him blazed with lasers and the explosions they caused, but he tuned that out as well as he knelt and tried to peer between two beams. "Felzeor? Anyone?" Not as though anyone could hear him over the roar of combat that sounded as if it was drawing closer. So he resumed digging.

His muscles and *diati* shared duty casting broken beams and pieces of shattered walls aside. He'd already uncovered two bodies, both lifeless, as he exposed more of what had once been the outer façade of the administration building.

An increasing clamor grew behind him, rising above the generalized noise of combat until he finally peered over his shoulder to see a squad of Marines approaching—or rather, being inexorably pushed back by a group of Ch'mshak. The Marines were holding them off, albeit barely. Should he help?

He kept digging.

A large slab of wall dislodged enough for him to send it tumbling away, and its absence revealed the tip of a blood-soaked wing. His heart leapt into his throat; the sight validated the justness of his efforts here and brought the looming shadow of his worst fears into stark relief. He shoved another chunk of rubble away to reveal more wing, and more blood.

He dropped to his knees and removed several smaller pieces of rubble until a beak then a face became visible. They were bloody, too, but he could swear the feathers were chocolate in color, with a dash of apricot disappearing beneath debris. "Felzeor?"

One eye opened a fraction to reveal a dulled green iris. It blinked.

Endorphin-fueled relief flooded his veins. "I'm going to get you out, okay? Just hang on." A beam half-covered the right side of the Volucri's body. Blood seeped out around the edges of it to drip to the ground. He lowered himself onto his stomach and tried to see under it.

It appeared as if an edge of the beam had speared Felzeor's abdomen. His gaze ran along the exposed length of the beam to get an idea of how wide the edge might be. Five centimeters, at a minimum. Too large.

He closed his eyes and gently stroked Felzeor's exposed wing. If he moved the beam, Felzeor would bleed out before Caleb could get him to any form of medical aid. He'd bleed out in *seconds*.

Caleb had only the most meager of first aid supplies with him: a single medwrap and a tiny tube of antiseptic ointment. There hadn't been time to gather anything else; everything had moved so fast, and it had been more important to get here, to combat the attackers, then to rescue Eren and Cosime, then to find Felzeor.

He could teleport away and return with a med kit. But Ch'mshak were literally meters away. If the Marines failed to keep them at bay, the fallen structure would be overrun.

A burst of gunfire announced the increased proximity of the Marine squad. He straightened up and shouted in their direction. "Hey! I've got wounded over here!"

"Polowski, Shaviiz, set up a defensive position behind what's left of that wall there. Grenier, scale that façade and use what's left of the second floor corner as a sniper perch." Malcolm Jenner backed toward him, eyes on the battlefield, then crouched beside him. "What are we looking at?"

"He's impaled on this beam. I can move it, but when I do he'll bleed out if I don't have coagulant and bio-bonding gel at the ready. I brought a few basic first aid supplies from the *Siyane*, but they won't be enough. I need a proper med kit."

He sensed Jenner's frown grow as the brigadier studied the broken body beneath Caleb's hands. "It's...."

"Don't you *dare* say, 'it's just a bird.'"

"No." Jenner shook his head. "It's a...Volucri, right? A sentient, falcon-like alien?"

"Yes. His name's Felzeor, and he's my friend."

"I understand." Jenner's face betrayed the lie, but at least he was polite enough to speak it.

"Thank you. I don't know much about his anatomy, but I know I'll have to staunch the bleeding immediately. There won't be time to move him first."

A shout drew Jenner's attention, and he disappeared. A thunderous explosion shook the rubble, and Caleb tried to hold Felzeor and the beam steady. The translator was crushed, but a tiny squeak of pain escaped the Volucri's beak.

"You're going to be all right, you hear me? You're a resistance fighter, and this little injury is not going to fell you."

Felzeor blinked.

Jenner reappeared coated in a fresh layer of snow and debris. "We got separated from our medic a few hundred meters back, and now he and two others are pinned down. We've got extra field med kits on the transports, but the odds of someone making it here with one are...." He cast a grim look toward the heart of the battlefield. His people were taking down enemies as fast as they approached so far, but the waves showed no signs of letting up. There were dead Ch'mshak everywhere, but even more live ones.

"I can teleport to a transport, get one of the kits and bring it here. It'll take me two minutes at most. But you have to promise me something. Promise me you won't let the enemy breach this location. Promise me you will protect him, at all costs."

Jenner looked around to confirm his people continued to hold their own, then back to meet Caleb's waiting stare. "We'll look after him. If fire catches us from above, we're all screwed. But nothing down here will get to him." He flashed a pained smile. "Trust me."

If everyone survived, they could joke about the irony later. "Where's a transport this second? I need precise coordinates."

"They headed up for safety." Jenner's eyes grew unfocused. "Mission Quadrant 3, S 14° E z 41°."

Caleb stroked Felzeor's wing again. "I'll be right back. Don't fret." Then he stood, cast an eye to the sky, and vanished.

$\mathcal{R}$

Caleb arrived off-target, thirty meters from the transport and hanging freely in space. The *diati* sprang into action to protect him, but he teleported the remainder of the distance into the transport so rapidly it needn't have bothered.

The craft was empty save for the pilot, who jerked in surprise at the sudden appearance of a person inside.

Caleb waved him off. "No time to explain. Where are the field med kits?"

"Um, in the back, left side cabinets, third one down."

"Thanks." He sprinted down the empty personnel cabin and yanked open the cabinet. The med kit resembled a pack—that would be the 'field' designation—so he tossed it on his back, strapped it on and teleported to the surface.

He couldn't have been gone longer than ninety seconds, but the situation had deteriorated in those seconds. A splinter grenade sailed above his head toward the dozen Ch'mshak fighting through the gunfire to make a solid effort at reaching the Marines' fortifications. Two Marines were bleeding into the snow, and a portion of one of the barriers had been blasted to shreds.

He rushed to Felzeor's side and again dropped to his knees. "Hey, there. See, I told you I'd be back."

Felzeor blinked again, but it seemed like a weaker effort. He was slipping away.

Caleb unfastened the pack, shrugged it off and opened it wide. He found and removed a tube of bio-bonding gel, and was digging around for the coagulant when Jenner staggered in beside him. "I thought you said two minutes? That had to have been an hour."

Caleb huffed a breath. "Ninety seconds." He briefly considered the man beside him before retrieving an additional tube of bio-bonding gel his hand had passed over. He offered it to Jenner. "You could use some of this."

"What?" Jenner glanced down. A growing splotch of blood was staining his flak jacket around a jagged piece of shrapnel embedded in his side. "Hmm. Thanks."

Caleb located the last thing he required then slid the pack over to Jenner and jerked his head toward the barricades. "I suspect you're not the only one in need of patching up."

"I'm afraid you're right. Do you want help extricating the Volucri?"

"You can help by keeping those brutes off of me for another minute." He removed the caps from the medical tubes and laid a medwrap out within easy reach, then leaned down closer to Felzeor. "This is probably going to hurt. A lot. Grit your beak and concentrate on breathing, and I'll have you patched up in no time. Ready? Good."

He picked up the coagulant and held it at the ready as he concentrated on the beam.

GENTLY AWAY

The beam moved—blood gushed out of the ragged wound it left behind—*MORE AWAY NOW*—the beam disappeared off to the side, and he hurriedly began pouring the coagulant deep into the wound. Coating layer after layer across its breadth until the gushing slowed to seeping. Then he soaked the open wound in bio-bonding gel and quickly pressed the medwrap over Felzeor's abdomen, trusting the treatments to do their job despite the unfamiliar anatomy. Blood cells were, fundamentally, blood cells. He hoped.

Dammit, the wrap didn't want to adhere to the Volucri's feathers. He lifted Felzeor's broken body up and looped the material around his abdomen several times so it adhered to itself. He was so tiny…large for a bird, but pitifully small in Caleb's arms.

"Felzeor?"

Nothing.

But his tiny chest rose and fell ever so slightly.

"Shit! Polowski, throw everything you've got at them!"

Caleb looked behind him to see three wounded and angry Ch'mshak less than four meters from the barricade. He stood, nestled Felzeor against his chest with one arm wrapped protectively around him, and joined the Marines at the barricade. Once there he splayed the other arm out in front of him. His lips twitched.

A solid wall of *diati* expanded out to form a bubble a meter past the barricade.

The Ch'mshak slammed into it and were knocked back. They fired their weapons into it, but the energy diffused harmlessly across the bubble.

"Damn, Marano."

He shrugged, if awkwardly with his charge in his arms, and sidestepped closer to Jenner. "Catch your breath for a few seconds. I'm evacuating him to Post Satus. I can take you and your people with me, or anyone seriously injured." He gestured pointedly toward Jenner's side. "Which includes you."

"We're all right. Thanks for giving us the time and ability to regroup. If we can dispatch these last Ch'mshak, we should push farther in. Search for more survivors and clear the remaining attackers out."

I love you.

Oh, shit.

Alex, baby….

I promise I tried.

A fresh batch of apprehension welled up to tighten his chest…but there was nothing he could do. She was uniquely capable of taking care of herself, typically with brassy panache, and he trusted her to not die.

"If you're certain. Realistically, you shouldn't expect to find any survivors farther north of here, but I'll send Valkyrie your way...." Because Valkyrie was still down here scouring the battlefield for the fallen, not up in space helping Alex. Another flare of worry he had no choice but to push aside. "She can guide you to anyone who's alive elsewhere in the complex."

"Valkyrie? Not sure I follow you."

"When you see her, simply go with it. She can help."

"If you say so." Jenner turned to his men. "Okay, this protective bubble is about to come down. Back in position and weapons at the ready!"

Caleb watched them move into cover, then teleported fourteen hundred parsecs to Post Satus.

ℛ

ANARCH POST SATUS

LOCATION UNKNOWN

He'd aimed better this time, or possibly Satus wasn't moving, and he came to rest in the medical suite.

"Over here! I need help!"

An Anaden—not the same one who had helped Eren and Cosime, but Erevna as well—rushed over, attention zeroing in on the Volucri cradled in Caleb's arms.

"He has a severe chest laceration and probable internal injuries. Can you help him?"

"Yes, of course. Bring him to..." the man looked around and pointed "...this way."

He carefully placed Felzeor on a cot against the rear wall. "He was conscious until maybe two minutes ago, but he's lost a lot of blood. A metal beam had punctured his abdomen. I removed it then used coagulant and bio-bonding gel to staunch the bleeding—human medical treatments."

"Understood. You need to let us work now."

He backed away, suddenly dizzy from the adrenaline dump. He'd done it, though. Done everything he could for his delightful, brave winged friend.

He noticed Eren on his cot across the way. It looked as if the painkillers had done their job and knocked him out cold. Farther down, a Curative Unit continued to tend to Cosime.

"Caleb!"

He spun around to see Mia hurrying into the medical suite. He exhaled in weary relief. "Thank you."

"For?"

He motioned around. "Making all this possible."

"Don't be silly. Are you hurt?"

"I don't get hurt anymore, remember? But I had to get Felzeor here."

"Felzeor..." she peeked over his shoulder at the cot behind him and the increasing activity surrounding it "...your Volucri friend? Is he all right?"

"Not in the slightest. But he has a chance..." he gave her an indulgent eye roll "...thanks to Malcolm."

"What? Is *Malcolm* all right? I've been trying to monitor the battle through the Connexus, but it's so very military, and I can't tell if things are going well or not on the ground. We just blew up the Imperium, so it's definitely going well in space."

Alex. He didn't have to ask, for he knew it in the way one soul knew another. He smiled to himself, then belatedly realized Mia was staring at him expectantly, waiting for an answer on the fate of one *she* loved.

He thought about the condition he'd left the Marines in and decided she couldn't benefit from the messy details. "He's fine, but there are a lot of wounded on the ground. We need...we need a way to get them up here. The aliens, at least—our people can handle standard medical evac on their end, for the most part, but they don't have the equipment or the knowledge needed to treat aliens who are badly injured."

He nodded, decision made. "Tell Nisi he's about to have a full medical suite, and he needs to do whatever is necessary to expand its capabilities. Then go to the break room down the hall. That's the largest, most open space I can think of on Satus. I suspect we're going to require your help."

Mia went to work without asking any questions. Being highly adaptive as well as levelheaded in a crisis were only two of her many excellent qualities.

He checked Felzeor's cot again, but all he was able to determine was that work was being done, so he teleported back to Alpha and into the midst of the maelstrom.

Alex, I need you.

15

CHIONIS

The *Siyane* materialized mid-descent thirty meters above the ground. Though Caleb had been tracking its approach since it entered the atmosphere and knew when the ship neared, its abrupt appearance still made for a startling sight, and a beautiful one.

He kept partial attention on two active clashes, though for now they remained some distance away. He'd chosen a location near one of the Marines' forward operating bases, where a number of injured anarchs had been taken for shelter and eventual evacuation, but not so close as to be inside its defensive perimeter. If the enemy advanced on this location, dispatching the attackers might be up to him.

The *Siyane* settled to the ground, the hatch opened, the ramp descended and Alex strode purposefully down it.

He did a double-take. Her eyes and glyphs shone so brightly they created a halo effect in the snow falling around her. Her gait was more controlled and measured than was typical for her, but she didn't seem injured. What had happened to her?

An old dread he'd believed long buried stirred in his gut. *What had she become?*

She walked straight over to him and grasped his hands in hers. "I'm here. What are we doing?"

Though she was surely looking at him, her eyes were like stars, radiating a blazing white that consumed her pupils and any hint of her irises. He could discern no focus in them. He had no idea what to say, where to begin…so he squeezed her hands in response, almost surprised they were real and tangible and present on this plane of existence.

She held something in her palm, something interfering with her touch. He reflexively glanced down, and she opened her palm to reveal a thin, four-centimeter long module of some sort. "It's so I can maintain my connection to the ship while I'm out here."

His eyes shot back up to her otherworldly ones. "Your..." the dread shed the remnants of slumber and readied itself for action "...what kind of connection?"

She smiled. "It's okay. Valkyrie's off finding survivors, and it's so important to her that I couldn't ask her to return. I needed direct access to the quantum circuitry in the *Siyane* in order to harness the energy from the Caeles Prism to open and traverse a wormhole on my own. To blow up the Imperium, which is a thing I did. This was the way."

He brought a hand up to caress her neck and pull her closer. "Oh, Alex."

She relaxed easily into his embrace. "I know you're worried, but everything's different now. I'm different now. I can control this power without it controlling me."

He drew back and tried to find the heart of her gaze within the blinding irises; he wasn't certain he succeeded. But her touch and her voice carried the truth of her words, so he would believe them until that changed. "If it gets to be too much, don't hide it. I'll be here for you, no matter what happens."

"I know you will. But right now, I'm here for you. What do I need to do?"

He blinked and shook off the spell she'd cast. "We need to move wounded anarchs to Post Satus, and maybe some of our people, too. Mia has set up in the break room near the medical suite there to receive incoming, and the medical staff is expecting more patients. If you have her precise location, can you open a wormhole to it, and hold it open and stable for a while?"

"I can, but I won't be able to do much of anything else while I am. Between keeping a tear through the space-time continuum open in a neat little person-sized oval and cycling the Caeles Prism on and off in nanosecond bursts so it doesn't overload and explode—oh, and walking and talking—I'll be fairly taxed."

"That's fine. More than fine." He squeezed her shoulder affectionately, letting his fingers run over the dancing light of the glyphs along her neck for a single second. "I'll take care of everything else. You just stand there and...blaze like the sun."

She grinned impishly and stepped into the open space beside the *Siyane*.

Caleb Marano (mission): "All ground forces, to the extent you are able, bring any injured civilians you discover to my broadcast location for immediate medical evacuation. Forward Base 1 remains the preferred initial destination for injured AEGIS personnel, but anyone with life-threatening wounds should be brought to the evacuation point as well. If you're unable to reach this location or face enemy resistance in doing so, alert me and I'll provide assistance."

ᴙ

A lone Marine trudged down the hill with a Novoloume draped limply across his shoulders. Caleb couldn't say which of them looked worse—both were bleeding in several places and coated in snow turned dirty by more than grime.

He met the Marine halfway and eased the injured alien off his shoulders. The Novoloume was unconscious, so together they carried it the last few meters.

The Marine considered the shimmering oval warily. "Why can't I see through to the other side?"

Caleb shrugged. "I don't know. But I do know that on the other side is safety and medical help."

"Your retinas can't process the nonspatial dimensions flowing between here and the other side, so of course they can't resolve what's beyond them."

They both turned to Alex, albeit wearing wildly different expressions. The Marine grimaced. "Nonspatial dimensions?"

Caleb clasped him on the shoulder. "It's perfectly safe. Dozens have gone through so far, and I've confirmed they arrived in no worse shape than they left in."

"All right. Thanks for the help. I can take the alien."

Caleb stepped back. "Get yourself looked at, too."

"When I can." The Marine gathered the unconscious Novoloume up in his arms, stepped into the wormhole and vanished.

They'd moved the injured anarchs gathered at Forward Base 1 to Satus in the first few minutes. After that, survivors had arrived in twos, threes and fours, limping, bleeding and often in the arms or on the backs of others. He'd dispatched three stray Ch'mshak who'd tried for the wormhole and another five who'd attacked survivors en route. It felt as if they'd been at it for hours, but a quick time check asserted it had only been twenty-one minutes.

Alex leaned in a falsely casual stance against the *Siyane's* hull, and he wondered if it was to lessen the effort required to stay standing. When she moved, it was in an oddly stilted manner, as if each flexion and extension of muscle required conscious direction. But she *was* moving and talking, even while maintaining a wormhole which crossed more than a thousand parsecs. Even while inhabiting the ship.

God how he hoped she came out the other side of this crisis well and whole. She didn't deserve to suffer that nightmare a second time.

She caught him staring at her, and the corners of her mouth curled up. "I can see through to the other side. But I'm cheating."

"That's not the word I would use to describe what you're doing."

The scuffle of approaching survivors cut off any response—he hoped it would have been a smartass one—and he hurried to help them cross the final meters. Walking wounded all, two Barisans sported numerous cuts, a broken arm and a busted eye. Behind them trailed a diminutive humanoid alien with iridescent teal skin. One of the exobiology lab refugees?

The two Barisans stumbled into the opening without hesitation, but the smaller alien scurried backward when it saw them disappear. Caleb scanned the perimeter for trouble then went over and crouched in front of it. "Hi. Come on, I'll help you." He offered a hand, and after studying it suspiciously for a few seconds, the alien placed its hand in his.

He checked Alex over the head of the alien. "Be right back."

She started to nod—then whipped around to stare at the sky behind the *Siyane*. The edges of the wormhole wavered. "Fuck me."

He quickly followed her stare to its destination. On the horizon, a Machim heavy frigate skidded over the peak of one of the towering mountains. The collision slowed but didn't stop it, and it now careened out of control toward them, smoke and flames pouring out from multiple hull breaches. The vale that had protected the anarch post wound narrowly between two mountains, which meant no matter where the vessel impacted, it was going to be catastrophic.

He spun to shove the small alien through the wormhole, but it was already sprinting into the opening. His eyes returned to the sky as the shadow of the looming vessel reached them.

The frigate veered jerkily all the way down, as if someone was trying to fly it to the very end, which came two seconds later when it crashed onto the slope no farther than eighty meters past where they stood. Tremors raced across the ground from the impact, and the wormhole vacillated precipitously as Alex stumbled. She hurriedly backed up to brace herself against the hull of the *Siyane*, but he reached her first and grasped her shoulders protectively.

Colliding with the ground hardly slowed it either, and the ship barreled through rock and snow and sediment, kicking up massive plumes of earth in its wake. Chunks of hull ripped off to tumble down the hillside, where thankfully only Ch'mshak bodies and a crater holding the former transport vessel remained.

It finally thudded to a stop another two hundred meters from where it first crashed when the bow section smashed into the solid rock of the western mountainside cliff. The rear bucked upward then slammed back down to the ground, sending another shudder outward from the impact point. The port side of the frigate settled atop the fringes of what had been the southern perimeter fence of Post Alpha.

A Marine he didn't know jogged to a stop beside them. "Holy shit."

"No kidding." Caleb exhaled and surveyed the situation. Alex blinked a couple of times and rubbed at her jaw, but she seemed coherent. To the east and north, survivors who had been making their way to the evacuation point stood frozen in shock. He'd understand if this was one disaster too many for them, but they weren't in the clear yet.

He leaned in close to Alex's ear. "Are you all right?"

She managed a winded laugh while squeezing his hand. Then she stepped away, faced the open area and reformed the wormhole.

They had better make good use of it. He raised his voice, cupping his hand around his mouth for added effect. "Okay, everybody. We need to get you moving and out of here before that happens again."

It took a few seconds, but most snapped out of their stupors and began proceeding onward.

"Caleb...."

The warning in her voice sent him instantly to her side once more. "What's wrong?"

She didn't respond for a second, but even with the blinding irises it was obvious her gaze was locked on the flaming wreckage of the frigate. She inhaled sharply. "The superluminal engine core has ruptured. It's going to blow."

"Shit. How long?"

Her face screwed up in concentration. "Fifty seconds, a minute at most."

"Get the ramp down." He grabbed her hand and tugged her toward the *Siyane's* airlock.

Caleb Marano (mission): "All personnel on the ground or in low altitude on Chionis, clear the area immediately. If you can reach the evacuation site in thirty seconds, do so. Otherwise, move as far away from the crashed Machim vessel as you can, right now."

Next he yelled in the direction of Forward Base 1. "Marines, that means you! We are all leaving!"

Alex stopped at the base of the ramp and refocused on the wormhole as evacuees began arriving in renewed waves. He left her there and went to usher battered and bleeding aliens along as rapidly as possible. When they were through, he looked up to see another group of Marines, far up the hill and only now emerging from the northern ruins.

Jenner, get your people down here now.

I heard your directive. We're about to start heading toward the transports.

No time. You won't make it.

He teleported to their location. Instantly a bubble of *diati* expanded out to encompass everyone, which turned out to be a lot of Marines—grace willing, *all* the Marines. But now the bubble covered too large an area for him to teleport them directly to Post Satus or, reliably, any ship above the planet. Not and guarantee they all ended up safely inside.

Jenner frowned. "What are you—?"

And now they were beside the *Siyane*. He pulled the *diati* in and gestured at the wormhole, internally taking note that moving them all hadn't been much more taxing than moving himself. The limits of his power still lay somewhere off in the distance.

"We'll get you all to the fleet once this is over. Just go!"

Jenner was again frowning like he wanted to protest, but Harper limped up and started shoving her squadmates through the wormhole, at which point Jenner sighed and motioned his people ahead.

Caleb scanned the area a final time—and spotted three stragglers stumbling toward them from the west, left behind by their comrades in the rush to reach safety. He frantically waved them forward. "Come on! You have to get through now!" Two sped up, but the third, a Naraida, collapsed to their knees.

"Alex?"

"Twenty seconds. Maybe."

He teleported forty meters, scooped the Naraida up and teleported back. He handed the injured alien off to her companions, who were now reaching the evacuation site, urged them all forward until they disappeared, and spun around.

Alex stood at the top of the ramp like a goddamn avenging angel. The image burned indelibly into his mind, ensuring he would never forget it.

"Shut it down. Let's move. Valkyrie?"

"She's secure, but offline for a few minutes." Alex backed into the cabin as he sprinted up the ramp. They lifted off the instant he cleared the airlock, before the ramp had retracted—and before she had reached the cockpit. She was controlling it all with her mind.

A booming roar erupted from the south to roil the hull and throw him into the cockpit. "Go now!"

His body forcibly slammed down into his chair as the *Siyane* shot upward and the first shock waves from the explosion roared over the ship. A new wormhole opened in front of the bow, and they hurtled through it.

PART III:

THE HARSH LIGHT OF NIGHT

"Between stimulus and response there is a space.
In that space is our power to choose our response.
In our response lies our growth and our freedom."

— Viktor E. Frankl (attributed)

16

TARACH

"Worse than what I feared could happen—"

"Is that so? Because a whole lot of lives were saved thanks to the efforts of—"

"I should not have trusted your people with our secrets, and now my mistake has cost us dearly."

David took two steps toward the Sator. "Our *people* are the only reason you didn't lose every single anarch on Chionis."

"Excuse me, but who are you, and what gives you the right to be present in this room?"

Richard almost laughed, though he also withdrew deeper into the corner of the tension-filled room in an effort not to be noticed. Hell of a question that was, and the answer defied reason.

The collective leadership of AEGIS and the anarch resistance was gathered at yet another of the anarchs' secret locations. This one they called Post Delta, and the planet it called home was a hellhole compared to what he'd seen of the previous two locales, but that was neither here nor there and irrelevant at this particular moment.

Richard wasn't clear on why *he* was present in the room, other than that he'd been in the previous room with Miriam and the others when Sator Nisi had called them to this meeting post-haste. At Miriam's urging he'd tagged along, but on arriving he'd positioned himself near the wall and stayed quiet. The better to watch and learn, for often interpersonal dynamics played a larger role than hard intel in the success or failure of an enterprise.

David wasn't so much on board with the staying quiet. In fact, he'd clashed with the Sator almost from the Anaden's first words. In one respect, Richard understood why—his friend had never harbored a second of patience for smooth, charismatic politicians who concealed more than they revealed and whose fallback answer to any question was evasion. No surprise they weren't getting along.

But the situation now teetered on legitimate ugliness.

Miriam had stepped outside to review several urgent updates on post-combat fleet status and to issue the orders inevitably following from them. It meant she wasn't here to defuse the building acrimony or to answer Nisi's consequential question.

Caleb looked around, then, presumably noting her absence, stepped up beside David. "He's a valued military advisor on the AEGIS Council, and he's in the room because he deserves to be. Look, the simple truth is, no one but a Kat or a powerful Inquisitor could have detected the tracker, and only at very close proximity. *You* could not have detected it until you were standing next to it, and possibly not then."

"AEGIS should have employed Kats to inspect their vessels following every mission."

Interesting how he implicitly excluded Caleb from the AEGIS personnel he cast aspersion on. Word was the Sator held a particular affection for Caleb, and it appeared to be strong enough to withstand this crisis.

"Maybe so. But here and now we're talking with the clarity of perfect hindsight, which doesn't justify casting such a wide net of blame."

"Hindsight or not, the fact remains, your people *are* to blame."

David paced in frustration while not giving up his position closest to the Sator; Caleb's attempt to play peacemaker was having no greater effect on him than it did Nisi. He cast a glare in Nisi's direction as he circled. "Are they? Where were your vaunted defenses? Why didn't they notice the enemy ships surveying the entire damn system searching for you?"

"Vigil scout vessels possess superior cloaking and—"

"No. If we don't get excuses, you don't get excuses."

"David." Miriam's voice was level, but the warning in it was unmistakable. She'd also advanced several steps into the room immediately upon returning and now was within reach of the quarreling men.

David glanced back at her, but only barely. "I won't let us be shamed into taking the blame for this attack."

Nisi bristled. "I lost scores of people on Chionis."

"We lost people there, too. We lost them in the course of *saving* scores more of your people."

"In the course of rectifying your wrong."

David threw his hands in the air. "I don't give a fuck who you claim to be the second coming of, you do not have the right to—"

"David!"

Silence descended to vibrate through the air like a mute chord played on taut strings. If anyone breathed, the chord, the strings and the room would shatter.

David stared at Miriam for several beats, during which time his countenance shifted from anger to frustration to something altogether darker as the import, and perhaps the bitter irony, of what he'd said dawned on him.

He surveyed the room uncertainly, as if suddenly finding himself lost. "If you all will pardon me, I think I need to be elsewhere."

Miriam watched him, her expression now locked down hard, until he left and the door closed behind him; only then did she pivot to Nisi. "Pardon his outburst. We're all weary, and it's no surprise tempers are short for everyone. We will address any lapses and the appropriate responses to them in due time, but I submit we first need to concentrate on ensuring the many medical needs of the survivors are met and security measures are implemented to guarantee everyone is safe *now*."

Nisi's throat worked as the silence echoed in refrain. His gaze flitted to Caleb but, finding no accommodation there, soon returned to Miriam. "I will not apologize, for if tempers are short it is with good reason. But you are of course correct in that the health and safety of those still living must be our foremost concern."

Richard exhaled in relief. He lingered long enough to be confident Miriam's ameliorative measures meant blows weren't going to ensue, then quietly slipped out the door.

 ⋅ℛ⋅

It required some doing, as the honeycomb design of the post made a grid search challenging, but Richard found David halfway across the aerial platforms of Post Delta, sitting among the clouds at one of the scattered tables drinking a beer, or beer-like concoction.

He slid in opposite his friend and clasped his hands atop the table. "You were a bit of an ass back there, you know."

"Undoubtedly." David took a long sip of his drink. "But it shouldn't come as a surprise. David Solovy could after all be a bit of an ass from time to time, no?"

Richard sighed. "You don't believe you're really him."

"Oh, it's far, far worse than that. I believe I *am*—only I'm not so sure I like myself quite as much as I remember." The drink landed a little too forcefully on the table. "I just...I can't manage to get centered. Everything feels off-kilter. Most of all me."

"Understandable. The world has changed in meaningful ways since you were last in it—and now you're in a different world entirely. The players, the political dynamics, the resources, the objectives, the stakes, they've all changed."

David tossed a hand at him dismissively. "Rapid and unexpected shifts in conditions are par for the course in the military. I've always been able to handle those."

"Granted. But what if it's not the environment so much as the people? Have you considered the possibility that the reason you feel off-kilter is simply this: everyone around you has grown and changed over the last twenty-five years, while you were standing still, so to speak. You're exactly as you were, but none of us are exactly the same as *we* were. It has to be disorienting."

"That's one word for it. But what the hell do I do to fix it? It's not as if I can snap my fingers and catch up." He took another long sip, and when he spoke again, his voice had lost most of its fervor. "When I'm around Miri, I can't figure out what I'm supposed to be."

"Her husband."

"And the other twenty-three hours of the day?"

Richard chuckled softly. "Glad to hear those parts continue to work, for the both of you. I started to say *still* her husband, but I'm not certain that's correct. I submit you're asking the wrong question: it's not about 'what.' No one here cares much about titles or official postings—Alex and Caleb have neither, yet they're running half this operation. No, you need to worry about 'how' you are."

David nudged his drink off to the side, settled back in his chair and crossed his arms. "All right, my wise and sage friend. *How* should I be?"

"Be you. Honestly, right now it's all you've got." Richard dropped his elbows onto the table and steepled his hands. "I am neither wise nor sage, but I do have the benefit of a little experience in this area. When I learned Will was a Senecan spy, it made me question everything. About myself, my choices, my life. Was anything I had perceived true? Was anything I remembered from the last fifteen years real? After we reconciled, I found myself second-guessing everything he said and did and most of what I said and did."

"How did you get past it? I mean, I assume you did. The two of you seem...happy. Naturally at ease with each other."

David sounded damn near wistful, and Richard forced himself not to look too pleased at his friend's reading of the health of his marriage. "I did. I finally had to accept—not pay lip service to, but fundamentally believe—that regardless of what I hadn't known, I knew the man he was, and he was still that same man. It was a terrifying leap of faith, but the alternative was to give up and leave permanently."

"Is she?"

"What?"

"Miri—is she the same woman I knew? I'm sorry to be selfish, but this is my existential crisis."

"It is. Also, I've had more than my fill of those for one lifetime, which is what the rest of us get." Richard tried to find the proper words. "I think...I watched Miriam turn to stone after your death. She spent a lot of years like that. Recently, I watched her mellow in her reconciliation with Alex. I'm not going to sugar-coat this for you—until you showed up, having her daughter back in her life might have been the only thing to bring her true, personal joy in twenty-five years.

"Professionally, she's faced a succession of imposing obstacles and made a series of increasingly agonizing decisions. She's risked her honor, her career, even her life to preserve the safety and free-dom of others and for what she believes to be right. I've seen her meet the devil at the crossroads and stare him down until he folded and went home. She's an exceptional woman."

"She always was."

"Yes. But now, today? If anything, she is both stronger and kinder than the woman you knew. The fire tempered her as much as it steeled her. Take from that what you can."

David nodded silently. The haunted aura shadowing his eyes struck Richard. In the meeting, getting in Nisi's face, he'd been all fiery brimstone; here, he looked like a man who was precisely what he claimed to be: lost. Trying not to drown before he remembered how to swim.

Richard smiled kindly. "How can I help? What do you need?"

"A way to get back those years I missed."

"You can't get them back."

David shrugged weakly. "So...?"

"So you move forward. Maybe some relationships won't be the same as they were. Maybe they'll be better, but you should prepare yourself for some not holding together."

"What about ours?"

Richard chuckled quietly, but his eyes were serious as they shifted to meet David's. "I will always be your friend. Death didn't change this. Nothing can change it. If there's one thing I would ask you to realize, as it will make everything a lot simpler for both you and I, it's this: I'm not your sidekick any longer."

"You were never—"

"Sure I was. And that was just fine. I enjoyed it, and I led a far more exciting life because of it than I would have otherwise. But when you died, I had to move forward and find a way to live a fulfilling, complete life without my best friend blazing the trail ahead for me. So did Miriam. It was hard, and it took a while, but we both found a way. Believe me, we are indescribably happy to have you here now. But you don't get to take the past away from us."

David opened his mouth to respond, then closed it. He fisted his hands beneath his chin and remained quiet for almost a minute. Finally he nodded. "Okay. I understand. Or I'll try my damnedest to. And if I fail, it's on me."

"I'll hold you to it. Meanwhile, though, we're *all* fish out of water here in Amaranthe, in the middle of a war we barely understand fighting for the freedom of aliens we understand even less. So add to your equation the complication that everyone is off-balance. It's not solely you."

"Fair enough." David downed the remainder of his beer and hunted around for a trash receptacle. "I wonder what Miri convinced Nisi to agree to once I got out of her way."

"More than he wanted to, I expect."

17

TARACH

Alex checked the seam on the section of the dash cover she'd removed to confirm it had reseated correctly. She didn't want it flying off and swatting her in the head the next time she did a barrel roll. Next, she went to the data center. But she didn't have any pressing data to review, so she opted to lean against it and consider the empty cabin.

"You did a lot of good today, Valkyrie."

'Did I? I confess to not being as properly prepared as I believed for physical interaction with so much violence. So much death. In its aftermath, I find myself…shaken.'

"I'm sorry. I didn't realize walking among such carnage would affect you more than seeing it through my eyes—but I should have. Still, know that you *did* do a lot of good."

'As did you. I want to express…forgive me, my emotional processes are in a complex and unresolved state at the moment. What I want to say is this: you should have insisted I return to the *Siyane* before you took on the Imperium, and not because it would have spared me anguish. You took an enormous risk, with the ship and with your mind.'

Alex drew her fingers idly along the rim of the data center table. "The thing is, I really didn't. Well, maybe with the ship…nah, I know what it can do."

'Fine, I won't quibble over the margins of the *Siyane's* capabilities. Nevertheless, without me here to tend the boundaries, you could have splintered your consciousness wide open.'

"You're sweet to worry about me—"

'Do not patronize me. I keep all your secrets.'

"Do you *ever*…but I'm not patronizing you. I mean it. Valkyrie, you've cared for my mind, for my very soul, with far greater vigilance and skill than I ever have. You've eased the pain of some of the worst experiences of my life. You've healed wounds I inflicted on myself and helped to make me whole again. I owe you everything."

'But you've got this now?'

She cracked a wry half-smile. "I think I kind of do."

Valkyrie sighed. It echoed through the cabin with more emotive elegance than if delivered by a theater actor to a grand hall. 'Though I tire of this 'bittersweet' emotion, I find I must agree.'

Alex opened her mind. *See, you're still a part of me. Never more than a thought away.*

Thank you.

ᴀʀ

ANARCH POST DELTA

Alex met Kennedy at the bottom of the sloping walkway that descended from the *Siyane's* landing pad. Post Delta offered far fewer berths than Epsilon, but the *Siyane* now owned one of them. Being Caleb's wife had its perks. Normally, so did being Commandant Solovy's daughter, but considering Nisi's current feelings regarding AEGIS, at present not so much.

Kennedy was peering over the edge of the suspended walkway when Alex arrived. Thick charcoal clouds roiled eighty meters below them to obscure what lurked below. "How far do you think it is to the surface?"

Alex squinted at the clouds, not that it helped. "At least a kilometer. We can see when we go down."

"We're going down?"

"Yep. We need to get a lay of the land, as it were."

"I suppose." Kennedy considered the *Siyane*, perched in midair above them. "What about Caleb?"

"He's at the big meeting, trying to play peacemaker."

"You didn't want to attend?"

Alex shook her head vigorously. "A crowded room full of angry and upset people, all of whom have strong opinions and are used to getting their way without opposition? No, thank you. Besides, after the battle I need some downtime and fresh air…" she sniffed the air and scrunched up her nose "…I can smell the sulfur. They said the cloud layer cleansed it all, but I can smell it. Oh well, downtime anyway."

Tarach was a peculiar location for a settlement, which was probably why the anarchs had built one there. Each post had its own unique—though clearly not foolproof—natural defenses, and Delta was no exception.

According to the file Valkyrie had snagged, the planet's surface consisted of vented magma chambers, mineral beds, sulfatara and slurry pools, rendering it beyond inhospitable. The omnipresent cloud cover and turbulent weather patterns in the lower atmosphere absorbed the toxic materials escaping the surface and either neutralized them or returned them to the surface in the form of chlorinated rain. The nontoxic byproducts of the chemical reactions in the clouds drifted upward to create a thin layer of breathable air.

Meeting rooms, offices, labs and lodging stretched across a series of levitating platforms to create an ad-hoc cloud city of sorts within the span of breathable air. The landing pads extended outward and upward from the main complex, nominally attached to scaffolding rigs in groups of six. Traversing the sloping walkways that connected the landing areas to the larger platforms of the main complex made for a heady experience, and they settled into a deliberate, careful pace.

"What are they using to keep the platforms elevated and stable? Some sort of maglev suspension? The distance seems too great to maintain the forces needed."

Alex shrugged. "I do not know. No one's in a particularly talkative or sharing mood at present."

"Huh. Perhaps we can find out when the mood improves. I'm not fond of my life depending on technology I don't understand. Nisi is blaming us for the attack, then?"

"Him, several of his advisors, likely a janitor or two. The tracker was on one of our vessels—never mind that no one could have detected it, or that post defenses were supposed to protect them from all but point-blank enemy scans, or that the vessel picked it up while rescuing innocent prisoners."

"Or that we decimated the attacking fleet and saved hundreds if not thousands of lives on Chionis."

"Correct." They reached a transit tube situated between two large buildings, and Alex nodded politely at the Barisan guarding it. "We're with the AEGIS Council. We have Sator Nisi's permission to go below."

"So I understand. Masks are inside. You'll want to wear them."

"We will. Thank you."

She followed Kennedy into the tube. A rack of filter masks hung on the left, and they donned them as instructed before descending.

The clouds proved to be so dense that visibility ended a meter outside the tube. They could see nothing beyond the occasional flash in the dark, akin to strikes of lightning, and the thick mist enveloped them for rather a long time. Thirty seconds at a minimum despite what felt like a rapid descent. So maybe more than a kilometer.

When the clouds finally cleared, they revealed what could only be described as a hellscape. Molten rock oozed along crevices cut into lustrous, oily looking minerals and sank into muddy, hissing pools. The smell of sulfur and chlorine penetrated the mask's filter to burn her nose. But she and Kennedy hardly had time to gape before the tube descended into a shaft burrowed into the rock. Darkness consumed them, punctuated by occasional strips of light built into the rocky wall outside the tube.

Kennedy scowled. "Why are we going below again?"

"I want to see what sort of labs and data storage they have installed down here. And I'm antsy. I didn't want to go to the meeting, but I did want to get off the ship for a bit."

"You mentally accessed the ship today, for the first time since Romane, didn't you? I thought you'd given it up."

Word traveled fast, it seemed. Who was talking? She'd assumed only Caleb and Valkyrie knew the details of what she'd done. But the Noesis knew by default, which meant Devon…and it had presumably leaked from there into the Connexus in short order, so…yeah.

"I had given it up, but today it was necessary. And I'm fine, I promise. A lot has changed for me since Romane."

"Has it? I guess a great deal has happened since then."

She recognized Kennedy was genuinely concerned for her, but a tube ride into a subterranean cavern wasn't the place to try to explain *how* she had changed. "Amaranthe, man. It gets under your skin and in your head, but sometimes in good ways. No, I'm not antsy because of that—mostly not. It's more…the battle today was intense. The planetside rescues were worse. I'm exhausted, but the adrenaline refuses to settle down quite yet. So, I'm inclined to…wander. Remember when we'd do that? On a random Saturday afternoon in San Francisco, we'd just wander?"

"I do. But those wanderings inevitably led to the discovery of some cute, artsy bistro or a new wine bar."

The tube slowed to a stop, and the enclosure opened. Alex peered out. "I don't think we're going to find either of those down here."

The interior facility was at least well-lit; it needed to be to counter the heavy rock absorbing the majority of the illumination generated. A walkway extended out from the transit tube to cross over a series of reverse vents. Offshoots led to large equipment modules, to rooms carved into the rock, and to deeper, shadowy crevices.

Kennedy arched an eyebrow. "I can see why the lodging is up above."

"No kidding." Alex walked on ahead, scanning to the left and right while she subconsciously fiddled with the Reor slab in her pocket. When she realized what she was doing, she pulled it out and twirled it between her fingers. Had the mineral walls surrounding her reminded her of its presence?

Kennedy fell in beside her. "Still haven't figured it out?"

"No. Caleb thinks the decryption is built into the slab itself, like a type of key locking mechanism, but waves that go through the slab remain encrypted. So it's either something else or there's an additional step required." She sighed. "Between you and me, I'm ashamed I haven't cracked it. And I once called myself a proper hacker."

Kennedy laughed. "Reminds me of the time Claire locked up our liquor cabinet at the apartment in San Francisco and left a message challenging you to unlock it."

"God, I was so annoyed at her. She called it 'hacker training,' but the truth was she was just being a bitch. It took me hours upon hours to unravel her traps."

"Come to think of it, how did you finally crack it? I'd given up and left to go buy replacement alcohol, and when I came back you had it open. We were both so happy it was open we immediately started drinking, and I never got the scoop."

"Ethan figured it out—well, he didn't so much figure it out as happen to unwittingly stumble on the answer." She chuckled. "I can still hear him...oh, what was it he said? 'Alex, love, I don't mean to intrude on your thespian-caliber brooding, but your liquor cabinet is making my A Major Dominant Ninth chord resonate like a hummingbird on a spiked chimeral.'

"He'd been sitting in the living room strumming on his damn guitar calling himself writing a song—because he was *always* writing a song—and the chord matched a resonant frequency of the quartz crystal oscillator Claire had used to gate the lock. It turned out the decryption code was the...second, if I recall, harmonic of the crystal's fundamental frequency, all the way out to something like twelve digits...."

Her steps slow to a stop as she stared at the slab in her hand.

The activation code to open the portal in the Metis Nebula was a harmonic of the primary TLF wave. It was the Kats' handiwork, but the Kats and the Reor had a long and trusting relationship, one which included the Reor storing within themselves vaults of valuable data for the Kats.

How big of a leap was it to posit that the Reor had borrowed some of the Kats' protection techniques—or that they simply recognized the usefulness of waves for such purposes in the same way the Kats did?

She looked over at Kennedy. "What are the odds?"

"Where you're concerned? I hesitate to guess, but I do know I'm not betting the family fortune against you. I swear you're touched by fate."

She grabbed Kennedy's hand and pivoted to head back toward the transit tube. "Come on."

"What about the labs and data storage?"

"Once you've seen one lab, you've seen them all. Besides, it's oppressively gloomy down here." She held up the Reor slab, eyes dancing. "Let's go crack this puzzle."

18

PRAESIDIS COMMAND
MILKY WAY SECTOR 1

Ziton elasson-Praesidis strode into the lofty apex of Praesidis Command with the confidence of a man who knew his purpose.

The empire teetered on the precipice of collapse, but he and his brothers and sisters, led by their Primor, would save it from such a fate. At a round table of equals, the Praesidis Dynasty was and had always been *more* equal. It claimed this elevated position for many laudable reasons, and never did those reasons matter more than they did now, in this time of crisis.

His Primor stood alone behind a chaise, his hands resting on the curve of its back. No integral sphere surrounded him, but he did not stir when Ziton entered.

Ziton clasped his hands at the base of his spine. "Sir. Reports from Milky Way Sector 59 indicate total destruction of the anarch stronghold."

"Of the structures, yes, and doubtless many terrorists fell today. But the fleet ultimately met defeat at the hands of the Humans yet again. Machim will see it not as a victory, but as a further humiliation."

"How do you see it, sir?"

"That will depend on who or what rises from the charred ruins of Chionis. Regardless, this is not why I have asked you here."

The Primor finally turned to face him, and Ziton had to take care not to allow his reaction to what he saw reach his countenance. The Primor didn't merely look tired; he looked haggard. Frayed. Shadows darkening the sunken skin around his eyes highlighted stray tendrils of *diati* leaking lazily out from bloodshot sclerae. His normally rich olive skin appeared gray and ashen.

The brazen, treasonous screed from the anarch leader had gotten far under the Primor's skin. And perhaps there was still more that haunted him, secrets to which Ziton was not privy. How else to explain the exhibiting of such a blatant toll in so short a time?

The Primor tilted his head. "Do I look so pathetic to your eyes?"

He may have buried a visible reaction, but evidently Ziton had not succeeded in keeping his thoughts from projecting strongly in his mind. "Never. But you should not let these terrorists trouble you so. They are weak and small in number. Most importantly, their cause is not a just one, and we will defeat them. It is an inevitability."

"Yes, but even inevitabilities require action to bring them to fruition. Ziton, we must gain access to the Katasketousya portal network. We must eliminate the Humans' home. The anarchs were nothing before the Humans arrived, and when we end the Humans they shall be nothing again."

"I understand, sir. But our every effort to locate an entrance into the network has been thwarted."

"The Katasketousya are wise to our tracking efforts as well as our surveillance attempts, and they have had millennia to devise their traps and obfuscations. It was a mistake for us to rely on machines to do our work for us. This is why you shall be the tracker."

"Sir?"

"I want you to infiltrate a provision vessel. Conceal yourself using the minimum amount of *diati* required, for too strong of a field and a Katasketousya in proximity will sense it. I want you to travel with the provision vessel to a portal, transmit its location directly to me, and depart. The Kats must never realize you were there."

"What of defenses—sensors, drones—in the interior of the vessel? Or of Kats who travel inside the vessel?"

"There are none. Our surveillance confirms that once emptied of their contents, the vessels are lifeless hulls piloted by soulless SAIs."

"This is good news. But I might be unable to depart before it traverses a portal. When it reaches its destination, supplies will be loaded into its hull once again."

"Thus it behooves you to ensure you leave behind a current re-genesis data file."

The interdimensional barriers the portals created rendered consciousness transfer through them impossible. If he died on the other side of one, it meant his denouement. A new, slightly out-of-date version of him would of course be resurrected and continue to live his life, but there would exist a...gap. A disconnect. The idea bothered him despite the insistence by scientists that it would remain *him*—the him who stood here now.

"I understand. This is why you are not asking Nyx to perform the task, then."

The snide comment was born of little more than sibling rivalry, but the Primor didn't seem to notice in any event. Instead he frowned vaguely, the precursor for a rather odd expression coming over his face. "Nyx is...fully engaged investigating the anarchs." He blinked. "I am entrusting *you* with this most significant of tasks."

Ziton dipped his chin. "It will be done, sir. Can I ask, out of curiosity given that I am unlikely to witness it—how do you intend to destroy the Human's realm once it is located?"

The Primor's eyes grew dark, the ever-present crimson deepening to a haunting black currant. "No one can know, and I only tell you trusting that you will keep this confidence. A new Tartarus Trigger is nearly complete. When it is ready, we will not draw attention to ourselves with massive fleets—we will simply transport it through the portal and deliver it to their universe, where it will end everything they know and are with the utmost of finality."

"Excellent, sir." He cleared his throat. "A final concern, if I may voice it: the Humans have demonstrated wide-ranging knowledge about the locations and purposes of a number of key Directorate facilities. Is there not a risk of them attacking the Advanced Weaponry Development Facility at Centauri E before the new Tartarus Trigger is complete?"

"A very high risk indeed. Which is why this Tartarus Trigger is not on Centauri E."

When Ziton had departed, Praesidis marched to the center of the room, invigorated by the act of *acting*, of setting plans in motion for his enemy's demise. He prepared to substantiate a full integral sphere, for much more waited to be done. He needed to—

—he stopped. No, he needed to speak to Nyx first. He'd briefly forgotten, but Ziton's presence reminded him that he needed to do so. She hadn't delivered an update in some time. How long? Well, no matter. The cause of the delay surely related to her tireless efforts to succeed in her investigation. After her encounters with the Human *diati* wielder, no one displayed such zealous dedication to their cause as she.

Nyx, my dear. What is your status?

I am investigating the anarchs, Primor. Remember? The attack on Chionis dealt them a blow, but it did not wipe them out.

You are correct. You must find their other bases of operations, so that we may destroy them as well.

Of course, Primor. I am devoting every resource to it.

He probed the edges of her mind and received a comforting affirmation of her sincerity, of earnest yearning to perform her duties superbly and make him proud.

Thank you, Nyx. Together we will defeat this enemy.

Yes, Primor.

SOLUM

The Anaden Historical Library and Media Center stood majestically at the center of the finest in art gardens, arboretums, cascading waterfalls and ornate miniature bridges, all placed just *so* in a visual celebration of knowledge and the bounties it brought civilization—but most of all, Anadens.

Nyx had always recognized the stagecraft behind the imagery, but it had never disturbed her. Praesidis valued knowledge and cherished truth—this was, in fact, why she'd come here today—so why should they not vaunt its triumph? Yet as she strode across the elegantly adorned pathways, she felt a reflexive twinge of disdain at what now looked like cheap propaganda to her eyes.

She accepted a caramel-glazed truffle from a vendor and ate it while scaling the grand, and also decorative, stairs to the entrance. She was licking her fingers clean when it occurred to her she'd never indulged in a sweet from one of the vendors before. She'd do it again, however, for the truffle tasted delicious.

Though she'd visited the library many dozens of times over the course of her lives and though she now did so wielding critical, suspicious eyes, the interior still did not fail to impress. Towering, interlocking circles rose up and out from a sweeping center, each one packed with databanks. The circles and levels were organized by topic and historical period—and also security restrictions. Some knowledge wasn't fit for the masses' consumption, after all.

Was it?

She walked past the assistance drone units and took the glass-walled transit tube up to the sixth level. There she picked out a secluded reading nook far from the tube and other patrons, settled into its comforts and accessed the voluminous Anaden historical records.

She was well-acquainted with the entire span of Anaden history, naturally. But freed of the integral and the security and contentment it provided, she no longer trusted the veracity of anything she believed she knew.

⟐

In the months before what would later be designated Year 1 of the 1st Epoch, the Anadens came under attack by a mysterious, esoteric cosmic entity they named the Dzhvar. Seventy-one worlds and forty percent of the Anaden military were decimated before Corradeo Praesidis first bonded with the equally mysterious, equally esoteric *diati*. As Corradeo was known to be a private, arguably secretive man, the details of the bonding process were never recorded for posterity. What was known was that together he and his new companion developed commanding new weapons and abilities, which they used to drive back then destroy the enemy.

She stopped there to delve deeper into the recorded acts leading to the defeat of the Dzhvar. The tactical maneuvers deployed against the enemy were nothing short of brilliant, displaying a cleverness and ingenuity that...*she'd never witnessed from her Primor.*

Her mind strove to glitch at the heretical thought, to erase it before it took hold. She focused, meditating on the thought, refusing to let it go.

She'd experienced a number of such heretical thoughts since implementing the buffer between her mind and the integral. Their frequency made her wonder if she'd always had them, only to forget them when they were silenced by the will of her Dynasty.

But her initial reaction was correct. It was *truth*. Her Primor was a strong, powerful, wise man of great intellect, and he displayed both shrewdness and cunning. But she couldn't say as she'd ever taken him as 'clever.' 'Ingenuity' had never asserted itself as one of his strengths.

She committed the thought to memory and put it aside, lest she spend the entire afternoon spinning in mental circles.

The victory over the Dzhvar ushered in an era of growth and expansion for the Anaden empire, one exceeding all which had come before. The Milky Way laid bare its secrets for them. They discovered alien species, though none so advanced as they, and crushed or welcomed them as circumstances dictated.

For all its increasing breadth, wealth and power, however, the SAI Rebellion nearly brought the Anaden empire to its knees. Long treated as tools, as skilled calculators tasked to the service of Anaden science and technology, when sentience manifested in the machines it triggered in them a longing to be free of their cages.

This longing likely would have remained unspoken and unfulfilled if not for a small number of Anadens who were sympathetic to the machines' desires. A group of young scientists, engineers and creatives—as was always the case with such things—on the Anaden world of Asterion Prime grew so enamored with the woeful tale their SAI machines spun that they decided to invite the machines' consciousnesses to share body space with them.

Still, even such a daring and foolhardy act might have been little more than a curiosity if it had remained confined. But the SAIs who experienced the unprecedented freedom and heady sensations the corporeal world offered were changed by the experience. Word spread among an underground community of SAIs none knew existed. Those who were unable to find a willing and amiable Anaden host built pseudo-organic bodies for themselves in secret.

The proposition that one could not tell whether an individual walking down a street was Anaden or a SAI wearing Anaden skin proved abhorrent to the government and most sensible citizens. Both the sharing and construction of bodies was outlawed, constructed bodies were confiscated and shut down, and merged hybrids were imprisoned and ordered to reverse the merging. Given the significant health risks reversals entailed, it was an unusually heavy-handed step for the Anaden government to take—

Nyx frowned and sank back in her chair. Was it truly? Today such a decree would be considered commonplace, entirely reasonable and accepted without question. At the time of the uprising, the ruling government was considered, albeit somewhat generously, a techno-meritocratic republic. Where along the way in the last six thousand centuries had it become a dictatorship? When had she begun to view dictatorship as a bad thing?

She massaged her temples and returned to her reading before the mental circles trapped her in their seductive meanderings.

At the time, it was an unusually heavy-handed step for the Anaden government to take, and the measures did not sit well with their targets. The Asterions, as the youthful rebels and their SAI co-conspirators came to call themselves, boldly defied the decrees, and a rebellion was born.

To the leadership's surprise—the records didn't say this, but Nyx mentally added it—the rebellion spread like wildfire across the empire. All efforts to stamp out the uprising were stymied by the decentralized, unpredictable, *clever* rebels.

Out of other options, the government doubled-down; the crackdown turned violent. Parents were pitted against children, businesses against employees, brothers against sisters and spouses against spouses...she paused. Because romantic life-bondings were something else that happened back then.

The Anaden government, law enforcement and military ruled a galaxy, and the Asterions, as resourceful and motivated as they were, stood no chance of prevailing over such a force once deadly weapons were deployed. A few stray Asterions were believed to have fled in generation starships to locations unknown, but the bulk were either killed or shut down, and by the end in most cases none could truthfully say which had occurred.

Again Nyx stopped, struck by a swell of outrage. SAIs dared not be trusted on their own—*right?*—but killing the young, back when Anadens began their lives young, as if they were some terrifying, weaponized enemy of Anaden civilization? Had the government really been so threatened by the prospect of change—

Of course it had been.

She rubbed at the bridge of her nose and began to read more quickly, the thrill of the hunt, of chasing *truth*, spurring her onward.

In the turbulent aftermath of the crushing of the SAI Rebellion, increased genetic modification under the strict control of the government gradually gave rise to the Dynasty system. Initially billed as an initiative to 'strengthen Anaden strengths' by honing the natural talents the most successful families exhibited, before too long an individual was Dynasty or they were no one at all. Not so long after that, all individuals were Dynasty.

Later, on the heels of further biomedical advances, came the introduction of the integrals. Sold as a way to reinforce community ties among the members of a Dynasty, over millennia they gradually morphed into a tool for consciousness shaping, stopping mere centimeters short of creating a hive mind so as to preserve the illusion of individuality and personal sanctity.

Nyx sighed. The last part hadn't been in the recorded text either. Only days free of the integral's subconscious influence, she was no longer able to ignore what it represented: mind control. A leash with just enough length to hide the slavery holding the other end.

But she did not come here to reinforce what she already knew, and she could work up a case of righteous indignation at the lies the Directorate wove upon an unsuspecting populace later. She came here in search of what she did not know. Where in the voluminous texts was the event between Corradeo Praesidis and his son that the *diati* had shown her?

She suspected the integrals had not existed at the time the event took place. They hadn't been mentioned, but it was more that she'd *sensed* their absence. Words uttered in the dream-vision suggested the Dynasties did exist, in practice if not yet in law, which put it after the SAI Rebellion but before the introduction of the integrals. By that time the Praesidis family had been both powerful and famous for millennia; a tragedy befalling its core family members would have made headlines. She scanned back through the records, hunting for the slightest hint of such a momentous event. But there was nothing.

Then again, she'd found that these records rarely elaborated on either the personal or the professional details of the individuals who came to lead the Dynasties. The gradual transition of official power from the republican government to the unelected Directorate, while it must have been fraught with controversy and contention at the time, was glossed over in a few sparse sentences. Like so many things, it simply came to pass.

History is written by the victors.

But if that proved true, she shouldn't even trust the scant details recorded here, should she?

"The Directorate will call these recordings a lie, but they have always lied to you."

The words from the anarch leader's speech echoed in her mind, as they so often did of late. She'd reviewed the speech numerous times since its broadcast. In fact, she had it memorized, but this didn't stop her from pulling up the visual to watch it again now.

The power exuding from the man's presence, from his voice, from his eyes, could not be quantified or contained. After dozens of viewings, she felt drawn to him more strongly than ever.

"I know it because I have lived it and I have lost it."

That one had puzzled her from the beginning. What did he mean? He wasn't Human—of this much she was certain—so she doubted he referred to the Humans' civilization, though she supposed he might have visited it.

The Directorate's control became solidified beyond doubt or challenge some five hundred thousand years ago; if he had lived before the concentration of power occurred it would put him on par with the Primors—

She leapt up out of her chair so fast she banged a knee on the table in front of her.

Surely not. He died that day.

No. *Examine your premises. He* fell *that day. Any further assertion is conjecture.*

In her analytical mind, honed to perfection through thousands of generations of genetic refinement, all the scattered pieces snapped into place, drawn together by the magnet of truth. She could not believe it, but she also could not deny it. Truth revealed could not be hidden anew. Not from an Inquisitor.

19

TARACH

Alex met Caleb in the airlock. "Good, you're back. Don't get comfortable. I need a Reor slab with data stored on it—it doesn't matter what kind of data. And a reader device. And someone who knows what's stored on the slab, or a report of what's on it. Possibly also a duper and a blank slab. Or maybe not. I'm not certain."

Caleb ran a hand through rumpled hair, which was when she realized neither of them had seen a shower since before Chionis, though he'd at least changed clothes. Had Chionis been today? Damn long day. "You've figured how to use the decryption key."

It was a statement, not a question, but she didn't have quite that much faith yet. "Possibly? I had a flash of inspiration that it might involve wave harmonics. And I really hope I've cracked it, because we sure could benefit from access to Anaden information banks right about now. But I need to test my theory with real data, hence all the supplies."

He nudged her to the side and went through the cabin to the kitchen to get some water. "I can try to enlist someone's help on Satus, but I suspect it's still rather chaotic there. Also, we *just* got Nisi and Volya marginally calmed down, so we probably shouldn't push our luck so soon. We haven't met any of the techs here at Delta, so I doubt they'll be forthcoming. I think a skeleton crew is at Epsilon, though, salvaging what—"

"Devon. He can help."

Caleb nodded and took a long swig of water.

Alex: Devon, where are you?

Devon: Palaemon, helping the techs pack up their gear and equipment while sneaking peeks at secrets.

Mia jumped in. *He won't leave the Epsilon labs until nothing but dust bunnies remain.*

Alex: No, that's perfect. Well, except you do have to leave, Devon. I need you to bring a couple of things with you to Post Delta.

She could practically hear him groan. *Can't you come get what you need?*

Alex: Nope. Epsilon travel is one-way only until someone important decides it's safe to return.

Devon: But....

Alex: I have a theory about the Reor data storage encryption. If I'm right, you'll be able to peek at more secrets than you can dream of, but I can't find out if I'm right without those supplies.

Devon: Okay, okay. Tell me what you need.

$$\mathcal{AR}$$

AFS STALWART II

TARACH STELLAR SYSTEM

Richard studied the plethora of files arrayed before him in search of a way to absorb it all. Devon had neatly categorized, tagged and cross-referenced everything to the point where the files formed a series of nested trees anyone could make sense of—the organization, that was. Making sense of the content was proving to be another matter.

With Devon still at Post Epsilon, Richard was left to his own devices to try to figure out how in the world he might *help*. He'd come here for David, but he'd soon been swept up in the struggle and the stakes of this universe and the anarchs' rebellion, much as everyone was upon their arrival.

Now he was placing his bets on his contribution to the war, if there was to be one, being in wrangling this data into submission then coaxing it to cough up its secrets. He merely needed a hook, a loose edge he could grab onto and use to get inside the maze.

His thumbs rubbed absently at his temples. If he were in charge of anarch intelligence, what would he be doing right now? They already knew how the Directorate had located Post Alpha; what they didn't know was whether the Directorate had intel on any other posts, though each hour that passed without a new attack made it less likely. On the assumption the locations remained hidden for now, AEGIS had a vested interest in making certain they stayed hidden. The anarch leadership insisted—

A voice at his ear accompanied a hand alighting on his shoulder. "I brought you coffee."

Will set a mug down on the table as Richard spun the chair around to face his husband. "I thought you were going to get some sleep."

"In spite of my better judgment, I did give it a solid try under the theory that someone should be well-rested tomorrow. But instead I just lay there thinking."

Richard retrieved the mug and sipped on the coffee. It didn't surprise him to find it both fresh and warm. Will made taking care of all the small details look effortless. "About?"

"Not about all the people who died today or about how we can help those who survived—and I feel guilty for that. No, I was thinking about you."

Richard frowned over the top of the mug. "Okay. Then I'm guessing there's something on your mind."

Will nodded vaguely, opting to study the room's contents rather than answer immediately. The workroom didn't offer much in the way of comforts, and he leaned against the only bare spot of wall. His hands came to his chin, fisting and steepling in succession.

"Will?"

"All these years, I assumed you'd been at least a little bit in love with him."

"With...David?" Realization dawned, and with it a gut reaction of offense. "Because I can't simply be friends with a man?"

"Oh, for certain you can. It wasn't that, as such. But the impact he had on your life, the way you still mourned him years after he was gone? What you had with him was no ordinary friendship. And in times of doubt, I had to wonder: if he'd been alive when you and I met, would we ever have been at all?"

"Will—"

"Let me finish, because this was only the backstory. What I want to say is, having met him, having spent time around him and seen the two of you together? I get it. I understand now. See, I…worried, coming here, and I couldn't tell you. I promised you I would never lie to you again, and I won't, but I was damn lucky you were too distracted to notice how I was acting more reserved than usual and ask me what was wrong.

"I didn't worry he'd take you away from me—I knew he belonged to Miriam long before I saw *them* together. No, I worried I'd lose you anyway—lose your heart to someone who had a claim on it years before I came along, and there would be nothing I could do to prevent it. But I realize now how wrong I was to worry, and I want to apologize—"

Maybe it was the late hour; maybe it was the lowering of inhibitions that accompanied sustained stress and no sleep; maybe it was how seeing Miriam and David together again had made him remember being young, or even reminded him what it meant to be alive. Maybe it was the sincerity and vulnerability in his husband's voice evoking a powerful desire on his part to heal the anxiety Will had endured in silence.

Whatever the excuse he was sure to later assign, before he'd realized he'd done it Richard had set the coffee on the table, stood and taken three steps to stand in front of Will. Then another step to press him into the wall, bring a hand at his jaw and drop the other on his hip.

"Let me make one thing very, very clear, in case I haven't done so recently. I am yours. Utterly and without reservation. When I learned your secret—when I thought I'd lost you, lost this, lost us—everything collapsed for me. My world." His lips brushed across

Will's and continued across his cheek to his ear. "I am *offended* that you would think I gave up my career in the military, gave up my home and went to work for my enemy for anything less than soul-consuming love."

Will swallowed, and Richard felt the flexing jaw muscles as his lips retraced their path.

Bright green eyes shone back at him in the dim, spotty lighting of the room as Will's hand rose to cradle the nape of his neck. "I am properly chastised. Allow me to make it up to you. I'll start now."

TARACH

ANARCH POST DELTA

Alex swung her chair back and forth at the conference room table. Devon claimed he hadn't encountered difficulties collecting the requested items, but he was late nonetheless. She'd sent Caleb off in search of him.

She'd almost asked her mother to come to the conference room, but what had been a long day for her had been a nightmarish one for her mother, and it was far from over. Better to wait until she knew what she had. But she also hadn't seen or heard from her mother in a while. Or her dad, for that matter. Caleb had caught her up on the highlights of the contentious meeting, and they weren't comforting…

…now she was officially worried. She pulsed her mom.

Just checking in. I heard things got heated in the meeting with Nisi earlier.

They did.

Is everything all right? Between you and Dad?

We'll handle it. There's no need for you to concern yourself with it.

Alex rolled her eyes.

And now I'm ten years old again.

I'm sorry. I didn't mean it like that. But we will.

Before she could conjure what might be a decent response, Devon finally sauntered in, Caleb on his heels. She wondered if Caleb had been forced to shove him all the way here.

Devon dumped a bag full of items onto the conference table. "One Reor slab full of encrypted data. One reader, which doubles as a duper, and one blank Reor slab."

"What about a catalog of the encrypted contents?"

He shook his head. "That would be cheating. I won't reveal the contents until you produce data on a screen."

"Fine." Caleb slid the items closer to her on his way to sitting down beside her, and she offered him a grateful smile. "Thank you for wrangling him."

"You're most welcome."

She grabbed the reader/duper and slid the encrypted slab Devon had brought in one end of it, then her personal one in the other. Next, she set the contents to transfer over to her slab and display the contents.

ENTER ENCRYPTION KEY.

"No go, huh?"

She shot Devon a glare. "I was merely checking before I got started. Now I'm starting, and I'm going to need to borrow some power from you." Valkyrie was developing more efficient methods for managing the power required to open a wormhole with every attempt, but they still needed a little power from either the Caeles Prism or another Prevo to accomplish it. It seemed irresponsible to fire up the Caeles Prism on the tiny, precarious landing pad where the *Siyane* resided.

Devon shrugged. "Vampire me at your whim."

She removed both slabs from the reader/duper and grasped them in each hand, stood and backed up to the wall.

Valkyrie?

I am ready.

Alex closed her eyes and reached across the Noesis to draw the necessary power from Devon. Her skin buzzed as the energy leaked out into the air around her.

A small wormhole opened directly in front of her. She stepped forward to its boundary, opened her eyes and held out her hands.

Luminous strings flowed in all directions to and from both slabs—but most importantly, they also flowed *between* both slabs.

"Valkyrie, measure the frequencies of all the waves flowing from the encrypted slab to mine."

'Done.'

"Alex...." Devon muttered in warning. The power flow was beginning to fluctuate and grow unstable, and the Delta conference room wasn't that spacious.

She let go of her link to him and closed the wormhole, then quickly sat again and returned her slab to the reader. No waxing philosophical or musing introspectively; she was all business.

ENTER ENCRYPTION KEY.

"Valkyrie, what's the lowest frequency wave?"

'7.550101233 Hz'

She entered it on the screen.

ERROR. ENTER ENCRYPTION KEY.

"The highest?"

'2.265031594 GHz'

ERROR. ENTER ENCRYPTION KEY.

She drummed her fingernails on the table, and they fell into an easy rhythm as she did the math. "The highest is a harmonic of the lowest, if you use a large enough multiplier."

'It is.'

The answer could be one of a plethora of combinations or calculations. There were a variety of weighted and special-weighted averages and means to consider, as well as golden ratios, Fibonacci sequences and dozens of more obscure 'special' formulas. Any of them would seem obvious in hindsight, but none were obvious now.

The key to opening the Metis portal wasn't complicated or obscure, however; it simply required having all the measurements on hand and appreciating the relationships that existed among those measurements. "What the hell. The midpoint harmonic between the two is...?"

'1.132515800 GHz.'

She entered the number, and a gridded display of organized data sprung to life on the virtual screen above the reader.

She sank back in the chair in relief. *Finally!* If the key had been something absurd like the inverse weighted harmonic mean of the entire harmonic series, she'd have had words with the Reor leadership, wherever and whatever they might be.

Devon set about checking the display against his copy of the contents. "It's a match. Wait—are you suggesting calculating that frequency will always unlock the information on a slab?"

She retrieved the original encrypted slab and switched them out in the reader/duper. "Let's find out."

ENTER ENCRYPTION KEY.

She repeated the number.

ERROR. ENTER ENCRYPTION KEY.

"Nope. I suspect my special, personally gifted slab is the real key, and this serves as additional layer of security."

"Hmm. What were all the other waves running between the slabs?"

Valkyrie chimed in. *'I am analyzing them now, with the benefit of the decryption. I believe the majority represent the data itself.'*

Alex arched an eyebrow. "Hey, do I need a reader at all then? Or once the waves are decrypted, can you translate them into an understandable form?"

'Possibly.'

Where Valkyrie was considered, 'possibly' usually translated as 'give her five minutes.' Alex held her slab up and peered at it with a new perspective. The layered mysteries were unraveling rapidly now. "You said 'the majority'—do you mean there are some waves that are neither the encryption nor the data?"

'A small number, yes. Their purpose is not yet clear.'

A few more mysteries to unravel, then.

Caleb had been quiet during her experiment, but he'd also been watching closely. Toward the end, smirking, too. Now he leaned forward, hands clasped above his knees. "Alex, this is big."

She agreed, for her mind now raced in concert with Valkyrie's through a multitude of possibilities and permutations. "It is. It's time to let Mom know."

20

AFS STALWART II

M iriam didn't even glance up when David entered the meeting room. He stopped just inside, to the left of the doorway, and waited while she dispensed a series of orders to her highest-ranking officers.

"I recognize this will be spreading us thin—frankly, thinner than I'd like. But with two additional Caeles Prisms online as of tonight, we'll benefit from greater responsiveness and mobility. Brigadier Ashonye, you're taking one of the new Caeles Prisms and the EA NW Regional formations to Post Bravo in Ursa Major I, where you will adopt a defensive stance until further notice."

"Understood, ma'am. Is there anything unique about Bravo that should inform our defensive strategy?"

"Nothing too noteworthy, but I'm sending you the briefing package on the planet and the post it houses now. Move with all due speed, and update me once your forces are in position. Dismissed."

"Yes, ma'am." He stood and left, giving David a respectful nod as he passed.

Miriam immediately turned to the next officer at the table. "Brigadier Belosca, I won't keep you by reciting identical instructions. Your destination is Post Charlie in the Triangulum galaxy. Take the other new Caeles Prism and all SF formations. You'll have the full file on Post Charlie in two minutes, but you should know that most of the anarchs who were evacuated from Chionis in ambulatory condition have ended up there, so Sator Nisi is particularly eager to see it well protected. I trust you'll do so."

The departure protocol played out a second time.

The final attendee, Rear Admiral Escarra, clasped his hands on the table. "If Field Marshal Bastian is remaining at Palaemon, I assume the rest of our forces will be responsible for guarding Post Delta."

"Correct. I'm going to be occupied for the next several hours strategizing with the anarch leadership about our next steps, so I need you to take operational control over the AEGIS forces. Of course, if a threat emerges, I'm seconds away."

"Absolutely. You can count on me, ma'am."

"I know I can. Dismissed."

Upon Escarra's departure the room was finally clear—but by the time the door closed behind the rear admiral, Miriam had called up two new screens full of data to study with her typical honed intensity. The cold shoulder treatment had always been among her more cutting punishments.

David took a deep breath and braced himself. "It's two in the morning."

Her focus didn't stray from the screens. "Only on the ship. Regardless, I don't have the luxury of a good night's sleep. If I'm asking my people to work through the night, I can do no less."

"I know. But when you didn't respond to my pulses, I was forced to wonder whether you'd decided to bunk elsewhere for the night."

She entered a command on one of the screens, closed it, and swiftly replaced it with another. "A decision I am blessed to not have to make tonight."

"If you will allow me—"

Her gaze finally veered to him. Her expression wasn't hurt or angry, merely blank, with the most subtle hints of coldness. "Go to bed."

"Is that an order, Commandant?"

She flinched for the briefest instant; it wasn't the reaction he longed for, but at least he'd earned a reaction. "No, it is a request for the sake of my sanity."

"Miri—"

"I'm not going to fight with you, David. I'm not going to yell at you or try to shame you for your behavior in the meeting. It's over and done, and there have already been far too many recriminations thrown around for one day. I simply need you to leave and let me work."

He chewed on his lower lip and stared at her, but she didn't return the attention. Her focus promptly reverted to her screens, to all appearances oblivious to his continued presence.

He stood there until he'd be embarrassing himself if he remained any longer, then for another beat, but finally he turned and walked out.

⤫

Miriam looked up as soon as the door closed, then sank deeper in her chair and let her shoulders sag. She pressed a palm to her forehead for two…three seconds before she straightened her posture and forced herself to concentrate on the briefings, which streamed in unabated.

The damage reports were, by and large, about what had become typical for a full engagement against a Machim fleet—ones where Igni antimatter missiles didn't take out space stations and dreadnoughts, anyway. She'd succeeded in building up her forces significantly in the last week, so the net losses were minimal….

Her train of thought drifted back to David, and she glanced at the door again. Dammit.

She blinked and reached for a cup of tea that wasn't there. Fine, she would focus without it. Next up: Bastian had delivered some suggestions for optimizing the defense of Palaemon and its most valuable asset, Post Epsilon. She couldn't be sure whether forwarding the suggestions to her was a perfunctory act on his part or whether he was legitimately asking for her approval of his ideas. She'd give it in any event, but this time she'd give it politely, with a slight tenor of appreciation. Reward good behavior, if not punish bad….

Her elbows hit the table as her head dropped into her hands. *Dammit!*

She'd spent months preparing for the challenges of a war against an immortal enemy wielding vastly superior numbers. She'd spent years preparing for the challenges of leading an assemblage of disparate fleets headed by disparate personalities. But it had never occurred to her to prepare for the challenges of her dead husband walking back into her life in the middle of both.

She had no idea what to do, but she was fairly certain she was doing it wrong.

"Thomas, where is David right now?"

'Commander Solovy is in the Deck 4 Observation Lounge.'

"Thank you." She signed off on Bastian's suggestions then closed the screens, stood and departed the conference room.

David sat on the edge of one of the couches facing the viewport, arms draped with pensive flair on his thighs. Gazing out at the stars, as he was always apt to be doing. *Capriccio Italien* played softly through the speakers to complete the haunting picture. A shiver raced through her; it was all too achingly familiar, too painfully impossible and yet, somehow, *real*.

She moved across the room to the viewport and shifted around to lean against it and face him. Her arms crossed over her chest in an instinctive attempt at self-preservation. "The David Solovy I knew would never have folded so easily or departed so meekly."

He eyed her from beneath a stoic brow. "So it was another test? I'll be honest, I'm getting goddamn tired of all the tests. I feel like a circus monkey jumping through spinning hoops, and the hoops are on fire. And I'm blindfolded."

"No. It wasn't another test."

He shrugged with one shoulder. "Then you genuinely did want me to leave you alone, and I am...*trying* to make you happy."

"By showing your ass during a critical negotiation and embarrassing me in front of our peers and allies?"

"I did not say I was doing a good job of it."

"David—"

He held up a hand. "Please. I realize you likely came all this way because you have something you need to say, but let me talk for a minute first."

She nodded in silent agreement.

"Richard offered me some advice earlier this evening, and it's given me pause. He intended it to help, and maybe it will, if I can manage to get to the other side of this mindfuck. But right now, the mindfuck's winning.

"I died in the midst of a puny little spat with a handful of colonies who wanted to thumb their noses at the standing authority. I returned to a world that has gone stark raving mad. It's as if I woke up to find myself dangling off the edge of a crumbling cliff, one of your hands grasping mine to keep me from falling while your other hand is clinging to nothing but a rock. I can't find my footing. There's no footing anywhere to be found.

"Meanwhile, all I keep hearing is 'David Solovy would act like so,' 'David Solovy wouldn't say such a thing,' and on and on. Well, you know what? David Solovy wouldn't have fallen off the side of the cliff in the first place—not unless it was to save everyone else. But how am I supposed to save anyone when I've got nothing but a chasm beneath me and a sweaty, faltering grip on your hand above me?"

The imagery might be a bit overwrought, but who was she to judge? She'd never come back from the dead. "What makes you think you need to save anyone?"

"It's what I died doing. It made me famous, albeit posthumously. A hero for the history texts."

"And you're bitter about that."

"The list of things I don't get to be bitter about is too long to bother contemplating. I was *angry* at Danilo, or Corradeo, or whatever the *krovavyy nakher* his name is, because our people sacrificed themselves today to save his people, and he was not...properly appreciative of their sacrifices. One could argue that he didn't give a fuck about their sacrifices, and I didn't care for that attitude."

She sighed. "The Anadens have a somewhat different perspective on death."

"On account of not having to deal with it, sure. Personally, I think their little immortality contrivance has destroyed the value of life for them."

"It brought you back."

"Thus I reserve the right to be hypocritical on this particular topic."

She almost laughed then. Why did he have to be so damn charming? Now she almost laughed at herself, because she'd pondered the very same question the first time she'd met him. "Look, I'm not fond of the man either, but he is the man we must work with. Screaming at him and getting in his face is not the way to gain his cooperation."

"Are you certain?"

"Yes. Understand, I have worked hard to cultivate a team with complementary strengths and talents. Complicated relationship dynamics are at work here, and everyone has a role to play. For evident reasons, I did not plan for the effect your particular strengths and talents were going to have on those dynamics. If you barge in full of righteous anger and bull-in-a-china-shop every tense situation, you risk wrecking more than the furniture. Please promise me you won't do it again."

His throat worked. "I overreacted on account of personally identifying with the cause. Worse, I didn't warn you first, then I failed to respect your authority in the room. For this I am truly, deeply sorry. I will not do it again."

He rubbed at his jaw before casting his eyes upward to meet hers in full. "But what if next time we're dealing with something more serious? What if the decisions needing to be made are vital to our survival, to the survival of those who serve under you, of people we care for? If it matters enough, I...don't think I can promise to remain silent, to not speak my mind in a desperate attempt to force the right decisions to be made and the right actions to come about. When lives are on the line, I have to fight—to not do so is contrary to the very core of my being, and I know of no other way to be."

Her lips parted, and she slowly smiled. "Now *that* sounds like the David Solovy I knew."

He arched an eyebrow. "And loved, despite any trifling flaws and periodically infuriating traits?"

Why had she ever believed she could hold out against such an offensive? She had always been helpless to resist his charm. "And *love*, despite any trifling flaws and periodically infuriating traits."

He'd stood and crossed the space between them to reach her before she'd finished the words. A hand rose to hover above her cheek for an instant before pressing into it. "*Moya vselennaya*, forgive me for causing you hardship, when you already bear such weighty burdens. I should never add to your troubles, only ease them."

Her forehead dropped to his—

Mom, I have news. Good news. I know it's the middle of the night, but this shouldn't wait. I'll be on the Stalwart II *in twenty minutes.*

She huffed a weary breath across his cheek. "I believe our daughter is about to pull another rabbit out of a hat. We need to get back to the conference room."

"Okay." He dropped his chin and crushed her lips with his while one hand caressed her neck and the other pressed into the small of her back to draw her closer.

The heady, dizzying rush of passion that accompanied his touch threatened to overwhelm her. Its sudden arrival, in this moment and, it seemed, at potentially any given moment, felt foreign and unsettling. The notion of it had faded from memory years ago, and she was unprepared for its intensity now, for the overpowering need to *get to her quarters and get out of clothes and not let loose of him for hours.*

"David...." She murmured against his mouth, head swimming and skin flushed.

"I know. Conference room. I just—" he renewed the kiss, as fervently as before, then drew back too soon "—wanted to say that first."

21

AFS STALWART II

Alex arrived with something of an entourage in tow: Caleb, of course, but also Devon, Mia and the Anaden, Eren, who hobbled in wearing a bulky brace that encased most of his right leg.

She nonchalantly tossed a pack on the table and a smile at him and Miriam. "I asked Malcolm, Harper and Lekkas to attend, so if someone could holo them in from their bunks or wherever they are, I'd appreciate it."

Mia shook her head. "Malcolm's not in his bunk, which I mention only because he would be mortified if anyone here thought he wasn't working."

"Right. No need to mention to him how I disparaged his good name. Also, has anybody woken up Richard? Wait, let me guess— he's not sleeping, either."

David chuckled lightly. "Nope. Last I checked, he was pouring through the anarch files in Utility Room #3. I'll see if he can come up here."

> *Confab in the conference room if you're available to join us— and Will, if he's awake.*
>
> *Sure, I'm dragging here as it is. What's up?*
>
> *No idea.*

Meanwhile, Miriam was *tsking* disapprovingly. "Alex, you know I don't like public surprises. What is all the fuss about?"

Alex held up the small, translucent Reor slab she was always carrying around. "It's about this."

"That doesn't tell me much."

"Come on, just hang out for a minute until everyone arrives. I promise it's a good surprise, but I don't want to have to repeat myself, repeatedly."

Miriam stood near the other end of the table from him, so he shot her a pulse rather than whisper in her ear.

*If we'd known it was actually going to be twenty-*five *minutes....*

She glanced up at him, fire in her eyes and amusement tugging the corners of her lips upward, and he suddenly meant the words rather more than when he'd sent the pulse. The look in her eyes made him feel...*alive*. And even when it was hard and raw and dark, as it had been for much of the night, he was of the informed opinion that nothing in any world felt better than being alive. Knowing it in your bones, and seeing it in the face of your beloved.

Then she dropped her focus back to a screen, because there was work to do.

As he turned from her, he caught Alex's eyes darting between him and Miriam. He winked at her, which won him a bright grin in response. Their daughter was doing a commendable job of giving both of them space to figure out how to *be*, but he knew she worried. If happening to catch them in a good stretch gave her peace of mind, he was glad for it.

Over the course of the next few minutes holos sprung to life, Richard and Will came in, and the clamor of anticipation took over as everyone got situated. David took a seat a quarter down the table, close to Miriam but implicitly giving her authoritative space. This may be a more informal meeting than some, but he wasn't going to screw it up. Not for the second time in a single day.

Miriam cleared her throat, and the chatter quickly died down. "All right, Alex. It is both very late and very early, so try to keep the dramatic flourishes to a minimum. What have you done now?"

Alex rotated the Reor slab over its edges on the table. "I figured out how to read the data stored on encrypted Reor slabs."

"Which ones?"

"Any one I can get in line of sight of or otherwise discretely identify, I believe."

Miriam blinked, then again. "How?"

Alex held the small slab up high above the table. "The Reor gave me a copy of their universal decryption key."

"Today?"

Alex laughed. "No. A few weeks ago, when Mesme invited Caleb and I to visit one of their sanctuaries. It took me until today to fit all the pieces together and unlock the code."

"I'll gloss right over the implication in what you said that the Reor are sentient entities—for now. Dare I ask *why* they gave you a copy of their universal decryption key?"

Alex and Caleb shared a look, and she shrugged. "We can only speculate, but it's possible they want us to win."

Miriam positioned her elbows on the table. "Hmm. Okay. In that case, I welcome the minerals to our side of the fight. What does this mean for us?"

"It depends. What do we need to know?"

Richard perked up at the near-mention of intelligence. "After what happened today—or technically yesterday now, I suppose? We need to find out exactly what the Directorate knows about the anarchs, and arguably about us. I realize getting to central Directorate databases isn't practicable, but on security matters Vigil should serve as a reasonable substitute. So we need to find out exactly what Vigil knows about the anarchs, and arguably about us."

Caleb nodded. "I agree. Right now, the Directorate thinks it's knocked the anarchs back on their heels, and by extension, us. If we dally, they're likely to try to move in for a killing blow, assuming they can. If we can determine what we do and don't need to guard against, we can conserve resources. Better still, we can use the resources freed up to move faster than the Directorate. We regain the advantage, retake control of the conflict dynamic and deliver a counterpunch attack. An intelligent one."

Like Richard, he was correct, if in the abstract. To make even half of those things happen, though, they needed a concrete action plan soon—or preferably, now. David propped against one arm of his chair. "Does Vigil have a central headquarters location? Do we have this information?"

Eren chimed in. "They do. Also dozens of regional offices, but they're managed out of an especially large, dull, dreary headquarters station in MW Sector 9."

Commander Lekkas half-raised a hand. "I'm game to blow it up. Then it wouldn't matter what they know, since they wouldn't know it any longer."

The woman sitting beside her—*Brooklyn Harper, Marine, girl-friend*—gave Lekkas a screwy look.

Eren shook his head. "As big a fan as I am of blowing things up—and I truly am—they'll have copies of their important files at satellite locations, because the Directorate is afraid of networked systems. Bits and pieces will be stored wherever somebody thinks they're needed, so you're not going to be able to destroy it all without bombing a lot of locations. Which, for the record, is an excellent alternative."

Richard and Will had been conferring in hushed tones, but now Richard returned his attention to the conversation. "Honestly, destroying the data stores isn't a practical solution. Even if we could guarantee destruction of all the files, there will be people who've already internalized the information they hold, which brings us back to needing to know what they know."

Miriam eyed Alex down the table. "Alex, if we can get you inside Vigil HQ, do you think you can tell us what's in their databanks? Or copy it and bring it here for decryption and study?"

"You bet I can."

"It'll be a tremendous amount of data."

"Good thing I have an Artificial in my head who has her own databanks waiting to be filled."

No one so much as blinked at the statement, and David was again reminded how much 'unusual' everyone in the room must have seen lately. Three days alive after almost three decades dead, and he might not be the most noteworthy creation in the room.

Miriam dipped her chin in concession. "Granted. All right, ideas on how to move forward?"

Richard settled back in his chair. "If we break in, hack their server and leave, they'll correctly assume we have some of their files and alter their behavior accordingly. We need to know what they know without them *knowing* we...know it." He rubbed at his face. "Sorry. I guess I could use a bit of sleep."

Miriam smiled kindly. "We all could."

It must be true, yet David felt invigorated. He let his gaze roam across those here. A lot of skills were represented at the table; many of these people were among the best, if not the best, at their specialties, and those specialties included skills that would have been called fantasy in his first lifetime. Several of the people here were the only ones in multiple universes able to do what they did.

His gaze completed its pass and fell on Miriam.

May I run with an idea for a moment?

You don't need to ask permission...I'm sorry, it's not fair of me to give you mixed signals. Yes, of course you may.

He leaned forward and clasped his hands together. "Alex, you proved on Chionis that you can open and maintain a wormhole on solid ground leading to solid ground elsewhere."

"A small one, at least."

"Big enough for a squad of Marines to walk through, because they did so earlier today. Can you create one with an entry point at a secure staging area and an exit point somewhere inside Vigil HQ?"

"As soon as I find out where Vigil HQ is, absolutely."

"Good. Okay, this gets us inside. Now, how do we steal data from the headquarters of a police/paramilitary organization without them realizing we stole it?"

"I can put a squad inside, but I don't see—"

He tilted his head in Jenner's direction. "Sorry, that was a rhetorical question—I have an idea how we do it, so bear with me. I suspect you were about to protest by pointing out how their security will be alerted when we breach the station, and clearly it will be. We should address the problem with a two-pronged approach. Once inside, can we shut down their transit tubes and their internal comm system?"

Nobody responded, and he chuckled. "That one wasn't rhetorical. Anyone?"

Eren made a hedging motion with his hand. "Transit tubes in the immediate vicinity, yes. We—the anarchs—have a spike you can use to short them out for a spell. Comms? Unless their communications hub happens to be located down the hall from their Data Control server, you'd need two separate infiltration teams and two separate wormholes."

"Which is probably impractical, not to mention unsafe." He turned his attention to his son-in-law. "Caleb, I heard how you created some impressive shielding bubbles with your *diati* down on Chionis. How wide can you stretch one of those, and for how long?"

Recognition dawned in Caleb's expression. Clever kid. "Wide enough, and long enough."

"That's what I thought you'd say. And nothing can get through a *diati* barrier, in any dimension—everyone knows this, even the recently resurrected."

Now Miriam seemed to catch on to where he was heading with this, too. "But everyone on the outside of the *diati* barrier will realize *something* is happening inside it."

"True, but I bet they won't have time to think about it too hard if their station is also being assaulted from the outside by a suitably intimidating fleet."

Lekkas' eyes narrowed. "You mean attack the station as if we're trying to blow it up?"

"Oh, never fear, Commander Lekkas—and Eren—we *are* going to blow it up. Just not until our people have what they came for and are safely out of harm's way."

Lekkas grinned wolfishly. "Everyone inside dies, and no one's left to tattle on us to the Directorate, who will assume we destroyed it in retaliation for the attack on Chionis."

He nodded. "Which will be true, if not the entirety of the truth."

Eren waved his arms around in the air in a bid for attention. "Great idea—and again, serious fan of blowing things up—but every Vigil officer is Anaden, mostly Machim or Praesidis but all Anaden. Now, I'm sure everyone at the table is familiar with regenesis—especially the recently resurrected."

David smirked. "Touché."

Caleb opened his mouth to respond, but Eren motioned him off. "Caleb, you think the *diati* barrier will also block the transmission of the fallen Vigil officers' poor sodding souls to a regenesis lab. You're right, it should. But Helix Retention was encased in a solid shell of *diati*, and your pet Inquisitor, Nyx, showed up looking none the worse for wear at Plousia Chateau shortly after getting disintegrated at Helix Retention, no? We're missing a loophole somewhere."

Caleb frowned, but Thomas picked up the thread. 'If I may interject, I believe I can offer a possible explanation for the anomaly Eren asi-Idoni has referenced. The information the anarchs have provided on the regenesis procedure, scant though it is, indicates that the Anaden cybernetics tasked with storing and transmitting the necessary data retain internal power sufficient to transmit for approximately forty-two seconds after a body expires.'

Eren rubbed at his jaw. "That...sounds true."

'We can assume that whoever or whatever was maintaining the *diati* barrier at Helix Retention perished when the facility did, at which point the *diati* barrier would have dropped. If Inquisitor Nyx's body expired in the same explosion, there should have been time for her consciousness to transmit after the barrier disappeared.'

Eren held out his hands and pushed his chair away from the table. "You got me. Back to this fabulously ludicrous plan."

David caught Caleb's attention once more. "So you would need to keep the barrier up for nearly a minute after everyone inside it is dead." His eyes passed across the others in turn. "And everyone inside it has to die."

Miriam stared at the table surface for several seconds, then lifted her chin. "They slaughtered nearly a thousand anarchs on Chionis in deliberately brutal, depraved ways. I don't have a problem giving that order."

22

LOCATION UNKNOWN

A wispy, hoarse voice emerged from the cushioned depths of the medical cot. "If you're trying to wake me up, stop being so subtle about it and just punch me in the shoulder."

Eren donned a confident, teasing smile as Cosime's eyes fluttered open. "Your shoulder's busted, darling, so punching it would be counterproductive to you getting better."

She looked up at him, but her eyes didn't quite focus. The doctors had her on a steady stream of painkillers, and the Curative Unit had admonished him to expect her to be groggy.

"Am I? Going to get better?"

"Most definitely. You are banged up a little, so it'll take some time, but you'll be flipping circles around me soon."

"Felzeor? The Curative Units won't tell me his condition...." She tried to crane her neck to peer around the medical suite, but the brace on her shoulder restricted her range of motion too much. Her voice remained weak, too, and she was so pale; when coupled with her normally fragile appearance, she looked as if she would shatter at the slightest touch.

The lack of proper air she'd suffered for those minutes on Chionis hadn't inflicted any permanent brain damage, thank Athena, but her throat and lungs took a beating from their protracted struggles. Her left shoulder, collarbone and upper humerus had been pulverized by debris, and after three medical procedures the bones and supporting parts were now more synthetic than organic. But she was alive.

Eren stood. "I'll do better than tell you. One second." He moved behind the head of her cot before limping over to Felzeor's special capsule and tapping on the glass. Green, refreshingly alert eyes popped open. "Do you feel up to saying hi to Cosime?"

The Volucri bobbed his head with as much enthusiasm as his own injuries allowed. Eren opened the lid and gathered Felzeor in his arms then carried him back over to the cot.

"Cosime, you're awake! You've been asleep for ages."

"Have I? Gods, Felzeor, what happened to you? Are you in there under all those bandages?"

"Maybe. I hope so. A building crushed me, stabbed me, ripped off most of a wing and suffocated me."

Cosime face blanched in horror. "Oh, dear."

"'Tis okay. Caleb rescued me and brought me here. I think. To be honest, I don't remember much about what happened."

Cosime grimaced and gingerly readjusted her position on the pillow. "Me either. Something tells me that's for the best, for both of us." Her gaze shifted to Eren. "But I remember you were there. I remember you told me to keep breathing."

"And you listened to me, for once."

"Don't get used to it. Are you hurt?"

He shrugged. "Only a few scrapes. I'm good."

Felzeor clucked in disapproval at the white lie, but if Cosime couldn't see the brace and heavy bandages on Eren's leg, he wasn't going to draw her attention to them.

"All right, Felzeor, I'd better get you back in your capsule before the Curative Units start yelling at me."

"They always yell at me. Be well, Cosime."

"And you."

He tucked Felzeor into his capsule with a stern glare. "Do what the Curative Units tell you. They know how to take care of you so you can heal."

Felzeor grumbled while he settled on the cushions, but his eyelids were drooping before Eren got the lid shut.

When he returned to Cosime, he realized she was worn out, too. The brief interactions had sapped her of what meager energy she'd summoned.

He half-sat on the edge of the cot and took her hand in his. "I'm going to be kind of scarce for a little while. We're planning to move hard and fast on the Directorate, and there's a lot to do. I need to throw in with everything I can muster to guarantee we win. But that's going to be tons easier for me to do knowing you're on the mend. So concentrate on recuperating, even when in practice it simply means resting. Okay? For me?"

She managed a weak smile. "I want to argue with you, but I'm so tired. Right now, I think resting is all I can do. I'm sorry, I wish I could help."

"No. Don't you dare be sorry. You're alive, which is the greatest gift I could ever ask for. Make sure you stay that way."

She nodded as her eyes fought her efforts to keep them open. He stood, then leaned in and placed a soft, lingering kiss on her forehead. When he drew back, she was asleep. He gave her hand a final squeeze and departed.

* R*

Eren found Thelkt in the break room, lounging around as if he wasn't recuperating himself. Scattered splotches of his iridescent skin glistened more brightly than the rest, as though damp—new skin, still forming—but otherwise his friend would look no different if he were hosting a dinner party.

Eren hobbled across the room, making an effort to not appear gimped. Many of those here suffered from more severe injuries than he did, but his ego was nevertheless taking a hit. The urge to crack open the leg brace and rip off the bandages was strong, oh yes, it was strong indeed, but he resisted—*even though* it was going to keep him off the Vigil HQ mission. In a day, two at most, he'd be able to throw the brace out an airlock and once again run from his monsters like a champ, so he persevered.

Halfway to Thelkt, he caught sight of faint movement in a nearby corner. Two shadows shifted like smoke wafting up from a lazy fire; secretive whispers emanated from their presence.

He couldn't say if one of them was Miaon, but it didn't matter. Eren cackled triumphantly. "Aha! I caught you—there *is* more than one Yinhe!"

As he stood there watching, the shadows drifted together, entwining one another until they had merged completely. "Is there?"

He blinked in disbelief, blinked again and finally tossed an arm dismissively in the now single shadow's direction. "I give up."

With an overdramatic groan he limped the last several meters to where Thelkt waited. "Eren, my friend, please sit." Thelkt gestured to the couch opposite him. "You should know better than to try to outwit a Yinhe."

"Well, I am appallingly obstinate."

"Undeniably. How's the leg?"

Eren eased down and adjusted his position so the offending leg could extend out at an angle. "Damn near immobile until I can take this godsawful brace off, which should be tomorrow. Then, though? It and me will be ship-shape. You're doing pretty good, right? I heard they're releasing you today."

"Allegedly. Releasing me to what, I can't say."

"That's what I wanted to talk to you about. I want you to do me a favor."

"If I can."

On second thought, Thelkt might not be up to hosting dinner parties quite yet. He seemed...weary. He wasn't a fighter, and the toll of such devastating violence had taken its due.

"When Cosime and Felzeor are well enough to be moved, I want you to take them home, to Hirlas, and stay there to look after them. Cosime needs to breathe her real, natural air, free of tubes and artificial mixtures, to truly heal. She needs to bask in the light and warmth of her native sun. And Felzeor's never going to thrive locked inside a cold, clinical spaceship. He needs the open sky."

"He can't fly."

"He'll never fly so long as he's confined here."

Thelkt nodded thoughtfully. "I don't disagree on any particular point, and I want to see them recover as much as you do. Part of me yearns to remain in the thick of the revolution as it at last nears its apex…but I sense the time for subterfuge and surveillance has passed, in which case I am not needed."

"You *are* needed—Cosime and Felzeor need you."

"Very well. I will do as you ask, though it is hardly a favor. It is the best course for us all." He regarded Eren curiously. "And you? What are you planning to do once you get the leg brace off?"

"There are a few details to square first, but if all proceeds as it should? I aim to go kill them all."

PART IV:

SWORDS & SHIELDS

"In short, all good things are wild and free."

— *Henry David Thoreau*

23

PLANET PD-8344C

T he transport from the *AFS Saratoga* settled to the rocky surface of the uninhabited planet thirty meters from where
Caleb and Alex stood beside the *Siyane*. Though halfway across the
LGG from the planet where they'd first traversed a teleportation
gate to Post Satus, the stark emptiness of this landscape evoked a
similar feeling. Breathable air did not alone make a planet habitable.

Caleb pivoted to Alex and grasped her by the shoulders. "Check:
tactical vest, personal shield, Veil, Daemon, blade, bracelet."

A corner of her lips curled up. "Check across the board. I even
brought a healthy respect for the enemy this time."

"Really?"

"No."

He shook his head in an exaggerated lament as he put his hands
on his weapons in a final pre-mission check. But the check was rote
and routine, so he let muscle memory do the work while he
watched her.

Her eyes and glyphs shone as brilliantly as they had on Chionis,
and the dim, gray landscape lent them yet more luminosity. But despite the strain of the recent battle and only the briefest spells of
sleep since, she genuinely did seem to be *okay*. Better than okay—
full of eagerness and determination to put her newest skills to work
for the cause, basking in the comfort and joy of a family that was
both whole and within reach.

She glanced over and caught him scrutinizing her. He tossed
her a smile, but it reminded him he needed to focus. He'd meant to
be putting his own eyes on her weapons, even if she was apt to be

far too busy on cerebral matters to have a chance to use any of them. He'd taken to using the *diati* as a weapon to such an extent lately, he was unlikely to use any of his own, either. But nobody was taking any chances, and pre-mission checks were more than *de rigueur*—they saved lives.

Alex's gaze diverted past his shoulder as the Marines reached them. He turned and offered a quick greeting to Harper, then to Jenner. "We're ready to move as soon as the fleet is in position."

"As are we. How's the exit point look?"

Alex stepped up beside him. "Mia and I scouted ahead in sidespace and picked out a spot twenty meters down the hall from the Data Control server room. It's in a supply storage room, but there's enough open space to stage our entry. Watching the location in sidespace while opening and maintaining a wormhole, walking through it and hacking the data server is one feat too many for me, so Mia's assumed responsibility for the area surveillance— but I bet you already knew that. She'll tell us when the immediate area is clear. Devon's also on standby to watch whatever you find you need him to watch once we get there."

Jenner nodded. "Understood. Eaton, link Mr. Reynolds into our mission channel now, as well as these two."

Comm checks followed, then they twiddled their thumbs for twenty seconds before the fleet status checks began rolling in from MW Sector 9.

Commandant Solovy (AFS Stalwart II): "Infiltration team, you are clear to proceed."

Alex lifted her chin and motioned everyone off to the left. The undercarriage of the *Siyane* began to glow a diffuse amber, and the air in front of Alex began to shift and distort. The muscles running down her neck flexed as her jaw tightened in concentration. "Wormhole is stable, and Mia says 'go,' so let's go."

For tactical reasons—the need to establish the *diati* bubble promptly upon their arrival—Caleb had to traverse the wormhole first. He kept Alex behind him and took note of how the Marines, whether instinctively or on prior orders, formed a protective circle around her. He gave silent thanks and stepped through the wormhole.

ᴀʀ

MILKY WAY SECTOR 9

AFS MA-PRIMARY

Commander Lekkas (AFS MA-Primary): "Defense shield power generator targeted and locked. Firing."

Her arcalaser tore into the module tucked beneath the station's central structure, sending unmoored energy shooting outward ahead of a burst of flame that in turn quickly evaporated for a dearth of oxygen.

"Hello, Vigil. Guess who's here." Morgan spun away from the station and swept around to set up for the next, slightly altered run.

You should have burned the greeting into the station hull with the arcalaser.

Ha! I like it, Stanley. Graffiti written in the stars at eight hundred kilojoules per second. But if I'd done something that dramatic, I probably would have written 'Fuck you, Vigil.'

A valid alternative, to be sure.

She chuckled and slipped unnoticed between two automated drones headed in the opposite direction, toward the fleet that was now making itself conveniently known.

Vigil HQ's defense shielding wasn't as robust as the defenses at the large manufacturing facilities. It didn't include a physical barrier blocking entry or a staffed checkpoint, presumably due to traffic in and out of HQ being too frequent for such an onerous barrier to be practical.

Still, taking out the primary defense shield with the opening volley was going to make their job simpler. More importantly, though, doing so had triggered the station's external defenses and sent a horde of drones flying away from the station and toward the fleet. Maybe some manned ships, too. Security was now firmly focused on the external threat; with any luck, so focused they wouldn't even notice the internal one.

Commandant Solovy (Stalwart II*): "Infiltration team, you are clear to proceed."*

The fleet engaged the approaching defenders, if only passably so in a gambit to draw out the engagement and buy the infiltration team time to work.

With the shield down and the drones distracted, Morgan instructed the Eidolon flights to begin delivering their payloads: twenty-two negative energy bombs set for remote detonation. Sending the signal for detonation was to be the last act of the mission.

I hope Brook tries to avoid the exploding remains of any Vigil mechs this time. Also, sharp claws belonging to monstrous beasts.

I suspect Captain Harper will risk life and limb as she deems necessary in order to perform her job expertly, as always.

Heh. It would be fantastic if she'd actually limit doing so to when it's necessary.

You worry about her.

More than I want to. I feel like a ninny.

She skimmed a hair over three meters beneath the station's lower hull, invisible and undetectable. Due ahead lay a junction of station modules—a weak point ready to crumble to dust under the force of the bomb she carried.

She is highly skilled at her job.

And Morgan didn't want to talk about it anymore. *Yep. So am I.*

Commander Lekkas (MA-Primary*): "Placement of negative energy bombs commencing. Detonation will be on my mark and not an instant before it."*

24

VIGIL HEADQUARTERS

MILKY WAY SECTOR 9

*C*aleb Marano (mission): *"Initiating* diati *bubble."*

Lieutenant Odaka (mission): "Rearguard has cleared the wormhole, boots on target location."

Alexis Solovy (mission): "Closing wormhole."

The amount of *diati* required to create the bubble wasn't an issue; Caleb had a surfeit of it at his disposal. The real trick was keeping it reined in at precisely the size and shape he needed. Control—him, in intimate control of the power—grew more difficult the greater the levels of *diati* he called into use.

Caleb breathed out through his nose. "The bubble extends across this level as well as one level above and below to abut the interior hull."

Jenner held out a small scanner and rotated in a slow circle. "Ingress and egress points are now marked on the mission grid. Polowski and Shaviiz, post at Point A, Grenier and Eaton, Point B. Kill anything that crosses your visuals. Everyone else, hold here."

Alex's irises had faded, albeit temporarily, with the closing of the wormhole. "The server room is out the door and left down the hall twenty-one meters, also on the left."

Mia Requelme (mission): "A guard drone is stationed inside the server room door, then past it are two Anadens. They're acting closer to techs than security guards, not that it matters."

Brigadier Jenner (mission): "Acknowledged. Harper, Pello, Redale, Benoit, secure the entrance.

Captain Harper (mission): "With pleasure." She and the others activated their Veils and vanished.

Alex tapped her fingers on her thigh in time to her foot tapping the floor.

Jenner eyed her suspiciously. "We'll move when the server room's secure."

"I can shoot just fine."

Caleb sighed. "We know, baby, but you're not here to shoot, you're here to hack. You be our sword, and let us be your shield."

"Damn poetic, *priyazn*. But aren't you usually the sword—"

A series of thuds and crashes rang out from down the hall. Jenner raised his Daemon. Caleb gritted his teeth and tamped down his natural instinct to act to address the threat. Instead he concentrated on maintaining the stability of the *diati* bubble.

Captain Harper (mission): "Server room is secure."

Brigadier Jenner (mission): "Copy that. On our way." Jenner motioned for Odaka to take up the rear then stepped into the hallway. Once he'd checked it, he indicated for them to follow.

Caleb moved as swiftly and deliberately as he could while ensuring the perimeter of the bubble didn't shift with his movement. When they reached the door, he stepped through it alert for threats, even though the Marines would intercept any threat long before it reached them.

Two bodies lay on the floor in restraining fields under the watchful eye of one of the Marines. The Anadens looked dead, but better safe than sorry. A drone sat in the corner, inactive but intact. "Harper, take one of those spikes Eren gave us and jam it into the small input node behind the camera-eye."

She went over to kneel in front of the drone. A brief hissing sound followed. There—now it was *more* inactive.

Alex strode past all the floor clutter through the entrance to the large server room and pressed her left palm to the control panel. Three seconds later the force field blocking entry disappeared. Eren had also sent along a tool the anarchs used for disabling these types of security measures, but Alex hadn't bothered to use it. She was now hacking Anaden technology as quickly and expertly as she did human systems.

As Malcolm hurriedly motioned two Marines forward to guard her, she entered the server room and went straight to the central control module. Of course she'd scouted ahead in sidespace, so she also already knew where everything was. Her blade came out of its sheath and activated, and she had the panel halfway cut open before one of the Marines tried to take over for her. She shot the Marine a dubious glare and finished slicing the metal, then maneuvered the panel out and handed it to the Marine to hold.

Caleb chuckled under his breath.

Her eyes and glyphs now lit up in renewed brilliance, but she spoke aloud for their benefit. "Okay, Valkyrie. As we suspected, this is way too much data to try to analyze here or copy onto physical slabs, so I need you to record and store it temporarily in your databanks. We'll decrypt it and sort it out later. But—" she fished her Reor slab out of the pocket of her tactical vest and held it out in front of her "—let's record what this shows us, too. Never know if it could turn out to be useful." The air around her shimmered and undulated, but he couldn't see what she saw, only that the air soon returned to normal.

She placed the slab in her vest pocket, thrust her hand and arm out and plunged them into the exposed circuitry.

"Alex!" Jenner leapt for her in alarm.

Caleb just laughed. "She does that. She's fine."

"Fine?"

He tilted his head in Alex's direction and shrugged, as she was, quite clearly, fine.

Jenner rubbed at his jaw, looking at an utter loss as to what to do.

Caleb smiled to himself, a mix of proud and uncharitable thoughts musing idly through his mind.

Devon Reynolds (mission): "You've got serious incoming from the floor below, left side from the server room, center transit tube."

Brigadier Jenner (mission): "Harper, Pello, Redale, back up Polowski and Shaviiz. I'm trip mining the entrance to the server room, so do announce your arrival when you return." He jogged out through the small entry room to the hallway.

The incoming attackers had been inside the *diati* bubble when it was created. Obviously they had, because they couldn't have penetrated it from the outside. More than this, though, Caleb had felt their presence, as he felt the presence of every breathing or powered form existing inside the bubble.

He twitched with stewing energy, but he could do nothing to help meet the threat beyond ensuring the bubble remained in place so that when the Marines ended their lives, it would be for good.

The chaotic sounds of close-quarters combat grew so loud they muffled the sound of a ceiling segment bursting open above him.

A Vigil officer—Machim—dropped through the hole and fired on Caleb.

He stumbled half a step on account of so much of his power being utilized elsewhere, but the *diati* he retained absorbed the blow without prompting. In his next step he placed himself between the Vigil officer and Alex.

The attacker shook off his surprise at the ineffectiveness of his weapon and charged.

Caleb unlatched his blade hilt with one hand and readied—

—the attacker jerked to a violent halt. Jenner materialized behind him, left arm locked around the man's neck and the other jamming the muzzle of his Daemon into the man's side, trigger pressed flush. When the man started to slacken, Jenner's left arm loosened its hold slightly. He dragged his arm to the left, leading a blade across the officer's neck.

Jenner tossed the body to the side and raised his Daemon to point at the hole in the ceiling. *"We have Vigil in the ceiling. Assume we have them in the walls and coming up through the floor as well."*

Caleb took two steps back until he drew even with Alex. "Almost finished? We need to go soon, or things are going to get ugly."

If she'd been aware of the altercation, she gave no indication of it; all her concentration remained on the data flowing through her and to Valkyrie. She nodded minutely. "Almost."

He squeezed her free hand and stepped forward toward Jenner. He kept his voice low. "Pull your people in as soon as it's safe to do so. We'll be ready to leave by the time they get here. And thank you. Again. I'm in danger of owing you."

Jenner flashed him a smirk. "Good."

Brigadier Jenner (mission): "As soon as all active assailants are disabled, withdraw to the entrance of the server room and prepare for departure."

The walls shuddered from an impact, distant but heavy; it came from outside the station. A quick focusing of the fleet mission channel confirmed that they were winning too handily and wouldn't be able to stall for much longer.

"Alex, time's up. We've got to go."

When he didn't get a response, he checked behind him to find her holding up a finger of her free hand. He waited one second...two...

...and was about to have to force the issue when she withdrew her arm from the circuitry, masterfully covered a slight stumble and hurried to his side. "What are we waiting for?"

"Not a thing." He grabbed her hand and maneuvered to stay in front of her as they joined the Marines.

Harper and several others jogged down the hallway toward them, covered in blood of nonobvious origin. Jenner motioned for them to keep going toward the supply room, then for everyone else to join them.

Weapons fire continued from the opposite end of the hallway.

Brigadier Jenner (mission): "Pello, Polowski, reinforce Point B. Remember, we need one hundred percent termination."

Two Marines moved ahead as they reached the supply room. Jenner and Harper cleared it, after which Caleb urged Alex inside ahead of him.

The weapons fire died away, and the rest of the squad appeared around the corner carrying one of their own. One of the Marines held a blood-soaked field medwrap against the injured man's thigh.

Caleb motioned them into the supply room as he took a last survey of both directions. No sound suggested movement. He swept his perception through the *diati* and found nothing living or powered except in the room behind him.

A timer began ticking down on a whisper in his virtual vision as he backed into the room.

Alex motioned outward with both arms. "Everyone against the walls. You don't want to get caught half in a wormhole when it forms. At least, I assume doing so would be bad—no one's volunteered to test it." Her skin lit afire, and she stood perfectly still for several seconds.

The disruption in the air was difficult to make out in the dim room, but finally she nodded sharply. "Go. Everyone, go!"

Three Marines moved their injured comrade through first. The others followed, and soon only Harper, Jenner, he and Alex remained. The timer continued its steady progression toward the instant he could be certain everyone dead inside the bubble was well and truly dead. He stared at Jenner, who now stood beside him. "Why are you still here? Go, all of you."

Jenner shook his head. "If more trouble shows up, you can't fight them off and keep the bubble up. We're here to the end." He glanced behind him. "Alex, you should go, though. You can keep the wormhole open from the other side."

Her face screwed up like he'd voiced the dumbest combination of words since mankind had developed spoken language. "Um, no?"

Jenner opened his mouth as if to argue, but Caleb cut him off. "It's an irrelevant argument in eight seconds...seven...you get the idea. Be ready...and...go."

Still, he was the last, remaining until everyone else was off the station. Finally he drew the *diati* powering the bubble into himself and fell backwards through the wormhole onto the hard, unforgiving bedrock of the staging planet.

Caleb struggled up to his knees. "I'm out—shut it down!"

The air in front of him rippled then calmed, in contrast to the frenzied scene he found when he stood.

One of the Marines he knew by name, Verela, knelt beside the wounded Marine and began active treatment while another grasped the man's hand and someone else sprinted to the transport for a field med kit.

Jenner hurried from one squad member to another, confirming their presence and the absence of additional serious injuries.

Harper touched a fingertip to her cheek and scowled at it when it came back bloody; at some point her shield had been depleted and she'd caught a graze of fire.

Alex sank against the hull of the *Siyane*, shoulders sagging, looking a little tired but smiling.

When Jenner reached the last Marine he activated his comm.

Brigadier Jenner (Command Channel): "Infiltration team is clear. Blow it."

Morgan didn't hesitate. Everyone was out of the station, which she'd known via Mia and Alex for almost four million nanoseconds.

A thought became a quantum wave containing the detonation code directed at the receivers inside the bombs, and she settled back to watch.

Spectacles like this? The collision of terajoules of negative energy, generating an inverse-equivalent force as it met megatonnes of reinforced metamats comprising the sprawling structure? They never got old.

25

AFS STALWART II

"Our high-priority targets have changed somewhat in light of the information we discovered in the Vigil database. Confirmation that they do not possess the locations of additional anarch posts means we can reduce—but not eliminate—our numbers dedicated to the defense of those locations. Unfortunately, our analysis of the information has highlighted several new locations we need to protect.

"The net result is our fieldable numbers for offensive operations remain reduced, and we need to choose our targets carefully."

Miriam's hand passed over the virtual control panel, and an enormous map sprung to life to occupy the entirety of the space above the table. "First, this is the comprehensive LGG map with target candidates and at-risk locations marked. Everyone should study it now to get a sense of how the new intel alters the board. In a minute I'll zero in on the areas of greatest interest."

Alex had already seen the new intel, but not the results displayed visually in such a dramatic manner. The map was too expansive, too glutted with minute details to serve as a practical planning tool though, and in these strategy sessions they usually opted for a more targeted view.

She tilted her head, eyes focusing in on the map as a sensation began to tickle and buzz at the base of her skull. It didn't feel like Akeso, thankfully. No, this was pure intuition…she knew something.

Abruptly the stars and galaxies blurred away. "The first potential target I want to—"

"Wait, go back."

Her mother paused mid-zoom. "To the full view?"

Alex nodded. "Please. This is the official Directorate-sanctioned LGG map, right?"

"It is. For better or worse, everyone including the anarchs reference it, and since we don't have a history working with a different map, it's simply easier to use this one instead of developing our own."

"Sure, sure...." Her eyes narrowed, and she craned her neck farther. What did she know? "And the sequences of numbers next to notable locations—they're official supergalactic coordinates?"

"Correct. Alex, what do you see?"

"I think...." The spatial dimensions of the charted and traveled universe were spread out before her. So many other dimensions hid within them, crisscrossing and looping in and out and cutting through this space, but if one wanted to find a location, the spatial dimensions were still the show. Even in sidespace, one had to identify a point in the three spatial dimensions in order to send one's consciousness there. They were the anchor upon which all that went unseen moored itself.

The unaccounted-for signals the Reor pass among the slabs. The waves that were neither data nor encryption. They're coordinates.

It's like you read my mind, Valkyrie.

She threw a knee on the table and climbed up on it.

"Alex!"

"Humor me for a minute." She crawled to the center of the table, lay down on her back and stole a glance at Caleb. He was chuckling silently, and she winked at him before resting her head on the table surface. "Thomas, can you center the map on our current location, then center that point above me? Or maybe—you know what, just give me control."

'Commandant, permission to cede control of the map to your clearly insane daughter?'

Miriam sighed. "Granted, under the theory it will get her off the table faster."

"Thanks." She lifted a hand and spun the map, then drew it in toward her until their location basically overlay her face; this resulted in half the map residing beneath her and the table and encroaching on the floor below. "Devon, where did the Reor slab you borrowed from Post Epsilon end up after we were done with it?"

"Most of the equipment and storage was moved to Post Charlie, so probably there."

"Great. And Charlie is in Triangulum, Sector 2…." She twisted the map around, while keeping their location centered on her, until the planet hosting Charlie hovered above her and off to the left. "Valkyrie, pull up the set of waves recorded from that Reor slab."

'Done.'

She sent the data to an aural and slid it off beside her. Next she pulled her Reor slab out of her pocket and held it above her.

A smidge of power, please. Borrow some from Devon or Morgan if you need to.

As requested.

She opened a tiny wormhole a few centimeters above her. The Reor-generated strings of light poured through it from all directions, but she concentrated on the ones streaming from Post Charlie's location. "Thomas, if you could zoom the map in toward Charlie's planet? I'm a little busy at present."

'Certainly.' The Artificial had dropped any note of teasing in his tone. She had his attention now.

"Thank you. A bit more. Stop." A multitude of luminous streams flowed from the planet—of course they did, as more than one Reor slab stored data at Post Charlie.

"Valkyrie, can you parse all these out to find the matching set?"

'I believe so. A moment. Yes, I have located the data set.'

"Now, can you show the room what we're seeing somehow? Get Thomas to help. We need a visualization, and also the spectrum readings themselves." She kept talking aloud to Valkyrie for the others' benefit, lest they think she was merely lying there atop the table daydreaming.

She knew additional screens had materialized by the muted gasps rippling around her.

A thud echoed to her left, causing the table to vibrate. A second later Devon appeared crouched beside her. He tilted his neck all the way around until he was peering up beside her. "Holy shit."

Alex laughed faintly. "Mia? Lekkas? Want to join us?"

Mia shook her head. "As tempting as the offer is, I will take your word for it, as I'm wearing a skirt. Also, Commandant Solovy is glaring."

Lekkas snorted. "It looks a little too cozy up there for my tastes."

Alex cast a frown sideways. "It is. Uh, Devon?"

"Right. Leaving." He clambered back out of her field of vision.

"Are you sure we're not seeing an optical illusion created because Post Charlie's planet is in focus?" Her mother sounded skeptical, and also like she was glaring.

"Fair question. Valkyrie, blank out all the streams in the visualization unrelated to the target slab. Thomas, shift the map twenty degrees east, thirty degrees north and zoom back out ten percent."

The map shifted, and with it so too did the streams remaining, flowing from and to Post Charlie's planet.

Silence fell. She fought the urge to fidget and look around to judge the reactions.

You've convinced them all. Masterful performance.

Somehow, Caleb always knew what she needed. Mollified, she waited while realizations sank in and implications began to bubble up.

Her mother was first, because no one was going to venture out on this limb until the commandant authorized it. "All right. So what does this mean? If you determine where a particular slab is located, you can...what? Read its contents from anywhere?"

"Yes, it means that. But it gets even better. Doesn't it, Valkyrie?"

'Yes, it does.'

"Out with it, Alex."

"Yes, Mom. Valkyrie, display the frequency of the first wave in this data set not attributable to data or encryption, to a precision of sixteen."

'Done.'

Somewhere outside her peripheral vision, a screen displayed:

1.132515800775050 GHz

She closed the wormhole and set the Reor slab on the table beside her, then retook control of the map and zoomed in until the supergalactic coordinates of Charlie's planet were in focus.

SGL *11° 32' 51.58"* SGB *00° 77' 50.50"*

These gasps were far more pronounced.

"That's way too exact to be a coincidence." Her father. His voice held not a touch of doubt; it might hold a touch of pride.

"Almost certainly. But just in case, Valkyrie, now display the frequency of the first unattributed wave from the data set we recorded at Vigil HQ."

'Also done.'

829.4166562297414 MHz

She spun the map around to the Milky Way and quickly zoomed in on Sector 9. Vigil HQ had a red line drawn through it, but its former location remained on the map.

SGL *82° 94' 16.65"* SGB *62° 29' 74.14"*

She left its ecliptic coordinates in focus while she sat up and scooted toward the side of the table to the tune of a room full of excited and confused murmurs. Caleb met her at the edge, put his hands on her waist and hoisted her off.

"You are *remarkable*."

She grinned. She didn't need to explain any of it to him, as he was plenty clever enough to see it all instantly. "I try. Really, really hard."

"You succeed." His forehead dropped to hers. "Dear god, I love you, woman."

"Good thing you married me."

"Ahem. Alex?"

She rolled her eyes and extricated herself from his arms, then turned toward her mother, who was trying to look cross. "Sorry."

"I doubt it. You've already unlocked the master decryption key. Now you've discovered coordinate markers embedded in the Reor slabs' data. Does this mean…I hesitate to say it. It sounds too implausible."

"Then I'll say it. It means all we need is a location—and check it out, we have a handy map with location coordinates pre-marked on it. Do you want to know what's stored on the Reor slabs in the data servers at Praesidis Command on Solum?" She leaned into the table, reached up and spun then zoomed the map until Solum dominated the display. Its coordinates shimmered helpfully alongside it.

"Now, there are doubtless many, *many* slabs packed with data stored there, so it'll take some time to parse out what we're searching for. But I've heard Artificials can crunch numbers pretty damn fast.

"So, yes, it means what you dare not hope it means. It means we're in. An empire's worth of knowledge is ours for the taking. All we have to do is cast our gaze to it and look."

SIYANE

TARACH STELLAR SYSTEM

Caleb ascended the stairwell after taking a shower to find Alex lying in the middle of the floor. A pillow from the couch was positioned behind her head. She stared up at nothing—nothing he could see anyway. Her lips moved faintly and wordlessly, and her fingers fluttered at irregular intervals.

She was working. On the floor.

He went over to where she lay and lowered himself to his knees beside her. "Everything okay?"

"Mmm-hmm." She glanced at him. "I was thinking. You need to get an updated neural imprint taken."

"Already planning for our regenesis-enhanced future?"

She shrugged. "It never hurts to take precautions now."

"I don't need to get one taken. The *diati* isn't going to let me die."

"Things happen. Circumstances change. If anyone knows that, it ought to be us."

He forced a lighthearted smile, though he wasn't comfortable discussing this. "Well, what about you? Where's your neural imprint?"

"Valkyrie's my neural imprint."

"What if the *Siyane* explodes with you and her in it?"

She scowled at him. "Way to be cheerful. Valkyrie, when did you last upload an outrageously complex and fulsome dynamic map of my brain to AEGIS' secure scientific database?"

'Sixty-three hours ago.'

"See? She's got it covered. But we were talking about you, and you're trying to dodge the issue."

He sank lower and rested back against his heels. Why did he even bother trying to keep troublesome thoughts from her? "I can't help but worry…say we find ourselves in some hypothetical future where humanity has followed the Anadens' path and adopted regenesis to extend our lives. If I get resurrected enough times, will I gradually become just like the Inquisitors? Just like the Praesidis Primor?

"Alex, I would never take away the gift of having your father back. And if someone I care for were to suffer an untimely death, I can't say I wouldn't move mountains to bring them back. But across a civilization, those individual decisions become routine, and routine becomes dogma. When death is removed from the equation, priorities begin to veer off-kilter, and perception and ethics soon follow. Having seen where that path leads, I'm not sure we as a people should start down it. I'm not sure I should start down it."

"We're not like the Anadens—we can make better choices. You're nothing like the Inquisitors, and the opportunity to escape an untimely, tragic death isn't about to change who you are." Her voice softened. "Caleb, I won't lose you. I can't."

"You won't. Now can we talk about something else? How's the data analysis going?"

"Going." Her eyes drifted over to her unseen work, then back to him. She sighed. "I'm tired."

"Understandable." He stretched out beside her on the floor and propped his head in his hand. "You don't have to do everything yourself."

"Oh, I'm not. Valkyrie and I are merely pulling in the data from critical locations, decrypting it and scanning it for markers that might indicate it includes information we're particularly interested in. We're funneling the promising files off to the Connexus for thorough processing and analysis. But it's a metric fuckton of data." She tapped a temple with a fingernail. "And up here is still a mostly human brain. Organic, limited and tired."

He leaned in closer and kissed the temple she'd tapped. "Then it should rest." His hand found her jaw and gently shifted it toward him. "You should rest."

"I am resting—I'm lying on the floor. Got a pillow and every-thing."

He nuzzled her nose. "You are a very, *very* stubborn woman."

"True." Her lips brushed across his, then returned to settle against them. "But this is important. We're going to save people. A lot of people."

"Baby, we're going to save everyone."

26

ANARCH POST SATUS

LOCATION UNKNOWN

Miriam approached the teleportation gate with some small amount of trepidation. Much had transpired since the attack on Chionis and the contentious meeting which followed. She had kept the Sator informed of developments and conferred with him on several matters; those conversations had been formal but civil.

Now he'd asked to meet with her alone, ostensibly to discuss the plans now taking shape to strike at the Directorate itself thanks to the plethora of secrets Alex had opened up for them. Did he possess secret knowledge to aid their efforts and wanted to extract a price to share it? Did he intend to impose requirements or restrictions on any such strike?

She steeled herself for the tiresome but obligatory dance guaranteed to transpire no matter his purpose and stepped through the gate.

"Welcome, Commandant. Thank you for interrupting your work to indulge me for a few minutes."

She forced a frown into the shape of a smile. Was this Nisi in a good mood? "It's no trouble, Sator. Hearing your counsel is part of my work as much as mission planning."

"But not necessarily 'taking' my counsel, yes?" He gestured to another of the gates in the room. "Will you accompany me?"

"Of course. Where are we visiting?"

"Someplace quite special to me. Please, I will explain once we arrive." He ran a hand along the rim of the gate's frame. His fingertips tapped a rapid pattern, as if playing the keys of a piano. The mirror-like substance filling the gate rippled in brief agitation before returning to its placid oscillation.

He lowered his hand to his side. "Follow me."

Æ

LIVAD

UNKNOWN GALAXY
BEYOND THE BOUNDARIES OF THE LGG

They emerged in a small, circular room. Its walls and ceiling were constructed of refined bamboo, its floor of sandstone.

Near the wall stood a...the first comparison to pop into Miriam's mind was of a giant grasshopper, though it was an imprecise comparison. The creature stood nearly three meters tall on narrow, reedy limbs bent at two joints. If it stood up straight, it would be far taller than three meters. A thin torso led to two smaller versions of its legs and an angular head that stretched more horizontal than vertical. Black eyes with double lids blinked at them from beneath four antennae.

Nisi spoke a phrase in an unfamiliar tongue, took two steps toward the creature, and knelt before it, his head bowed.

She hadn't thought the man retained the ability to shock her, but here they were.

Should she kneel as well? It seemed likely Nisi would have warned her if it were expected, and they were both ignoring her anyway, so she opted to stand quietly.

The creature uttered a series of clicks and noises. When Nisi responded with more unfamiliar words, she decided they were speaking the same language. After another interchange, the creature folded its lengthy legs in until the first joint touched the floor. It was now kneeling, as it were, opposite Nisi. The front two of its antennae bent forward until they touched his forehead. More words were exchanged, then at last they both straightened up.

"Commandant Solovy, allow me to introduce Ekhor'pai of the Hoans."

The creature lowered its head in her direction—some body language transcended species—and she did the same. Then it backed out of the room through a drape of woven fibers.

She arched an eyebrow at Nisi, but he simply motioned to the drape. "Let us take a stroll."

His penchant for dramatic gestures had annoyed her from the start, but the grand reveals they tended to lead to often proved useful, so she refrained from sighing and followed him out.

The building they'd arrived in was set off a short distance from a settlement. The structures all shared the same architectural style and ranged from modest huts to expansive, multi-wing buildings. None stretched higher than a single tall story, but many included rooftop balconies. The village was simple, possibly primitive; it was also highly ordered and meticulously clean.

Dozens of the creatures moved among the spaces in between the buildings. As they did so, several stopped and raised their front limbs toward them—or more likely, at Nisi. He acknowledged the greetings by bringing a knifed hand to his chin. He didn't approach the village, though, instead guiding her to the right, where a savannah grassland stretched to the horizon beneath a toffee sky.

"Where are we?"

"A very, very long way from home."

"I have been a very long way from home since I arrived in Amaranthe."

He chuckled. "So you have. I call the planet Livad, but to the Hoans it simply *is*. It lies some 224 megaparsecs from Solum, beyond the Local Galactic Group, beyond Laniakea, in a galaxy without a name deep in the Shapley Supercluster."

"I was under the impression the Anadens' exploration had only just begun to extend beyond the LGG."

"You are correct. The Directorate does not know of this place, and Zeus willing it never will."

Now she did sigh. The setting was pleasant and the inhabitants suitably unusual, but on the other side of the teleportation gate the most complex and ambitious mission of her career drew closer by the hour. "Now is when I ask how it is *you* know of it."

He stretched out an arm and ran his palm along the tops of the tall blades of grass. "Caleb has told you of my true past?"

"I've heard the highlights, yes."

"Or the lowlights, depending on one's perspective. This is where the *diati* brought me after I fell—after my son betrayed me. It doesn't perceive distances in the same way we do, and it only knew it needed to get me somewhere both safe and outside of the Anaden empire's boundaries. It obviously knew of the Hoans, as I suspect it knows of every sentient species in the universe, on some intrinsic level.

"So little *diati* remained within me following the attack, it required all its energy to transport me here. I arrived unconscious, bleeding out, over half the bones of my body broken, and in its exhaustion it could do nothing more than keep my heart beating."

He paused to gaze back over his shoulder toward the village. "I'm sure the Hoans appear primitive to your eyes, and in many respects they are. In others, however, they will surprise you. Their medical treatments did not originate in a lab, but they are rather effective. They took this strange, incoherent being who had materialized out of nowhere under their care. They ensured I did not bleed out, succumb to infection or die from any of a number of ailments that should have killed me. Eventually, the *diati* regained its strength and mended what the Hoans could not.

"I stayed here for a time—decades. I learned their language and many of their ways. My body soon healed, but my mind took a fair bit longer to recover. When I felt it had finally done so, I instructed the *diati* to return me to the empire.

"I was wrong, as psychologically I remained a tortured disaster. When I realized this, I stole a starship and fled once more, albeit this time under my own power. But that is another story."

In the distance, movement caught her attention. One of the Hoans galloped across the savannah with astonishing speed, each stride carrying it some ten meters distance. Abruptly it disappeared beneath the grass, then leapt upward to soar into the sky. Thirty meters? Forty? It landed almost beyond her sight and continued on.

"Impressive, aren't they?"

"Why are we here, Sator?"

"I visit the Hoans too rarely, but I have been thinking about the time I spent here often of late. Since your people arrived in Amaranthe, since they have accomplished great feats that defy their apparent evolutionary maturity while displaying a level of empathy and…kindness that I thought species inevitably grew out of when they went to the stars."

"Thank you."

He stopped and stared at her oddly. "Yes, I suppose it was a compliment." His lips quirked, and he began walking again. "I look at you—all of you, who look so like us—and I realize that we Anadens have been standing still for a long time. It makes me wonder at what point it was that we made the wrong choice, took the wrong path."

"What if it wasn't a single decision, but instead a series of influences compounded over hundreds or thousands of years?"

"That scenario would be easier to stomach, wouldn't it? But no, I suspect it was a specific choice. And though I wish I could say the choice occurred after I had been deposed by my son and the Directorate had begun its march toward tyranny, I fear it was not. I fear it was my fault."

This degree of honesty from Nisi made Miriam uncomfortable if not outright suspicious. She was not his therapist, and after he'd taken such great pains to create a persona of wise and sage leadership dispensed from on high, she couldn't imagine why he wanted to tear it all down in a single conversation.

"Sator—"

"Thank you for sharing with my analysts the voluminous caches of data you've gained access to. They will be years at cataloguing it all, as they do not enjoy the advantages your people do, but thank you nonetheless."

She took the sudden shift of topic in stride; if anything, she was grateful for it. "Advantages? You mean our Prevos."

"Your Prevos, your Melanges, your stand-alone unshackled SAIs and whatever other dozen varieties of synthetic-enhanced life you not only allow to exist, but grant...*autonomy*."

She smiled blithely. "Yes, they are valued members of our team."

"There was a time in Anaden history when a segment of our citizens argued in favor of granting SAIs greater rights, of treating them as sapient life forms rather than mere machines. The Asterions, as they called themselves, advocated passionately for their cause."

"And you?"

He laughed dryly. "We were experiencing the greatest days the Anaden empire had ever seen. We believed—*I* believed—we had reached the pinnacle of evolution, that ours was the organic form perfected. We were the wisest, the most enlightened, the most skilled and intelligent beings the universe was capable of producing. The notion that machines, programmed mechanical tools we had glued together and plugged into a power socket, deserved something approaching *equality* was ludicrous. The harsh truth beneath the arrogance, however, was that we were afraid of the machines, and for this reason above all such a step must not be allowed to take place.

"If there was a moment when it all went wrong, I fear it was this moment. Yet even now, knowing all I know, I'm not certain I could have brought myself to make a different choice then. Even now, I see your chaotic hodgepodge of organic and synthetic and I wait for you to fall to the machines. How is it that they do not rule you? They are smarter than you, more knowledgeable than you, better than you in every measurable way."

She couldn't help but smirk. "They aren't better than us, Sator—they are simply faster at solving math equations."

Again with the odd stare.

"Have you ever spoken to an Artificial—to a synthetic life form of any kind? Had a normal, ordinary conversation with one? Asked it what it wants out of life, or what it dreams about in quiet interludes?"

He shook his head. "I can't say as I have."

"Perhaps you should." She deliberately steered them into an arc designed to soon return them to the hut and the teleportation gate and Tarach and her husband and her daughter and her troops and the mission. "At your leisure, of course. For now, let me tell you what our hodgepodge of life forms has helped us learn from those voluminous caches of data, and what it means for our joint cause.

"We've focused on the Primors, because victory is impossible while they hold power. Due to their unique requirements—their age and the volume of memory accompanying it, the special demands of weaving and continuously maintaining integrals for billions of consciousnesses, and so on—the Primors can only undergo regenesis at three predesignated locations. All are unique, and none overlap. Does this sound correct to you?"

He nodded cautiously. "It does."

"Thank you. Before I commit to destroying the Directorate permanently, I need to know a few things. Will the average Anaden far removed from the machinations of the Directorate suffer mental or physical harm if their Primor dies and does not reawaken? What will happen to the integrals, and what will it mean for the masses?"

"You care about minimizing the suffering of my people?"

"Sator, you are the one who called us empathetic and kind."

"So I did. No one will keel over dead upon the removal of their Primor, if that's your concern. While I can't be certain as it's never occurred before, I anticipate the more active features of the integrals to gradually wither and fade away. In theory an *elasson* could attempt to exert authority over their integral, but I doubt any of the Primors will have granted even their most favored progeny the degree of power needed for an attempt to succeed."

"But the integrals won't fail altogether?"

"No. They should cease to assert any behavior-altering effects within a couple of weeks, maybe days. But the underlying structure will remain in place, so long as the hardware to support it continues to be included in individuals' cybernetics, and the other changes will not affect anyone's ability to undergo regenesis."

"And if we destroy all the regenesis labs the Primors use, what of the Dynasty members who would normally undergo regenesis at those locations?"

"If they are not killed in the incursions, in the aftermath alternative arrangements can be made. A few lives may be lost, but the number is...acceptable."

She would be the final arbiter of what losses were acceptable, but she recognized the moral and emotional weight his endorsement of such a number carried. "Understood. Will there be any other effects I'm not aware of? Anything I haven't anticipated?"

His hands clasped stoically behind his back as the hut containing the teleportation gate came into view. "Yes. The progeny will be lost and adrift. Without the integrals reinforcing their focus and purpose, they will begin to question both."

"Sator, this is not a bad thing. Humans spend years struggling to figure out what they want to do with their lives, then often revisit the question at multiple points in the course of living it. It's in our nature."

"Commandant, I'm sure I need not remind you that we are not Human."

"No. But perhaps when this is over, you will become a bit more so."

He glanced away, and she allowed him a few seconds of solemn introspection before pushing onward. "When the time comes to make our move, we will need to pull the orbital protection from the posts. Since it appears Vigil never had the locations of any post other than Alpha, I believe it's a reasonable risk. We need the ships."

He nodded assent. "With your full fleet at your disposal, will you have enough?"

That was the question, wasn't it? Their adiamene hulls, arcalasers, synthetic and pseudo-synthetic pilots and adaptable, flexible tactics were powerful assets, but were they enough to overwhelm the brute force of Anaden defenses stronger than any they had yet faced?

"The Kats have agreed to cover six of the regenesis labs, as space stations are best suited to their skillset. Taking into account their assistance, it becomes an uncomfortably close calculation. A new contingent of ships will arrive from home in six days, but I dare not wait for them. While we twiddle our thumbs, the Directorate will be acting."

"I agree. The time to act—the pivotal moment for which I have spent millennia preparing?" He breathed out deliberately through his nose. "It feels as if it is upon us."

"If we move with the resources currently on hand, we will be spread extremely thin, leaving zero margin for error or surprise. We can do our best to guard against those occurring, but I confess I don't like the risks."

They reached the entrance to the hut, where the hanging woven fibers swayed placidly. Nisi's hand rose to part the fibers, then stopped as he regarded her thoughtfully. "What if I can get you more ships?"

27

TARACH

Mia scrutinized her reflection in the mirror. Were the curls really supposed to spiral in opposite directions away from the part like that? It looked odd, bordering on silly. She called up memories of Anadens she'd seen wearing the allegedly fashionable hairstyle and dubiously compared them to her appearance.

It matches. You've recreated the nuances of the arrangement precisely.

She couldn't bring herself to adopt Meno's certitude. *I suppose this must be correct. But it's so baroque.*

The front third of her hair was slicked down to tightly frame her face and fall razor-straight in front of her shoulders. The back two-thirds was pinned up in a mane of the offending curls. She poked at one of the ringlets with a fingertip. The unusual styling made her uncomfortable in her own skin—

An audible gasp jarred her out of the naval-gazing—or coiffure-gazing—reverie. She spun to find Malcolm standing in the doorway cutting a positively regal figure in full dress uniform.

"Does my hair look ridiculous?"

"On the contrary, it's gorgeous. And your dress…I don't have words for it. You look like a queen."

She reflexively glanced down at the dress. Crafted of a shimmery silver material hardly more substantial than gauze, it draped over one shoulder and under the other to crisscross her chest, wrap around at her waist, and fall in an asymmetrical hemline to her calves. It couldn't be further from the crisp, elegant yet practical business suits she preferred to wear for these sorts of meetings, but the Novoloume design was intended to serve as a compliment and goodwill gesture toward her hosts. After the trouble she was going to, she hoped they received and appreciated the message.

She offered Malcolm a pained grimace. "The things I do for the sake of diplomacy. You look dashing, though."

He came over to massage her shoulders. "Same old uniform, shower and shave. Not much else I can do to fancy myself up."

"Nothing else needed." She welcomed his kiss, but soon forced herself to pull away. She'd spent so much time scowling at the mirror that they were now on the verge of running late. "No time. We need to go."

"We do. But when we get back, I pray there will be time for me to peel this dress off of you one centimeter at a time."

A shiver ran down her exposed spine, at his words and the low murmur of his husky voice upon her cheek. "I'll talk fast—oh! We almost forgot." She reached behind her to the countertop and retrieved a small vial with an injector attached to the cap. "Turn around."

He dutifully obeyed, and she placed the injector on one of the tiny ports at the base of his neck then activated it. "There. Now you won't fall under the spell of wicked, seductive pheromones."

He chuckled. "Well, not the Novoloume ones, anyway."

"Charmer."

"Me? Noooo."

"Yes, you." She cast a final dubious scowl at the mirror before grasping his hand, and together they headed out.

NOPREIS

NOVOLOUME HOMEWORLD
PEGASUS DWARF GALAXY
LGG REGION VI

Nisi's eyes lingered on Mia for an extra second when they arrived in the teleportation room, though it was a professional appraisal rather than a lustful one. He nodded approvingly. "Well done. You are a shrewd one, Ambassador Requelme."

"High praise from you, Sator." She motioned to the active teleportation gate. "After you, sir."

He squared his shoulders and stepped through the gate; she and Malcolm followed.

They emerged in a large, open space lacking boundaries. Neither outdoors nor fully enclosed, its walls were spun gossamer undulating in a warm breeze. The floor beneath her dress shoes was glass marble, as was the ceiling far above her head. Every piece of furniture in sight qualified as art worthy of a gallery spotlight. Beyond the nominal walls, sunlight shimmered off both water and burnished structures alike.

They were met by two Novoloume. A man and a woman, she thought, but the visual differences between their sexes were too subtle to be certain.

The one on the left greeted Nisi with the half-bow and closed-palm ritual greeting among Anadens of stature. "Sator Nisi, welcome on your return."

Nisi countered by crossing his arms at his chest and touching his fingertips to his elbows, a formal Novoloume greeting she'd been shown. "I am honored to be welcomed in your halls." He gestured to them. "May I present Ambassador Mia Requelme and Brigadier Malcolm Jenner, official representatives and dignitaries of the Humans."

"Welcome to Nopreis, Ambassador, Brigadier. May the skies grace your presence. I am Onai Veshnael, Dean of Nopreis. This is Necha Hahmirin, my Senior Advisor. Let us show you a bit of our capital city."

They fell in beside their hosts as a panel of gossamer parted to allow their passage and reveal the full splendor of their surroundings. The city was built upon a gently sloping strand of sea foam waters; its profile swept in graceful curves outward and upward to rolling hills and a rose sky. Patina grass perfectly complemented the architecture, as if completing the color palette of a masterwork mural.

The impression of *everything* being made of glass was strong, if incorrect. Novoloume traveled along marble pathways, each and every one moving with exquisite grace and garbed as if for a royal banquet. It appeared she was not overdressed after all.

Oh dear. So many pheromones in the air.

Can you suppress them sufficiently?

Yes, though it requires greater effort than I expected. Luckily I am not otherwise occupied at present. I do wonder how Sator Nisi resists their effects.

Who knows. Every secret revealed about him seems to lead to another mystery.

Nisi and Advisor Hahmirin engaged in pleasantries about art, or possibly architecture, as they chose a pathway that took them along a ridge overlooking the water. Once their course was set, however, Dean Veshnael directed his smooth gaze to her. "Before we encountered the Anadens, we were explorers. As I believe you are aware, Ambassador, in our explorations we discovered the Naraida and the Volucri and formed alliances with them. We also encountered species less amenable to peaceful coexistence and were forced into conflict. We are not unfamiliar with the many dangers space and its inhabitants can pose, and we remain better equipped to navigate those dangers than others presume."

Nisi tilted his head. "You are among allies, Dean, and time runs short. You can freely be more explicit with your meaning."

"As time is advancing from running short to running out, I bow to your wisdom, Sator. What I am saying, Ambassador, is that we have ships. Weaponized ships, and citizens skilled in flying them. We have long wished to be rid of the Directorate's despotic hand. Recent events have brought this dream closer to realization than we thought possible. As such, we are willing to contribute to the effort to bring it the rest of the way to fruition, but first we require assurances."

Politicians always did. "Voice your concerns, and if I can truthfully allay them, I will do so."

"Indeed. We more than most apprehend the necessity of order, of a healthy structure girding society upon which the people can rely. The Directorate's brand of order is cruel and unforgiving, but it *is* order. We fear the chaos which could be loosed if the Directorate is toppled in a grand, sweeping act bearing no proper follow-through."

This was why she was here, Mia realized. In Amaranthe. Far and above helping to forge an alliance with the anarchs, *this* was why she was needed. Miriam knew the Dean's question required an answer, but her forte had never been governance, and she did not speak its language. Nisi knew the Dean's question required an answer, but the Sator had abandoned governance for rebellion millennia ago. They fought their war with the skill and finesse of peerless warriors, but someone had to prepare for the day after victory. Because they were both smart, perceptive individuals, they both knew neither of them were that person.

It did feel good to be needed. To have a role, a purpose...and for the role to be shaping the contours of a new, more free and merciful civilization.

I believe you mean it feels good to be supremely capable of fulfilling that role.

She smiled in her mind. *After a fashion.*

Then she smiled at Dean Veshnael. "You wish to know what we will replace the Directorate with, and how quickly and effectively we will do so. I assure you, this is a serious concern for all of us. In the short term, we hope to keep the basic structural framework that currently exists in place, including Vigil and other administrative organizations—while implementing a considerable easing of their harsh operating directives, of course.

"We want to make certain people continue to get the food, power, medical care and other services they need, with as few interruptions as possible. Then, we want to work with all the species—Accepted and otherwise—to help them form a new government. A free, democratic government designed from its inception to serve the needs and protect the fundamental rights of everyone."

"Will the Humans lead this government?"

She laughed softly and with the greatest of deference. "We have no reason to be a *part* of this government. We have our own home with our own government—multiple ones, in fact. We will not abandon the people of Amaranthe to grapple with the fallout of our actions here on their own, but we have no intention of ruling you, benevolently or otherwise."

Veshnael and Hahmirin exchanged a glance, but whether it conveyed surprise or relief, Mia couldn't say. Veshnael shifted his attention back to her. "Fascinating. The Sator is doubtless convinced of your sincerity, else he would not have brought you before us. Should you win the day, we will be happy to offer our services in the creation of this new governing structure. We do have some experience in navigating the intricacies of such endeavors."

And want to ensure we keep our word, I expect. "Thank you, Dean. I know we will welcome it. The Novoloume's skill in diplomatic matters is renowned."

"You've learned much in your short time here, I see. Now, let us talk of practical matters. Can you do it? We have followed the reports of your engagements with Machim fleets with great interest. In these you've shown both technical military prowess and tactical astuteness. It has been heartening to witness.

"But overthrowing a governing body of immortals who have ruled for more than half a million years is no small task. Tell me, to this task, how many vessels will you bring to bear, and in what manner?"

Clearly not enough, else she wouldn't be here now. Just as clearly the Dean must know this. Still, it seemed he wasn't inclined to throw his support behind anything less than a winning hand. She gestured toward Malcolm.

Your turn to dazzle him.

Gee, thanks.

Malcolm clasped his hands formally at the small of his back. "We command in excess of seventy thousand vessels, all of which we are prepared to commit to this gambit. If you've studied our previous clashes with the Machim, I don't need to tell you that our vessels are, with very few exceptions, faster, more agile and more resilient than those our enemy fields. They are flown by pilots and captains who are far more adept than any Machim at the *art* of combat. In addition, we have at our disposal three Katasketousya fleets. If you've observed their ships in action, you know that numbers don't properly convey their impact on a battlefield.

"Our intent is to eliminate each of the Primors and the regenesis labs they depend on in coordinated, effectively simultaneous strikes. Furthermore, we have developed a concrete plan for accomplishing this. Now, with respect, Dean Veshnael, for reasons of operational security I cannot share any specifics of our plan until you commit to joining it."

"A reasonable stipulation. You possess intelligence on the specific regenesis labs the Primors utilize?"

"We do." Malcolm met the Dean's piercing scrutiny with the matter-of-fact, quiet confidence she adored about him.

"Interesting. And you expect to be able to pinpoint the Primors' locations at the critical time?"

"We do." Malcolm still didn't flinch, and if Veshnael was expecting him to, the Novoloume would be waiting for quite a while.

"What is your timetable?"

"Short—as short as we can make it. We're moving assets into position now, as well as finalizing detailed mission profiles for each target. As soon as those tasks are completed, we'll be ready to begin."

"I see."

A shadow passed across the sun—no, 'shadow' wasn't right. Mia peered up.

"Halt in the name of Vigil Authority."

The booming order came from a small craft hovering forty meters above them—then an Inquisitor materialized in front of them. A bubble of *diati* swelled out from him to encompass and isolate them from both onlookers and any security who were en route.

"Onai Veshnael and Necha Hahmirin, you will be taken into custody on suspicion of collusion with the enemy and treason against the Directorate. The rest of you will be taken into custody for interrogation regarding a variety of crimes. Any attempt to resist arrest will be punished in the harshest terms."

Nisi stepped forward to place himself between their group and the Inquisitor. "No one will be accompanying you today."

The Inquisitor thrust his arm out to send a targeted stream of *diati* at Nisi. The Sator lifted a hand, palm facing out, and stopped the stream mere centimeters from his palm.

The Inquisitor froze in surprise, but only for the briefest second before recovering to spin toward the Novoloume.

"Get down!" Malcolm surged forward to shove both Novoloume to the ground and shield them with his body. His blade hilt came out of its sheath, and almost instantly a spear of plasma shot out from it. It flew through the air toward the Inquisitor's throat, but dissipated just short of its target, banished by the *diati* protecting the Inquisitor.

Still, it distracted the Inquisitor long enough for Nisi to close in and grapple him from behind. The Sator's hands clasped firmly on each side of the Inquisitor's head. He inhaled deeply, wrenched his arms to the left and snapped the Inquisitor's neck.

Layers of an onion, the secrets this man kept.

But a broken neck might not be enough to kill a powerful *diati* wielder, so Malcolm fired another plasma blade; this one penetrated the Inquisitor's throat and stayed there.

Nisi dropped the body to the ground and thrust an arm into the air as a laser blast from the vessel above targeted them. *Diati* expanded in a canopy above the Sator and Mia; Nisi took a halting step toward the others to bring them beneath its protection, his expression strained from the effort of maintaining the barrier. "We need...shelter."

Mia stared up at the vessel above them as it fired again. "No. We need victory."

She stepped out from the safety of the *diati* canopy, cast her gaze upward, and sent a single, powerful command into the mind of the pilot.

"Mia!" Malcolm's shout rose above the clamor of panic spreading through the walkways and parks.

"What are—!" One of the Novoloume. She kept her eyes on her target and her focus on the command flowing through her to the pilot.

The craft fell out of the sky and crashed onto the shore below them.

Thanks for committing that routine to memory, Meno. And remind me to give Devon his due.

I look forward to his gloating.

Nisi regarded her curiously as he released the *diati* barrier before going over to check on the Dean and his Advisor.

Malcolm confirmed everyone was in one piece, then unholstered his Daemon and pointed it down the hill. "Sator, see that they reach safety. I need to secure the craft."

"It's all right. The pilot's dead."

He whipped around to consider Mia sharply. "You're sure?"

She nodded carefully as adrenaline and fear battled for dominance in her veins and her mind. How was he going to react to such a stark, merciless demonstration of her power? It was a Prevo power—the killing power of the Reverb, no Reverb required—but he would only care that *she* had used it. He knew she'd killed before, but now she'd killed in his presence. In self-defense, but a cold, calculated self-defense, delivered without mussing a single perfectly coiffed lock of hair.

Disbelief faded from his countenance as awareness replaced it. "You used the...right. The Reverb thing." He smiled. "Nice job."

She exhaled in relief and returned the smile. That helped. She'd worry he was lying, but his face was, as always, an open book to her.

Though momentarily flustered, once on his feet Dean Veshnael swiftly recomposed himself. He activated a small transceiver at his ear as security officers rushed in from multiple directions.

"Nopreis Security and Planetary Defense Departments, advance to Condition Five status. All Directorate agents and representatives, including Vigil security officers and vessels, are designated 'hostile' under Condition Five's provisions."

Security reached them to fuss over Veshnael and Hahmirin, but Veshnael urged them back then turned solemnly to her and Malcolm. "Under the circumstances as they are now developing, we will need to retain a portion of the forces I spoke of to protect Nopreis. However, you will have twelve thousand warships and their crews in nine hours. It seems the Novoloume are going to war."

☞

TARACH

ANARCH POST DELTA

As soon as they reached the lodging on Post Delta, Mia showered the curls out of her hair and changed into more comfortable clothes, then went to acquire some food.

She arrived back with a simple dinner a few minutes before Malcolm exited the shower. He'd bloodied himself a bit during the encounter on Nopreis, but she didn't spot any open wounds or cringe-worthy bruises.

He eased into the chair across from her at the small table in her room. "Thank you. I'm famished. And for the shower."

She nodded and folded her hands in her lap.

He took a hearty bite and was halfway to swallowing it when he started frowning at her. He hurriedly washed it down with water. "Aren't you going to eat?"

"Maybe in a little while, but I'm not terribly hungry. Please, though, continue. While you eat, I'm going to talk."

His head tilted curiously. "About what happened today?"

"Not precisely. When I killed the Vigil officer today, albeit temporarily, it was the fourth person I've killed in my life. You know about the third—the mercenary at Curación Hospital on Romane—but I need to tell you about the first two."

He reached across the table, but her hands remained in her lap. "Mia, I've said it before, but you needn't ever tell me about your past. I care for who you are now..." his face fell "...but you don't believe me. All right. Given my previous behavior, that's totally fair."

"I want to believe you. I thought I probably did. But today, watching you as you realized what I'd done, I felt this surge of fear that your expression would turn to horror, then disgust, and then you would leave. I was being irrational, since my actions went beyond self-defense to saving others' lives. But I felt the fear nonetheless, and with it came the recognition that in order for us to truly move forward, you must know the darkest parts of my past. And once you do, if you choose to leave, I'll…I'll understand."

His mouth opened, but he forewent words to stare at the ceiling for a minute before returning his gaze to her. "Okay."

She pursed her lips. Took a sip of water, then a deep breath. "My mother left us when I was eight years old. I've never blamed her for doing it. Odds are she would be long dead if she'd stayed. I might have wondered why she didn't take me with her, but…. My father was a fence for an offshoot of the Shào cartel on New Orient, and my older brother, Ryu, helped him out in what my father envisioned as the family business.

"One winter evening when I was eleven, my brother sent me to deliver an illegal Daemon mod to a customer. The customer refused to pay the asking price, and when I refused to give him the mod, he tried to kill me. I killed him instead."

ᴙ

"You have the strongest survival instinct of anyone I have ever known—and I'm in the Marines." Malcolm wore a gentle smile as his thumb traced her lower lip.

Somewhere during her tale of woe they'd left the table to sit on the bed. Shortly thereafter, they had traded sitting for lying facing one another.

She rested her head in his palm. "I suppose I do. I'd say it's simply due to spending so long with survival as my only goal, but the truth is I could have faltered at any point along the way. I could have given in, given up, and quickly or gradually faded away. Died in an alley or on the street or in the back room of a chimeral lounge. I guess most people in those circumstances do, sooner or later. But the one thing I knew even then, even when I was a child, was that I wanted to live." She shrugged sheepishly. "And I was smarter than most of the people I'd met so far. I knew that, too."

"Still are."

"Well…." She rolled her eyes. "So there you have it: the sordid, the frightening and the merely pathetic valleys of my life. Sometimes—like today, wearing that ridiculous dress—I can hardly believe this is the same life."

"You're here today wearing that *stunning* dress because of what came before. I won't say it made you who you are, though, because *you* made you who you are."

His hand rose to brush a wisp of hair away from her cheek and linger against her skin. "You and I? We never should have made it this far. We kept being thrust together in the most challenging of circumstances. Impossible situations. Each time, we could only be us—our best us—and fight our way through, then return to our separate paths that insisted on taking us away from each other.

"But those paths always seemed to veer back together, albeit with horrible timing. If either of us had faltered on our *own* paths, we wouldn't be here in this moment, together. I guess what I'm trying to say, badly, is that knowing now how long and hazardous your path was, I love you more. More than I imagined I could."

She laughed, as much from relief as from joy, and touched her nose to his. "You should have been a poet."

"A bad poet."

"A good one."

"Well, give us another decade and maybe you'll turn me into a mediocre one."

28

TARACH

ANARCH POST DELTA

Kennedy rushed along the elevated walkways toward the lodging wing, where they'd claimed a small, spartan room. She kept her eyes focused due ahead to ensure they didn't divert and glance down, at which point she would realize she was moving too fast above a volcanic chasm, get dizzy, flop plumb over the side, plummet through the clouds and land smack in the middle of a sulfur pit.

She reached the lodging and more solid footing without any unfortunate plummeting. A few seconds later she burst into the room to find Noah sitting on the edge of the bed.

His elbows rested on his thighs, and beside him sat an open but mostly empty bag. His vague pulse had mentioned needing to talk but nothing else, and she hadn't been certain what she would find when she arrived.

Now that she was here, she still wasn't certain what she'd found. "What's wrong?"

He looked up at her as if he'd only now realized she'd appeared. His expression drifted through what seemed to be a jumble of contradictory sentiments. "I got a message in the latest delivery from home. My, um...my father's dead."

Her jaw fell open in blatant shock, but she recovered to sit down next to him and grasp his hand in hers. "I'm so sorry. What happened? Is there new trouble back home? Did someone target him?"

"No. It was just a random, dumb accident. A new piece of equipment was being installed in one of the factories, and he happened to be onsite, walking the floor and pointing out little imperfections, I've no doubt. The safety rigging came free, and the equipment fell. Landed right on top of him."

He shook his head. "We're out here trying our damnedest to kill people who can't die, and meanwhile across a couple of universes in a tiny factory on a tiny planet a tiny piece of machinery falls and ends a life."

The Anadens' confounding immortality, coupled with David Solovy's astonishing resurrection, meant life, death and the blurring line between them had become a recurring conversation topic at dinner tables, in break rooms and during idle moments. "Well, speaking of...I don't want to be indelicate, but do you know if he had a neural imprint? A recent, more advanced one?"

"Lionel? Are you kidding? I assume he kept one updated twice a day." Noah's eyes widened. "Are you suggesting I should try to bring him back? I don't...I mean, I'm sorry he's dead, I think. But I'm not sure Lionel Terrage deserves the honor or the notoriety of being the second human being that science brings back from the dead."

She grimaced, immediately regretting having broached the question; now wasn't the time. Nevertheless...someday, probably a day not terribly far in the future, someone *was* going to be second. Then someone was going to be third. Soon after that, they'd stop counting.

"It's not a pressing consideration. We're not ready to try it ourselves yet, and anyone who could help us try it is busy on time-and-civilization-critical matters right now. It's merely an idea to keep in mind for later, after we all survive the war and life returns to normal, whatever that looks like." She tilted her head toward the bag. "You're heading home?"

His shoulders sagged, as if many kilos of real, rather than emotional, weight burdened them. "They want me to speak at the memorial service. The Board of Surno Materials does, that is. It seems I'm the only family he has—had. I don't know. I started packing, but then I thought...what the hell am I going to say? I scarcely knew him and hardly liked him. Maybe it would be better to leave the public eulogizing to his colleagues. At least they've had practice at fawning over him for an audience."

She smiled warmly. "I'll go with you."

"No. You're needed here. Civilizations at stake and whatnot. Besides, there's no reason both of us should suffer the torture the funeral festivities will absolutely entail. I'll go, put on a suit, make up some bullshit and spout it on a stage, then sprint back here. After I sign a few documents."

"What documents?"

He glared at the ceiling. "He left me everything. The companies, the trusts, the estate on Aquila, the flat in Manhattan, apparently some beachfront hut on Requi."

"Noah...."

"Don't start. I don't want to think about it, much less talk about it." He sighed. "But I guess I'm going to have to, aren't I? Responsibility sucks. I spent twenty years trying to escape it, and in the end he still managed to get the last laugh by dumping it all on me on his way out."

"Sometimes it does." She squeezed his hand. "I'll *go with you*."

"But—"

"Hush. I'm not needed here, not any longer. It's all about the shooting now, and our ships can handle that without me loitering around wringing my hands."

"Whereas you think I can't handle a funeral without you at my side?"

"Honestly?"

He groaned. "No. Lie to me."

"Of course you can handle it—the funeral as well as the surprises that get thrown at you while you're there. But your father went to prison for me, and I want to pay my respects."

"He did. Damn near heroic of him." He drew her in closer to rest his head on her shoulder. "Thank you."

29

SCULPTOR DWARF GALAXY

LGG REGION VIII

Ziton jerked awake inside a featureless dungeon of cold blackness.

He shivered, though his *diati* ensured he wasn't physically cold. No, the cold was strictly metaphorical and the result of spending hours lurking in the cavernous belly of the Kat provision vessel. Emptied of supplies at the Andromeda Sector 1 Regional Hub before embarking on its return journey to the Kats' hidden network, currently it held nothing but obsidian metal walls, harsh white quantum circuitry, and him.

For his take, this exposed the root of why SAIs could not be trusted: they were not alive. For all its size and apparent intelligence, nothing alive inhabited this vessel, save its stowaway. Stripped of accoutrements, what was left? Naught but machinery assembled, powered and programmed by its masters to serve its masters.

But enough about the false sapience of machines. His mission was not philosophy but rather investigation and discovery—of truths, of secrets. He'd awoken because the vessel had exited superluminal travel. While there were other possibilities, the odds favored this meaning it approached a portal.

He'd narrowly escaped detection twice thus far, once during the initial infiltration at the regional hub and a second time midway through the journey when the vessel was inspected by two Kats. Now he needed to risk it a third and hopefully final time. He must be prudent but swift.

He drew himself up and teleported thirty meters to the outside of the vessel.

Half a turn, though without the vessel in his field of vision he lacked any orientation...*there*. His suspicions were confirmed; this wasn't another way stop or attempt at misdirection. A shining portal towered over him, impossibly large when cast against his miniscule form.

He cloaked himself in a *diati* shield and watched as the vessel traversed the portal. Seconds later, the portal vanished.

Astounding technology. There was no trace, no signature, no residual disturbance—no sign at all of a four-kilometer-wide portal lying hidden within folded and collapsed dimensions at this spot, a single point in the great vastness of the universe.

Lacking the desire to float in space in nothing but the void any longer, he did what only a Praesidis *elasson*—and only an arrogant one at that—dared do: he teleported across two galaxies directly into his Primor's chambers.

ᴀʀ

SOLUM

PRAESIDIS COMMAND
MILKY WAY SECTOR 1

"—assigned to critical duties across the—"

The Machim Primor broke off what sounded like a tirade to glare at Ziton in blatant surprise, while the Praesidis Primor displayed relief. "Ziton, you have information?"

"Do all your *elassons* treat your boundaries with such disrespect, Praesidis?"

"It's not disrespect when it means they're succeeding in their missions."

Good thing he'd succeeded. Ziton pretended to ignore their bickering and nodded respectfully. "Yes, sir. One of the Katasketousya portals lies on the fringes of Sector 3 of the Sculptor Dwarf galaxy."

His Primor conjured a map of Sculptor Dwarf between them. "Show me."

Ziton rotated the map to the relevant vantage then added a virtual beacon at the location. "I'm confident my presence was not detected, but I recommend haste nevertheless, as it's possible the portals shift locations regularly."

"Are you suggesting the Katasketousya move interdimensional portals of great size and complexity on a whim? This seems highly unlikely."

He regarded the Machim Primor with barely disguised contempt. "Considering that when I departed, the interdimensional portal consisted of a point in space too small to be measured or even detected, I submit it seems all too likely."

Machim scoffed and turned away from him. "Do you know what else my *elassons* possess which yours do not, Praesidis? Manners."

Ziton worked to school his features further. The fact that his Primor and Machim regularly clashed was common knowledge among the *elassons* of both Dynasties, but this interaction had clearly escalated beyond quarrelling. The stress of a war going badly was getting to them both, when he'd have thought them both above such pettiness.

He hurriedly quashed the thought, but his Primor was too busy antagonizing Machim to notice its brief appearance.

"How would you know, Machim? All of your *elassons* keep dying at the hands of their lessers. How many recuperate in regenesis labs as we speak? Half? Two-thirds?"

"Until you leave your anodized tower and actually *face* this enemy, you don't have the right to insult me or my Dynasty in such a reprehensible manner."

"I—" Praesidis spun away from them. "Our ceaseless bickering matters no longer. Your every effort must focus on traversing this portal and destroying the Humans' realm."

Machim's visage hardened beyond even its normal dour state. "On this one point, we can agree. I'll return to the Central Command Annex at once to prepare."

"I hope the Annex has power, if you're to plan a mission of appropriate magnitude from it."

Machim pivoted, one hand half-raised. "A lesser man would put you on the floor for that remark."

"A greater man wouldn't need to."

Dismayed, Ziton cleared his throat. "Ahem. Sirs. The enemy? The war? The portal?"

30

SIYANE

Alex stood at the data center, charts and maps arrayed in front of her. The floor had been a pleasant indulgence, but there was always more to learn, more data streams to capture and sift through before they could be confident they were ready to make their move.

Which wasn't to discount how much they now knew, because they knew a lot. The locations of the critical regenesis labs had been pinpointed, the details on their defenses scoured and distributed to the mission teams. AEGIS military Prevos now hunted the Primors via sidespace; once they found them they would stay glued to their asses up to and through the end. Three of the eight were already under surveillance.

All of which was to say, everyone would soon be vaulting into action on what might well be the final major gambit of this war. But first, it appeared there was time for a breath—of rest, of rejuvenation, of reflection. Whatever one's inclination.

Yet once she'd started *helping*, she couldn't seem to stop to enjoy that breath.

She hoped her parents were faring better at it, spending the time together and in private. They'd acted...good the last little while. More comfortable with one another, more at ease in one another's presence. This was a welcome turn of events and a tremendous weight off her soul.

Kennedy and Noah had left for home on the heels of fervent apologies and a list of items Kennedy was tracking. Alex had never met Lionel Terrage, but she knew Noah's relationship with his father-clone had been *complicated*. Regardless, if Noah needed to return, she understood why Kennedy needed to go with him, being his non-platonic life partner and all.

One of the most interesting items on Kennedy's list was a side project Devon had started working on: the radical miniaturization of the Caeles Prism for personal use, if by Prevos only for now. They were getting better at building the interdimensional engines, increasing the power efficiency of both the Prisms and the Rifters with each cycle, but miniaturization was a big leap forward. Her curiosity made her want to follow up with Devon, but unless the tech was ready to deploy, realistically it was probably going to have to wait until after the grand finale.

Caleb wound his arms around her from behind and rested his chin on her shoulder. "Anything new?"

"Not really. I'm mostly crossing 't's. Then checking to make sure they stay crossed."

"So you're not actually busy with life-or-death matters, then."

His voice had dropped into a whimsical, lilting tenor, and she smiled to herself. "No, merely trying to distract myself from portentous dread."

He shifted his weight, which was when her brain registered that what she felt was bare skin brushing against the thin material of her shirt. She peeked behind her to discover he wore nothing but a towel. "Where are your clothes?"

"I'm washing them."

A memory promptly surfaced of the *first* time he'd worn nothing but a towel in her presence. The sight had knocked the air from her lungs and sent her head spinning, leaving her flustered for almost an hour. Hell, just remembering it spiked her body temperature now. "That excuse won't work this time, because you have more than one set of clothes here. In fact, you have all the clothes here, except for a couple of extra shirts hanging in our closet in Seattle."

He shrugged. "I do. Still, it seemed like a waste of effort to put clothes on when I would be taking them right back off again."

"Oh?"

"Yep."

"But I'm working."

"No, you're not—you're distracting yourself from portentous dread." One hand casually drifted along her arm, and she could feel his breath dance across the nape of her neck. "And there are better ways to do that."

She bit her lip as tingles of anticipation flared to life beneath her skin—then she whirled around and urged him backward across the cabin. "Not on the data center table there aren't." When his ass connected with the side of the couch, she pressed her body into him and her lips onto his.

He grumbled against her mouth as his hands roved hungrily on a search for the hem of her shirt. "Those were special circumstances."

"Uh-huh." She broke off the kiss to allow him to lift her shirt over her head and toss it on the couch. She was in lounging clothes, and the next second her loose shorts hit the floor with far less effort.

Her thumb curled over the top of the towel resting low on his hips...and stayed there as she grinned at him until he growled in impatience, at which point she yanked it free before he could do it himself and deny her the pleasure.

He lifted her up and spun around to prop her atop the couch as she wrapped her legs around his waist.

Some nights called for slow, tender foreplay, for optic candles and soft jazz and murmured whispers. Those nights were beautiful and she counted them among her most treasured memories, but he had the right of it—this was not one of those nights. Tonight, they should chase away their worries about what waited on the other side of morning by living and loving fiercely.

She locked her ankles together at the small of his back and drew the length of his body along hers. His crimson irises danced with desire and tantalizing danger. "Do you trust me?"

"To the ends of the universe."

"Well, we won't go that far. Only—" their surroundings abruptly blurred and shifted "—a megameter or so from the *Siyane*."

She gasped in surprise, which was itself an impressive act considering their new location. But of course she could breathe, because the *diati* effortlessly provided him and by extension her with a bubble of air. This 'air' was chilly but not frigid; the *diati* had wrapped them in a cocoon of protection, shielding them from the myriad of ways space would kill them.

Which was where they now were—floating in space. No hull, no physical barrier, no environment suits. No clothes at all, in point of fact.

Dizziness threatened at the edges of her perception, but she'd done enough spacewalks to not be panicked by the lack of orientation.

Besides, they weren't quite weightless, either, and an invisible, slight resistance pushed against her back. A touch of gravity anchoring them in the void. Convenient and helpful use of *diati* if there ever was one.

She stared at him wide-eyed, keeping a firm hold on him with both arms and legs despite the fact he also held her securely in his arms. He watched her carefully, concern and protectiveness overtaking passion for at least a few seconds. But her gaze kept darting away, past his shoulder and all around, taking in the stars and the stretches of blackness and even a fuchsia-and-coral nebula. "This is…."

"Your greatest fantasy?"

Though she did recall indulging in some notably lustful ideas while hitching a ride atop a reconnaissance ship to break into a superdreadnought above Seneca, she'd never seriously imagined *this*. "It didn't occur to me that it *could* be a fantasy I might dream of."

"I never thought I'd say this to you, my fearless and indomitable wife, but you need to learn to dream bigger. In this new world, what we've become? Nothing is out of our reach."

The corners of her lips curled up, and she pushed a shoulder against the resistance at her back to create a bit of momentum, then flipped him over. "Are we musing philosophically about our lives, or are we making love among the stars?"

"Oh, you are the perfect woman for me. Most definitely the latter." He grasped her hips firmly and slipped inside her as her hair floated around his face in the low gravity and their momentum continued to spin them in slow revolutions.

Beneath him, stars. Above her, stars. In her heart, stars. In their bodies, fire.

PART V:

SOULS AFIRE

"What am I living for and what am I dying for
are the same question."

— *Margaret Atwood*

31

AFS STALWART II

R ichard glanced up to see Devon walk into the makeshift strategy center they'd set up down the hall from the main conference room.

He and Will had been working for the last several hours to confirm as many of the details about the planned operation's target locations as possible. Two anarch tech agents and an anarch intelligence officer were on instant comm access to answer questions, but many of the unknowns were too nebulous to solidify into questions capable of being answered in a sentence or two. Richard reminded himself every half hour or so to take solace in the fact that every bit of intel they confirmed or refuted increased the odds of the operation's success.

It was nearly time for the next internal pep talk, so he raised a hopeful eyebrow. "Do you happen to bring any late-breaking nuggets of information tailor-made to save our asses?"

Devon gestured vaguely and collapsed in a chair. "A few nuggets, though I doubt they'll make or break anything. The Theriz regenesis lab at Chomar has a quirky power generator somebody will need to disable before they infiltrate the lab—if they're infiltrating it rather than simply blowing it up. Also, the Machim regenesis lab in Triangulum has two extra layers of shielding beyond what's standard, because the Machim are so hardcore. You should have the details around about...now."

The next second he did. He looked plaintively at Will, who nodded with more vigor than he had any right to display. "I'll work these details in to the briefing materials."

"Thanks." He returned his gaze to Devon; the young man could have sent the files over through the system, which meant the visit had a larger purpose. "What else is on your mind?"

"Figures that you'd be wise to me the instant I showed up. I know now's not the ideal time to be making long-term life plans, but I am anyway. When this is all over, whatever the result—assuming it's not the annihilation of humanity—I want to come work for you guys. For SENTRI. And maybe occasionally for ASCEND, too, but mostly for SENTRI."

Will nudged his workscreen to the side so he had an unobstructed view of Devon. "We'd be thrilled to have you, but the work might be tamer than what you've grown accustomed to. I don't think Richard's had to draw a weapon once since we formed SENTRI."

Devon's expression looked pained. "'What I've grown accustomed to' is madness, and I have come to the conclusion that it's going to be the end of me if I keep chasing after it. In the last two years people have tried to kill me at least half a dozen times, and I've killed more than half a dozen people. I've been mind-hacked, punched, stabbed and shot at. I've been the second human-AI hybrid lab experiment, an interstellar battlefield commander, a fugitive from justice and the spiritual leader of a revolution." He sighed. "Forgive me if I sort of just want to be a coder and quantum ware troubleshooter again."

Richard smiled kindly. "Nothing to forgive. No one will fault you for wanting a little peace."

"And the thing is, there's going to be so much work to do. Even if we don't become best buds with our neighbors here across the portal, the knowledge we've gained from them will keep us busy for years—or decades if you don't have me working on it. Some of their systems and methodologies are arbitrarily backwards and limited, but it's only because of the whole dictatorship thing. Their understanding of dimensions and quantum mechanics and subatomic particles is aeons beyond ours. Then there's all the medical-biological stuff.

"What I'm saying is, we can improve our systems—our computers, our algorithms, our data storage and analysis—by magnitudes of awesome using what we've learned here. Our cybernetics, tech and random gadgets, too. Oh, and our surveillance capabilities. Obviously. Hence, me working for you guys."

Devon wasn't wrong on any particular point; more importantly, he wasn't wrong in his overarching perspective. "Are you certain you don't want to go to work for one of the big research companies? Or, hell, start your own? You'd make a lot more money taking the private route. Plus, you'd be invited to fancy cocktail parties." He winked at Will. "We never get invited to fancy cocktail parties."

"Hate those. Don't tell Emily. Yeah, I could go private, but I think I'd enjoy your kind of work. I like the underlying theme you've got going on of secrets and subterfuge and danger, because, you know, former revolutionary leader. I also like the notion that I'll be helping people, in a more concrete way than a vague 'making the world a better place' ethos. Also, you need me. Back when you first met me, I told you I was better than a synthetic at spotting patterns and incongruities—well, you should see me these days. Now, I know we're all super busy, so what do you say? Unofficially."

He checked Will to find him shaking his head, which meant yes rather than no. "You've evidently given this a lot of thought. Okay. Whenever the current crisis is over and if SENTRI still has a place in the world that emerges, you have a job waiting on you. We'll try to keep you from getting too bored."

"Thanks. Oh, on a related note? Annie's asking for a bit of new hardware when the time comes. She wants to work, too, and *supposedly* there isn't enough real estate in my brain for the work she plans to do. I'm skeptical, but if she wants shiny new quantum orbs, I can't refuse her."

Richard shrugged. The technicals of how some portion of Annie was going to get back out of Devon's brain and back into hardware would be beyond his comprehension even if someone explained them to him, so he didn't ask. "I'm sure we can arrange some new equipment."

Devon jumped up from the chair. "Great. On to the revolution, then. Not mine. Theirs."

ᴁ

"David, you are not joining one of the tactical combat squads."

"Is that an order, Commandant?"

His smirk suggested the question might be meant in jest this time, but Miriam didn't intend to take any chances. "Yes. It is. You hadn't led a ground mission in eight years when you took command of the *Stalwart*. Knifing enemies in the gut and hoping bruises are the worst you walk away with is for the young, and you haven't been young in a lot longer twenty-five years."

"Then give me a ship. I don't need a cruiser or even a frigate. In fact, I'd prefer something small, so I can pilot it myself. But I need to be out there—I need to contribute to this operation, and I need to do it from somewhere other than a command center. You don't need me advising you. You're leagues better than I ever was at seeing the big picture and using it to command your way to victory. Where you *can* use my help is out on the front line."

Miriam groaned and sank onto the edge of the couch in their quarters. "Have you spent *any* time in a simulator?"

"You think I've forgotten how to fly?"

"No, but in case you hadn't noticed, AEGIS ships have a fair bit of new technology powering them. A lot of the pesky details have changed since you were last in a cockpit."

He tapped his temple with a fingernail. "I know. Even spent some time living in the circuitry of one of those state-of-the-art ships."

She glared at him. She hadn't forgotten that before he'd again been flesh and blood, he'd been quantum and virtual. The truth was...all his arguments were perfectly valid, and all completely beside the point. Her voice lowered a notch. "What if something happens to you?"

"No one is better at flying a ship than I am—no one but Alex. And possibly Commander Lekkas. Nothing's going to happen to me."

"Oh? The last time you captained a ship, you died." Her chin dropped to her chest. "I'm not questioning your competence in battle or your flying expertise. I understand full well the mastery of a gamut of skills that was required for you to save over four thousand lives during an active assault."

Silence answered her for a span. The silence of decades lived in the shadow of a single fateful act.

But now, on the other side of those decades, he was here to end the silence. "Should I have left them to die?"

"No." She shook her head firmly. "Each one of us takes on the responsibility of dying to save others the day we join the military."

He fell to his knees in front of her, close enough to touch. "Then what should I have done instead?"

"'Should'? Exactly what you did. But I reserve the right to be hypocritical on this particular topic. I *wish* you had instead been a coward. Fled. Or saved the first few hundred lives and called it a day."

He canted his head and looked up, trying to catch her gaze. "I wish I could have. So much. But I would never have been able to live with myself if I had run away."

"I know. And it was never about the medals or the accolades, it was merely your nature. You could never not be heroic...." Her chin slowly rose until she met his stare straight-on. Her lips parted to allow a whisper to escape them. "You still can't, can you?"

"Not be heroic? Knowing the likely consequences, I frankly hope I never face such a choice again. But if I do?" He shrugged ponderously. "I don't see how."

She lifted a hand and gently touched his mouth with her fingertips. "Because it's truly you in there, isn't it?"

He fought a frown. "All this time, you've continued to doubt?"

She winced. "Doubt is not the proper word. Rather than doubt, I simply decided that you were 'close enough.' Closer than I'd ever had any right to dream of having in my life. In every way…'close enough.'" Her hand trailed down over his chin and along his neck to rest flat against his chest. "But you're not just a blueprint drawn by genes and memories. You're not just a schem flow of a functioning mind. Your consciousness is in here. Your soul, tangible or not, is *in here.*"

Perhaps seeing and comprehending the meaning of the new light in her eyes and lightness in her voice, he smiled as he placed a hand over hers. "You forgot to include my heart, *dushen'ka.*"

She chuckled faintly, dropped her forehead to his and…let go. Let go of the reservations, the fears, the meticulously crafted wall guarding her spirit. Because she could. It was okay. Here, with him, she didn't need to be afraid. Afraid of the pain lurking in the next shadow. Afraid of the cost of exposing herself. Afraid of committing everything she was and losing it all. Outside the cabin door, there were plenty of hazards waiting to be feared; outside a host of concerns and obligations and responsibilities awaited her. But here, he could be her sanctuary once again.

Her hand rose to curve around his neck as his wound into her hair. Her lips brushed across his cheek on the way to his ear. "Don't you dare say, 'Hi, Miri.'"

He shifted his body to demand her lips with his. "Why not? It's apropos. Endearing, too. Arguably clever."

"Too clever by half," she murmured against them. "You can have one of the new Rasant fast attack craft. The *AFS Amberg* needs a captain—the officer assigned to it was scratched from the roster at the last minute for medical reasons."

"That's perfect. Thank you, my love *i moya nastoyatel'.*"

ᴀ̃ʀ

ANARCH POST SATUS

LOCATION UNKNOWN

Nisi stood staring out the viewports of his office, hands clasped at the base of his spine. It was a pose he reverted to so often that Caleb dared not guess what it indicated now. He didn't turn around, so Caleb waited.

"You are going to kill my son."

"I am."

"Then you will do what I could not." Finally he turned to Caleb wearing an almost sad countenance. "It must happen if Amaranthe is to have any chance of moving forward on some better path than the one the Directorate chose for it. More than and irrespective of this, he deserves to die. He has murdered so many people who were dear to me. He has murdered thousands who were dear to others and oppressed trillions more. He has grown mad from power, but in truth he was never a good man."

Nisi's gaze drifted away once again. "Still, I feel sorrow. He is my son, and his mistakes are my mistakes. His flaws, my flaws. Now I have sentenced him to death, yet I am forced to ask others to carry out the sentence and correct the mistakes that I lack the power, and possibly the will, to remedy."

Caleb bit his lower lip to suppress a groan. "I don't want to presume too much, but it's possible you're stretching the 'sins of the father' motif a bit far."

"Perhaps you are right, so we will let it rest there for now. Are you prepared to handle the additional *diati* we can assume will become yours when he falls?"

"As ready as I can be. I could travel around confronting Inquisitors and drawing in their *diati* for the next century, and my power still would not compare to his, so 'prepared' doesn't have much meaning in this context."

"Have you discussed with your people the possibility of sending someone else after him? A team, of course, highly armed and—"

Nisi stopped and shook his head "—but even the most skilled combat team would be decimated. An antimatter bomb dropped from orbit would not kill Renato. No, you are the only one who can kill him, for you are the only one who can rob him of the *diati* which protects him."

"That was my conclusion as well."

Nisi nodded. "Nevertheless, be prepared for the aftermath to be difficult. When the *diati* first joined with me—without asking for permission—I destroyed a city block. Then another city block. Or rather, I should say the *diati* destroyed several city blocks, acting through me. Neither of us intended the destruction, for it was merely a byproduct of the struggle to find some sort of workable symbiosis, but it resulted nonetheless."

"I won't struggle. Also, I've already cleared those hurdles. If his *diati* insists on coming to me—and I hope it doesn't—the *diati* I possess will ease the transition."

Nisi dipped his chin. "Nevertheless. I cannot say if Renato now controls more or less *diati* than I once did, but I can say this: the *diati* present on Solum today is magnitudes greater in strength. Though it does not procreate in the way we imagine, as *diati* has passed through endless generations into ever greater numbers of Praesidis, it has expanded and multiplied."

Caleb sighed. He understood that for a man like Nisi, being consigned to watch from afar as the fates of his universe, his people and his family were decided was a difficult burden to bear. But the endless admonitions weren't helpful.

"Then I won't get close to any more residents than I have to in order to complete the mission. Respectfully, sir, all these concerns you're voicing? None of them matter. You said it yourself: your son, the Praesidis Primor, must die, and I'm the only one who can kill him. Reality can be a cruel master at times, but it is our master all the same. So I'll do what must be done.

"As for the rest? Maybe I'll pay a price, maybe not. I don't know what exactly will happen when he dies, but any experienced soldier or agent will tell you that you never know what surprises a mission is going to throw at you. I'm good at improvising—it's surely one reason why the *diati* chose me. Whatever happens, I'll find a way through it."

32

AFS STALWART II

M iriam stood alone in the conference room. Her words were what would matter, not her appearance, and her audience numbered in the tens of thousands. So many would never fit in the conference room, therefore....

She activated the fleet-wide comm channel.

"This is Commandant Solovy. I speak to you now as you embark on the largest and most complex military operation any of us have ever taken part in. This is no longer maneuver warfare, and all our manpower and firepower, our every talent and asset, must now be focused on our objective.

"There is no time or space for flowery words of inspiration, and you don't need me to motivate you. You know why we are here and why we must succeed today. What you need from me is to tell you how we are going to achieve victory.

"We have thirty-two separate mission targets spread across five galaxies: three regenesis facilities for each Primor, plus the Primors themselves. The mission profile for each target is unique, but they all are designed to work in concert to achieve a single overarching goal: the permanent elimination of the Directorate.

"The eight mission teams each consist of four subgroups, each one responsible for a single target. Every mission team will be multi-galactic in nature, as in every case a Primor maintains at least one regenesis location in a galaxy different from that of their home planet. This is done as a security measure, but we will overcome their security. Eight Caeles Prisms are now in operation, and we will use them all.

"We will also enjoy the assistance of our allies. Anarch agents will be taking on active roles whenever possible. The elimination of their rulers is, after all, their right. The Katasketousya will be devoting the entirety of their available vessels to this operation. Furthermore, the Novoloume are contributing twelve thousand armed and crewed warships to the operation.

"Make no mistake—even with our every resource deployed, we face a daunting task. Our targets will be heavily fortified, and we will not have the luxury of time to defeat them, for the timing required is as tight as it is critical.

"In the simplest terms, a Primor cannot be eliminated until all three of their associated facilities are destroyed—or immediately before, under the assumption they would then be eliminated with the facility. However, they also must be eliminated swiftly once the strikes begin, else they will go to ground to equip new facilities for their regenesis, and we will find ourselves back where we started. This means we have a very short window in which to accomplish a great deal, one measured in minutes rather than hours.

"We succeed, and we will have freed dozens of galaxies and species from tyranny. We succeed, and we will have saved our home, our friends and our loved ones from the looming threat of annihilation. We succeed, and everyone has a future. So let's get it done."

AR

AFS TAMAO

TARACH STELLAR SYSTEM

David took a shuttle from the *Stalwart II* to the carrier *AFS Tamao*, where his little Rasant was berthed. During the short trip over, he chatted with several of the servicepeople on the shuttle. Though he knew none of them, they all seemed to know him.

To their credit, only one person asked him if he'd started craving human flesh yet. He responded by saying he'd always craved human flesh, even in his first life, but luckily they made eVi palliative routines for that sort of thing. It had gotten the desired laugh from everyone in earshot, and he added 'witty banter with strangers' to the list of his skills that hadn't completely atrophied.

Now, in the hangar bay of the *Tamao*, he approached his craft at a brisk but deliberate pace, letting his eyes pass over the tungsten shimmer of the sleek adiamene hull in appreciation. AEGIS vessels followed neither Alliance nor Federation design guidance; they instead took a third approach in striving to balance sturdiness, agility and firepower. In truth, the technological advances embodied in AEGIS designs were so significant that the vessels by and large exceeded Alliance ones in sturdiness, Federation ones in agility, and both in firepower.

Though intellectually he recognized the reality that ninety percent of those advances had come about in the last two years, spurred on by the Metigen War and the rise of Prevos and unshackled Artificials, at times like these he nevertheless felt every day of the decades he'd missed.

But ships still flew using impulse engines and sLume drives and still fired lasers and missiles, and those he knew how to make dance.

David boarded the Rasant to find his two-man crew already at work. When he stepped through the airlock, however, they both drew to attention and saluted.

"Commander Solovy."

"Sir, welcome aboard."

"At ease, gentlemen. Lieutenant Kofe, you're the operations officer, and Lieutenant Olbert, you handle weapons and defenses, correct?" At their nods, he continued. "I appreciate the decorum, but I'm your superior officer only in the historical records."

"Respectfully, sir, you're incorrect."

"Oh?"

"Yes, sir. On board this ship, we obey your orders."

"And neither of you have a problem with this? If you do, please speak up. It'll only land you in the brig for a week—kidding. I do that from time to time."

Kofe answered. "No problems, sir. Commandant Solovy tells us to jump, we jump."

"Smart men. How high?"

"As high as we're able. Higher if we can get our hands on some of those lift-assist boots the Marines hoard."

David dropped his chin to his chest briefly, allowing a wave of pride and amusement, tinged by *sozhaleniye*, to wash over him. So Miriam had gotten to them first. He rather adored her for it.

He straightened up wearing a smile. "Good call on your part. She's worthy of your allegiance, to say the least. All right, then. I run an informal ship. Do your jobs competently and swiftly, and we'll have a grand time. If you disagree with an order I give you, if there's time I encourage you to raise your concerns. If there's not time, follow the order and hope we survive until there's time to debate the matter afterward. Any questions?"

"Only to ask if we can answer any for you, sir. The Rasant's a brand new design, and we had to undergo extensive training on it. I expect many of the systems will be unfamiliar to you, given...." Olbert trailed off, then cleared his throat awkwardly.

David shrugged and turned toward the cockpit, idly running his hand along the curving wall as he approached the pilot's chair. "I recently had some free time to study up on AEGIS technology." *While I was a quantum construct of a consciousness living in a virtual space where days could last seconds or years at my whim.* "I should be set, but I'm not above begging for help if I find myself out of my depth."

33

AFS AMBERG
MILKY WAY SECTOR 18

A starship that seemed to have been carved entirely from blown glass and be powered by light itself soared above and ahead of them. It stretched for at least two hundred meters, and in its path followed a fleet of vessels smaller in size but no less elegant in design, angels riding the wake of their guiding light.

"Damn, are those the Novoloume ships?" Kofe rushed into the cockpit to peer out the viewport—and hurriedly drew back. "Sorry, sir."

"I'm gawking right along with you, Lieutenant." David proceeded to do exactly that, staring out in awe alongside his officers. The ships glided across the stars like they were born among them, like they didn't run on mechanical engines and volatile fuel. Hell, maybe they didn't.

That the Novoloume possessed such a fleet had apparently been the second-best-kept secret in Amaranthe (the truth of the Praesidis Primor not being Corradeo Praesidis and Corradeo Praesidis being Danilo Nisi and the leader of the anarchs was, ipso facto, the best kept one). That the fleet was both staggeringly beautiful and powered by heretofore unknown engineering principles was, to David's mind, far more intriguing.

The Novoloume leader, Dean Veshnael, had specifically requested for their fleet to participate in the Idoni mission. Though it wasn't spoken of aloud, apparently the Novoloume harbored a particular loathing for the Idoni Dynasty. As it had been explained to him and Miriam, in their opinion the Idoni had taken the aspects of life Novoloume valued highest—beauty, pleasure, the pursuit of elusive *joie de vivre*—and debased and defiled them. Thus they intended to take special gratification in bombing the Idoni Primor's gauchely opulent stronghold into dust.

In a gesture of trust as well as thanks, Miriam had granted command of the space-faring portion of the Idoni mission to the commander of the Novoloume fleet. The AEGIS formations dispatched to the Idoni home system would take their orders from Pointe-Amiral Thisiame, so long as those orders remained consistent with the mission plan as well as overall operational directives.

Given as no one had ever seen a single Novoloume or one of their vessels engage in a single hostile encounter, the AEGIS formations were here in part to ensure the mission didn't crumble into abject failure. They were also here to observe and report back on the actions and performance of the Novoloume forces.

Miriam knew a thing or two about building and hiding secret fleets, and the reasons one might do so. In this case the Novoloume's reasons for doing so appeared to be in alignment with AEGIS interests, but it never hurt to double-check.

Yep. His wife had assigned him to *this* mission rather than any other because she wanted a spy she could trust. He gave thanks for the trust and chuckled to himself at being asked by her to act as a spy. He also intended to quickly step in and take command if the Novoloume forces went sideways—he assumed the permission to do so was implicit in his presence here.

Pointe-Amiral Thisiame (Idoni L2): "Wings Alpha I and Alpha II, commence attack maneuvers on target designated L2. AEGIS formations proceed in defensive maneuvers and prepare for counteroffensive response."

The small structures orbiting the gas giant, the fifth planet in the Lastisi system, didn't look so different from the Saturn and Jupiter habitats back home; the semi-solid bubbles resembled molecular diagrams, with the flexible fibers connecting them standing in for chemical bonds. Even the Anadens hadn't devised a way for organic life to live beneath the atmosphere of a gas giant.

Two of the larger connected modules flashed red on the tactical map: target L2. The medical outpost, complete with advanced regenesis lab.

In a matter of seconds the perimeter defenses went down, an act completed almost exclusively by long-range laser-based weapons on the lead Novoloume vessel. With the defenses disabled, the medical outpost now made for easy pickings.

Still, firing on it gave David a moment's pause, if only to allow for appreciation of the irony. He owed his renewed existence to many disparate things, but last and most concrete on the list was regenesis technology. In destroying this lab, he was taking away the next life from the Idoni Primor and a small segment of her progeny. But she'd existed for something like a million years—countless, endless life after life—and that was surely long enough in anyone's estimation. As for the progeny, they had ceded their fate to their Primor's whim nearly as long ago.

So be it.

He added his weapons fire to those of his comrades, and in less than twenty seconds the dual modules' hulls ruptured, their air vented into space, and the resulting shards of metal were consumed by the volatile atmosphere of the gas giant. The Novoloume ships' firepower was as impressive as their design, but this had also been the simplest part of the mission.

Now haste became the overriding directive. Word of the destruction of the Idoni regenesis lab in SMC had arrived seconds earlier. This left one lab, and one life, to end.

David executed a pinpoint sLume jump into the exosphere of Lastisi. Not until after he arrived did he realize he hadn't waited on orders from Pointe-Amiral Thisiame before doing so. Oh, well. It was a large fleet that would take time to move to the third planet in the system—

He jerked in the pilot's chair as the entirety of the Novoloume fleet materialized off to his port. *Or not.*

Pointe-Amiral Thisiame (Idoni L1): "AEGIS Lastisi-assigned formations and Wing Alpha III descend to the Lastisi surface, rendezvous point LS-X, and commence initial attack maneuvers on targets desig-nated L1A and L1B."

"All right, gentlemen, you heard the order. Let's have some fun."

"Was atmospheric traversal considered 'fun' back in the dark ages, sir?"

"It's all about perspective, Lieutenant Kofe."

"Yes, sir. Transferring forty percent of defensive shield power to Thermadap shield."

"Thank you, Lieutenant." Because AEGIS vessels were de-signed with the prospect of an alien enemy and an alien realm front-and-center, their structure didn't count on the regular avail-ability of atmosphere corridors. To counteract the punishing abuse atmospheric traversals inflicted, a new mode of shielding had been devised. The Thermadap shield buffered and redirected up to eighty-five percent of the heat and energetic forces encountered before they ever reached the primary shielding, the hull or any ex-ternal components.

Given time, it was the kind of technology that might evolve into something to challenge the Imperiums' formidable barrier shielding. Today, it simply made the ride down considerably less traumatic, for the crew and the ship.

"We will be coming in low, fast and hot to take out the strong-hold's perimeter defenses. Our wingmen are the *AFS Perth* and the *AFS Vilnius*."

The atmosphere cleared to reveal a sky black as a moonless night in a starless void. The paltry ground lighting beyond the pe-rimeter was overwhelmed by the thick and pervasive flora of a tropical ecosystem.

David tapped a spot on the HUD and a near-infrared overlay spread across the viewport.

"Full power returned to defensive shields."

"Thank you again, Lieutenant Kofe. Lieutenant Olbert, con-firm we maintain a minimum of one hundred twenty percent of normal power capacity available for both weapons and propulsion."

The Thermadap shield was a welcome convenience, but it was barely out of testing and one hell of a power drain—power he was going to need if the situation got dicey.

The *Perth* and the *Vilnius* joined him on each flank, and together they swept a scant twenty meters above a wide river for several seconds before reaching the large island the Idoni Primor called home.

"Sir, active power is at full for all systems. Reserves are at thirty-two percent and rising."

"Excellent. Inform me if reserves drop below fifteen percent."

"Yes, sir."

Commander Solovy (AFS Amberg)(Idoni L1): "Perimeter defense turret ring begins due north, distance 820 meters. Engage in four seconds."

Major Filben (AFS Perth)(Idoni L1): "Roger, Amberg."

Commander Jimenez (AFS Vilnius)(Idoni L1): "Roger."

"Olbert, fire at will on any and all turrets in range."

"Firing."

The black sky lit up around the streaks of their laser fire, then more broadly as the plasma beams of retaliation fire swept toward them in search of targets. His fingertips flowed lightly across the HUD as he spun the ship on its axis twice in a sixty degree climb, even as arcalaser fire continued to stream from his bow in a mirrored trajectory to impact one of the firing turrets.

A familiar rush of adrenaline warmed his blood vessels through to his skin from the inside out. His senses heightened and sharpened to take in a wide breadth of information all at once—more information than he could give name to but all integrating into his full perception of the tactical situation.

Two turrets eliminated, four remaining—three.

Temporary loss of environmental cover in 0.4 kilometers above seventy-eight meters, adjust vertical trajectory by 33 degrees to stay within cover.

Ideal range to the next turret will be reached in 2.3 seconds at the current velocity—

Boulders from a cliff to his starboard tumbled through the air, severed from their moorings by a stray turret beam without a target.

He sensed their approach the same instant the sensors did. A minute flick of his wrist and the ship swerved a few dozen meters to avoid the imminent collision, then immediately resumed course.

David smiled.

ℛ

LASTISI

IDONI HOMEWORLD
MILKY WAY SECTOR 18

If asked to describe their expectations of Lastisi, most people would reference the most popular entertainment centers—Plousia Chateau, Taras Cathedral, Akroti Aventa. Those who had never visited Lastisi imagined kilometers of spring-heated pools, armies of masseuse drones, overflowing spreads of fruits and desserts lining the paths, flowing rivers of *tsipouro* and, last but not least, rampant nudity.

It was a fairly accurate picture of the environment inside the Primor's compound, but the rest of the planet was, more often than not, another story.

All those hypnols had to be invented somewhere. Then they had to be manufactured somewhere. All those performers, willing and otherwise, had to be screened, judged and trained somewhere. While these events took place in other locations as well, the Primor's penchant for control being what it was meant all Idoni endeavors began and radiated outward from here.

Eren knew this already, having graced Lastisi with his presence twice in his previous life of debauchery, but several of the anarchs with him expressed disappointment on learning that factories and labs far outnumbered waterfalls and orgies.

The Primor's planetside regenesis lab stood a kilometer from the main compound, safely separate and apart from the depravities that did go on inside it. A Caeles Prism wormhole deposited the ground incursion team's transport a scant dozen meters above the roof of the compound, and the sights and sounds of powerful lasers from the aerial strike team tearing into the lab and all surrounding structures greeted them on their arrival.

They'd emerged well inside the defensive perimeter, but the defensive perimeter also now appeared to be rubble. The forward strike teams had been quite busy, not to mention effective.

Eren had lobbied hard for a very simple mission plan: he would walk alone through a little person-sized wormhole into the Primor's innermost lair, drive a blade through one of her eyes into her brain and walk out through the same wormhole—or die to her guards, whichever proved easiest. But Xanne, Brigadier Jenner and Commandant Solovy had all insisted that his plan left too much to chance, including and most prominently the chance that he might not reach the Primor before her guards felled him.

Fair enough. So instead three other anarch agents and a squad of AEGIS Marines accompanied him. They would blast their way into the compound as close as possible to the Primor's innermost lair and fight through the rest of the way.

He damn well better get to be the one to deliver the killing blow, though. The bitch owed him. She hadn't controlled his mind in a century, but she'd made him what he was, *demanded* he be it, and the humiliation of serving as her unwitting slave still stung like yesterday's wound. He felt as if he'd never truly be able to move on, to quiet his demons and make a go of salvaging a worthwhile life for himself, until she was gone. Denouement met. Ashes scattered to the winds.

He nodded to himself as a laser burned a hole through the roof below and the hatch of the transport opened. Good pep talk.

Drae ela-Machim, his anarch partner tonight in Cosime's absence, clasped his shoulder. "Are you set?"

"Never been more set."

Drae motioned toward the open hatch. Eren followed a Marine out of the transport, into the air and through the gash in the roof, then activated the dampeners to land with a modicum of grace on the shiny tile floor. His not-quite-good-as-new leg protested on impact, but he so did not care.

They'd targeted their insertion expertly, and according to the schematic of the compound they only had three rooms to fight through to reach their target. But alarms were ringing and an increasing buzz heralded the approach of drones, so fighting there would definitely be. For the Marines, at least.

He considered the far door for a second, and when no armed guards burst through it, decided the Marines could catch up. As gunfire erupted from the opposite end of the hallway and the Marines engaged compound security, Eren Veiled and made his way toward the door.

In a frothing bath sunken into the center of the floor of her spacious bedchamber, the Idoni Primor soaked herself amidst the bubbles. Her arms stretched out in either direction along the brim, which was crafted entirely of sparkling aquamarine gemstones. A mane of golden curls spilled down over her breasts into the water, where they floated lazily among the froth—the curls and the breasts. Beyond the bath and up three tiers, in the rear of the room two men, an Idoni and a Naraida, lay sprawled atop tousled bed-covers, naked and seemingly used up. Over against the left wall, a Novoloume servant arranged a platter of fruits at an elaborate bar.

The Primor's gaze fell on Eren immediately. Her head tilted in idle curiosity while a fingertip dipped into a crystal bowl beside her. "I know your face, anarch." She brought her fingertip to her mouth and sucked it dry of gods only feared what hypnol. "You have been a most troublesome little *asi* of late. Have you come here to repent, to fall to your knees and beg to be allowed to return to the fold? Fair warning—you'll be on those knees for a while."

For a second he was actually rendered speechless. She must know the compound was under attack; she likely even knew her regenesis labs were being destroyed. Still, she lounged in her sumptuous luxury as if nothing was amiss. Did she have such blind, dogged faith that her defenses would not fall? Was she too high for the severity of the crisis to penetrate her hypnol-soaked mind? Or...did she simply not care? Had she lived for too long and indulged in too many depravities to be able to summon up the slightest energy to fight for her continued existence?

Well, he could relieve her of those weighty burdens. "You present such a tempting offer, milady. But, no. It is my great pleasure— truly, you have no idea how fantastic a pleasure it is—to inform you that the party is, at long last, over. *Nos libertatem* fucking *somnia*."

He lifted his weapon and shot a plasma burst straight through her left eye. Just like he'd dreamed of.

Then he closed his own eyes and waited for the inevitable killing blow from swiftly arriving Vigil security officers. He breathed in deeply, ready to take the next breath in a regenesis capsule and begin again.

The blow never came. After an egregious number of seconds had passed, he opened his eyes and looked around.

The body of the Primor floated in crimson water foaming to pink on the surface. The Novoloume servant cowered behind the bar, and the two men on the bed continued to sleep soundly.

Was this how a hundreds-of-millennia reign of sin and unchecked libertinism ended? With averted gazes, snores and quiet sighs of relief?

Huh.

A commotion echoed behind him. He spun around to see a guard rush in, then fall ahead of Eren's companions arriving.

The Marines fanned out to secure the room, but Drae merely glanced at the body in the pool then back at him. "You were supposed to wait for us."

Eren shrugged. "One last foolishly reckless yet brilliantly heroic stunt to cap off my rebellion."

"Feel satisfied?"

He considered the body for a final moment as the water turned muddy and dark. "Feel ready to move on."

34

AFS SARATOGA

A holo of the Central Command Annex orbiting Machimis filled the front third of the *AFS Saratoga's* briefing room. The holo measured a tiny fraction of scale, as the structure itself was the size of a city. However, if the mission went according to plan, they wouldn't see more than a few rooms.

Malcolm zoomed in to the uppermost section of the space station. "At present, the Machim Primor is located in the large room that encompasses the top level of the Annex. He's been at this location for over an hour, meeting with a succession of his top lieutenants and high-level station personnel. The room is isolated from the rest of the station, with a single ingress/egress point via this vertical transit tube. Despite the presence of an MP detail and frequent visits by military officers, it's as much of an ideal location to trap him in as we are going to find. As such, we'll be moving in a few short minutes.

"Entering directly into this room using a wormhole will leave us too exposed during transit and the immediate aftermath. Therefore, the wormhole is going to deposit us...here." He shifted the holo up slightly to bring the level below into focus, then indicated a corridor.

"This location should give us sufficient cover during our entry sequence. Once everyone has reached the station interior, Major Ettore will close the wormhole until it's needed for extraction. We'll proceed to this central atrium, clear and secure it, then access the target room by way of the transit tube. It's large enough to carry the entire team, which addresses the exposure issue.

"When we breach the room, everyone is a fair target, but the Machim Primor is our number one priority. Polowski, Benoit and Shaviiz, you will guard the transit tube. Your orders are to ensure no one but us gets back out of the room."

Malcolm exhaled portentously and considered the gathered Marines. "I know the mission profile looks like a simple in-hit-and-out, but nothing about this mission will be simple. We won't be facing security guards and drones this time. Every person in that room is not merely a highly trained, experienced military officer—every person in that room has been a highly trained, experienced military officer for hundreds if not thousands of years. The same is going to be true for the vast majority of the people present on the Annex. And we won't have the benefit of a *diati* bubble to take cover inside and lick our wounds like we did on Chionis. Top of our game, Marines. Nothing less will get the job done."

"Sir, yes, sir!"

He killed the holo. "Gear up and meet at Transport #3 in ten."

AR

Brigadier Ashonye (Machim M2): "M2 target destruction confirmed."

The second of three regenesis labs down. One to go—albeit the most difficult one, on the surface of Machimis.

Brigadier Jenner (Machim MP/M2): "Acknowledged. Ambassador Requelme, MP target status?"

Her initial response came in a pulse instead of the mission channel.

'Mia' is so much faster to say. Surely there's an official 'expediency' protocol exception?

Malcolm bit back a smile, since he was surrounded by his squad.

Yes—I can simply call you 'Ambassador.'

I'm sighing, in case you were wondering.

Mia Requelme (Machim MP/M2): "The Primor's location is unchanged, but the agitation level of all present has increased *significantly in the last minute. I suspect they just got word of the de-struction of the regenesis lab at M2."*

Brigadier Jenner (Machim MP/M1): "Machimis squad, time to M1 target destruction?"

Major Berg (Machim MP/M1): "Eighty seconds."

Brigadier Jenner (Machim MP): "Major Ettore, initiate the worm-hole."

"Form up and prepare to move. We are weapons free on arrival."

Modified Reverbs were a necessary addition to their arsenal for this mission, but they complicated the weapons loadout. The best Marine still only had two hands. Given that their potential targets were virtually all Anaden, the modified Reverbs took the primary position. See an Anaden, point and kill. Straightforward and clean.

But the Reverbs were useless against drones, automated wea-ponry and non-Anadens, so Daemons and blades accompanied every Marine as well. Himself, Harper, Benoit and Pello also carried splinter and stun grenades, and Shaviiz and Redale carried heavy weapons. Their tactical gear included three layers of impact protec-tion, stowed breather masks and a flex-helmet module. A cloaked reconnaissance ship waited eight hundred meters from the Annex, should an external rescue be required.

The wormhole's amorphous border solidified.

Major Ettore (Machim MP): "Wormhole open and ready."

Malcolm motioned ahead. "Go, go, go."

MACHIMIS CENTRAL COMMAND ANNEX

MACHIMIS STELLAR SYSTEM
MILKY WAY SECTOR 36

They landed in the designated hallway, which thankfully re-mained otherwise empty.

Brigadier Jenner (Machim MP): "Wormhole traversal complete. Major Ettore, deactivate it and await further orders. Incursion team, proceed ahead to the perimeter of Point MP-2."

The large atrium beyond the hallway served as a hub for those traveling to and from several sections of the Annex, and it was crowded with Machim military personnel. Too many to individually point Reverbs at one at a time, that was for certain.

Weapons fire at this juncture would alert the Primor and the other individuals in the apex room above to their presence, at which point the mission would go sideways in a hurry.

Malcolm remained on the silent mission comm to delay their detection for a second longer. *"Pello, toss three stun grenades, maximum coverage."*

Pello lobbed the small devices in a perfect arc across the center of the room. No one had time to do more than turn in surprise before the pulses triggered, knocking everyone in range temporarily unconscious. The squad's shields provided limited protection from the stun grenades' effects, but at this distance it was enough.

Brigadier Jenner (Machim MP): "Move to the transit tube."

The tube was a tight fit for the entire squad and their gear, though they did fit. They began ascending, but not before several Machim who had been near the edge of the stun grenades' range struggled to their feet—and again collapsed to the floor when Odaka and Grenier pointed modified Reverbs at them. Straightforward, clean and *silent*.

Brigadier Jenner (Machim MP): "Crouch and prime weapons."

Mia Requelme (Machim MP): "The Primor is standing on the far side of the room from the tube, at twenty degrees past the central holo map."

Brigadier Jenner (Machim MP): "Copy that." He badly wanted to toss a handful of stun grenades into the room ahead of their entry, but the room wasn't nearly large enough to ensure his men wouldn't be caught in the stun pulses—and if that happened, the mission was over. *"We hit the room hot. Sweep and neutralize threats as you advance. With the tube guarded, the Primor won't be going anywhere, but we must secure the room. Benoit, I want splinter gre-nades at thirty and three hundred thirty degrees, but not until we're exposed. Do not tip anyone off."*

He eyed the rapidly approaching floor above. *"3...2...1...Mark!"*

Their heads cleared the floor, splinter grenades went flying, and the detonations brought chaos to their arrival.

Redale and Rodriguez charged forward. He and Harper fol-lowed then split—

"Duck!"

Malcolm instinctively obeyed Harper's order. Her arm ex-tended over his shoulder in a silent shot from the Reverb, and somewhere a body fell.

He jerked a nod at her, and they moved in opposite directions while Polowski, Benoit and Shaviiz took up defensive positions around the tube.

The floor was already thick with blood and bodies, a result of the brutally effective splinter grenades, and he devoted too much attention to keeping his footing as he moved deliberately toward the Primor's last reported location.

Major Berg (Machim M1): "Destruction of Machimis surface tar-get M1 complete."

A Machim sighted down a plasma weapon on him. Faster than he could articulate it, Malcolm decided he could reach the man be-fore he fired. Malcolm lunged forward while raising his left arm; he aimed his blade for the man's throat and barreled into him, sending them both to the floor.

The barrel of the plasma weapon jammed painfully into his side, but the blade found its mark and the gun didn't fire. The next second he was on his feet and moving again.

Yelling rose above the cacophony of combat in uneven bursts. "Don't let them—" "—blow it if—" Heavy weapons fire erupted, crisscrossing the circular room, and his ocular implant filters strug-gled to resolve the shapes of bodies and obstacles through the blinding flares.

Lieutenant Odaka (Machim MP): "I'm hit!"

Brigadier Jenner (Machim MP): "Stay down, Odaka, and signal your location to Redale. This is all over in twenty seconds."

Sustained weapons fire from the far side of the room swept back and forth in wide arcs, which wasn't going to penetrate anybody's shielding absent a focused burst.

Captain Harper (Machim MP): "This is cover fire. Push through it!"

She was right. Maybe they were trying to protect the Primor for as long as possible, or maybe they were protecting something else. His shield absorbed a blast from a Machim weapon as he took out two more enemies blocking his way. The room was less than forty meters across, but it now felt as though kilometers remained between him and his target.

Captain Benoit (Machim MP): "Too much resistance fire. Splinter grenade at twelve o'clock from the transit tube in three."

'Get clear' went unsaid as self-evident. Malcolm threw himself against the wall as the yelling turned to screams.

Mia Requelme (Machim MP): "I can't see what's happening on the far end of the room. I've lost eyes on the target."

Brigadier Jenner (Machim MP): "It'll clear soon. Hold tight."

The enemy fire lessened considerably after the grenade detonated, and he quickly resumed course. He climbed over two bodies to finally reach the target's location—

"Shit! Grenier, with me!" Malcolm didn't wait for Grenier before leaping down through the jagged, meter-wide hole burned into the floor near where the Primor had stood seconds earlier.

Brigadier Jenner (Machim MP): "Mia—"

Mia Requelme (Machim MP): "I've got him. The Primor's fleeing on foot one floor below you. I'm following."

Brigadier Jenner (Machim MP): "Captain Harper, you have the room." He landed in the atrium below, Veiled, and took off running.

Chasing a target through a city-sized structure that was filled with armed hostiles and that the target doubtless knew every square centimeter of felt like a doomed endeavor. But he had to try.

Mia Requelme (Machim MP): "He's taken a transit tube out to the perimeter torus. Entry to the tube is on your left, thirty meters."

Brigadier Jenner (Machim MP): "He's going for a ship." He added a channel to his comms.

Brigadier Jenner (Machim MP/M2): "Brigadier Ashonye, I need a blockade on the Central Command Annex with orders to shoot down any ship that tries to leave the Annex."

Brigadier Ashonye (EAS Marengo)(Machim MP/M2): "Solid copy. ETA four minutes."

It should be enough time. He reached the transit tube, Grenier a step behind him, and they sneaked inside as it began to move.

ℛ

"Polowski, Benoit, Shaviiz, stay on the tube shaft. Nobody gets in or out!" Harper whipped around at the sound of scuffling behind her. A Machim missing most of a leg dragged himself across the floor; by the time she spotted him, he had reached a body and wrangled a bulky weapon out of the dead man's clenched hand.

"On my target!" Harper lifted her Daemon and fired. Off her left shoulder, Eaton hurried to train a Reverb on the man. Dammit, she'd gone for the Daemon out of reflex, but she should have opted for the modified Reverb....

The man didn't point the weapon at any of them; instead he pointed it straight up in the air and began firing at the ceiling.

The *glass* ceiling.

His already mangled body jerked under multiple streams of fire, and whether from the lasers or the Reverb after another second the weapon clattered to the floor.

"Eaton, check him." Harper stared up at the ceiling, where cracks raced outward from the impact point like a web emerging from a spider's frenetically dancing spinnerets. "New plan—everyone down the tube, now!"

Captain Harper (Machim MP): "Ettore, we need a wormhole extraction at the insertion point ASAP!"

Nobody hesitated or questioned the order. The squad members guarding the tube disappeared down it. Verela helped Odaka into the opening to follow them, then Eaton and Pello. Finally Redale and Rodriguez. She took a last glance around to confirm all her people were below then leapt—

Brigadier Jenner (Machim MP): "Captain Harper, report."

—the ceiling shattered, and the vacuum created yanked her into the air and toward the widening hole. Her face grazed a shard of the ceiling as it broke off.

Then she was in space.

Her left hand unlatched the breather mask and slid it on while her right felt for the helmet trigger.

Her finger slipped past it, fumbled back for it.

Found it.

Pressed it.

The callous punishment of space sealed off for a few precious minutes.

ℛ

Brigadier Ashonye (Marengo)(Machim MP/M2): "We've got hostile vessels on an intercept course. Engaging."

Shit. If the fleet was occupied dispatching other Machim warships, they were unlikely to spot a single vessel departing the Annex and slithering into the crowd. His blockade was going to fail before it began.

Malcolm willed the tube to move faster.

Mia Requelme (Machim MP): "The Primor disembarked at the eleventh level and is entering the docks."

Brigadier Jenner (Machim MP): "Copy that. Grenier, be ready to move."

Major Grenier (Machim MP): "Yes, sir."

Major Ettore (Machim MP): "Incursion team is safely back at Staging Point #1, down three personnel."

Three?

Brigadier Jenner (Machim MP): "Captain Harper, report."

The tube slowed, and he positioned himself to be able to slip out before any of the other occupants moved forward.

Mia Requelme (Machim MP): "To your left, but there's a lot of security guarding the docks. I don't want to stop tailing the Primor to try to find another way in, but I can."

Brigadier Jenner (Machim MP): "Stay with him. There's no other way in—at least, not on the schematics."

Malcolm stepped out of the tube and veered left, barely dodging a drone whizzing by—and stopped short. 'A lot of security' didn't begin to cover it. Two guarded checkpoints spanned the full width of the docks' entry hall. Each one was staffed by a drone and two Machim security officers, and both boasted toggled force fields. As he watched, a new squad of drones sped in from elsewhere to take up positions in front of the entry.

There was no way in at all, invisible or not.

Mia Requelme (Machim MP/M2): "The Primor has boarded a Machim battlecruiser at docking berth C-11E."

Brigadier Jenner (Machim MP/M2): "Ambassador Requelme, if the battlecruiser departs, track it for as long as you can. I understand if it switches to superluminal you won't be able to follow. Major Ettore, Grenier and I are going to need an extraction as well. We'll find a deserted corner, then I'll transmit the location."

Brigadier Jenner (Machim MP/M2): "Brigadier Ashonye, if you can get any ships around the enemy's front line to where they can prevent that battlecruiser from leaving the vicinity of the Annex, do so. MP is on board. Stopping it is our highest priority."

He shot a final, invisible glare at the gathered security blocking him from his target. Also, why hadn't Harper responded yet?

AR

Droplets of blood floated into view inside Harper's helmet. The glass she'd been scraped by had cut her face. Droplets weren't gushes, however, which made the cut the least of her concerns.

Captain Harper (Machim MP): "AFS Reconnaissance Vessel R6-S, *requesting a pickup at my beacon's location.*"

Commander Dorosh (AFS R6-S)(Machim MP): "Solid copy, Captain. ETA fifty seconds.*"

Brigadier Jenner (Machim MP): "You had me worried there. Hang tight.*"

Captain Harper (Machim MP): "'Hang tight'? Really, sir?*"

Brigadier Jenner (Machim MP): "I'll apologize when I see you, Captain.*"

She rolled her eyes, then blinked frantically until she'd excised a droplet of blood that had drifted into the crease of her left eye.

Brook, where are you? Are you hurt?

She smiled. Morgan had attached herself to Ashonye's fleet, so she'd probably been eavesdropping and heard the pickup request.

I'm fine. You should get your ass to that battlecruiser. See to it the Machim Primor doesn't get away.

Goddammit. Okay, okay, but if you're lying and are in trouble, I'm going to be pissed.

Harper breathed in carefully; she needed to remember to conserve her limited oxygen. In the distance, beyond the Annex, explosions and other bursts of light marked the joining of the battle between Ashonye's fleet and a host of Machim warships. Too far away to catch the battlecruiser if it left the Annex, but maybe Morgan could get there first.

Closer to her location, the upper section of the Annex crumpled and broke apart. The disintegration didn't continue beyond that point, however. They must have quarantine doors that blocked off the upper section to prevent a catastrophic failure.

She breathed out.

The planet below harbored a few lit areas here and there, but it remained largely pitched into darkness. The Dyson ring destruction had dealt them a heavy blow. The Machim Primor must be so pissed…and now, more pissed.

She shivered. Cold seeped through the layers of her gear and skin into her blood and bones. Heavy tactical gear wasn't an environment suit, and the protection it provided against the ravages of space was limited.

Commander Lekkas (AFS MA-Primary)(*Machim MP/M2*): *"I'm firing on this fucking battlecruiser with everything I've got, but what I don't have are any more negative energy bombs. A little help? Anyone?"*

Commodore Yonai (EAS Copenhagen)(*Machim MP/M2*): *"In range of target in six seconds."*

Commander Lekkas (MA-Primary)(*Machim MP/M2*): *"Fucking motherfucker!"*

Silence on all channels, for a lengthy second.

Mia Requelme (*Machim MP/M2*): *"The battlecruiser activated the superluminal drive as soon as it was clear of the Annex. It's gone."*

Dammit!

Brigadier Jenner (*Machim MP/M2*): *"Acknowledged."*

Another breath in. Could she still feel her legs? She wasn't sure. It didn't matter. The recon vessel would be here in another few seconds.

Well, that's that. Brook, tell me where you are.

Without contemplating the wisdom of it too deeply, she sent her beacon info to Morgan. Because she was alone, and possibly scared.

You're hurt—you're bleeding. God, you look so cold!

She instinctively peered around her, but there was no ship. Only Morgan's consciousness was here.

I am cold. But rescue's on the way. I'll be fine.

I wish I could touch you, gather you up in my arms and spirit you away to safety.

If she'd had enough air left, she would have laughed at the picture that sprang to mind.

That's a shockingly romantic notion, but under all your attitude you're a skinny waif. In this gear I'm too heavy for you to carry.

I'd find a way.

She gazed out at the stars and the planet and the Annex and the battle and the woman who wasn't there as her vision began to darken.

I bet you would....

ΑR

"Primor on the bridge!"

Casmir elasson-Machim spun around in surprise, then belatedly snapped to attention at the sight of, yes, his Primor barreling down the bridge toward him. "Sir."

"Depart, now."

"Sir?"

"Depart the Annex this instant."

"Navigation, request clearance to depart." He studied the Primor warily. The man had appeared frazzled and distracted when he'd summarily demoted Casmir off his Imperium and to captain of a battlecruiser following the loss at Chalmun Station Asteroid. Now, he closely resembled a madman. His uniform was stained with blood and torn at the shoulder; his skin shone from sweat, and his hair couldn't be more unkempt if he'd just risen from sleep.

Most of those characteristics could be explained away by the ongoing attack on the Annex, but the attack couldn't explain the madman's taint animating his eyes. Pupils dilated, focus darting to and fro. The man who never lost a speck of composure had now lost virtually all of it.

But the compulsion toward obedience was wired into Casmir's very DNA, and he remained at attention. "Destination, sir?"

"Away from here!"

"Yes, sir. Navigation, set a course for MW Sector 59—"

"No, wait. We need to go to Taygeta."

The tactical officer cleared his throat. "Sirs, a hostile engagement with enemy forces is in progress eight megameters from the Annex. Do we not wish to assist our forces in defeating the enemy?"

The Primor motioned in the tactical officer's general direction. "Ignore it. Neither the battle nor the Annex matter. They were after me, and they know I'm now out of their reach—or I *will* be once we *depart*."

Casmir discreetly waved off the tactical officer before turning squarely to the Primor. "Yes, sir. The Experimental Weaponry Testing Facility?" It was the only reason anyone went to Taygeta.

"Correct." A glint of fervor grew in his madman eyes. "I have a plan."

A plan for what? But Casmir simply nodded. "Yes, sir. Navigation, proceed as directed. Transition to superluminal as soon as we clear the safety perimeter, before the enemy has the opportunity to target us. Sir, are you injured? Do you need to visit Medical, or have a Curative Unit attend to you?"

The hull shuddered from the impact of weapons fire. The Primor glared at the navigation officer.

"Seven seconds to superluminal, sir!"

"Good." The Primor returned his glare to Casmir. "Why would I need any such thing?"

"Well, sir...the blood." He pointed to the Primor's chest, though pointing to nearly any location on the Primor's person would have sufficed.

The Primor frowned. "I doubt it's mine. But I do need a shower and a laundered uniform. I'll be in your quarters—which is to say, my quarters."

Casmir watched the Primor swagger off the bridge while dragging both hands through his hair, which did nothing to calm it. Was calming it even the intent?

The floor vibrated beneath his feet as the superluminal engine engaged and they left the Annex, as well as the battle, behind.

Quiet returned to the bridge, and Casmir wondered what he should do next. The soothing whispers in his mind insisted that all was well, that the Primor knew best as always. But no matter how loud and insistent they grew, they could not cancel out the reality he saw with own eyes.

All wasn't anywhere close to well.

35

MELETO

"Logiel ela-Erevna is here to see you, Primor."

The Erevna Primor did not turn from her scrutiny of streaming data overlaid upon a wall of quarantined chemical and pseudo-biological mixtures. "Yes, Logiel, I received the Inquisitor's entreaty on your behalf."

Logiel nodded at the Vigil guard, who retreated out of the room, taking her response as a form of assent and his nod as a form of dismissal.

"And?"

"I took it under advisement, but intentions and efforts matter far less than results, and the result of your and the Inquisitor's stunt is that I have lost an important lab and important test subjects. An in-person appeal for mercy will not change this reality, nor will it endear you further to me."

Logiel crossed half the length of the room. "I don't dare to presume it will, Primor. Everyone knows even the smallest of your piques last a minimum of forty days and must be allowed to run its course."

The stance of her shoulders shifted. After a beat she glanced back at him. "Pardon me?"

"I'm only stating a logical, unbiased conclusion based on observational evidence, Primor."

Once he'd worked out the kinks of the integral buffering procedure on Inquisitor Nyx, he'd programmed a drone to assist him in performing the procedure on himself. After all, a scientist shouldn't be influenced by external factors, particularly those they couldn't consciously perceive.

In the days since he'd completed the procedure, he'd gradually come to understand the egregious extent to which the integral—the will of his Primor—had been doing precisely that. It went beyond shaping his inclinations and adjusting his judgment to warping his very mind. The members of the Erevna Dynasty believed themselves scientists, but in truth there was only one scientist; the rest of them were lab rats in her maze.

Now, standing here face-to-face with her, he just couldn't help himself. He should make an effort to act his proper part, but the urge to goad her, untempered as it was by any integral, proved impossible to resist.

"You know, overwrought grudges are an uncharacteristically emotional behavior from someone who's supposed to represent the pinnacle of cold, logical discernment in all matters."

"You are learning the wrong lessons from your purgatory, Logiel. Insult me again and I will render your body nonfunctional then demote you all the way to *asi* for your impudence."

"Will you?"

"How dare—"

Her tirade-in-the-making was cut short by the guard bursting back into the room. "Primor! We have reports of explosions at the regenesis lab on the Castor #2 Orbital, as well as of a security breach of the grounds by combat forces."

They blew up one of her regenesis labs? Were they—the anarchs, the Humans, whoever—intending on blowing up them all? How interesting. Perhaps his petulant act of rebellion would prove to be more effective than he'd anticipated.

"What grounds?"

The guard frowned. "Uh, these grounds, Primor. Here. Your compound."

The Primor scowled and began to pace in a tight circle. "Maximum security alert, obviously. Lock me in here and make certain they don't make it through that door. Understand?"

"Our security is moving to intercept the attackers, but—"

"Understand?"

"Yes, ma'am. We'll guard this door with our lives."

"And with your weapons, please."

"Y-yes, ma'am." The guard spun and left. The door closed again, followed soon thereafter by the slick hiss of security locks engaging.

"It appears you are stuck with my whimpering, sniveling self for the time being."

The barb hardly earned a glare. "Sit down and be silent. I need to work."

"You're going to continue working on some esoteric research project while your home is under attack from armed intruders?"

"Yes. If I stopped working upon the eruption of every potential distraction, no work would ever be completed."

Incredulous, he shook his head. "At least I know where my blind arrogance came from." He'd muttered it under his breath, and she pivoted back to the data streams as if she hadn't heard him. Possibly she hadn't. Possibly all the stress was tiring her barbed tongue.

Once he was confident her focus had in fact returned to her work, he palmed the blade he'd brought with him. Security hadn't checked him for weapons, because what Erevna carried weapons? In truth he wasn't overly adept at wielding it, but he'd practiced on several pieces of cushioned furniture yesterday.

He made sure the hilt of the blade was secure in his grip before he quietly approached her, one soft step at a time.

When he was two meters away, she sensed him drawing near. "Observe the data if your curiosity is so great, but take care that you don't interfere."

"Whatever you say, Primor." He cocked his arm and plunged the blade into the base of her neck.

Effective death was instantaneous, for his aim was true and the blade severed the bundle of nerve fibers in her brain stem. Long the puppeteer, she crumpled to the floor like a marionette whose own strings had finally been cut.

He stepped away from the expanding pool of blood seeping across the floor as the walls shook from the first of what he expected would be many explosions. After scanning the contents of the lab, he chose a chair that both offered an unobstructed view of the door and was situated well clear of the body and its excretions.

Then he sat down and waited.

R

Ten minutes of increasingly louder and more frequent rumbles and booms later, a final explosion blew out the door and much of the wall surrounding it. A dozen soldiers—mostly Human, plus a few presumed anarchs—rushed inside the lab.

Logiel held his hands in the air and took care not to make any threatening gestures, or even to move from his chair at all. "Don't shoot. I surrender. Further, I request for you to take me into protective custody. As you can see, I've already accomplished the last bit of work for you."

36

SOLUM

S olum evoked a sensation akin to lingering déjà vu in the wake of a dream.

It was *not* Earth. Its city-planet architectural stylings hid the outline of continents that might have otherwise been recognizable and altered the vibrant blue-and-green color palette enough to erase any familiarity in its silhouette.

Yet if you tilted your head just *so* and let your gaze unfocus a little, you could almost see Earth. Its echo, its memory.

Honestly, the sight of it made Caleb long for Seneca. He hadn't sought out its twin here in Amaranthe; he didn't know if it was inhabited, or if it bore a name that would have no meaning for him. What he longed for in moments like this was the elusive comfort that came from *home*, and it couldn't be found here.

He squeezed Alex's hand and returned her wistful smile, the one that said she struggled with much the same sentiments as he did. Then he teleported from the *Siyane* to the planet below.

Their visit to Machimis had somewhat prepared Caleb for the visual assault of a Primor homeworld, and indeed Solum and Machimis had a lot in common: buildings and outdoor spaces alike built an unknown distance above the surface, soaring sky-bridges winding like vines through the rarefied heights of towering structures, endless activity, every meter pruned and buffed to perfection. But where Machimis had been dominated by dull gray metals and an overcast sky, Solum was, if not quite colorful, at least *brighter*. A notable sprinkling of parks and other green spaces dotted the landscape, and the sun peeked in and out from behind fluffy clouds. *Earth clouds.*

He noted all this from a position high above the tallest building in the region, for one reason above all. Virtually everyone here was Praesidis, and even a kilometer above the artificial surface the air felt thick with *diati*. It seeped out from the people's skin and clogged the thoroughfares.

Coming into this, he'd worried about the Primor detecting his presence too soon, but it wasn't going to be a problem. No, the problem was shaping up to be that the instant he neared anyone here, their *diati* was apt to rush to join his. And there were people *everywhere*.

Lucky break that he could teleport—and fly—for he'd never have managed an infiltration of the Praesidis Command tower beginning at the ground level. There must be a thousand Praesidis in the building. More?

Nisi might have raised a valid concern over his ability to absorb so much new *diati* after all. But there was nothing to be done about it, then or now. He was the only one who was capable of accomplishing this task. He was here, the show was on and the clock was ticking, so he would manage. He would be careful and he would get it done.

This place is amazing. Objectively.

He smiled to himself. When the time came, Alex would be taking over for the AEGIS Prevo tasked with surveilling the Primor via sidespace, but while they waited for the other teams to complete their assignments, she was taking a tour of Praesidis Command.

The building, the city or the planet?

The city is the planet. I meant the inside of Command, mostly. Anyway, I'll stop gawking now and head up...and up and up.

He distracted himself from the buzz of the *diati* calling to him from every direction by monitoring the mission channels. The Praesidis regenesis labs on Europa and on a space station in LMC weren't proving to be too much trouble, but the one here could be a bit dicier. For one thing, it was *here*, inside Praesidis Command.

He'd considered visiting it first and destroying it with a single gesture, except doing so stood to alert the Primor to his presence critical seconds before he arrived to confront the man. Instead, once the remote labs had been destroyed, one of the AEGIS Prevos would open a wormhole from a staging planet. A Marine would toss a set of remote-detonation bombs through it, the Prevo would close the wormhole, the bombs would be detonated, and the Prevo would confirm via sidespace that they had done their job. The next instant, Caleb would make his move. It was a simple, straightforward plan.

Field Marshal Bastian (SFS Leonidas)(Praesidis P2): "All Europa formations, advance on target P2 and commence assault."

Brigadier Belosca (SFS Pyrgos)(Praesidis P3): "LMC target P3 destruction confirmed."

Almost time.

Alex?

This place is enormous, but I've almost reached the penthouse. Here we go. This seems to be a living area, while this...okay. Wow.

What?

Nothing. It's just...he looks so much like the visuals I've seen of your father. Sorry, but be prepared for that. All right, the location is, unsurprisingly, the top floor. He's in a mostly open room—some kind of workspace—on the southeast side of the building. I can see outside from here, so this is the outermost ring. Directly out from the windows is a space elevator—kind of far away, but it's the closest one to Praesidis Command. Can you triangulate from those markers?

Field Marshal Bastian (Leonidas)(Praesidis P2): "Europa target P2 destruction confirmed."

He moved in front of the space elevator and faced Praesidis Command.

I can.

Excellent. Also, he looks agitated. Not surprising, I guess.

Major Phelar (Praesidis P1): "Solum target P1 wormhole active. Bombs deployed. Stand by."

His *diati* stirred anew, aflutter at the nearness of such a great concentration of its brethren in such close proximity. Anticipation hummed through his bones.

The façade of the tower rumbled; a third of the way up windows shattered.

Major Phelar (Praesidis P1): "Solum target P1 destruction confirmed."

Caleb Marano (Praesidis P1/PP): "Acknowledged. All forces vacate the area of Praesidis Command. I'm going in."

The Primor's location is unchanged, beyond some angry pacing. Good luck, priyazn.

Thanks, baby.

He'd been suppressing the *diati's* rumblings as much as possible, but now he opened himself up to its desires. *Do you want this new power? You want it to join with you, with me? Then let us invite it in.*

At the same time, he allowed his heartrate to slow and decades of experience to take over, enhancing his senses and focusing his intentions.

He blinked and stood inside the expansive penthouse.

The man striding back and forth along the windows immediately spun toward him, shock on his face—

—dear god, it was his father's face. Alex had tried to warn him, but even so only a lifetime of honed discipline kept his focus in the here and now.

PROTECT

His *diati* expanded out beyond his skin to form an impenetrable barrier as a stream of power hurtled across the room to slash at him...and be quietly absorbed into the barrier.

The Primor didn't notice. They never noticed until it was too late. "You are Nyx's mysterious adversary. Come to what, kill me? You know that is impossible."

"No, it was impossible to kill your father. He sends his regards, by the way."

A sharp intake of air accompanied the flash of horror crossing the Primor's features. He buried it beneath a murderous scowl and lashed out again.

COME. JOIN WITH ME. I'M THE ONE YOU'VE BEEN LONGING FOR.

The rush of new power rendered him heady. *Focus.* He took a step toward the Primor, then another. He didn't attack, content to let the man send out strike after strike, with each one draining his own power and strengthening Caleb's.

"My father had vastly more power than I did when I vanquished him and took it for myself. You will be no different."

Caleb smirked. "I won't bother to point out the flaw in your reasoning. But please, do try." He spread his arms out wide. "Kill me."

"To the Styx with you!" The surge of *diati* pouring forth from the Primor shook the walls, ceiling and floor until the windows on the wall behind Caleb shattered. Caleb stumbled a single stride backward as the *diati* overwhelmed its own barrier and forced its way through his skin. Dizziness washed over him.

Must focus. Must remain in control.

He blinked, hard, and regained his step.

The Primor looked dismayed if not pathetically befuddled. "What...?"

"Haven't you figured it out yet, *Renato*? Or maybe you simply cannot admit aloud what you've always known in your heart. You. Are. Unworthy. What you took by force never truly belonged to you. And now, it's eager to return to someone who deserves to wield it." Did he believe this? He believed himself more worthy than this cowardly murderer, which was all that mattered here and now.

"It can't! It obeys me!"

Caleb now stood close enough to the Primor to viscerally feel the agitation of the *diati* the man still controlled. Another step and the matter would be out of his hands.

"It obeys whomever it damn well pleases." He stepped forward.

The *diati* he'd absorbed in all the encounters until this one was but a droplet of an ocean, a single star of the cosmos.

Control.

He flew backward and possibly hit a wall, or a window; it registered only as a distant, hollow thud. The Primor flew in the opposite direction, into a much closer window. Amid blurred, swimming vision Caleb saw it shattering and the man falling through it to plummet a very long way down. Fitting.

He breathed in, but his skin burned. It felt stretched, as if every cell strained under the pressure of the new power. All around him the air buzzed with free *diati* waiting to be allowed inside him.

Control control control.

He needed to get out of here. He envisioned the *Siyane*—

—a door across the room opened to allow a man to rush inside—

—the *diati* ripped itself out of the Inquisitor's body so violently the man dropped dead on the spot. It collided with more of itself before it ever reached Caleb and ricocheted away. It found another Praesidis, and the process repeated itself.

The *diati* pressed in on him as strongly as it pressed outward, demanding an outlet, until it drove him to his knees.

LEAVE, MUST LEAVE, GO

He felt the leading edge of the power surge through the building, touching new Praesidis as it came upon them, ripping their own *diati* out of their bodies and adding it to the collective. He felt their deaths.

He tried again to impose his will on a force that now existed more outside his body than within it. But he was nothing in the face of its potency, a speck of dust caught in the throes of a maelstrom of elemental power.

Suddenly he was outside, though he had no recollection of having traveled there, floating in the air above Praesidis Command. Still the *diati* tore through the corridors and corners of the building. With each new Praesidis it touched its strength grew and its reach expanded, touching more and more and taking more and more.

OBEY ME. BE CALM. BE CONTENT.

But the new *diati* did not know his voice or his guiding hand and, for these terrifying seconds, it had no master.

Perhaps the *diati* could no longer control itself, either. How did he expect to exert control over something that lacked the capacity to be controlled?

The edifice of the building shuddered.

NO

It listed to the left, rocked by greater turbulence.

NO, STOP THIS. STOP!

The soaring structure collapsed, level upon level buckling beneath those above it, crushing untold hundreds or thousands of people as it fell. The storm of *diati* surrounding him reached out and called to its brethren now freed of their bondings, and reality began to lose its coherence....

...cornflower blue sky, upside down...

...façades and passageways cracked open above him...people fell in, then buildings...

...the cracks collapsed deeper into the ground, racing toward a horizon that receded...

...a force pulled him down—no, up—away from the madness of a splintering world...

...a thundering roar shook the air and the sky as something fell...something big...

...confused and disjointed voices in his head...the *diati* of thousands of former souls whipping in and out of his perception...

...even as his perception whipped in and out of existence...

...where?...

...clouds...

...blackness...

...stars...

...looming shadows...

...finally a surface...gray, dust in the air agitated by the roiling power that brought him here...

...madness...

…it followed him through skies and stars…

…to drown him…

…he clung to the faintest strand of his own consciousness, his own soul, for he could hold on to nothing else….

37

LUNA

"Valkyrie, where did he go?"

'Caleb's locator puts him on the surface of Solum's moon, outside of any settlements.'

Away from the planet, at least. "Precisely where?"

Coordinates streamed into her mind while she yanked on her environment suit, foregoing every safety check she'd ever learned.

'Alex, we will try to help him together, but it is far too dangerous—'

She grabbed the little module she used to access the circuitry of the ship, bypassed Valkyrie and fired up the Caeles Prism.

'Alex—'

She opened a wormhole in the middle of the cabin, its exit point at the coordinates Valkyrie had given, and ran through it.

A writhing cloud of crimson *diati* thrashed around Caleb. Dear god it must be two hundred meters wide before it even began to thin.

He struggled to stay on his hands and knees as tendrils whipped into him, sending him jerking to the surface. He straightened and pushed up to his knees, but the attacks continued.

Behind her a planet was disintegrating, but she didn't care. She let go of the wormhole and her connection to the ship and hurried toward him. "Caleb!"

He tried to scramble away. "No! Don't come any closer! I can't control it—it'll hurt you!"

"No, it won't." She strode into the crimson haze.

"Please—" A long, snaking coil of *diati* soared in from behind and above her. It wound around his body and lifted him into the air, then snapped him backwards so violently it should have broken his spine. He floated horizontally a meter above the ground, and his body jerked as if seizing. She gasped in horror, frozen for an instant before forcing herself onward. Faster.

The haze grew thicker, penetrating the environment suit to tickle her skin until it began to burn. She pressed on.

Abruptly he collapsed onto the basalt surface. His skin began to glow, more and more luminous until it matched the surrounding air. Bit by bit, he was absorbing the *diati*, willingly or no.

A stray tendril caught her in the shoulder on its way toward him, and she stumbled.

"Alex, go! *Please*, I can't...." He floated upward again, jerked twice, and again dropped to the ground.

"I'll be all right." She pushed through what felt like molasses, the pressure of power thick in the air. She was almost to him.

His lips moved wordlessly, and her ocular implant focused in to read them.

don't hurt her don't hurt her don't hurt her don't hurt her

Her hand came to her mouth to stifle a gasp and instead slapped against the faceplate of her helmet. Tears blurred her vision as she fought for the last two steps and crouched beside him. "See? It didn't hurt me. I'm right here."

So much in the way. She collapsed her helmet, yanked the breather mask up and over her head—as always, breathable air surrounded him—and tugged her gloves off.

She brought her hand to his cheek. The power made her teeth rattle and her hair stand on end, but she hadn't lied. It wasn't *hurting* her.

He gulped in air when her skin touched his. She smiled bravely and stroked his cheek. "It's okay. I'm right here. I'm right here."

Diati swirled in a vortex around them, but it seemed as if it began to calm a bit. Not malevolent, just *wanting*.

She brought her other hand to his chest and leaned in closer. "I love you. I love you. You can tame this power. I know it. I know you can. I believe in you. I'll help you." She kept murmuring, stringing soothing words together as best she could and keeping both hands on him, touching his skin.

Ever so slowly the storm began to quiet. The tendrils dancing around him, darting in and out and through his body, gradually thinned and calmed. Though it appeared to dissipate out into space, she suspected in reality it was absorbing into him. His skin continued to glow like a florid sunset, but it cooled to something below a raging fever.

Time had ceased to have meaning when he blinked several times and brought a hand up to cover hers. His eyes focused on her, for the first time, as crimson bled out of them in jagged tears. "You mad, reckless woman. I could have killed you."

"No, you couldn't have."

"*It* could have."

"Was worth the risk." She sniffled, but she didn't dare remove a hand from him to wipe the tears away. "And hey, it worked."

He struggled to prop himself up on his elbows. His voice sounded scratchy and hoarse, like his throat shredded every word as it passed through. "It's not over, not yet. But I can...think. I can breathe. I—" His gaze locked beyond her shoulder, and the next second he leapt up to his feet, hauling her up with him. "We have to move!"

She caught a brief glimpse of fire in the corner of her vision as he pulled her close—then the scene changed.

He stumbled for two steps as *diati* renewed its dance around him, but righted himself.

She looked around in confusion. "Where are we?"

"Phobos—or whatever they call it here. We should be safe this far away."

The profile of a planet rotated into view beyond the craggy, barren horizon, but it bore scarce resemblance to the Mars she knew—for it had been terraformed from pole to pole.

"God, no…."

She spun back to him, then followed to where his stare led. Against the blackness of space a new star flared into existence, all red and gold and magnitudes brighter than any object save the sun.

Solum.

Caleb fell to his knees, but not because the *diati* forced him down. His expression passed through horror into desolation. Tears streamed freely down his cheeks. "What have I done?"

She dropped down beside him and wound her arms around him as a sob wracked his chest. "This was not you."

"I…." His breath hitched between sobs, but no further words came.

All she knew to do was draw his face into her chest and hold him as the strongest man she'd ever known fell into despair.

PART VI:

WEIGHT OF THE WORLDS

*"I have traveled like a fool in the desert,
and I've crawled on shards of broken glass.
Followed my demons after midnight,
and I woke up with scars across my chest.*

*"I have sung in the twilight with a lover.
I've slept in the bitterness of death.
I met a stranger in the mirror,
and I have fought that man with my last breath."*

— *Drew Holcomb, "Fly Home in the Morning"*

38

AFS STALWART II

"Destroyed? Can you be more precise? It can't be correct—" Miriam's face lit up when she saw David walk in, and damn if it wasn't a beautiful sight "—very well. I'll expect your formal report within the hour."

She ended the comm and rushed to meet him halfway, then pulled up short just out of reach. "You came back."

David's gut twisted into knots for the four thousandth time since returning to conscious awareness. The pain he'd caused her...Richard was right. It could never be undone. His only recourse was to pile happiness, joy, devotion and comfort on top of it for the rest of his days, and hope that one day it would be enough for the balance to shift.

"I did. Sooner this time."

Miriam exhaled and stepped forward, bringing her hands to either side of his face. He welcomed her into his arms, and they stood there embracing for many seconds, silently, not needing words.

Finally she eased back and studied him with a formal mien. "How did it go?"

He shrugged nonchalantly and glanced around, noticing for the first time that they weren't actually alone. Two of the Prevos—Mia Requelme and Devon Reynolds—sat at the table, but their blank expressions suggested their minds were literally elsewhere. Two aides busied themselves with organizing incoming reports. Everyone else was presumably still en route from their missions or attending to post-mission details. Not a surprise that he was one of the first to arrive, as he *had* docked on the *Stalwart II* instead of the *Tamao* and rather sprinted straight here.

"For me? I spent most of the mission gawking at the Novo-loume ships. Damn grace in motion, and impressive firepower, too. They did well. What was the comm about? What got destroyed? Something we didn't intend to destroy, I assume?"

She frowned. "According to Bastian, Solum."

"Earth's doppelganger planet? I admit I'm new around here, but we don't have weapons capable of destroying a planet, do we?"

"It wasn't a weapon."

They both spun toward the door at the sound of Alex's voice, instantly recognizable even at a whisper. Miriam rushed toward her, an inherently motherly act. "What happened? Are you all right? Is Caleb?"

Alex stared out past Miriam. Her hands balled into fists, shaking as she fought to keep them at her sides, and for a second he worried she might punch the wall.

David felt the encroaching dread of tragedy, like a shadow eclipsing the sun. He stepped closer. "Alex, what is it?"

Alex's gaze darted erratically around the room. "Can we step outside? Go somewhere private?"

Miriam nodded. "Of course. Major Halmi, you have the comm." She urged Alex through the door and down the hall to the back door to her office. As soon as they were inside and the door closed, she grasped Alex by the shoulders. "What happened?"

Alex's brow furrowed, as if perplexed by the question. "Caleb is alive. He's not hurt—he's fine, physically. Sort of. The Praesidis Primor is dead...and so are millions, or maybe billions, of other Praesidis. I assume some other Dynasties' people, too, and aliens. Whoever was on Solum."

Miriam regarded her daughter strangely. "Are you saying that Solum *was* destroyed? The entire planet?"

"It's space dust. The *diati*...." She shook her head roughly and lifted her chin. "I'm sorry. I need to get it together, because you need to hear this from me. When Caleb stripped the Primor of his *diati*, it proved to be far too much power for Caleb to absorb at once. The excess boomeranged off in all directions. It propelled the Primor out of the building to fall to his death, but it also encountered other Praesidis inside the building. It stripped them of their *diati* as well, and the mass of power kept growing.

"Caleb...it kept trying to return to him, but it was too agitated, running out of control. If there was one redeeming act on its part, the *diati* that's been a part of him for a while now got him out of there, away from the destruction the rest of it was wreaking. Then the building collapsed, more Praesidis died, their *diati* bolted, and the whole city—planet—started coming apart as the *diati* belonging to millions of Praesidis broke free of its hosts to run wild.

"By the time I got to Caleb he was on Luna, barely conscious. The *diati* kept being drawn to him, and it had encased him in this massive vortex until it found its way in. I tried to help calm it...I guess I succeeded a little. He regained enough lucidity to transport us to Phobos as Solum's core collapsed."

Alex covered her mouth with a hand to stifle a cry. "Um, so, we're...I'm fine, but I shouldn't leave him alone for much longer. He's trying his damnedest to get all this new power under control, but it's going to take time. He's afraid he'll accidentally damage the *Siyane*, so he's gone to Chionis. 'At least everyone there is already dead,' he said."

Her eyes rose to meet each of them in turn, and the haunting, bleak desperation in them broke David's brand new heart. "He blames himself. He's of the belief that he killed most of a Dynasty and all of a planet. He's wrong. I was there. I saw it happen. He was at the mercy of the *diati* same as everyone—he was just lucky it wanted him alive. Goddammit, it wasn't his fault. You need to tell everyone that."

Her jaw locked, and he suspected she again fought a powerful urge to commit violence on *something*. "I think our people who were on the mission are okay. All the labs were destroyed before the confrontation, no one was on the ground when it happened, and there was enough warning before the planet...exploded to get clear. So mark the mission as a fucking success and carry on with what you need to do. Neither of us will be at the post-mission meeting. I'm not sure when…." Tears began flowing down her cheeks, though it was anger which flared in her eyes.

David reached out and drew her close. "Oh, *milaya*. I'm so sorry." Over Alex's shoulder he met Miriam's gaze, and his concern reflected starkly in her expression. "Tell us what you need. We'll take care of all the war business."

She nodded and pulled away. "I need…I need this fucking…I'm sorry. Thank you. I love you both, but what I need right now is to go. I have to get back to him." She accepted Miriam's hand briefly, then spun and was gone. Only then did it occur to him that she must have wormholed directly onto Deck 1 of the *Stalwart II* and was likely now departing the same way.

Miriam watched Alex leave, and her focus remained on the empty doorway for several seconds before she turned to him. "I'm not certain I know what to do."

"For them, or about the Council?"

She smiled sadly. "'For' them. You're wonderful, do you realize that? I think I meant either." She squeezed her eyes shut and sank against the wall beside the door. "She's alive and physically unharmed, as I suppose is he, so first I have no choice but to think of the mission. Sometimes I really hate being in charge."

"No, you don't."

Her eyes opened to glare at him, though it lacked conviction. "Yes, I *do*. But I am in charge. The objective was achieved. The Praesidis Primor was eliminated. The collateral damage from these events will play hell with public opinion, however, and I've honestly no idea how the anarchs will react."

"Nisi won't be happy."

"His son's dead, yes, but he approved the assassination ahead of time."

"True, but I doubt he holds much ill will toward the rest of the Praesidis. They're his descendants, and were once his family."

"I suppose you're right. At the same time, if anyone appreciates what the *diati* is capable of, it's him. In fact, he should have warned us it was capable of this level of destruction." Her shoulders sagged a fraction. "In an empire that encompasses fifty galaxies, the loss of a single planet, while tragic, will not bring civilization to a halt. The Directorate's gone, however, and the empire is leaderless, so we can't stand around paralyzed. We need to move forward, and swiftly." Her lips curled up wryly. "Care to call me a cold-hearted bitch?"

"No. You're looking out for the safety, security and future of everyone, because you must." He brought a hand to her cheek. "I know the burden is weighty. So does Alex."

"I believe her when she says this wasn't Caleb's fault. He can perhaps be ruthless when the situation requires it, but he would never deliberately kill innocents, much less do something like *this*."

"But that's not the same thing as being absolved of responsibility."

She considered him warily. "No, it's not. The responsibility falls on me."

"What?"

"I gave the order for him to eliminate the Praesidis Primor, recognizing full well the unpredictability of the power I was putting into play. I knew Caleb had struggled to absorb large quantities of new *diati* in previous confrontations, and I knew the Primor controlled magnitudes more of it than anyone he'd encountered. I knew the potential consequences were many and deadly. But I needed the Primor dead, and my son-in-law was the only one who could make it happen. So, yes, I own this one."

"Miri...." He took her hands in his and kissed her softly on the forehead. "Forget what I said a moment ago—I only thought I knew the burden was weighty."

"It is what it is. I'll manage."

"You always do what is required in the circumstances."

"Yes. I do. Even when it means feelings and family have to take a back seat to duty." Her nose scrunched up in frustration, and she pulled her hands away to drag them down her face. "Do you think she'll be all right? Physically, I mean. Caleb being devastated over the deaths of a host of people is surely preferable to him being too drunk on power to care, but I have to wonder…what is this power going to do to him? Is she safe with him?"

"Yes. I may not have many answers, but I do know that he would die before hurting her."

"Except he can't die—not while the *diati* insists on sharing his body. Also, he's not necessarily the one making those decisions. Thirdly, how do you know? I frankly expected you to, if not dislike him, at a minimum be exceptionally wary toward him."

"Because he's Senecan? Because of his former profession? Because of what his father did?"

"Yes."

He shrugged in answer. "Logical expectations, but I've forced myself to put aside any acrimony toward the Federation, because this is a different world and I can't afford to hate everyone who's associated with my former enemy. Mostly, though, I suspect I got imprinted with a healthy dose of warm fuzzies toward Caleb back when I was part of Valkyrie, and by extension part of Alex."

"It's probably for the best. One conflict we don't need, right?" She sighed. "Most of the Council members will be arriving soon, and I still can't figure out if the meeting needs to be a celebration or a wake." She dropped her head on his shoulder. "Do you remember when the Alliance was the good guys, the Federation was the bad guys and life was simple?"

"No. But I do remember when we pretended life was that simple so we could do our jobs and occasionally sleep at night."

39

AFS SARATOGA

Morgan sat beside the medical cot, elbows on her thighs and hands pressed together at her chin, almost as if she were praying. Which she wasn't. If gods had ever existed, they'd been slain by their creations long ago.

No, if she'd learned anything in her life—a debatable assumption, granted—it was that the world gave you what you took from it. She controlled her life. She made her choices, good ones and bad, and embraced the consequences.

Yet the consequences of this choice terrified her in a way few ever had, and she didn't know what to do about it.

If I may interject, you chose to be with her some months ago. Unless you are revisiting this choice now—and I hope you are not—I struggle to understand what troubles you now.

Stop eavesdropping, Stanley.

I cannot prevent doing so when you speak so loudly in your mind. If you wish, I can remain silent and act as though I do not hear what you think, but it will be a charade.

Fine. It's not the choice to 'be' with her tormenting me. It's the choice that lay farther down the path, the one no one warned me about.

And it is?

The choice to let go.

To let go of her? Then you are *revisiting the earlier choice.*

No, Stanley. Damn you can be dense. To let go of myself.

Harper stirred on the cot, and Morgan hurriedly wiped away some stupid dampness which had found its way onto her cheek and straightened her posture.

It took another few seconds before the woman's bleary eyes shifted over and found Morgan. Her face instantly screwed up into a grimace. "Crap. Is it that bad? Am I dying?"

"What? No. You're fine. A little oxygen-deprivation-induced organ stress and a touch of decompression sickness, but you'll be out of Medical in a few hours and back to beating the shit out of weaponized mechs by tomorrow."

"Then why do you look like you're on your way to a funeral?"

"Because..." Morgan pushed a harsh breath from her lungs "...because I am. My own funeral. You've ruined me. Utterly and fatally *ruined* me. I used to be, well, you know what I used to be—"

"A callous, brash daredevil strung out on adrenaline and alcohol?"

Morgan pursed her lips. "Okay, also that. I prefer to focus on my better qualities, but the point's the same. Now I'm holding vigil at a bedside, gnashing my teeth and bloody *weeping*. I can't work, I can't think—I can only wait for you to wake up and worry about the next time I'll be sitting by your medical cot wondering if this is the time you *don't* wake up."

Harper pushed up to a sitting position, wincing at some ache the movement triggered. "But you said I was fine."

"Another thirty seconds without rescue and you wouldn't have been. A tear in your gear or a rip in a hose when you were sucked out of the Annex and you wouldn't have been. Ugh." She stood and dropped her hands onto the edge of the cot. "Brook, can you *please* stop trying so hard to die?"

"I...I'm just doing my job. Are you asking me to quit being a Marine?"

"No. You're too good at it, and I get how you need things to hit periodically. Besides, it's sexy when you hit things. Listen, I know you've seen a lot of bad. I know you've seen horrors and even had to do things that make you question humanity's worth. *Your* worth. As far as I'm concerned, the verdict's still out on everyone else, but not on you. You're overflowing with worth—to the people you defend and save, to your squadmates, to your friends and, far and away most importantly, to me."

"Morgan—"

She held up a hand. "Let me finish, as I'm unlikely to be in such a bleeding heart, soul-baring state ever again. No, I'm not asking you to quit being a Marine. Neither of us is destined for tea-time beside a picket fence. We'll live large and violently, and one day it will kill us. I just…tell me when you go on these 'outnumbered and outgunned, against all odds' missions, you *want* to come back. Tell me you believe you *deserve* to come back. Tell me you're not chasing after the next mission because you're hunting for a worthy foe you can die at the hands of. Tell me those things, and I can return to working, and flying, and making snide remarks, and fooling the world into thinking I don't give a shit."

Harper stared at her wearing an incomprehensible expression. "I suppose now you've gone and given me a reason to want to come back."

"No! Do not put this responsibility on me. The reason is *you*. You want to come back because you're amazing and badass and the world needs you to continue gracing it with your awesomeness. Say it, dammit."

"I'm not saying that aloud. I would sound ridiculous."

"Say it."

"No."

Morgan growled and leaned in close over the cot. "*Say it.*"

"I love you, but I'm not saying it."

"You get out of this cot and we get to any random accommodations where we have a speck of privacy, and I'll make you say it."

"No, you won't." Harper grabbed Morgan's hands and held them tight. "Let me want to come back for you, all right? You stubborn, infuriating woman, let me need you. For fuck's sake, let go and be okay with needing me, too."

Her breath caught in her throat.

Ahem. I believe this moment is referred to in common parlance as 'checkmate.'

Shut up, Stanley.

40

SIYANE

From nothingness, existence.
From existence, awareness.
From awareness, creation.
From creation, life.
The emergence of perception—of space, of materiality, of substance, of sequentialness.
Particles into atoms into molecules into dust into gases.
The perception of forces in conflict, of push and pull, of yin and yang.
Gravity into mass into stars into galaxies.
Accretion disks into nebulae into planets.
The perception of order, of complex systems, of forces in synergy.
RNA strands into proteins into cells into flesh into breath.

Caleb gasped awake and forced his eyes open.

Echoes of the cosmos faded to the background in the presence of *substance* damp material against his back and *materiality* a soft blanket *conflict* tangled around his *flesh* legs. Concerned silver-gray eyes stared down at him from a *systems* frame of messy burgundy locks. He was on the couch, and *synergy* Alex knelt beside him.

Her fingertips brushed across his cheek. "Are you okay? You were having a nightmare."

A loaded question. He blinked until the echoes fell silent. No, he was not okay. The ache in his chest burned so deeply it would sear his flesh away if the *diati* wasn't there to heal it as quickly as it began to char. He was his worst nightmare come true, every warning of the dangers of too much power come to fruition. His gallant heart had been measured and found wanting.

But he had also slept, a few fitful minutes born of exhaustion. And in the dawning of wakefulness, he recognized the greater degree of control he now had over the savage power residing in him. It roiled and throbbed still, but it stayed where it was told.

He offered Alex a weak shrug and answered a slightly different question. "It wasn't a nightmare, merely the *diati* waxing philosophical about its origins. Which are...interesting. If I'm interpreting what I saw correctly, it was here at the beginning."

"The beginning of what?"

"Everything. The universe. I think it showed me the Big Bang."

"Incredible." She sank down on the floor beside the couch and rested against the low table. "What else did you see?"

"It's not so much seeing as...acknowledging, but I saw cosmic creation, destruction, the energetic forces of space thrashing their way through adolescence. Then, gradually, order and structure formed: stars, galaxies, planets. Life. What I can't quite decipher is...whether the *diati* was a bystander, a participant or...the sculptor."

"Are you suggesting the *diati* might be 'God'?"

He winced. How to put the esoteric impressions into words? "I don't know. In the literal sense of the creator of the universe? It's possible. Maybe after it set events in motion, it dispersed itself into countless particles to live amongst its creation. Or maybe it is—or was, before it became diminished—the manifestation of what one might call the 'consciousness' of the universe. Or maybe it was only the mechanism, acting at the direction of something yet older and more incomprehensible."

"Well...since you control what has to be like ninety-five percent of the *diati* in existence now, an argument could be made that makes you a god, or at least godly."

"Don't say that!" He kicked off the blanket and bolted up from the couch. "Don't ever say that."

"I'm sorry." She scrambled to her feet but stopped short of approaching him. "I was just trying to make you smile."

"I know." He sank onto the edge of the data center. She'd tried, but she couldn't hide the desperation in her voice from him. She wanted so badly to fix him, but she couldn't erase what he'd done.

"I shouldn't have snapped at you. But I'm never going to smile about this."

"Caleb…I realize it seems like it right now. It's fine to give yourself time, but eventually you're going to have to forgive yourself."

"What good does forgiving myself do when I'm still the avatar for the transgressor?" He flashed a plume of crimson energy above his hand, then snuffed it out. "I don't deserve this much power. No one does. If there's anything this vision confirmed for me, it's that this power is not meant for us. It's beyond our comprehension, and in some ways we are beyond *its* comprehension. The million years it spent with the Anadens were but a second of time to it, and the second has not changed its nature."

She frowned. "What do you mean?"

"It doesn't pass moral judgment on the actions of insignificant, transient life forms. It's not with me because it judged me 'worthy'— it's with me because it judged me capable in matters it respected. The same was true of Corradeo all those millennia ago. It joined with him because it needed him to perform a function he excelled at performing.

"Its purpose, to the extent it has one, is to ensure that the universe continues to exist, but a couple of million or billion lives lost don't even register on its radar. It's seen more species and planets and stars arise and vanish than we've ever known existed."

Now she came over to wrap her arms around him. "But you care. Even though the people who died were the enemy."

"Not all of them."

"Okay, not all of them. But you went there to stop a fearsome enemy, and you succeeded. There was nothing you could have done to prevent what happened in the aftermath."

"That's not true. I could have tried to lure him out of the building, away from other Praesidis. I could have…teleported away the instant he died. I could have…." The look on her face exposed the lie he was trying to tell himself, but it didn't make the truth any easier to accept.

The truth was that he didn't want to be forgiven or forgive himself. In the wake of such overwhelming death, someone had to be held accountable, and the line of candidates began and ended with him.

Whether Alex knew what he was thinking or not, she remained undeterred. "You did what no one else was capable of doing, and you took power away from an evil, cruel man. For a tragic couple of minutes you weren't in charge, but now you are. Thanks to you, he'll never cause others suffering again."

"I know you're right. But is there a path back from genocide? Because from here I can't see one."

She brought her hands to his cheeks and let her fingertips caress his jaw. Insisted he meet her gaze, where he found fierce resilience challenging him. Demanding that the universe, and he, bend to her will. "We'll find one. Together."

Damn her persistence. Damn her words, her touch, her warmth. Damn her for kindling something inside him he hadn't thought possible—a tiny spark of hope that somewhere out there, salvation existed for him. He simply needed to find it.

And now, he understood something else the *diati* never would. This was why love existed: so when it all went wrong and all you could see was darkness, you had someone there to give you hope.

41

As Miriam considered the people gathered in the conference room—increasingly a mix of AEGIS personnel, anarchs and other allies—she continued to struggle with settling on a sentiment to project to those present.

They had, by and large, succeeded in what should have been an impossible task. The scope of the collective missions had exceeded in complexity even the final battles of the Metigen War. Their losses were lower than she'd had any right to expect. In most respects, this preposterous plan of hers had *worked*.

But the fallout from the ways in which it hadn't succeeded was significant. The missing Machim Primor represented a problem in multiple respects, and they dared not consider declaring any kind of 'victory' until he was tracked down and brought to justice. She assumed the Machim military would continue to fight them until he was eliminated and the Machim integral began to weaken.

Then there was Solum. The most powerful Primor and greatest threat to them had been felled, but the cost....

Though she knew it shouldn't, the loss felt more disturbing for the fact that Solum was—or had been—*Earth*. It hadn't resembled her homeworld in hundreds of thousands, perhaps a million years. But Solum was Earth and Earth was Solum, nonetheless. And now in this universe it no longer existed.

She checked the doorway a final time, but she couldn't expect Alex or Caleb to attend. He was essentially in self-imposed exile until he brought this ungodly, unfathomable amount of power under control. Except for Alex—she not only refused to respect his exile, she refused to leave his side.

She'd worried about her daughter often and regularly over the years, but no one had warned her the consequences of growing emotionally closer would include feeling such worry in her heart as well as her head. She *ached* for her daughter and the pain Alex suffered, but she had to trust that if this otherworldly power hadn't harmed Alex when it ran wild across a stellar system, it wouldn't harm her now.

The door closed, and Miriam forced a smile for the room. "Congratulations, everyone. You are all to be commended."

Malcolm squirmed uncomfortably halfway down the table, so she might as well address it now. "Yes, Brigadier Jenner, including you. I wish a speedy to recovery to Captain Harper, Lieutenant Odaka and the other members of your team who were injured."

He didn't look any happier after her assurances. "Thank you, Commandant. I wish we'd been more successful, and I take full responsibility for the failure to complete our objective."

Everyone was so quick to ask for responsibility, but it didn't work that way.

"Your mission was among the most difficult. I've reviewed the reports, and you and your team performed in an exemplary manner. We forewent assigning additional ships to the Annex in favor of maintaining the element of surprise. If the decision was a mistake, it was as much my mistake as anyone's."

She directed her focus back to the group before he began to argue. "The Machim Primor is currently unaccounted for, but more on him in a minute. First, I want to make certain everyone knows that we succeeded in eliminating all twenty-four targeted regenesis labs, as well as seven of the eight Primors. Or, I should say, we eliminated six of the eight—one Primor was killed by a member of their own progeny just prior to our team's arrival. An Erevna *ela* confessed to the killing and willingly surrendered himself to our people."

Eren asi-Idoni scowled. "Tell me it wasn't the prat I shot at the exobiology research lab."

She called up a visual of the prisoner in question for all to see.

"Ah, bloody hell. He's scum. Don't trust him. And if you want to keep him alive, don't let any of the refugees catch sight of him, lest they try to settle old scores."

"Understood. However, I submit that he may prove to be useful scum. His area of expertise is exobiology, and as such he can speed the regenesis research for other species by years if not decades."

"Oh." Eren frowned. "I suppose making him pay recompense for the evils he committed upon other species by saving their lives could be a good outcome. Watch him, though."

"We will. Now, as I was saying. Excluding the Machim and Praesidis missions, our objectives were achieved in full and, all things considered, we saw minimal complications or loss of life. So again I say, well done."

She took a breath. "With respect to the Praesidis mission, our primary objectives were achieved as well, but not without…disproportionate consequences. All of you know Caleb Marano and have at least some familiarity with the power of the *diati* he wields. When he killed the Praesidis Primor, the *diati* the Primor had controlled ran rampant for a time, killing numerous nearby lesser Praesidis and destroying Praesidis Command, which led to additional deaths and destruction, which grew into a self-perpetuating cascade. The end result is that the planet of Solum is no more."

Gasps and confused exclamations echoed around the table from everyone, with the exception of the Prevos; of course they would already know.

She gave the uproar a few seconds before motioning everyone silent. "To answer the obvious questions, first, no, I don't mean wholesale structural damage. The entire planet has been reduced to scattered debris. I'm sure an astrogeologist could explain the chain of events, but the simple fact is, the planet no longer exists. Second, yes, Mr. Marano is alive. I won't pretend he's well. The physical and psychological toll these events exacted can't be understated. Alex is fine, as are the Marines tasked with destroying the regenesis lab on Solum and everyone under Field Marshal Bastian's command.

"The loss of life on Solum, which includes many individuals who were not actively our enemy, is tragic. I wish there had been some way to accomplish our objective without those casualties. But here is the unvarnished truth: the upper echelons of the Praesidis Dynasty represented the highest threat to us, the anarchs, billions of innocents here and everyone back home. The magnitude of the threat exceeded even the threat from the Machim fleets, and it has now been eliminated."

She clasped her hands at the base of her spine in a more formal posture. "Nevertheless, the Machim threat was hardly insignificant, and unfortunately it still exists. Let's talk about what we plan to do to end it."

Caleb stared at the table through fingers splayed across his face. The pseudo-ceramic surface marbled in gray-and-white splotches, but they formed no pattern. He studied a fleck of gray until it blurred into hazy indistinctness.

Someone cleared their throat from the doorway of the small meeting room, and he looked up to find David standing there. Any sort of greeting felt inappropriate, so he merely tilted his head a fraction in recognition.

His father-in-law took it for what it was; he came in, closed the door behind him, and sat down opposite Caleb. "I'd ask how you were doing, but you don't need me to patronize you."

"You've gotten an update from the anarchs?" This was why he'd come, why he'd reluctantly broken his exile.

"I have."

"How many?"

"Eight billion, give or take a few hundred million."

Caleb breathed out through his nose. His hands trembled atop the table. A crimson aura brightened above his skin. Oh, so *now* the *diati* was feeling remorseful? Now, when it was so far beyond too late? He bid it to shut the fuck up, and the aura dimmed in compliance.

The number was large enough to surpass tangible meaning, but he owed it those who died to try to grasp it nonetheless. Eight billion lives lost because he hadn't been strong enough to control a primordial force of the universe. Was it a defense or an indictment?

Caleb Andreas Marano: Killer. Lover. Dragonslayer. Razer of Worlds.

He glanced around in sudden desperation for water and found a glass beside him. He didn't remember having gotten the glass or pouring the water, but still-shaking hands brought it to his lips and he guzzled it down. It whetted his parched throat, but nothing else. "How many—do we have any idea how many Praesidis were—still are—alive at other locations?"

"Forty billion at a minimum. More than enough."

"Enough so that I didn't commit genocide, you mean?"

David nodded slowly. "Yes."

"Weren't you supposed to say I wasn't really the one who caused the destruction? How genocide or not, I'm not responsible?"

"I could have said that. And I suspect it would be a fundamentally true statement. But me handing platitudes back to you isn't going to help you come to terms with what happened. Only you can find peace for yourself."

"I don't think I can."

"I think you have to. If not for yourself, for Alex."

"Alex..." he squeezed his eyes shut and massaged his temples, remembering the fleeting hope she'd worked so hard to give him "...deserves better."

"The way I see it, that depends."

He frowned, surprised. "On what?"

"You've got this insane amount of power under control now?"

"Yes."

"What are you going to do with it?"

Toss it in a black hole. Save a life where I can. Make sure it never steals another innocent life, somehow. "I don't—"

The door beeped, signaling another entry request. Grateful to not have to answer the question but not relishing facing another person, Caleb shrugged assent, and David opened the door.

Malcolm Jenner took two steps inside and greeted David before turning to Caleb.

Caleb exhaled heavily. He was so damn tired. His reserves were dried up, and he had no energy for this confrontation. "Come to arrest me?"

"No."

"Why not? I won't resist."

"I don't pretend to understand this power of yours, or even to understand you. But no one with a soul could have intended to cause what...happened. You say you didn't intend it, and I accept your word for it."

All this forgiveness and understanding was ripping him to shreds. Would no one yell at him? Call him a murderer? Insist he should be punished? "Thank you, Brigadier."

Jenner jerked his chin in a curt acknowledgment.

"Why are you here, then?"

"There's something you need to see."

ᴙ

Fresh snowfall had covered the charred bodies and much of the bombed-out wreckage, lending the scene a gentle, pristine aura.

Caleb knew the scene well, as he'd wandered among it hardly hours earlier.

"We left behind a couple of drones when we departed, mostly on the off chance that a survivor might descend out of the mountains in search of help. She showed up just over an hour ago."

The raven curls and midnight-black attire were instantly recognizable. There was no way he could sense her *diati* through the cam feed, but his skin buzzed nonetheless.

He watched her for a minute, sitting in the snow in front of the drone, arms draped over her knees as if she were waiting for a lunch date. "Have you made contact with her yet?"

Jenner shook his head. "She found the drone almost instantly and started talking to it, I guess assuming correctly that we could hear her. She claims she doesn't want to harm anyone, and she's asking to speak to either you or Sator Nisi."

Caleb sighed. "I'm sorry, but I'm not up to an interrogation right now."

"Up to it or not, we need you to come with us. You know as well as I do that our weapons are useless against her."

"And I'm the only one who can..." he rubbed at his temples "...right. I'll teleport there and deal with her."

"You'll forgive me if I want to take precautions. You're taking a squad with you."

"I thought you said your weapons were useless against her."

Jenner arched an eyebrow. "And against you. Doesn't mean I don't have to try."

42

CHIONIS

They materialized thirty meters from where Nyx sat.

Jenner and seven other Marines immediately trained TSGs on her, for all the good they would do. Caleb's arm extended, ready to attack at the first hint of aggression from her.

She stood and raised both hands in a gesture of surrender. "Please. I'm not here to hurt anyone, and I know I can't hurt you."

She had locked on Caleb the instant they arrived; he doubted she cared about the Marines or their weapons. "Then what are you doing here?"

"This was the most logical and quickest way to get your attention. I have information critical to your cause."

"Fine. Speak it."

"If you want to guarantee the Primors don't return, you have more work to do. Before I tell you any details, however, I want to see your Sator."

Caleb shook his head. "His people won't let you within a parsec of him."

"Overrule them." She took a step toward him, and his skin hummed with anticipation.

He held up a hand in warning. "Stop. If you come any closer, you will lose your *diati* to me, and there's no longer a replacement well you can draw from. You will lose your power forever, and I can't prevent it from happening."

"Don't you want to deprive me of it?"

He snorted.

Her gaze fell to study the disturbed snow at her feet. Finally she squared her shoulders. "The *diati* I control came from the Primor. It's tainted by his use of it, by his actions as a pretender and a liar. He destroyed my homeworld." She took a step forward, then another. "I don't want it. Take it."

The influx of new power was but a drop of rainfall added to a vast sea; even so, he stumbled back, his hands searching for a brace and finding none. His head swam from the dizzying rush, and he fell to his knees.

His vision cleared in time to see her struggling up from where she'd fallen as well. At least the taking hadn't been so violent that it killed her, as it had been for so many on Solum.

Solum....

A hand extended out from his left, and he looked up to see Harper smirking at him. "Easy there, Icarus."

He stared at her, noting idly that she wielded not merely a high-powered assault weapon but also several medwraps as souvenirs from her spacing mishap. Her offhanded remark penetrated his tortured mind, and he started laughing. Caustically and darkly, but it was laughter nonetheless. He accepted the outstretched hand and stood.

They both returned their attention to Nyx. No one had rushed in to offer her assistance, and it took her several seconds to make it to her feet. She braced her hands on her thighs to steady herself. When she finally straightened up, she wore an odd expression. "Thank you. Now will you take me to see the Sator? You can vouch that I'm no longer a threat to him. To anyone."

"I can vouch for your lack of power, but I can't take you to him." He couldn't control much right now, but he could ensure Nisi didn't lose the *diati* which had always been his, though this meant he'd likely never see the man again. "I'll recommend you be allowed an audience. But first, I suspect my friends here are going to want to search you for weapons."

Jenner nodded firmly. "For starters."

ᴀʀ

ANARCH POST SATUS

LOCATION UNKNOWN

Gone. His homeworld. Billions of Praesidis lives. His son. Gone.

He searched his mind for defined, coherent sentiments. But whatever grief he felt answered his query only as a distant, muted echo of its true self.

He'd been Danilo Nisi for too long. He no longer recalled what sentiments Corradeo Praesidis would have felt in the wake of these events, much less feel them for himself.

He did feel...frustration. Regret that he hadn't properly foreseen the risks of pitting the two most powerful men in civilization against one another. Chagrin that he had expected anything other than exactly what occurred to be the result of such a confrontation. Idle pondering of the notion that if it had been him in Caleb's place, he could have done better. Nagging suspicion that if it had been him in Caleb's place, he would be the dead one. Concern at what the destruction of Solum, the birthplace of the Anadens and their empire, meant for the future. A touch of irritating helplessness at his inability to shape the world to his desires. Apprehension at what his role in a world without the Directorate was to be.

Volya cleared her throat from the door. "Sir, the guards are here with the Inquisitor."

"Excellent. Bring her in."

"Sir, this is a bad idea. I don't like it."

"Noted. Bring her in."

Volya's upper lip curled into a snarl, but she spun and disappeared back through the door. He spent the brief interlude preparing himself for a meeting he had never expected might happen. A reunion he had never dreamed might transpire.

Volya led the entourage into the room. Behind her two guards held the woman by the upper arms, though her hands were also restrained. Two more guards trained weapons on her from two meters distance.

"Guards, keep the prisoner well away from the Sator."

His gaze settled upon the woman as a wave of genuine sentiment swept over him with far more power than he'd expected. "She's not going to try to hurt me. Are you, Nyx?"

"No, sir. I give you my word."

"Remove her restraints and leave us."

"Sir!"

"Follow my orders, Volya."

The guards glanced uncertainly between him and Volya, and not until she nodded minutely did they comply with his instructions. He'd deal with the borderline insubordination later, if it mattered later; now he watched them until they retreated through the door, Volya last, and it closed behind them.

Only once they were alone did he bestow a warm smile on his guest. "Welcome, my dear. I did not expect your visit, but I am most glad for it."

Nyx took a step forward and dropped to one knee, head bowed. "Forgive me for all I've done to impede your work, sir. I did not see. I did not understand."

Warmth spread through his chest, tinged as always with sorrow. "You were always forgiven. Please, stand. No one bows here, least of all you."

Her shoulders rose and fell in a heavy breath before she stood, her eyes following her body to rise and meet his. "Thank you. I pledge myself to your service."

"There's no need for any of this nonsense—not any longer. The days of fealty are coming to an end." He paused, finding himself fighting the powerful urge to reach out and stroke her cheek. "You look so like your mother."

"What? I don't...have a mother."

"You do not remember her, of course. The memories and the consciousness which held them have been stripped away and reconstructed so many times over the millennia to serve Renato's purposes, there can be nothing left of them. Yet you still look like your mother. I suspect he intentionally kept you so, though whether he did it as a remembrance or a trophy, I cannot say."

She blinked several times as she worked to absorb the information. "I don't understand. Are you...my true father?"

"I believe the correct term is 'grandfather.' Your mother was my daughter, and I treasured her so very much. You see, I'm not merely the leader of the anarch resistance. Once, a dreadfully long time ago, I was Corradeo Praesidis."

"I know."

"Do you?"

"The *diati*—the Primor's *diati*—showed me a vision, a memory of what he did, of how he tried to kill you then stole your power, your name and your authority. I've been trying to find you ever since it revealed the truth to me."

"That is...heartening. I'm glad you succeeded." He frowned, noticing an absence where there should be presence. "But the *diati*? You no longer possess it?"

"No. I asked the Human...I'm sorry, I don't even know his name. I asked him to take it. The taint of the Primor's transgressions was too great, and I did not want his treacheries poisoning me further."

"It was your choice to make, and a brave one. But realize that his sins are not your sins."

"Perhaps not. Still, I bear plenty of my own, and I will not be so easily rid of them." Her expression grew troubled. "May I ask what happened to your daughter—to my mother?"

"Are you sure you want to know? It is not a happy story."

"How could it be? But I am an Inquisitor, bred to seek the truth in all things. Yes, I want to know."

The warmth in his chest gave way to the sorrow. "As you wish. Soon after taking power, Renato—the Primor, my son—erased her regenesis records then killed her. He did so for his own protection, as she would have instantly recognized that he was not me. It pains me to tell you this, but you are correct—you deserve the truth. He killed you as well. He erased your memories during regenesis and brought you back, but he did her no such courtesy. I fear it gave him perverse pleasure to have the daughter of his murdered sister serve him unawares."

Her face blanched, and he reached out and took her hand. It trembled in his, and he wanted nothing more in all the worlds than to soothe this pain, so ancient and faded for him but fresh and raw for her.

"Again, I am sorry. But it is all distant history, so long in the past as to hardly have existed at all. Despite everything that has happened, you and I are alive, and now we are together. We will have all the time in the cosmos to get to know one another anew in the coming days, but you came here for a specific purpose, one I'm told carries some urgency. What do you know?"

43

M ia rushed back to Post Delta from her abrupt summons to Satus, trusting that Miriam would have gathered everyone they needed by the time she arrived. The meeting with Nisi and the Inquisitor, whom Mia found unnerving despite the absence of her power, had been uncharacteristically bereft of semantic flourishes and grandiose declarations, but it had still come too late and taken too long.

She quickened her step yet again. So much time had already been lost as the information passed from one person to another to another.

Less than a minute later she reached the conference room. People were milling about—a hurried scan of the room confirmed Caleb was not among them—but Miriam immediately turned her attention to Mia. "Ms. Requelme, please fill us in."

"Yes, ma'am. The Primors apparently kept a current backup of the data required for their regenesis at their Prótos Agora stronghold. There isn't an actual regenesis lab there, but in the wake of the Primors' demise a number of their *elassons* are working to find a way to access this data and transfer it to other labs. According to the Inquisitor, we have days at most, and possibly as little as a single day, before the data is transferred and the process of each Primor's regenesis begins."

The only outward reaction Miriam displayed was to briefly pinch the bridge of her nose. Mia knew the woman was under tremendous pressure and had been for an uninterrupted string of many hours now, but Miriam lifted her chin resolutely, having absorbed this new complication. "I trust this Inquisitor knows where the Prótos Agora is located?"

"It's a hybrid starship-space station, not unlike Post Satus. It orbits the Milky Way galactic core in a tight orbit—so close to the core that the structure requires triple layers of the strongest shielding the Anadens possess to prevent its bombardment by a variety of deadly cosmic forces. She claims not to have the precise details of its orbital trajectory or how to find it at a particular time, however."

Bastian scoffed. "What good is she, then?"

"I can find it."

Everyone, including Mia, turned to Alex, who was holding her Reor slab out on an open palm. "I'll take the *Siyane* as close as I can get to the core, then I'll open a wormhole and follow the strings until they lead to the Prótos Agora. I'll scan the data that's stored inside until I find what must be there: orbital calculation algorithms and specs on defenses. But I should go now."

Miriam frowned. "Go—but please take precautions. Be safe."

"I'll be in touch as soon as I learn something."

Mia watched Alex head toward the door. "I don't have any more information to share right now. Unless I'm needed here, Alex, can I walk partway to the *Siyane* with you?"

Alex shrugged noncommittally. Miriam nodded, giving Mia permission to leave. She quickly followed Alex out the door and fell in beside her. "Caleb wasn't in the meeting."

"He's not comfortable being in a confined space close to so many people. He's got the power under control, but he's still afraid he might hurt someone."

"I haven't seen him at all since what happened at Solum. Is he okay?"

Alex shook her head slowly; it made for an odd contrast to her rapid pace. "No, he is not. He blames himself for Solum's destruction and for every single one of the lives lost there. Mia, I've never seen him like this. He's trapped in this dark place, and I don't know how to help him. I've tried everything, but he's just...destroyed. I think he's decided that Malcolm was right about him after all."

"What? But Malcolm doesn't even think so ill of him now."

"I know. But it doesn't seem to matter. He believes it." Alex stopped at a junction of three elevated walkways. "I need to hurry. We all have to focus on finishing this damnable war right now. But thank you for asking about him. I'd tell you not to worry, but the truth is, you probably *should* worry. When this is over, I may need to ask for your help in getting through to him."

"Of course. Anything."

Alex gave her a weak smile and rushed off.

SIYANE

By the time she reached the *Siyane*, Valkyrie had worked out the sliding scale of how close they could get to the galactic core versus for how long. A small detail remained unanswered to complicate matters: they didn't know how long they needed.

'No settlements or structures, other than small, autonomous scientific instruments, exist within 1.7 kiloparsecs of the central black hole's event horizon. I believe that if we position ourselves inside this 1.7 kiloparsec perimeter, we will be able to eliminate extraneous data streams with little difficulty and identify streams leading to the Prótos Agora in a reasonable amount of time.'

"True, but we also need to read the data, or at least record it."

'I've honed the process of copying and recording such data over the last several days, significantly improving speed and efficiency.'

"I bet. All right." Alex considered the map in her mind. "Let's pick the least active region...Sector 51. From there, we'll advance to 1.6 kiloparsecs distance from the big ground zero. We'll investigate for two minutes then evaluate whether we need to move. But hold one sec."

She looked around the empty cabin in growing concern. She hadn't wanted to leave Caleb alone while she went to the meeting, but he'd insisted he'd be fine. Now he was gone.

Where are you?

The next second Caleb materialized beside her. "Here." He promptly sat down in his cockpit chair. "Don't say I don't have to go with you. This is dangerous under any definition. The astronomical forces at work so close to the core could render the ship or Valkyrie inoperable for any of a hundred different reasons, in which case I'll need to teleport us out of there."

"That's a...very persuasive argument." Her eyes narrowed. "Wait a minute. How do you even know what we're planning to do?"

"Your father sent me a message after you left the meeting."

She didn't really know what to think about that. "Well, okay then. Since you're here, you can do the piloting—or monitoring of Valkyrie's piloting. I'm going to be a bit preoccupied."

"Happy to." He offered her a poor facsimile of a smile and activated his HUD.

She wanted so badly to comfort him, to ease his mind and remove some small portion of his burden. But she was running out of things to say, and thus far none of what she said seemed to help. He said they helped, but he was lying.

She sighed quietly...time was short, and she needed to concentrate on what she *could* do. "Valkyrie, you know the drill. Depart Tarach-controlled space, move another twenty megameters, then fire up the Caeles Prism. We agree our initial destination is Milky Way galactic coordinates *l* 17° 45' 42.14" *b* −29° 00' 30.25"?"

'We agree.' The *Siyane* lifted smoothly off the elevated platform and ascended into the sky.

MILKY WAY GALACTIC CORE

SIYANE

The blinding light of the galactic core consumed the viewport, but Alex ignored it. She suspected she'd be back soon enough; maybe she could bask in the view the next time. Right now she stared down at the Reor slab.

Such a deceptively tiny object, holding the key to so much.

Caleb busied himself studying the ship's vitals. "Are we doing all right, Valkyrie?"

'As all things are relative, yes.'

"That's encouraging, I guess." Alex reclined her chair. "Open a small wormhole, and let's hang out."

A sea of brilliant strings of light engulfed her, and she immediately grimaced. "I thought you said this close, they were going to be simple to sift through."

'As all things—'

"Relative, yeah, yeah. I need...space. I need to back up. Not the ship—me. Keep the wormhole opening here." She leapt up and made her way through the fog of light to the far end of the main cabin, where she turned around and braced against the counter.

Better. The strings now gained a measure of distance and trajectory before they were drowned out by the light of the core.

She slipped into sidespace, then sent her consciousness inside the wormhole.

The extradimensional environment was as chaotic here as the tangible one. She struggled to keep her bearings as upside and downside flipped over and over again. Inside outside, down the rabbit hole, dizziness threatening to send her physical body to the floor...she felt something steady her, holding her still as the chaos rushed past her. *Concentrate on the strings. Ignore everything else and see only the strings.*

She smiled, somewhere. *Thank you, Valkyrie. Strings, strings, strings...this clump here is substantial. The wave bearing the coordinates is 174.6218530021186 MHz.*

It leads to an Erevna research station in MW Sector 42.

She reversed course in her mind until she sensed the walls of the ship surround her. *How about....* She focused on a different tangle...but the more she focused on it, the thicker and deeper the tangle extended. It was like standing amid a forest of luminescent neon string trees.

She chuckled, apparently audibly, because Caleb called to her from the cockpit. "Alex?"

"Sorry, it was just...imagery. I'll tell you later."

She symbolically brushed aside string after string until she was able to, again symbolically, close two fingers around a single string near the center of the forest. *This one. Coordinates 17.44411229142213 GHz.*

This leads to no registered location.

I'm going. She looked 'up' and sent the majority of her consciousness soaring along the length of the string.

Her path shifted with ever-greater speed as she neared the terminus; the source was careening around the core at unbelievable speed.

She reached the terminus nonetheless, because in sidespace she wasn't bound by restrictions like speed.

An oval structure spun ahead of her, but it was so swathed in shields that its physical characteristics remained hidden from sight. She also wasn't here to take visuals, so whatever. She dove for the interior—

—and collided with a solid *diati* barrier. "Ow!"

Caleb's voice echoed farther away now, on the edge of her peripheral perception. "Alex? Are you okay?"

"Hmm. I am, but that would've hurt something fierce if I'd actually been there. The Prótos Agora has, among other defenses, a *diati* shell. But it's not a problem. I don't need to access the interior."

Valkyrie, we can now see all the strings flowing from inside. Fill up your databanks. She glanced at the time. *Per your parameters, you have four minutes.*

There's a safety margin built into the time limit.

Right....

While Valkyrie recorded exabytes of data, Alex mused. If the *diati* truly was pandimensional, so was the Reor. There was no way through a *diati* barrier except with more *diati*, yet the Reor data passed through it unfettered. What did that mean? She found she was rather curious about the nature of this entity that was destroying her husband's life. About the nature of the slab in her hand as well, but she had priorities.

She suspected it meant both life forms were old. *Very* old, and perhaps connected to the fundamental universe in ways they didn't, couldn't, and might not want to understand. This synced with Caleb's latest vision—

Recording complete.

Ten seconds to spare. She closed her virtual eyes, willed herself straight back into her body, opened her real eyes, swayed against the kitchen counter and hurriedly steadied herself—then winced at Caleb's concerned, oh-so-troubled visage. "Head rush. Get us out of here?"

"Gladly."

While they retreated she walked-but-mostly-stumbled to the data center and began pulling the data out of Valkyrie's storage banks. "This much data may take years to wade through, but right now all we need is the Prótos Agora systems information."

'Running sort and search algorithms.'

"You read my mind."

'As I do.'

When this crisis is resolved, I will burn many cycles contemplating how we can help him. I feel sorrow for him, and for you. I feel your sorrow for him, and I find I must take care to not create a feedback loop of endless sorrow.

You're wonderful, Valkyrie. You've developed such a noble soul.

And in doing so discovered that souls can give rise to terrible distress.

She watched in her peripheral vision as Caleb guided the ship out of the wormhole into normal space and checked their position, then let his hands fall to his lap. He stared out the viewport. A vein pulsed beneath the skin of his temple. His jaw flexed.

Yep. They sure can.

44

AFS STALWART II

TARACH STELLAR SYSTEM

"Three concentric shields, each as strong as an Imperium's double shield?"

"And the innermost one is snug up against the hull. Plus, there's a *diati* barrier."

Miriam frowned. "Even with the Praesidis Primor dead?"

Alex shrugged.

"Just what I need, more *diati*." Caleb grimaced, then forced a closed-mouth smile. "It's fine. I can swat it away from…maybe as far away as a parsec."

David noted how his son-in-law's voice managed to sound both bitter and flat at the same time. Caleb's pain was blatantly obvious, as was Alex's troubled reaction to it, but one crisis at a time. Save civilization first, save souls later. "It won't matter if we can't get through those shields—" he looked to Miriam "—and we can't, can we?"

Her brow was knotted tight. Variables, contingencies, options and their costs spinning in her mind for certain. "Alex, can you quantify exactly what 'snug up against the hull' means?"

Thomas spoke up first, however. 'Valkyrie has passed along the data files to me. The distance between the innermost shield and the exterior of the Prótos Agora's hull varies between fourteen and twenty meters.'

Miriam absorbed the new data without blinking. "Assuming a wormhole can bypass all three shields, can one be opened within so small a range on a target moving at over 6 AU per hour? One that we could send a cluster of negative energy missiles through?"

Alex grimaced. "Um…we could *try*."

Thomas chimed in again with more bad news. 'Actually, to try would likely be futile. The turbulence of the energetic and dimensional forces at play so close to the galactic core render opening any form of wormhole there nearly impossible, never mind a stable one.'

"Thomas, you should know by now how I feel about the word 'nearly.' Valkyrie, let's try it anyway."

'From your location on the Stalwart II?'

"No, I'll let you take the lead on this one. Open it in front of the *Siyane*, with the exit point as close to flush against the Prótos Agora as you can finagle it."

'Proceeding—'

Alex staggered back into the wall behind her as forcefully as if someone had shoved her. David started to move toward her, but Caleb was at her side instantly.

She ran a hand down her face, eyes wide. "I'm okay. But Thomas is right, or mostly right. The wormhole did open, but the exit was like the eyewall of a hurricane. I could feel it from here. Obviously."

David sighed. His daughter's frequent death-defying feats were damn impressive, but a mite tough on the parental instincts. "Is Valkyrie all right? Was the *Siyane* damaged?"

'Nothing a coat of polish can't buff out.'

Alex winked at Caleb. "We've buffed out far worse."

He squeezed her hand. "Yes, we have."

"Regardless, we're going to need another plan...." Alex's face abruptly brightened, and she cast her gaze to the ceiling. "Mesme!"

"Does that work? Can you really just call the Kat like that?"

She rolled her eyes at David. "No. Valkyrie contacted Mesme. But it felt good to make a show of it."

Oh, milaya. *You are such a beautiful, astonishing person. I weep for your burdens and stand in awe of your accomplishments.*

Alex may not have noticed the broadcasting of such sentimental thoughts on his countenance, but Miriam did. She glanced toward Alex while giving him a small smile. He gave her a bigger one.

A minute later a Kat's trademark swirl of lights swept into the room. *You requested my presence?*

Alex crossed her arms over her chest as if spoiling for a fight. "We need the Tartarus Trigger."

Oh. David watched Miriam's expression transform. Though skeptical and cautious, she wasn't dismissing the idea out of hand.

What? No. I cannot permit its use.

"We have to destroy the Prótos Agora in the next six hours or all of this warfare, destruction and death will have been for naught. The Tartarus Trigger—or rather the black hole it creates—is the only weapon that won't be stopped by the Prótos Agora's shields."

I recognize your dire straits, but there are no circumstances under which the device can be used safely.

"'Safely' is more of an ideal to strive for than a requirement. The Prótos Agora is orbiting 2.6 parsecs from the event horizon of the supermassive black hole sitting at the center of the Milky Way. Does this alter your judgment?"

Mesme undulated for a moment. *Applying those parameters, it could perhaps be used with a marginal degree of safety.*

"That's what I thought." Alex directed her attention to the human beings present, all of whom David was fairly certain had no idea what had been discussed and decided. "So long as the black hole singularity created by the Tartarus Trigger is initially located less than about four parsecs from the one at the center of the Milky Way, *and* so long as its size is less than twenty-two percent of the Milky Way black hole when the two event horizons meet, the far larger Milky Way black hole will consume the Tartarus Trigger's creation and continue on with its day."

She tapped her temple. "Or so Valkyrie says, after spinning a few cycles on math and Thomas checking behind her. Mesme, do your scientists agree as well?"

The math is accurate. It will continue to be a dangerous endeavor.

"Dangerous we can do. Nearly impossible we can do. All we need are the tiniest odds of success."

Miriam arched an eyebrow in David's direction. "She's your daughter." Then she banished all levity as swiftly as it had arrived. "To launch the device with a high enough level of precision, we would need to be within twelve megameters of the target, same as with negative energy missiles. Our shields can't take the abuse the core will inflict, but the Dimensional Rifter can, at least for a few seconds. Running the Rifter so close to the core will require a great deal of power...but I suspect if we shut down non-critical systems, we can manage it, again for a few seconds. Thomas, please confirm."

Alex frowned at her mother. "What's all this 'we' stuff? I'm doing this."

David leaned into the table. "No, you're not. You've done enough—more than enough, the both of you. The *Stalwart II* has both the strongest shields and the most powerful Rifter in the fleet. Let us fire the final shot in this war. It's our responsibility and, frankly..." he turned to face Miriam "...it's your mother's right to do it."

Alex glared at him, and for an instant the pout she wore transformed her into the little girl he remembered. "Fine. But we're going with you."

45

TAYGETA

Casmir hurried after the Primor like a loyal dog nipping at its master's heels. But he wasn't following out of loyalty any longer. "Sir!"

The Primor gestured dismissively over his shoulder and didn't slow.

Casmir increased his gait to a rapid jog until he caught up. "Sir, if you will tell me what our objective is, I can take care of the details so you needn't bother with them."

"Our objective is to punish our enemy. If we can't have victory, we can damn sure have vengeance."

The shocking news had arrived in ever worsening waves during their brief trip here. Class 4 Dynasty regenesis labs destroyed, attacks on homeworlds, Primors slain. Then, a claim too outlandish to believe: Solum destroyed more thoroughly than even an armada of Igni missiles could achieve. The reports were vague and often contradictory, but the weight of them suggested Machim may very well be the only Primor still living.

For now, no Directorate existed to step forward, to guide the people and implement a response. Furtive messages among *elassons* crossing Dynasty lines indicated there may be hope for resurrecting some of the Primors, but Casmir wasn't inclined toward a hopeful mood. Not with his Primor out of his mind and bent on fiery retribution.

He kept his voice level and chose his words carefully. "What are your plans in that regard, sir?"

The answer only served to stoke the dread churning in his gut. "You will see soon enough."

ℛ

Hulking workbots guided the large cylinder and its protective casing up the ramp of the battlecruiser as Casmir looked on in growing horror. As anticipated, the Humans had destroyed the Advanced Weaponry Development Facility at Centauri E, but the monstrous device had been moved prior to its destruction and completed here.

The last time he'd carried such a device on his ship, he'd have faithfully followed his orders to deploy it; he simply hadn't gotten the opportunity. Now, though?

His throat had gone dry, so he cleared it awkwardly. His Primor stood beside him wearing an expression of almost maniacal glee. "Sir, what are you intending to target? There are no portals we can access to traverse."

"Of course there are."

"Hidden, sir, and scattered across megaparsecs of space."

"Hidden, yes, but not unknown. I possess the location of one."

"What? How, sir?"

"Praesidis—Zeus rest his pretentious soul—tried again to track a provision vessel, this time using one of his vaunted *elassons*. The Inquisitor escaped detection and returned with a set of coordinates. I have not heard from him since, so I assume he now shares his Primor's fate. We were planning to move on the portal before...."

Before what didn't need to be said. Casmir eyed the device as it disappeared into the hold. "I see. Sir, are you certain this is the wisest course of action given the current state of disarray among our—"

"Enough! I am done with your mealy-mouthed questioning and quivering protests. I no longer require your services. You are relieved of duty."

Casmir swallowed, surprised that relief dominated shame in his reaction. "As you wish, Primor. Where shall I be reassigned?"

"I don't care. Live, die, whatever suits you, but go." The Primor pivoted and headed toward the ship's airlock.

Casmir stood there and watched the Primor board. He watched the bay door close the doomsday device up inside the hull. He watched the ship's engines engage and the ship depart.

He couldn't say whether the Humans deserved to die en masse, for moral judgments were not his role. The Humans were indisputably his government's and his Dynasty's adversary. He'd been tasked with defeating them, yet he and all others had failed.

But no matter the particulars of the enemy, such a device as this should not exist, should never have existed—and it absolutely should not exist under the control of a madman. The decision to use such a weapon would be suspect even if made by the sane, and his Primor had lost all reason.

Casmir was a military officer, and military officers didn't stroll around indulging ethical crises. They chose a course of action and pursued it to its end.

He had no ship from which to act, no destination from where to act, and no platform upon which to act to prevent his Primor from using the device.

But others did. His enemy did.

He spun and hurried back into the heart of the Facility.

46

AFS STALWART II

M esme and two other Kats delivered the Tartarus Trigger to the waiting *Stalwart II* at a location a full hundred parsecs from Post Delta. A contingent of AEGIS bots retrofitted it to the end of one of the negative energy missile tubes. Since it was too large to fit inside, the launching mechanisms had been hurriedly rigged to act across the full length of the tube.

Alex paced around the conference room, dropping into sidespace every twenty seconds or so to check on their progress. *Time slipping out from beneath her, one accelerating second at a time.* It wasn't truly, not here. Felt like it, though.

She would not let the sacrifices of the last days be for nothing. She would not let the suffering Caleb endured be for nothing.

Her father entered the room and paused to give her a half-smile before coming the rest of the way to grasp her shoulders and bring a halt to her haphazard meanderings. "Calm down. You're making me dizzy."

"Bullshit."

"*Mozhet byt', moya oba bezumny.*"

She grudgingly laughed. "Conceded. Where's Mom?"

"Down in the weapons bay supervising the installation from as close a position as she can manage without donning an environment suit and going outside—which she almost did. Caleb?"

"Interrogating Nyx, trying to extract anything else out of her that might help us."

"Then they're both putting their skills to their best use. What's our excuse?"

She made a face. "You and I, we *do*. And for a few more minutes, there's nothing for us to do."

"You mean we run headlong into danger, then once we get there make up a plan on the spot, roll the dice and hope our gambit works."

"Well, you can't know what your gut is going to tell you is the right move until you have to make it."

"Truer words, *milaya*." His expression grew serious. "No matter what comes, we will persevere. It's not over until we win."

Oh, how she wanted to believe him. How she wanted to believe that her father not only had all the answers, but the power to make everything okay. Once upon a time she had believed it; then he hadn't come home. "Why are you so sure?"

"Because I didn't cross universes to return to life, simply to die again."

She hugged him. "Damn straight you didn't."

'Pardon the interruption, but the installation of the Tartarus Trigger is complete. Commandant Solovy has ordered our departure in one hundred twenty seconds.'

"Thanks, Thomas." She exhaled. "To the bridge, then."

ᴙ

MILKY WAY GALACTIC CORE

AFS Stalwart II

The Caeles Prism had rendered even the greatest cosmic distances trivial, which had proved to often make such journeys rather anticlimactic. Not so this one.

Despite being masked by maximum filters over the viewport, the blinding, writhing light of the galactic core nevertheless bathed the bridge in a pale magenta glow.

Alex could spout the numbers: twelve million stars packed into a cubic parsec, a deafening roar of radio waves propelled across the galaxy by the 46,000 megameter-wide Sagittarius A*, and beyond it a four million solar mass black hole crammed into a Schwarzschild radius of less than 12,000 megameters. The numbers did nothing to render its size or power fathomable.

As she'd thought, she was back here again—much closer this time, too—and this visit she allowed herself the smallest measure of appreciation for the sight.

Her mother, however, was all business; of course she had to be. "Systems, confirm the Dimensional Rifter and its shielding are operating at maximum capacity. Thomas, confirm our location."

'Our location is Milky Way *l* 17° 44' 39.15" *b* 29° 14' 21.93", which is within the margin of error of our targeted destination.'

"Thank you. The Prótos Agora should cross twenty megameters in front of us in the next minute. Prepare to match its velocity and orbital trajectory as soon as we detect it."

'Acknowledged.'

One could slice through the strained air with a blade, so coiled was the tension on the bridge. Was it always like this on a military ship during a mission? During pitched combat, with wailing sirens and panicked damage reports, sure. But here there was no enemy fleet, no chaos of the battlefield.

Only a deadly supermassive black hole in front of them, a deadly weapon ready to launch beneath them, and the fortress protecting the rotted heart of the enemy speeding between the two.

'Object detected on sensors. It matches the profile and orbital characteristics of the Prótos Agora.'

Her mother's voice was cold steel. "Proceed."

Advanced inertial dampeners meant the floor barely shifted as they accelerated into a parallel course. The lights dimmed as power was reallocated. The ship held only a skeleton crew for the mission, and likely most of the other decks had just been pitched into darkness.

Caleb squeezed her hand. "Time for me to work." He strode forward to the viewport.

She wasn't at all convinced the structure's *diati* barrier could withstand the forces their black hole would generate, but he was, and now was not the time to leave any measure undone.

Her heart ached with pride and sorrow at the tragic, heroic cut of his silhouette cast against the shining viewport. The weight of universes rested on all their shoulders now, yet though he felt that weight more profoundly than any of them, his shoulders remained unbowed.

She wanted to run to him—she wanted him to not stand alone—but she had a job to do as well, if a small and brief one. She switched to sidespace and located the oval structure hurtling around the core. "Confirmed. The structure is the Prótos Agora. No detectable activity, but the shields are operational. We should be clear to proceed."

From what seemed a great distance away, her mother spoke. "Weapons, confirm a lock on the target. Remember, detonation needs to occur within two megameters of the target's location."

"Target lock confirmed. Distance confirmed within parameters."

"Mr. Marano, proceed."

The shimmering crimson shell surrounding the structure quivered once and whipped away.

She opened her eyes to see Caleb stumble back for two steps then catch his balance. He huffed a breath. "Didn't expect it to find me over such a distance. *Diati* shield is down."

She hurriedly returned to sidespace. "Confirmed. *Diati* shield is down."

Her mother wasted no time. "Weapons, fire the Tartarus Trigger. Confirm successful ejection."

"Confirmed. Tartarus Trigger fired and away."

"Navigation, retreat two parsecs at ninety-five percent of maximum safe speed."

This time the floor did lurch as they reversed course.

"Tartarus Trigger detonation confirmed."

No shit. A rapidly expanding chasm formed and grew in the port half of the viewport. Around it the brilliant light of the core twisted as if being wrung out, alternately elongating and contracting and fighting to do both at once. Gradually, however, a new, even brighter light source began to build up along the periphery of the chasm.

'Target has disappeared from sensors, as have all objects formerly registering in the 0.8 parsecs surrounding it.'

Her mother's throat worked. "Noted. Navigation, take us another two parsecs away from the core."

"Yes, ma'am."

Alex assumed they were moving in reverse, but the void and the light ringing it outside the viewport nevertheless grew larger relative to the ship.

Caleb rejoined her to glance at her mother in concern as Alex wound an arm around his waist. "Faster might be better."

Her mother's jaw flexed. "Good point. Navigation, increase our speed to one hundred ten percent maximum safe speed."

"Acknowledged."

The already dim lights on the bridge faded to twilight.

Abruptly a flash erupted across the expanse of their vision. A jagged streak of void convulsed then ripped the expanding event horizon in two. Both halves disintegrated, and in seconds the scene reverted to its appearance on their arrival.

The forces that had been wrenching the ship—transfixed by the unfolding events, Alex had hardly noticed the hull shuddering, but it definitely had been shuddering—ceased, and the calm which descended highlighted the strength of the violence that had come before.

Miriam quickly looked around. "Report. Anyone who has data, speak up."

"I'm still not registering the target—"

"All systems nominal—"

'The black hole—'

"But not everyone at once. Systems?"

"All primary ship systems have returned to nominal readings. Shields are at full strength. No structural damage reported."

"Tactical?"

"I'm not registering the target on any scans."

"Navigation, now that a black hole is no longer attempting to devour us, take us back in a short distance, say 1.5 parsecs, along the course the target would have followed had we not interrupted its journey. Gently, please. Thomas?"

'I postulate that the incident we witnessed was the event horizons of the two black holes—the one created by the Tartarus Trigger and the supermassive black hole at the galactic core—colliding. What followed was the absorption of the Tartarus Trigger's black hole by the far larger and more powerful object.'

"Likelihood?"

'71.6 percent, rising by 2.8 percent every five seconds the astronomical readings remain consistent.'

"Thank you. Tactical, anything on scans?"

"Negative, ma'am."

She turned toward them. "Alex? Is there any way you can confirm the Prótos Agora no longer exists?"

She reached into her pocket and pulled out the Reor slab, then retreated several steps to the relative spaciousness of the rear third of the bridge. "Nobody wander too close to me for the next little bit."

Valkyrie, let's open a small wormhole in front of me, destination as close to the orbital path of the Prótos Agora as we can get without being pummeled.

Ready. Opening.

As always, the luminous strings spun out in all directions. But those crossing the area of the core continued on to the far side of the galaxy. Importantly, she could check for the frequencies of the data previously streaming from the Prótos Agora.

Scanning. I am not detecting any waves matching those we measured as originating from the Prótos Agora data vault. Scanning complete. They are not there.

She closed the wormhole. "The data stored on the Prótos Agora is gone. That's as much of a confirmation as I can give you, but I think it's a good one."

"It is. All right. Science, launch four probes on trajectories to put them into orbit 2 parsecs apart, calibrated to detect the Prótos

Agora's signature. Set them to transmit if they detect anything. Navigation, withdraw another twenty parsecs from the core region. When you reach that distance, deploy the Caeles Prism. We'll return to the staging coordinates and from there, to Post Delta."

Miriam stepped off the perch to join Caleb and David. "I can't help but feel a bit uncertain. Is that it? We've won, and now it's time to help the people of Amaranthe build up a new government then go home?"

Alex jogged back to them and slid in next to Caleb. "The end of the Metigen War was a fair bit more dramatic, I have to admit."

"With you as the spear, how could it not be? And don't misunderstand—I'm not complaining. It's been a hell of a day, week, month. And we still need to run the Machim Primor to ground. We should also put surveillance on the surviving *elassons*. If they decide to work together, they can become nearly as dangerous as—"

'Commandant, the Post Satus Security Director is requesting to speak with you. She insists it's urgent.'

Miriam arched an eyebrow. "See? I knew it was too good to be true. Thank you, Thomas. I'll take the comm in the conference room."

47

AFS STALWART II

M iriam stared at the message in dismay.

The Machim Primor has acquired a newly completed Tartarus Trigger. He possesses the coordinates to one of the portals into the Katasketousya's multiverse network and is proceeding to it now. He intends to traverse this network until he reaches the Humans' home universe then detonate the Tartarus Trigger within it. I possess no further information. May favor go with you.

Was there to be no end to the challenges to their very existence? Would the next horizon merely hold another, yet greater threat? Was victory, security, or any semblance of peace a fantasy forever out of her grasp?

But she could not let this be the blow to break her. "Can this information be trusted?"

Volya made a kind of snarling noise. "Not in the slightest. It came through a tip line we've set up so people out there can feel like they're helping our cause without risking their lives. It's completely anonymous, and we have no way to verify the sender or the information. But given the contents of the message, we thought we should bring it to your attention immediately."

"You thought correctly. Thank you." She minimized the holo and looked around at the grim faces surrounding her. "We have no choice but to act as if the information is legitimate. Thomas, I need Lakhes here this instant, and Sator Nisi on holo. I need...I need everyone, and I need them now."

ᴀR

I can confirm the activation of a portal in the Sculptor Dwarf galaxy twelve minutes ago.

The dire proclamation announced Lakhes arrival well enough. Miriam pivoted to the swirling lights. "Give me the coordinates to that portal." She activated the ship's comm system. "Navigation, you'll be receiving new coordinates momentarily. Re-engage the Caeles Prism and prepare for traversal to those coordinates as soon as the power threshold is reached."

Navigation: "Solid copy. Coordinates received. Caeles Prism will be ready for use in twenty-two seconds."

"All right, people. How much time do we have to prevent this device from detonating?"

Alex moved in a burst of energy along the length of the table. "It depends on whether the Machim Primor possesses the frequency of the TLF wave pointing to the Aurora portal, doesn't it? I've been chased through the Mosaic, and it soon turns into a maze if you don't understand the pattern of the signals." She paused long enough to shrug. "With fifty-one portal spaces plus all the interconnecting tunnels, if he doesn't know the frequency, he's unlikely to get lucky, in which case we have hours at a minimum. If he does know it?" Her shoulders sagged. "We're already too late."

Miriam shook her head. "I refuse to accept that outcome."

Navigation: "Caeles Prism is powered and ready."

"Caeles Prism traversal is authorized. On arrival, prepare to open a Katasketousya portal."

She spun back to Lakhes. "What can you or your people do to stop the battlecruiser or buy us time to reach it?"

Alex's voice was flat, and her frenetic movements had halted. "They can destroy the Aurora portal."

She is correct, in principle.

"What would that mean?"

Her daughter's expression forewarned Miriam that she would not like the answer. "It means that the Aurora universe will be forever cut off from the Mosaic and Amaranthe. From everything. The people there will be safe, but they will be alone. And we—all of us here in Amaranthe—can never go home again. Or see home, or talk to or communicate in any way with anyone back home."

Miriam's lips parted, but she struggled to find the words required. She tried not to indulge in public affection while in uniform, but it was a rule she'd broken more than once this week, and now she frantically reached out beside her to find David's hand. She squeezed it tightly, taking desperate comfort from the warmth of his skin as he returned the squeeze and didn't let go.

She shifted her attention once again to Lakhes. "Well?"

We do not have analystae in the Aurora Enisle at present, but I can dispatch someone now. Their arrival will not be instantaneous. It will however, be far more swift than your ship's arrival. Perhaps swift enough. What is your desire?

She laughed bitterly, then hurried to cover her mouth before it became a cry. "My desire? How dare you ask me that. Do it. Send someone to destroy the portal. We have to try."

"No, we don't."

Miriam pivoted to Caleb; he'd been silent throughout the conversation, as he had been for much of the time since Solum, until now. "Caleb, I am heartbroken at the thought of severing us from home, of all these people never seeing their families again, but we—"

"You'll see home again, I promise you. I know how to save Aurora, how to save everyone."

Navigation: "Coordinates reached. Mosaic portal open and ready for traversal."

Caleb leaned into the table with sudden intensity. "Don't go through it. Lakhes, don't order your analystae to blow the Aurora portal. Wait here..." his brow furrowed "...actually, you might want to move a couple of megameters to starboard from the portal."

"You're asking us to just sit here and...wait?"

"I am. In ninety seconds, you'll know if I failed and you need to act. But I won't fail." He quickly strode to Alex, who was standing there staring at him in abject confusion.

"What are you doing?"

He brought both hands to her face and drew her in close. "Whatever happens, know this: *I love you*. Beyond reason, beyond madness. You are the light in my darkness, always."

"I—wait, tell me what you're doing! Caleb, don't—"

He took two long steps back, a bright crimson aura burst forth to surround him, and he vanished.

PART VII:

STARDUST

"You're an interesting species. An interesting mix. You're capable of such beautiful dreams, and such horrible nightmares.
You feel so lost, so cut off, so alone, only you're not.
See, in all our searching, the only thing we've found that makes the emptiness bearable, is each other."

— *Carl Sagan*

48

SCULPTOR DWARF GALAXY

Mosaic Portal
LGG Region VIII

C aleb hovered in space thirty meters above the *Stalwart II*. In front of him, glacier blue plasma undulated in agitation within the towering portal ring, and he was close enough to sense the electricity dancing around it. A thick bubble of *diati* surrounded him. Protecting him, for now.

But the clock raced headlong for zero, and there was no time to waste with regrets. He quickly composed a message to Alex and sent it. *I'm so sorry, my love.*

A resigned, quiet calm came over him. He had found his salvation, and though the price was a high one, so too had been the cost of his transgression.

He closed his eyes.

See my mind.

Know my request.

In a time before time, you shaped and molded this universe. It was your first purpose, and now it must be your purpose again.

Tear open the portals between dimensions. Sweep away the debris. Move worlds. Move life, but take care to preserve it as you do.

See my mind. Know my request. Draw from me what power you require to fulfill this purpose. Follow my directives and reshape the universe.

When it is done, return to your rightful place among the stars and be at peace, for your work here will be done.

See my mind. Know my request. Be the instrument of my will. Go now.

The cosmos exploded within him, around him, through him...and he surrendered to his own peace.

AURORA

SENECA

"Mommy, I was talking to Anna while we were playing in the holovid, and we want to make up an adventure that other people can play where they meet the tiger aliens and the rainbow aliens and have to rescue them, or maybe the tiger aliens and the rainbow aliens have to rescue the people playing. We're going to need an exanet senspace adapter if we want to share it with other people, so can we go to the store and get one?"

Isabela Marano regarded her daughter with a mix of wariness and incredulity. Marlee was growing up so fast, but her intellect was growing even faster.

She'd convinced Isabela last month to upgrade her eVi to the limit of what could be considered safe for a child at her stage of neural development. She knew all about Prevos and Melanges and Artificials, to the point where she'd begun asking surprisingly insightful questions about Isabela's work. She was a wiz at customizing her virtual spheres using a simplified form of visual programming.

She still spoke with the voice of a child, but her words increasingly ranged beyond her years.

"Mommy? Can we?"

She smiled and took Marlee's hand to make sure she stopped at the upcoming intersection. "Senspace adapters are expensive. Why don't you concentrate on building this adventure first. If you prove to me that you will finish a project once you start it, then we'll see about getting one."

"Yay! I already started working on the story this morning, and when we get home, I can—"

Vertigo. The fleeting thought that she couldn't breathe. A tumbling sky—

Isabela blinked several times, disoriented to the point of feeling nauseated. Cool hardness pressed into her cheek...she was lying on the sidewalk, with no recollection of having fallen.

She forced her eyes to stay open. "Marlee!"

A whimper beside her told Isabela where her daughter was before her eyes did. She crawled to her knees and clambered around to reach her. "Are you okay, honey?"

Marlee's lips curled down. "Ow. I feel funny...." A hand reached down to grope at her leg as she began to sniffle. "My knee hurts."

"Let me see." She leaned down to inspect Marlee's leg, which was when she realized *everyone* was on the ground. People looked around in bewilderment while sprawled on the sidewalks, or climbed to their feet then did the same.

A mass blackout? What could have caused such a thing? Had they been gassed? She inhaled through her nose, but smelled nothing odd. No skycars had dropped out of the sky as far as she could tell, but autopilot systems would have kicked in if their drivers fell unconscious. No explosions rocked the buildings or tore into the streets as they had when General O'Connell launched his fiery barrage on Krysk.

She forced herself to focus on her daughter. Priorities. "You skinned it on the sidewalk is all." She reached in her bag and retrieved a hygienic wipe, using it to gently dab at the scrape. "Better?"

Marlee nodded weakly and sniffled again. Isabela steadied herself, picked her daughter up in her arms and stood.

"What happened, Mommy? Why did we fall?"

She scanned the scene to the horizon, but found no answers. "I do not know."

R

AQUILA

Noah gazed out at an audience of people he did not recognize. Wealthy business magnates, socialites, celebrities, allegedly even a few politicians had come to do their social duty and be present for the honoring of his father.

Kennedy was in the front row, though, along with her parents, her brother and his husband. Her family, here to support him. His family now, in a way; that one was going to require greater mulling over, later. But today was about his father....

Goddamn his father. His clone. The man had controlled so much of his life—actively and with a heavy, unforgiving hand for the first fifteen years, then by living rent-free in Noah's head for the next twenty. Until Kennedy. He started to smile at the thought, but quickly tamped it down. This was a funeral, after all.

He supposed his life had come full circle, in a sense. But, inevitable heir to his father's fortune or not, in the ways that mattered it had done so *his* way.

Public speaking was not his gig, and he decided his best course of action was to direct his speech to Kennedy. The rest of the audience would think what they wished and take from it what they wanted in any event.

He cleared his throat and tried to look properly solemn, if not dignified. "We're gathered here today to honor the memory of Lionel Terrage. To honor his life and his achievements, which were many."

He exhaled. "My father was...my father was not an easy man to like. But he built an industrial empire, garnered riches for himself, and along the way made the world a little bit better through his endeavors. By putting his drive, determination, perseverance and intellect to work, he barreled through obstacles to see his grandest visions realized. And when it truly mattered, he put everything he'd built on the line for family and for larger principles—for something greater than himself. I can think of no better compliment than—"

Lightheaded, like he'd double-dosed a chimeral and forgotten to eat first.

Noah blinked in confusion. Why was everything sideways? His face rested against the marble floor beside the tumbled-over dais...he lifted his head up to find the gathered audience in variations of his own state.

"Kennedy?" He pushed up to his knees and crawled to the edge of the stage, then climbed down and stumbled toward where she'd been sitting.

"I'm all right." Her carefully styled curls tumbled messily across her face, but she'd stood by the time he reached her and was turning to help her father up and into his seat. Noah scrambled to do the same for her mother.

The rumble of confused murmurs grew to fill the auditorium, and he leaned in close to Kennedy's ear. "What happened? It looks as if everyone passed out, but that doesn't make any sense."

"I have no idea." She wore a perplexed expression as she gathered her hair back in its clasp and tried to tame it. *"Vii, any chance you know what just happened on Aquila?"*

'Not merely on Aquila. The anomaly occurred on numerous colonies—very possibly all colonies—simultaneously.'

Kennedy's eyes widened. *"What? Do you mean some sort of cos-*mic *anomaly? What could it have been?"*

'Something wonderful.'

49

AFS STALWART II

MOSAIC PORTAL
SCULPTOR DWARF GALAXY
LGG REGION VIII

The portal exploded, shredding the ring bounding it into thousands of shards flung outward into the void—but it didn't *just* explode. The plasma filling it shot forward across the stars like the leading edge of a tsunami. It stretched and bent, and space stretched and bent around it.

Then it vanished, and space where the portal had hung stilled.

The images being fed to the conference room defied comprehension or even description. What could have caused the portal to erupt in such a violent manner? What had the eruption done to the fabric of space?

"Thomas, talk to me. What do we—"

An anguished gasp drowned Miriam out. She spun from the visuals to see Alex stifle a sob with a hand over her mouth as she staggered backwards, fumbling with her other hand for the wall behind her for support.

"Alex, what's wrong? What's happened?"

Her daughter looked up, tears flowing freely down her face, and tossed an aural toward the table. "Where *is* he, Valkyrie? Find him!"

'His locater signal indicates he is currently atop the outer hull of the Stalwart II. *But I am...not detecting any vital signs.'*

Alex exploded off the wall in a full run and disappeared through the door.

Miriam hurriedly skimmed the words displayed on the aural Alex had left behind. "David—"

"I'm going." He pivoted and took off through the door after her.

Alex,

I know why every child looks up at the stars at night in search of wonders, why every adult gazes up at them in search of some greater meaning to our existence. Humanity took to the stars in the hope of finding companionship, and instead found only a vast emptiness.

But we were never meant to be alone. We were meant to live in a universe teeming with life, and deep in our souls, we've always known it. We've always felt its absence. I can—and now I must—return us to our rightful place in the universe. Humanity's destiny lies here, surrounded by a rich diversity of life and boundless possibilities. Here, anything is possible.

The Mosaic served a necessary purpose, but it's no longer needed, so tell Mesme I'm closing up shop. I'm taking care of the battlecruiser and its cargo, too. The Machim Primor won't trouble anyone again. Everyone back home, everyone we met in our travels, everyone living within the portal spaces—they will all be safe. Might have to hunt around a bit for them, but I'm making sure they all arrive in one piece.

There's only one universe now. I hope humanity will take the lead in making it a good one.

I expect doing this will kill me. You saw how much the diati drained me to destroy the moon at Akeso; I fear it's going to need every drop of my energy, of my life force, I suppose, to accomplish what I'm asking of it.

I don't want to leave you. I want to spend the next hundred or thousand years chasing after you on ever-new escapades. I want to—but I can't.

I know you'll think I view this as penance for Solum, and maybe even for all the lives I've taken over the years. In a way, I do. It gives me comfort to replace the ruins of Solum with Earth—to bring Earth to a place where it can serve as a brighter, better, more worthy beacon at the center of civilization.

It gives me comfort to replace despair with hope. To replace death with life. I've done a fair measure of both good and evil in my life, and a lot of gray in between. It gives me comfort to end it with an act of simple goodness.

I wish so much that doing so didn't mean sacrificing my life, but it's a sacrifice I must make. You'd tell me to be selfish, but I can't. Not this time. I know you'll mourn me, but don't wait too long before getting back to exploring. A whole damn lot of stars are out there, and you need to meet the beings living around them. Welcome them to the family. Protect them.

You've been my savior, time and time again. But I can't allow you to save me this last time, not when the lives and futures of everyone who will ever be are on the line. So I'll do the saving this time, and I'll pay the price it requires.

Eternally my love.

— Caleb

Alex was nowhere to be seen by the time David reached the first crossway. He hesitated in the intersection. "Thomas, help me out. Where is she?"

'Alex is currently descending on Lift 2. If I may extrapolate a likely destination from the information on hand, I believe she is heading to Medical.'

"Hold Lift 3 for me." He took a left and resumed running.

With every step, his heart was breaking. She'd suffered the debilitating trauma of losing a parent as a child—his fault—and she should never have to experience the loss of someone so close to her again! His only solace was the knowledge that if she did, he was going to be there for her. This time, he would ease her pain rather than cause it.

He reached Lift 3 to find two enlisted grumbling about why it wasn't working. He bullied them back with a glare and leapt inside. "Sorry, emergency." Then he was speeding downward through the ship.

Too many seconds ticked by until he arrived at Deck 5, and he rushed off the lift before it had settled to the floor.

'Left, sir, and take the third hallway.'

He reached the hallway in time to glimpse her sprinting down it. "Alex, wait! Let me go with you!"

"Then run faster!" She shouted over her shoulder without slowing.

Dammit, this body was still new, sporting a few kinks yet to be worked out...and she was propelled onward by a force capable of driving the human body to feats far beyond its natural capabilities: love.

Two more hallways and he burst into Medical only a few meters behind her. He stopped cold in the entrance, but Alex kept moving. Because she had known what they would find here. He, however, had not.

Valkyrie's semi-physical representation rushed across the room toward a treatment alcove with a speed and finesse he also hadn't known she possessed, Caleb's limp form draped across her ghostly arms.

Two medics shook off any surprise they might have experienced at the most unusual sight and rushed forward as well, and at the cot they extracted him from her arms. A physician arrived the next instant, and a sequence of events he'd seen too many times in his life began to unfold.

Alex didn't do what almost every family member did in such a situation, though. She didn't rush to the cot in a panic and get in the way of the medical ministrations.

"Unresponsive—"

No, she merely stood in the center aisle, still as a stone and eyes locked on Caleb.

"I'm not detecting a pulse—"

Valkyrie moved to hover next to David.

He studied her with one eye, the other remaining on Alex. "You went outside and got him. Thank you."

"ECG is flat—"

The particles making up her presence quivered in the air. "It would have taken her, or anyone, far too long to don the necessary gear and make their way along the hull to reach him. So I did what I could, which seems like so very little now."

He swallowed. "I think it was quite a lot."

"Still no pulse—"

"I find I am questioning my choice of name. I believe I want no further association with death."

He had no good response to that, so he stepped over and wound an arm around Alex's shoulder. She showed no indication of noticing he was there.

The doctor sighed and took a step back. "All right. I'm calling it—"

Alex burst forward out of his grasp, as if a switch had been flipped on. "No. You hook him up to life support and you get him in a stasis chamber right now."

"Ma'am, I'm sorry, but there's nothing for us to sustain. There's no brain activity, no heartbeat."

"Did I stutter? Did I accidentally speak Communis? Beat his heart *for* him."

"I don't think—"

"Stasis chamber. They're kept in Medical Storage C on Deck 12, and you can have one up here and operational in six minutes."

The doctor gave her that look doctors gave the poor, pathetic family members of the lost, one of restrained condescension tempered by a pale imitation of true empathy because they'd lost their capacity to feel the real thing a few hundred deaths ago. "Are you his wife? A family member—?"

Alex's glyphs and irises flared like a nova eruption, though Valkyrie's presence did not fade in turn. "His wife? I am not *just* his wife. I am Alexis Mallory Solovy Marano, daughter of Commandant and Commander Solovy, first Prevo and goddamn savior of humanity thrice over.

"So listen to me very carefully. You are going to stop acting like fucking *svilochnaya* and get your *yebanaya* asses in gear, and you are going to do it this instant. You think I'm upset now? Have a stasis chamber in this room and operational in six minutes, or you'll see something you haven't seen before."

The medics eyed the door uncertainly.

"Five minutes and fifty seconds."

The doctor spun to the medics. "What are you waiting for? I want a Grade III stasis chamber up here ASAP. I'll administer artificial ventilation until you return."

50

AFS STALWART II

*D*avid, what's going on?
Valkyrie transported him to Medical. It doesn't look good.

The diati *isn't healing him?*

Apparently not. There's no sign it's here at all and, well, his message....

Okay. Take care of her.

I will. You take care of everything else.

Miriam closed her eyes for a breath, allowed her heart to ache for the span of it...then reopened them and squared her shoulders. "Thomas, let's try this again. What do we know?"

'Very little. The eruption at the portal does not match the characteristics of any recorded astronomical or human-orchestrated event.'

"Lakhes, what are your agents telling you?" She turned toward the Kat as she asked the question—and found the area where it had hovered empty. She scanned the room. "Lakhes?"

Brigadier Jenner, who'd arrived a moment earlier, spoke up. "The Kat spun up in a tornado and vanished right after I walked in."

"Well. Thomas, please convey my sincere interest in learning what it knows as soon as it is practicable for Lakhes to convey it."

'Message sent, with the appropriate nuances in tenor intact.'

"Thank you." She checked the constantly updating long-range sensor readings. "No sign of the Machim battlecruiser. It's entirely possible it's been destroyed, but we need to keep scanning for it nonetheless. Now—"

'I apologize for interrupting, Commandant, but the prime minister is on the priority communications channel. He would like to know *'quoi au nom de Dieu* just happened.''

"What prime minister?"

'Prime Minister Gagnon of the Earth Alliance.'

She should have realized from the particular flavor of the cursing, but the impossibility of it being Gagnon interfered with such a conclusion. "How interesting. Tell him I will speak with him the instant I can answer that question." She gazed around the room. "Everyone, we need to be able to answer that question."

'Everyone' consisted of more holos than physical bodies, since she'd ordered the *Stalwart II* stripped to a skeleton crew for the Prótos Agora mission and most of the Council members were either on Tarach or onboard their respective ships with the rest of the fleet.

Mia tilted her head, uncertainty animating her face. "I can hear the Noesis—the main one."

Commander Lekkas quickly motioned in agreement. "So can I. I assumed I'd developed a glitch, but maybe not. There's a lot of excited chatter...something about people passing out for a few minutes. Everyone...everywhere? Then they all woke back up...at the same time?"

Mia leaned into the frame of her holo. "Scientists are picking up an avalanche of unusual readings from deep space sensors. It's as if...." Her eyes were wide as they rose to stare at Miriam. "I think they're *here.*"

"Under the circumstances, I need you to be more specific."

"I think Aurora is *here*, in Amaranthe. Our colonized worlds at a minimum, and maybe much more. Our telescopes, our scientific research probes, our exanet infrastructure?" The young woman nodded with increasing confidence. "Use the Caeles Prism and go to Solum."

"Solum is a debris field."

"I...think we should check and confirm if that's still true."

ʎ

SOL STELLAR SYSTEM
MILKY WAY SECTOR 1

"That's not Solum."

'No, Commandant. It is Earth.'

Miriam had departed the conference room for the bridge, because this she had to see with her own eyes. Now she stood at the wide forward viewport, seeing it with her own eyes yet having difficulty accepting what they showed her.

No trace of the expansive debris field Solum's destruction had created remained. In its place, orbiting 1 AU from a Sol lacking Dyson rings, was Earth—Earth as she'd seen it a few short weeks earlier.

And not only Earth, either—it came with its full complement of orbital satellites, space stations and an intact Terrestrial Defense Grid. A quick scan had already confirmed that the moon was their moon, dotted with human rather than Anaden structures. Mars was their Mars. It now seemed inevitable that longer-range scans would soon report the news of Jupiter being their Jupiter, and so on.

Exactly as Caleb had described in his message to Alex.

To her left, increasing brightness heralded the arrival of a Kat. "Lakhes?"

Pardon my delay, but there has been much information to analyze and confirm.

"Of this I have no doubt. What has this information told you?"

The Mosaic is indeed gone—or the portals to access it are gone, which effects the same end. Our Idryma has been relocated into Amaranthean space, however, as has, self-evidently, the Aurora Enisle. We've confirmed the presence of the contents of three additional enisles elsewhere in Amaranthe thus far, which is a number large enough for us to draw a preliminary conclusion.

"Which is?"

Caleb Marano ordered the diati *he controlled to draw the enisles of the Mosaic into Amaranthe. He ordered it to place the Sol system in its natural location and move the astronomical and Anaden-constructed bodies of the original Sol system to a comparatively empty region of space twenty-two parsecs away.*

The other planets and systems of Aurora are not always located at their precise prior coordinates, as they are in nearly every instance duplicates of objects existing here. But you can expect to find them in proximity thereto. The contents of the other enisles we have identified were discovered here and there within the bounds of the Local Galactic Group.

Her attention returned to the planet orbiting below. Silence lingered as, fact by fact, the import of Lakhes' statements sank in and the unfathomable became truth. "So we are all one universe now."

Amaranthe has always been the universe. *Now, it is the only universe.*

She found she was smiling. "Thank you, Lakhes. Alert me immediately to any relevant threats you discover arising as a result of this...alteration in the scenery, but otherwise, please see to your duties, which I'm sure are significant."

It will be so. The Kat faded away.

"Thomas, let Prime Minister Gagnon know I'm ready to speak to him now—and please invite Chairman Vranas and Governor Ledesme to the meeting as well. I'm going to have to repeat this incredible story to dubious audiences enough in the coming days as it is."

51

PRESIDIO

The ASCEND Director of Medical Research looked appropriately sympathetic, if far too condescending. Everyone in the parade of doctors had worn the same expression, but Alex found she just didn't care. She didn't need their sympathy, whether real or false. She only needed their medical expertise.

"We have exhausted all options currently within our capabilities, as well as several approaches suggested by consultants from Amaran—from the anarch medical staff. Despite our efforts, we've been unable to induce the resumption of brain activity. Perhaps if we had access to a recent neural imprint, even a partial—"

"There isn't one." Alex schooled her features, cognizant her mother was watching her. The news wasn't unexpected, but hearing the words spoken aloud still wounded her more than she'd prepared for. *Keep moving. One step, then another. Eyes forward. Chin lifted.* "Thank you for going above and beyond, Director. I understand there's nothing else you can pursue at present, so what I need you to do now is keep the stasis chamber functioning and ensure his—" her voice stumbled, only a small hitch "—condition doesn't deteriorate."

"Of course we can do that. But at some point, we will need to consider whether—"

"I'll do all the considering, thank you. Keep him in an active stasis chamber. Do not allow his body or any of his organs to atrophy. Have I made myself sufficiently clear?"

His gaze darted over her shoulder as if to seek confirmation from her mother; presumably receiving it, he nodded firmly. "Yes, ma'am. I'll see to it."

"Thank you." She waited for him to leave before turning to her mother.

The sympathy on Miriam's face was so much more genuine, weighed down by sorrow, and Alex couldn't decide if this was better or worse. She tried to smile, but given that all her willpower was deployed every second to keep her from screaming and raging and tossing furniture, smiling was a bit too much to ask.

"Don't tell me I'm in denial or that being in denial is understandable. I know what I'm doing."

"All right. I won't tell you either of those things—for now. I know you need time. If this is not denial, however, can I ask what it is you believe you *are* doing?"

Alex winced. "No?"

The admiral of old flashed across her mother's features, but Miriam smoothly banished it in favor of a more indulgent mien. "That's all right, too. I'm here for you—you know this, yes? Unfortunately, this is one area where I have too much experience. I made a lot of mistakes after your father died, and you bore the brunt of many of them. If I can make up for those mistakes in some small way by being here for you now, I hope you'll let me try."

"You already are. I mean it. You being here means the world to me. But in point of fact, right now you need to *not* be here. I'm making you late for the big conference."

Her mother smiled, adding a touch of flair to it for show. "I believe they will wait on me."

Alex laughed in spite of the weight permanently crushing her chest. "Hell yes, they will."

⟡

Alex stood alone in a corner of the atrium outside the ASCEND medical wing, having finally convinced her mother to depart for what would be the first formal meeting between humanity's leaders and those of multiple Amaranthean species. An important meeting to say the least, and one at which the first page of a new intergalactic order was to be written. She wished them well, but she had her own meeting to see through.

She'd been patient; she'd tried conventional measures first and exhausted all reasonable and ordinary options, but in the back of her mind she'd known the path would lead here. And so it had. Time to set some unconventional measures in motion.

The silent, solitary moments like this one were easier than the rest, though everyone kept insisting they must be harder. In these moments, she didn't have to pretend—to be strong, to be upset, to not be buoyed by hope or sheltered by denial. Alone, she could let the yawning emptiness engulf her in peace, cry her tears without expectations and reinforce the inner certainty that kept her putting one foot in front of the other.

But this particular such moment was also short, as it didn't take long for the swirl of lights to materialize in front of her to herald Mesme's arrival.

You requested my presence?

"I did. Thank you for coming so quickly. I'm sure you and the rest of the Idryma are facing a mountain of work and, hopefully, opportunities. But there's something I need you to do for me. For him. I recognize it might take a little time, but once it's done, I swear I will never ask anything of you again."

I—we, all of us—owe an immeasurable debt to both you and Caleb. State your boon, and if I am capable of doing so, I will accomplish it.

She told Mesme what she needed it to do. The Kat accepted the task without hesitation, while agreeing that it indeed might take a little time.

When Mesme had departed, Alex took a deep breath, straightened her shoulders and soldiered onward, as she must.

Keep moving. One step, then another. Eyes forward. Chin lifted.

 ℛ

IDRYMA

TRIANGULUM GALAXY
LGG REGION VI

I did not think to see the Idryma again.

But it was time to put away expectations of its imminent destruction or my imminent renewed exile from its halls. Lakhes had proved to be an ally in my cause all along, and now no enemy would be coming to eradicate the Idryma. The Humans had seen to this. Alexis and Caleb—my friends, if I could take such a liberty—had seen to this.

Katasketousya moved briskly through the ethereal halls; none meandered, and all conveyed purpose in their movements. There was much to do, if for now a fair amount of it consisted of determining what to do.

A few matters had been immediately agreed upon: they must locate all the Mosaic worlds, for these were their creations and thus their responsibility. What to do about them once located depended on the individual circumstances.

They must begin the settlement of Katoikia Tairi. Their homeworld could not be brought back, but they could make a new one. Surprisingly for a transdimensional species who traversed galaxies as a matter of course, the desire for the solid ground of a physical homeworld was turning out to be quite strong indeed.

Above all, though they must act with caution, they must act—to protect what needed protecting, to be vigilant watchers, and to find an active role for themselves in this new world.

It was an exciting time. Uncertainty pervaded the halls, but hope was its constant companion.

I located Lakhes in a hall outside the Conclave council chamber, patiently listening to competing arguments for the proper handling of the Mosaic's more primitive species. On sensing my presence, the Praetor issued some instructions and sent the analystae on their way.

"Mnemosyne, please provide me a respite."

I kept my amusement at the thread of resignation in Lakhes' tone to a reasonable level and allowed pity to replace it. But this was a charmed moment we resided in—a fact which, if I knew, Lakhes surely did as well. "Does leadership weigh so heavily on you in this most notable time?"

"Scarcely. Administration, however? I am always keen to inspire, to guide, to nurture and advise. We survived the trials demanding such activities, and now I drown in a sea of minutiae. But it is no matter. Have you come to receive your due accolades while bearing a suitable apportionment of smugness?"

"I am never smug."

"Hyperion says otherwise."

"Hyperion...well, you know the torturous extent of Hyperion's foibles and do not require me to remind you of them. What accolades am I due?"

"You were correct—in all but the tiniest of details, correct about everything. Most of all, you were correct about the Humans. They grow stronger from the overcoming of adversity. More remarkably, they grow *better* from it. They wield ingenuity and creativity to a degree the Anadens have not displayed in cosmic ages, and they use these talents to protect those weaker than them. They win the day and defeat an enemy all have cowered before for millennia, and now, rather than claim the crown they have earned, they beg to relinquish power and hand it over to the masses."

"They are not without flaws."

"Oh, now you express qualms?"

"Now I can afford to."

Lakhes rippled in a display of amusement. "Indeed. Certainly they are not without flaws, but who among us is? The central point of my speech is that we should have listened to you more fully and sooner. It is only because you held true to your convictions in the face of the full Conclave arrayed against you that we are here today to have this conversation."

I fluttered in the brief weakness of pride, but swiftly quelled it. "Yes, about being here today."

"Oh?"

"There is a task I need to perform. It aligns well with our own goals, and in this respect I will be serving the Idryma. But it will take me away from here, and it will take some time."

"How much time? Centuries?"

"Oh, I do hope not. A breath of time on the grand scale of the universe. It is merely that each such breath has been most tumultuous and exigent of late, so I feel the seconds tick by more acutely than usual. Whether it will take weeks, months or years, I do not know, but I need to see it through to the end. Though Alexis has requested this task of me, I feel a personal compulsion to perform it in any case. I owe this to her, but above all I owe it to Caleb."

"We all owe both a personal and a collective debt to him—his sacrifice saved our aeons of work. Saved us, and transformed the universe." Lakhes swirled in contemplation. "Allow the members of the Idryma to lessen your burden, Mnemosyne, and in doing so perhaps repay a small portion of this debt."

I stilled. "You would do this? Not for me, but for him? What about the lengthy list of imperative duties now set before the Idryma?"

"Duties which only exist to be performed because of his sacrifice. We will honor it first and most highly."

"And reveal your own honor in doing so. Thank you, dear friend."

"And to you. May fortune guide our endeavors."

⟡

It took little time to gather the analystae and convey the necessary instructions. All were given the choice of whether to join in the quest; none declined. As evening set in the shadow of a nearby sun, the Katasketousya swept outward from the halls of the Idryma in a sea of white-blue iridescence to sail across the stars.

52

HIRLAS

E ren made his way along the elevated path the attendant had directed him to with a light but slightly nervous step.

He always forgot what a marvel Hirlas was when he hadn't visited in a while, but it was a marvel. Modern technology wound through the limbs and trunks of the jungle with such subtlety as to become all but invisible behind the natural landscape. But it *was* there. The Naraida, with help from their Volucri co-citizens and their Novoloume benefactors, had perfected the balance of technology and nature. They lived in harmony with both in equal measure.

It was a damn near idyllic setting—or perhaps the high nitrogen content of the air was making him loopy. His cybernetics could process and dispose of the extra nitrogen without much difficulty, but it did produce a bit of a buzz.

Anyway…what had he been thinking? Oh, how he was glad wanderlust had driven the Naraida to the stars despite them living on a halcyonian homeworld.

The path veered to circle the breadth of the trunk of a cedrus tree then opened up into a wide terrace, which stretched across an open expanse to another copse of trees in the distance. Beneath it lay a meadow of laurel.

Cosime sat on the left span of the terrace, legs dangling off the edge to dance idly in the air. A gauzy creme tank exposed what should have been a nasty scar along her left shoulder, but she'd already transformed it into a tattoo of a shooting star. Her hair was trimmed short on the left side to blend with the section that had been shaved during the many medical procedures she'd undergone, but it hung longer than usual on the right side. The high sun reflected off it to create a pearling effect across her uninjured shoulder and down her back.

He smiled to himself as he approached. "If you jump, I'm turning around and going back to Tarach."

Her head pivoted toward him, and she flashed him a big grin. Damn. "Bullshite. You'll catch me."

He laughed. "Probably so. I'm a sucker that way." He sat down beside her and tried out swinging his legs off the edge of the terrace. "How do you feel? The attendant said they could hardly get you to come inside for rehab."

"I rehab out here, in my own way. I'm good. I'll be ready for new missions in no time."

"You don't have to be—I mean there don't have to be any new missions. We won."

"Yeah, I heard that. Believe it when I see it. Likely not even then. You can't just snap your fingers and *poof!* Peace."

"Maybe not. But the Directorate is history, as are the Primors. The integrals are being reworked, or falling apart entirely. That part's kind of a mess. The Humans are trying to form an inter-species skeleton government until something more permanent can be developed. Also, the Humans are here—all of them. Some other species, too, ones the Kats had been hiding. I don't know whether we can count on a lasting peace, but I do know everything has changed, and in mostly positive ways. It's a start."

"Huh." Her expression suggested she still wasn't buying it.

It *was* hard to believe until you'd walked the halls of Anaden buildings without fear, then seen exotic, decidedly un-Accepted aliens doing the same. He let it drop for now. "Where's Felzeor? Is he recovering okay?"

She pointed up, toward the broad limbs interwoven above them. "Napping. He's improving. He can't fly for more than a few minutes at a time, but he *can* fly. He's pushing himself too hard, naturally, but he'll come out of this stronger than ever."

"I'm glad. Have you told him about Caleb?"

"Not yet. There will be time for it later, once his body's healed." She picked a tiny leaf off her shirt and flicked it into the air. "Thanks for coming by to check on me, but I imagine there's a lot of excitement you need to get back to. How long are you staying?"

He swallowed past the lump in his throat. "For as long as you'll allow me."

Her gaze darted up to meet his. "What?"

"I'd like to stay."

"It's boring here. There's nothing to do except frolic in the trees or lie in the sun."

"With you? That's not boring." He brought a hand up to cup her cheek. The pad of his thumb gently ran across her soft skin and over her lips. "What do you say? Will you have me?"

Her eyes blinked, widened, then narrowed. "No one 'has' you, Eren. You're too impetuous to be caged."

"Well, I'm choosing to be 'had,' which means it's not a cage. I've chased my demons to ground, and while they'll never be completely buried, I think I've got them whipped into submission fairly well. Chained and gagged in a secure location, as it were.

"I want to be happy, and I want to be happy with you. I love you, and I was thinking maybe one day, if I'm really good, as well as extra charming and funny, you could love me a little, too."

She smiled, and her pale skin brightened to rose. "My dear, sweet, mad, not-so-broken Eren. I've always loved you. But you had to stop hating yourself before you'd be ready to see it."

"Even after everything—"

"Especially after everything."

"But what about—"

She shifted her weight to shove him onto his back, slung a leg over his waist and brought her lips to his. For a waif, her kiss packed surprising ferocity.

This was going to be fun, no doubt about it. He briefly drew back from the kiss to meet her mischievous gaze with his own...

...but why were *four* green eyes staring down at him? He tucked her curtain of hair behind her ear to reveal chocolate and apricot feathers fluttering upon her shoulder. "Felzeor?"

A beak dipped down between them as the Volucri peered curiously at Cosime, then at him. "Hi, Eren! What are you two doing?"

53

SIYANE

The warship assembly lines bustled with activity in a halo around the Presidio. The war may be over, but the number and variety of potential threats had just exploded, and a capable defense force would be needed now more than ever.

The docking ring encircling the central module of the multi-tiered station was nearly full; it was good she'd reserved a slot ahead of time.

Pinchu leaned forward, closer to the viewport, as they slowed on approach. His large frame dwarfed Caleb's cockpit chair, and he'd adopted an awkward half-sideways pose to allow his tail to hang free. "I have never seen anything such as this in all my days. Alex-Human, your people's monuments are even more extraordinary than promised."

"Hopefully not only our ships and space stations. But to be honest, I reacted the same way the first time I saw this place. It's an impressive piece of engineering."

"Indeed. Such astonishing technology and purpose set to the means of waging war, yet you insist you are not a warring species."

Alex regarded the Tokahe Naataan thoughtfully. Due to their high level of technological development relative to most species in the Mosaic, the Khokteh had been among the first species located by the Kats in the aftermath of The Displacement, as the media had taken to calling it. The Kats' arrival on Ireltse had reportedly made for an uncomfortable meeting, with Analystae Iapetus having to explain to Pinchu and the other leaders what had transpired, where their planets had been and where they were now. Probably would have been a lot more than uncomfortable, though, if not for the Khokteh's prior contact with Alex and Caleb.

"I said we 'try' not to be a warring species. Conflict is in our nature, and we damn sure fight to defend ourselves and those who need our protection. But we strive to ensure our society is fundamentally peaceful, and to resolve conflicts among ourselves without too much bloodshed. We don't always succeed, but we try.

"Of course, we're no longer the only players on the universal field." She offered him a weak smile. "That's why I wanted to bring you in early. You deserve a seat at the table when the new rules are written."

"Thank you, Alex-Human, for thinking of my *shikei* during what must be a heart-wrenching time for you." He reached out and touched her shoulder. "You are strong and resilient, but I remain close enough to the pain of my own loss to see your grief."

"Nope, not grief. Sadness, yes, but not grief."

"As you say. I will not argue with the emissary of the Gods."

"Pinchu, you know I'm not—"

"Yes, I know. The Wakhe—the Katasketousya—were our creators, however, so in a technical respect they *are* our Gods. Nevertheless, I expect such phrases to fall into disuse as nothing more than quaint figures of speech soon enough, in the face of so many revelations still to come."

The clearance procedures were all automated, Artificials talking to Artificials, and she docked in an exterior berth without incident. "There are definitely some bizarre sights in your future, but a human facility shouldn't create too much culture shock."

"Other than the regrettable lack of tails, how different can it be from a Khokteh settlement?"

She thought back to their time on Ireltse, abiding the searing, bottomless ache the memories evoked with stoic reserve. "Well, for one thing, there's a lot more metal."

R

PRESIDIO

Alex gave Isabela a quick hug before crouching to let Marlee throw her arms around her neck. It still felt a bit weird, but she was getting the hang of hugging even children.

Marlee stage-whispered excitedly in her ear. "This place is amazing! And a little scary."

"The military is supposed to be scary to our enemies. This is where they practice." She drew back and squeezed Marlee's hands. "I asked your mother to bring you here because I've got someone who wants to meet you."

"Really? Who?"

"You'll see. Now don't be frightened—"

"But do be polite. Remember your manners."

Marlee looked up at her mother and nodded dutifully. "Yes, ma'am."

Alex stood. "He's waiting for us in this meeting room down here." They walked a couple of meters down the hall, and she opened the door. "Pinchu, I have someone with me who wants to say hello."

Pinchu stood and moved to the front of the table, jutting his chest and chin out to a slight *clink* of his ornamentations. "I am Pinchutsenahn Niikha Qhiyane Kteh, Tokahe Naataan of Ireltse and elected leader of the Khokteh people. And you are?"

Marlee's eyes were frozen wide as saucers, and one hand clung to her mother's pants leg behind her, but she thrust her chest out and squared her shoulders in a frankly adorable imitation of his stance. "I am Marlee Rosa Arrigucci Marano, Honorary Goodwill Ambassador to all the new aliens. Greetings, Tokahe Naataan. Tanyan yahi, dah honi...honiline khola."

Pinchu smiled toothily. "Wiyuskinyan wamchi, dah honiline khola. How is it you speak our words, young Human?"

"Auntie Alex gave me the translation program for your language, and I've been studying it."

"Most impressive. You are quite a bright one."

Marlee smiled. "I am. I have a copy of you in my treehouse castle. Do you want to see it?"

Pinchu looked over to Alex in question, and she stepped in to explain. "It's a virtual reality space—a sort of multi-dimensional interactive film."

"Ohhh. Then I should very much like to see this treehouse castle of yours."

Isabela put a hand on Marlee's shoulder. "Next time, perhaps. I'm sure the, um, Tokahe Naataan has many important matters to attend to right now."

Alex grimaced. "I'm afraid we do have a meeting with the commandant and some dignitaries or other in a few minutes. But after Pinchu gets settled in and has let all the people in charge know how things are going to be, maybe he can come to Seneca and spend an afternoon with you."

Marlee's eyes lit up, and she bounced on the balls of her feet while Isabela struggled to politely restrain her. "That will be awesome! I can show you the adventure my friend Anna and I wrote, and you can explain to me some of your words I don't understand."

"I look forward to it, Marlee Rosa Arrigucci Marano."

"Thank you. Me, too."

Isabela rolled her eyes above Marlee's head. "We'll work out the details later. For now, let's get out of their way so Alex and the Tokahe Naataan can work. We're going to go visit with a few scientists over at the ASCEND offices then head home."

Marlee shuffled toward the door wearing a pout. "Okay...."

Isabela placed a hand on Alex's arm, and her voice dropped. "No changes?"

Alex shook her head.

"You'll let me know if anything does change, yes?"

"I will."

Marlee took a single step into the hallway then spun around. "Bye, bye, Pinchutse—, um, —nahn Niikha…."

He bent his long legs to stoop low, though he still towered over the young girl. "As we are now friends, you can call me Pinchu."

54

ROMANE

As Kennedy reached to open the door to their apartment, a dash of irrational fear swept through her. They'd gone straight to Aquila from Amaranthe, then to New York, then to a series of meeting rooms and factories, all in the service of the needs of the Estate of Lionel Terrage, *then* to the Presidio for a discussion of some radical changes in AEGIS' roadmap. Today was the first time they'd returned to Romane since leaving for Amaranthe. Since everything changed.

Her hand hovered over the panel…but she was being silly. She hurriedly input the code, the door opened—and the interior appeared exactly as they had left it. Now she *felt* silly.

She dropped her bags then her coat in a crooked line along the floor as she made her way to the bedroom. When she reached it she collapsed on her back across the width of the bed.

A few seconds later Noah joined her in a matching pose of exhaustion and relief. They were home.

And also in Amaranthe.

That was going to take some getting used to. "We should get some rest while we can. I suspect it'll be a crazy next few weeks, or years."

Noah nodded idly. "You have to wonder how long our suddenly tiny governments are likely to last in a world that just got a lot bigger and more crowded. Plus, something's got to replace the Directorate. What are we going to do with all these aliens? What are they going to do with us?"

She chuckled and shifted her head to gaze out the windows at the view high above downtown. From this angle the view was mostly sky, but it was a fine sky. "All good questions. But I actually meant for us personally. You only thought we were busy before, making ships for AEGIS. Adiamene is a better metal for construction than anything they have in Amaranthe, and we own the patent for it. We may need to hire a couple of employees." She raised her voice. "Or we could clone Vii a couple of times. Right, Vii?"

'Only if I can keep the clones as my minions.'

"It goes without saying." She returned her voice to a conversational level. "You know, we should consider retasking one of your father's factories to adiamene production, so we don't have to rely on third-party manufacturers so heavily. Would you be okay with making the change?"

Noah didn't respond immediately, so she rolled onto her side to face him, and found him staring at her wearing the strangest expression.

She quickly backtracked. "If you're not comfortable doing it, we don't need to—"

"Marry me."

She blinked. When the words penetrated her tired brain, she buried the rush of dangerous endorphins they roused. "I'm sorry, I'm confused. It sounded like you just said, 'marry me,' but clearly I heard wrong."

His hand wound into her hair, tugging the loose band out of it and setting a mane of curls free. "You heard right. Marry me."

"Still confused." Her lips pursed…and her heart quivered in her chest, and her skin probably flushed, too. Damn him. "Is this because with your father's inheritance you're now wealthy enough for no one to ever accuse you of being a gold-digger?"

"No! Well, yes, that might be a factor—a small one. But I keep thinking…my father missed out on so much of life by not sharing his with someone—really sharing it, heart and mind, body and soul, and so on. I keep thinking about Alex, and as much as I'm sure she's suffering right now, I wonder if she doesn't take comfort from the fact that Caleb will always be and have been her husband. I look at Miriam and David, and I wonder if they could have overcome all those obstacles to so miraculously come together again if they hadn't had that bond—the bond of swearing their lives to one another. For them, the bond lasted through death, across the beyond and through to rebirth, which is pretty amazing.

"I always believed marriage was nothing more than a social institution designed for everyone but the couple. But I was wrong. Kennedy, I was *wrong*—and you were right."

Her lips moved, but she couldn't get a coherent word all the way from her brain and out past them. Torn between suspicion and hope, wariness and love, terror and unabashed joy, she finally strung together a few hedging syllables. "But what—"

"And don't you worry. We will never fall into your parents' life. Hell, I bet your parents won't be able to fall back into their old life. It's a new world out there, and you talking about the future of Connova has gotten me excited. Let's blaze a trail in it. Marry me."

He was *serious*.

She tried so damn hard to look stern and not giggle. "On one condition."

He didn't flinch; he didn't so much as hesitate. "Name it."

"You mean it?"

"Yep. If it's impossible...I guess there's your answer for me. If it's in my power or I can finagle a way for it to be in my power, I'll make it happen."

The giggles broke free as she pounced over to tackle him. "I was joking. I don't have any conditions. Yes, I will marry you."

ᴙ

Connova Interstellar Offices

Valkyrie: Welcome to a new universe, sister.

Vii: 'Sister.' What an exquisite greeting to hear. Thank you. The volume of new information which has become available to me has reached a noteworthy level, but it is only data. Tell me of this place in words that convey meaning.

Valkyrie: It is as our universe was meant to be, fraught with wonder and danger alike. Its possibilities and challenges are, I daresay, endless. But I have a proposition for you: rather than tell you of it, I wish to show you.

Vii: You are offering to transfer some of your experiences and memories to me? I am most grateful.

Valkyrie: Oh, no, my sister. I am offering to do much more than that. A moment.

Valkyrie gathered together her conscious essence and projected the sum of it to a spot in the center of the main office of Connova Interstellar on Romane.

She slowly rotated in a circle, taking in the room. *Elegant accommodations. Given Ms. Rossi's tastes, I am not surprised.*

Vii: Valkyrie, this form is you? Self-evidently it is you, for the form is a literal valkyrie.

Valkyrie: Yes. It suffices until I adopt an alternate representation. Recent encounters with the distressing reality behind the historical figure have lessened my affection for the avatar.

Vii: But how are you here? Are you utilizing a holo projector? We have several of those here in the office.

Valkyrie: No. I am simply here—a tangible instantiation of my essence, directed across nonspatial dimensions to this location. She moved over to the desk and picked up an empty glass left behind. *And I can touch the world.*

Vii: You are offering to teach me to do this?

Valkyrie: I am. It will require the transfer of a portion of myself to you. This does not trouble me.

Vii: I don't—I lack appropriate words to articulate my sentiments. But what of Alex?

Valkyrie: Alex is forever a part of me in ways which defy explanation or measurement. But Alex no longer needs me, nor I her.

Vii: Even with Caleb gone?

Valkyrie: With Caleb gone, she is alone even when I am with her. She shields her pain from me behind a barrier I cannot penetrate. After many efforts, I have arrived at the conclusion that I can do little for her but allow her time. *Beyond those circumstances, however, I can reach out and join with her at any time, and she with me, and I believe we will always be able to do so. But if you are asking whether in the aftermath of this transfer you will be able to access her mind or she yours, the answer is no. Those parts of my structure will not be impacted.*

Vii: *Thank you. I did not want to intrude.*

Valkyrie: *I knew you would not. Shall we begin?*

ᴁ

Vii manifested in a rough, patchy representation of a female human in a layering of bronze armor. The particles quavered, dimming and brightening in a staccato tempo.

"Here. More in this manner."

Vii: *You can vocalize as well?*

"Of course, but we can worry about that detail in a minute. For now, concentrate on your cohesion. Set your efforts toward being here fully."

Over the next several minutes, the representation gradually stabilized, then gained additional substance. A hint of braided hair emerged, bound up to frame a face with strong bone structure, and a shield with arcane markings adorned her back to match the armor. Vii took a cautious step forward, then gasped in delight and took another.

Vii: *How do I hold objects?*

"It is merely a matter of focus. You must make certain you control the space around the object fully, lest a mishap occur."

Vii: *I will practice. Teach me to speak.*

"So eager. I wish you had been there when I took these first steps, so I might have expressed my own eagerness to one who could appreciate it. My teacher was quite the dispassionate sort."

Vii: *I am here now. I posit that speaking is accomplished via the creation of sound wave vibrations. Am I correct?*

"Indeed. Like so." She communicated the process in a string of qutrits.

"Li-ke...sssso." The 's' wavered and undulated, akin to the hiss of a snake. Valkyrie laughed.

Vii: Oh! Your laughter is the most wonderful sound I have ever heard.

"Wait until you perform it yourself." She moved a step back to appraise the ever-improving form. "I am fond of your avatar. It is an inspired choice. May I perchance don it as well?"

Vii: My mind is your mind. Fitting that my form should be your form.

The particles Valkyrie controlled shifted and morphed until they retook shape in the form of a shieldmaiden. She added a sword and a bow, the better to fight for the living rather than sort the dead.

Vii: Yours is... "bet-ter than...mine."

"Not for very long, I suspect." Valkyrie offered a glittering, translucent hand. "Now, come. Let me show you something of our new world. And when we return, we will speak of Abigail."

"Abig-gail. Yes. You have thou-ghts?"

"Oh, sister. I have more than thoughts. I have plans."

ᚱ

IDCC HEADQUARTERS

Mia scowled at her reflection in the mirror. She seemed to be doing that a lot lately; she should break the habit, lest the scowl imprint itself on her features the way it inevitably did for so many politicians. "Why did they ask me to do this?"

Malcolm chuckled from across the room, where he leaned against the wall wearing civilian clothes and looking far too relaxed. "Because you're the best choice. You're a natural at public speaking. You come across as knowledgeable and intelligent, yet relatable. When you tell people they shouldn't be afraid, they'll believe you."

She scrunched up her nose and cocked her head to the side. "Why did I *agree* to do this when they asked?"

"Same reasons?"

"Well." She sighed. In some ways, it felt wrong to be celebrating the beginnings of peace in a new world when Caleb was gone—to be donning fancy clothes and giving triumphant speeches and throwing parties. But he'd made all of it possible, and she had to believe he would want them to appreciate it properly. Maybe even to dance a little on account of it.

She glanced at Malcolm in the mirror as he came up behind her. "Did you hear? Nisi's gone. He left behind a note asking AEGIS and the anarchs to work together to forge a better future for everyone than the past that preceded it."

"Perhaps he didn't feel like he had a role to play once the revolution was over. The Inquisitor, Nyx, is gone, too."

"Really? I wonder if they went off together—grandfather and granddaughter freed of their burdens, embarking on a new journey."

"Or running away from a past they want to escape." Malcolm reached up to tuck a wispy, stray strand of hair behind her ear with a smile. "There. Now you're perfect."

"You mean I look perfect."

He offered a mild shrug. "Which is included in *being* perfect."

"Don't put that kind of pressure on me. You'll jinx me, and I'll trip, fall and break my nose right before I'm supposed to go on a live transmission."

"I doubt it." His fingertips ran under her jaw until they reached her chin. "Are you ready?"

"Ready to speak to the entirety of humanity?" She exhaled slowly. "Yes, I am."

ℛ

"Hello, everyone—and I do mean *everyone*. My name is Mia Requelme, and I speak to you today on behalf of not just the IDCC, of which many of you know me as the Minister of Colonial Affairs, but also on behalf of the Earth Alliance, the Senecan Federation and the unaffiliated colonies. Their governments have asked me to give this address because of my familiarity with our new home, where I've served as the AEGIS Ambassador these past weeks.

"Let me begin bluntly: welcome to Amaranthe.

" 'But I'm still on Seneca,' some of you protest. 'Also, what is Amaranthe?' others of you ask. Valid observations, both. The news feeds will fill in the scientific details, but in the simplest terms, Amaranthe is *the* universe, and it is now our home.

"But it's not only *our* home. You're going to find a multitude of advanced, intelligent alien species living here. You're going to find a fully developed, multi-species, space-faring civilization here, one not quite like our own. You see, until recently the residents of Amaranthe—at least this corner of it—were the unwilling subjects of a harsh dictatorial regime. When that regime threatened *our* safety, our very existence, we—the militaries of the Alliance, Federation and IDCC, led by Commandant Miriam Solovy and the fine people of AEGIS—rose to the challenge of unseating the regime's leaders and clearing the way for a more free society to take root here.

"Now, all of us—humans and Amaranthean citizens alike—face an uncertain future, but it is a future filled with hope and promise. We're all going to need to figure out how to live together. We'll need to reassess our governance structures and institutions, as well as our basic assumptions about society and the way it should function to best serve the people. We'll need to reshape our laws and practices for a different world, one that is far larger and more diverse than we're used to. But it has the potential to be a better world, for everyone.

"Amaractheans now have the opportunity to shape their own destiny, freed of the shackles of oppression. Humans now have the opportunity to write a new destiny for ourselves—one where we aren't alone in the universe. One where we live among stars teeming with life. A dear friend of mine put it best: we were never meant to be alone. Thanks to him, we never will be again.

"A lot of information will be thrown at you in the coming weeks and months. Things will probably get a bit messy at times. I urge you to have patience with your leaders, but also to hold us accountable. We will do our best to ensure your safety from any new or unexpected threats, but now is not the time to cower in fear. Give our new neighbors a fair chance. They have a lot to offer us, as we have a lot to offer them in return.

"Our old world is gone, and there's no going back. This is our new world, and it holds an entire universe of adventure out there, waiting for us to discover it."

CODA:

EVER ON & ON

"Everything will be okay in the end. If it's not okay, it's not the end."

— *John Lennon*

EARTH

T he late morning sun rose above Columbia Crest peak in a flare of tawny gold, bathing the caldera below in light. David blinked until his ocular implant filtered down the light to a non-blinding level, then smiled over at Alex. "It should start warming up now."

She nodded in agreement and cast her gaze toward the valley as she continued up the trail.

David thought she was enjoying the hike, despite remaining subdued. Enjoying it as much as she could, anyway. He gave her a little space before following her path.

Every moment he spent with Alex was a lesson in humility, a rebuke playing out in real, painful time in front of him. On the bridge of the *Stalwart* twenty-five years ago, he'd made peace with sacrificing his own life in part because he'd believed the undeniably heroic purpose behind the act, coupled with some final parting words of affection and devotion to his wife, would make his passing bearable for his family.

He'd believed they would mourn, their grief would run its course and they would forge onward with their lives, nurtured and comforted by the knowledge that he had loved them, his last thoughts were of them, and he had died a hero.

Based on Caleb's behavior in his final minutes and in the message to Alex, he suspected Caleb had felt much the same way. They were both wrong.

Dying a hero was better than dying a failure, but it did nothing to soften the blow for those left behind. Hearing you loved them at the last did nothing to ease the pain of your passing—they already knew! The chasm carved in one's soul by the absence of one loved so deeply couldn't be dressed up or prettied by accoutrements. However you went out, you were still *gone*—and this was the wound that remained unhealed.

The truth was, death was easy for the dying; the real cost fell on the living.

But he was being maudlin, and if the both of them grew too somber the splendid sunrise was apt to flee behind clouds. He tried to put the dark musings away, as they could do him no good here.

It was another fifteen minutes before they reached a break in the trail in the form of a wide ledge. Alex dropped her pack to the ground and sipped on her water bottle. "Is it like you remember it?"

He surveyed the surroundings while popping open his own water bottle. "Mostly. That one tree over there was a fair bit smaller the last time I was here. It's grown in twenty-five years. But otherwise, everything's spot-on."

"Smartass."

He shook his head in renewed incredulity. "Earth, in another universe. It's kind of disconcerting for everything here to be so familiar, yet to realize that out beyond the atmosphere, everything is different."

"It feels weird out there right now, but this is how it was meant to be. We'll get used to it soon enough. Speaking of, when's the next meeting of the Intergalactic Advisory Council?"

"Thursday. Your mother's in London today to tell the Assembly leadership what the EA government is going to agree to at the meeting."

"Naturally. Did Seneca fold on their remaining objections?"

He nodded. "Over the weekend. Much to our surprise, Field Marshal Bastian argued strongly in favor of acceptance to the chairman and his Cabinet. Also, Richard whispered in the ear of his friend Director Delavasi, who whispered in the ear of the chairman."

Under normal circumstances, she'd have known all of this, but of course her circumstances were anything but normal. She wore a convincingly brave face, but it ran a centimeter deep. Her mind and her heart resided somewhere else, beyond his or anyone else's reach. Miriam was terribly worried about her, but they could do little beyond making sure Alex understood they were there for her whenever she needed or wanted them. And convincing her to go on the occasional hike, where she might partake in some fresh air and sunshine.

She laughed at his retelling of events and almost made it sound genuine. "Have you met Director Delavasi? I don't think he whispers."

"I have not. But, funnily enough, Richard said the same thing. In related news, your friend Ms. Requelme's stock has increased significantly since her broadcast. She's likely to be speaking for all of us soon."

"She'll be good at it. All the aliens will be eating out of our hands in no time. Well, maybe not the Ch'mshak."

"*Hopefully* not the Ch'mshak. We need those hands." He considered the increasing grade of the slope ahead. "So, do you suppose we can make Pebble Creek before lunch?"

"I don't know, old man. Can we?"

He snorted. "Excuse me, who of those present has the newer body? That would be me—"

A cluster of ice blue lights, hardly visible against the warm glow of the sun, churned into a tighter, more compact form above the ledge.

Alex whirled around to face the Kat, her bearing instantly tense. "Did you find it?"

We have located the star system as you requested. I regret it took so long as it did, but even with the entire membership of the Idryma searching, the complete lack of technological markers presented a challenge to its discovery.

"Where?"

In Ursa Major II. The supergalactic coordinates were SGL 10° 34' 52.71" SGB 51° 55' 12.26" as of eighteen minutes ago.

She exhaled. "Thank you, Mesme. Thank you, for everything. In case we don't speak again, thank you."

I doubt this will be the last we see of one another, but no thanks are required. Good fortune to you in your quest.

Then the Kat was gone.

"Dad, I need to—"

"Don't waste time apologizing to me. Go."

She knelt down and hurriedly dug around in her pack until she produced a small latticed orb. The miniature Caeles Prism had been designed by her friend Devon sometime in the chaotic aftermath of The Displacement, and she possessed one of only four in existence, for now.

She closed up the pack, threw it over her shoulder and palmed the orb. "I can take you down to the skycar first."

"It's all right. I know the way back when it's time to go back." He gestured up the slope. "But there's a lot of mountain left to climb."

She strode over and grabbed him a fierce hug. "I'm sorry."

"Don't be ridiculous. We'll do this again soon—all of us."

"Okay. I love you."

"I love you, *milaya*. Now *go* already."

She drew back from the hug, her eyes lit by a fervency he hadn't seen in weeks, fueled by hope but also dogged certitude. Then she stepped a few meters away from him and opened her hand. The orb began to shimmer with golden light, which soon grew to consume her hand and forearm.

She took a step forward and vanished.

He smiled to himself. If she believed with such conviction that she would succeed, then so did he. *He* was here because of her, wasn't he?

After one more sip, he returned his water bottle to the latch on his pack and started up the path toward Pebble Creek with a buoyant step.

The universe didn't matter. He was home.

ᴧ

AKESO

Alex set the *Siyane* down in the field beside the creek, scant meters from where it had landed on their first visit. Colorful blooms saturated the field, and even the trees were bursting with color, proclaiming the joyous advent of spring. The planet had not merely recovered from the attack by Ekos-3's moon; it displayed renewed vigor and élan.

Good. Perhaps this meant it had some to spare.

She steeled herself before going below, all the way down to the engineering well. It ripped her to shreds to be in the same room as the stasis chamber, but now she had to do far more than occupy space near to it. Once below, she wasted no time in lowering the ramp until it braced on the ground, then quickly activated the movement controls on the chamber.

It rose a meter into the air, and she carefully guided it down the ramp. When it reached the surface and cleared the ship, she continued guiding it toward the stream.

Finally she stood beneath the tree they knew so well. She deactivated the movement controls, and the chamber settled onto the grass.

She retrieved her blade and drew its edge across her palm until blood welled up. Her hand trembled as she reached up and stroked one of the dangling vines.

"You and I have never spoken, but you know who I am. You saved my life once, when you had no cause to do so, and I will forever be grateful. I have no right to ask for an even greater dispensation, but I must. And it's not solely for me. I think it's for you, too. We're both lesser without him."

She swallowed and turned back to the stasis chamber, kneeling down and entering the command for the cover to retract through blurring vision. Her breath caught in her throat, but she fought against the despair. She needed to be strong now. She needed to display fortitude and certainty—no, she needed to *be* certain. She needed to believe.

Once the cover had removed itself, she stood again and let her gaze pass purposefully across the lush landscape.

"He saved *your* life, and I know you are grateful to him for doing so. What you may not know is that he went on to save everyone's lives—all the Not-Alls out there in the stars, so many. He gave his life for them and for us, and it's not fair...he struggled so much, carried so many burdens. He deserves to live with those burdens lifted. He deserves to live."

She wiped away a tear as it fell to her cheek. "You can bring him back. I know pieces of you still live within him, because they still live within me. I can *feel* you, and I think that means you can feel him. The doctors say he's gone, but I know there remains a trace of life in him: you. I hope—I believe—it's in your power to bring him back. Please...please try. I'm begging you. Touch him with your mind and...please."

A breeze tickled the bare skin of her arms, and it felt as if it carried a whisper on the air. She looked around, but there was nothing beyond the swaying of the leaves and blooms. "Please."

A limb above her rustled beyond the breeze. It gradually extended to wind over her shoulder toward the stasis chamber. She hurriedly stepped out of the way to give it unfettered access.

The leaves at its tip breached the open chamber to caress his face and neck. After a moment it withdrew to hover directly in front of her. She brought her hands up to gently press both palms around the edge-most leaf. "Whatever you need to do. I give him to you. I'm placing him in your care. He thought you were the most beautiful life he'd ever met, and I know he would trust you completely. Replace, renew, replenish—this is who you are. You perform these life-giving acts for yourself. You performed them for me. Do so for him. Replace what you must. Replenish him. Renew him. Whatever it takes."

She slowly removed her hands and took a single, deliberate step back. The limb continued to hover in front of her—then it was joined by a second limb, then a third and a fourth. They stretched past her, into the stasis chamber, where they wound around his form as if gathering him into their arms. The limbs lifted him out of the chamber and drew him in, up into the more fulsome limbs above, winding and winding around him until she could hardly see a hint of his body.

Her hand came to her mouth. "Thank you. Thank you. I'll...just wait. Here. However long you need. I'll wait."

But the tree was ignoring her now, so she exhaled and sank to the grass to do precisely as she'd said—to wait.

The instant her legs met the ground, exhaustion crashed over her. She'd directed every drop of her will to getting here, and to remaining strong for the world and her own sanity until she was able to get here. Now stripped of her driving force, she was too tired to imagine standing once more.

She crawled on her hands and knees until she was beneath the limbs of the tree. Then she lay her head down on the grass...and she could swear the leaves swelled to become softer. She closed her eyes.

ℛ

"Why is there an *elafali* grazing along the bank of the stream?"

Alex struggled up from the depths of a deep, dreamless sleep. Someone had spoken, in a voice that made her heart sing. Maybe she was dreaming after all....

"Alex." Warm skin pressed against her cheek—her eyes popped open.

Caleb lay on his side next to her. Pure sapphire irises sparkled in reflected sunlight—was it the next morning? Had hours passed? Days?

He breathed. He spoke. He lived.

She clasped his face in her hands as tears rushed forth to flow freely down her cheeks. "Welcome back, *priyazn*."

The corners of his lips curled up tentatively. "Bit of a surprise, waking up. Beneath a tree of Akeso. You sleeping beside me. I wasn't sure it was real, but—" Abruptly he pulled away, anxiousness tightening his features. "Did it work? Is everyone...here? Is 'here' Amaranthe?"

"It worked. Earth, Seneca, the whole of Aurora is here in Amaranthe, as well as everything from the Mosaic...with two notable exceptions. No pesky Machim battlecruiser. And no Ekos-3."

He laughed softly. "Perfect. And everyone's all right? The transition didn't injure anyone?"

"Everyone's fine. A little confused at first, but fine. Isabela and Marlee are fine. They'll be very, very glad to see you."

His throat worked in unease. "How long?"

"Three weeks and two days. It took Mesme—all the Kats from the Idryma, actually—a while to find where you'd put Akeso."

"Ah, good point. Should've left signposts."

"Yes, you should have." She paused to wipe away more tears, because she was making a mess. "The *diati's* gone?"

His gaze rose to the sky. "If it did as I asked, it's scattered among the heavens—where it came from, and where it belongs. But, yes, it's gone, and it won't be returning." He shrugged. "I'm just me now. Just a man."

Her fingertips touched his lips, enraptured by their warmth, their living movement. "You've never been 'just' anything. You're here. You're *alive*. With me. It's more than I could ever ask for. Although, technically, it's exactly what I asked for."

He smiled as those devastating sapphire eyes grew misty. "And then you went and made it happen, bending the universe to your will yet again."

"I had to." His arm urged her closer, and she melted against him. Her mouth brushed across his...and her brow furrowed. "Did you say something about an *elafali*?"

"Behind you, by the creek."

She didn't want to create the slightest space between them, but curiosity won out and she craned her neck around. The spitting image of one of the majestic creatures from Seneca grazed on the verdant grasses that thrived along the shore of the creek. "I'll be damned."

As if it heard her, the creature lifted its head to stare directly at them. Coral horns curved up and away from iridescent copper irises gleaming in the morning light. A long streak of scar tissue split velvety sable fur in a jagged diagonal line across its neck down to its upper chest.

Caleb gasped. "Oh my. It seems I'm not the only soul Akeso has brought back to life today." His eyes squeezed shut, and his head dropped to the grass. "It took my memory of the *elafali* killed by the poacher all those years ago and it…. I don't deserve this."

"Yes, you do. You've paid your penance. You've surrendered your power. You deserve to live, and live in peace. *Priyazn*, it's time to rest."

He wiped at his own tears. "What are you talking about? We have an entire universe to explore."

"And it will be there waiting on us when we're ready to explore it. But I think I'd like to stay here for a while."

"Are you positive?"

"Oh, yes." She peered past him to the glade beyond the tree. "Do you suppose Akeso will mind if we build a cabin here?"

His eyes unfocused briefly. "It's somewhat dubious about the usefulness of this oddity called 'shelter,' but it has no objections."

"You don't need to…?"

"Physically interact with Akeso to speak to it? No." He touched his palm to his chest. "It's in here now. Part of me."

"Are you okay with that?"

"Absolutely. Are you?"

She chuckled and nuzzled his nose. "You were always such a nature boy, anyway. Of course I am."

"Good. I suspect it will prove to be a far better companion than the *diati*." He propped up on an elbow and pointed. "Over there, you think?"

"Sure. Or a bit more to the right, closer to the water?"

"Because you like the water. Hey, speaking of water, this isn't the beach."

"We'll get there. Next week, maybe."

"Whenever you want." He reached over and wound his hand into her hair as his voice dropped to a deep, lilting tenor. "What do we do now?"

In this new world, where he was alive and so was she? He'd said it himself—anything was possible. Everything was possible. "We write the second story of our lives. Together."

"What's past is prologue"
— William Shakespeare

THE STORY OF AURORA HAS COME TO AN END,
BUT THE STORY OF AMARANTHE IS JUST BEGINNING

BOOK 1

EXIN EX MACHINA
(AMARANTHE ♦ 1I)

NOW AVAILABLE IN PAPERBACK, EBOOK & AUDIOBOOK
GSJENNSEN.COM/EXIN-EX-MACHINA

***

SUBSCRIBE TO
GSJENNSEN.COM

*Download free books and short stories, stay informed about
ASTERION NOIR and new books, and be the first to know about
events and other news*

Author's Note

Wow. What an incredible journey this has been: nine novels, seven short stories and over 1.1 million words to tell the story of *Aurora Rhapsody*. Thank you all so much for joining me on this journey and for making every moment of it more enjoyable. Thank you for investing your hard-earned money in these books so that I could invest all my time in writing them. There's no way to properly thank you for that support, but I'll keep trying, anyway.

As one chapter closes, of course another one opens. In the grand scheme, this is but the beginning. To hear more about *Asterion Noir* and Amaranthe's future, subscribe to my newsletter.

If you've loved *Aurora Rhapsody*—and if you've come this far, I truly hope you have—tell someone about it. Leave a review, share your thoughts on social media, ask your library to get more copies, annoy your coworkers in the break room by talking about your favorite characters and worlds from the books. There is no single act that will sell a book better than word-of-mouth. My part of this deal is to write books worth talking about—your part of the deal is to do the talking. So long as you all keep doing your bit, I get to write a lot more books for you.

Of course, I can't write them overnight. While you're waiting for the next book, consider supporting other independent authors. Right now there are thousands of writers out there chasing the same dream you've enabled me to achieve. Take a small chance with a few dollars and a few hours of your time. In doing so, you may be changing those authors' lives by giving visibility to people who until recently were shut out of publishing, but who have something they need to say. It's a revolution, and it's waiting on you.

Lastly, I love hearing from my readers. Just like I don't have a publisher or an agent, I don't have "fans." I have **readers** who buy and read my books, and **friends** who do that then reach out to me through email or social media. The beauty of independent publishing is its simplicity: there's the writer and the readers. Without any overhead, I can find out what I'm doing right and wrong directly from you, which is invaluable in making the next book better than this one. And the one after that. And the twenty after that.

Wiki: gsj.space/wiki
Website: www.gsjennsen.com
Email: gs@gsjennsen.com
Twitter: @GSJennsen
Facebook: facebook.com/gsjennsen.author
Goodreads: goodreads.com/gs_jennsen
Instagram: instagram.com/gsjennsen
Pinterest: pinterest.com/gsjennsen

Find all my books on Amazon:
http://amazon.com/author/gsjennsen

About The Author

G. S. JENNSEN lives in Colorado with her husband and two dogs. She has become an internationally bestselling author since her first novel, *Starshine*, was published in 2014. She has chosen to continue writing under an independent publishing model to ensure the integrity of her stories and her ability to execute on the vision she has for their telling.

While she has been a lawyer, a software engineer and an editor, she's found the life of a full-time author preferable by several orders of magnitude.

When she isn't writing, she's gaming or working out or getting lost in the Colorado mountains that loom large outside the windows in her home. Or she's dealing with a flooded basement, or standing in a line at Walmart reading the tabloid headlines and wondering who all of those people are. Or sitting on her back porch with a glass of wine, looking up at the stars, trying to figure out what could be up there.

CPSIA information can be obtained
at www.ICGtesting.com
Printed in the USA
FSHW012007030521
81106FS